'Fallout is the best yet in one of our genre's cr...
best-ever series. Paretsky is a...
to dig a li...
Lee C...

'Simply superb! As a fan of V.I... beginning, I can say without dou... both author and protagonist at t... of their games'
Jeffery Deaver

'Paretsky's legion of fans will rejoice in her heroically scaled twentieth novel'
Kirkus Reviews

'An astonishing tour de force – thrilling, moving, illuminating – from an author of matchless intelligence, craft, and power. This is why Sara Paretsky reigns as one of the all-time greats'
Karin Slaughter

'V. I. Warshawski is one of my all-time favorite investigators. Doesn't get any better than this!'
Lisa Gardner

'Sara Paretsky is a legend, and FALLOUT is her finest novel to date – an extraordinary read from an extraordinary author'
Harlan Coben

'Even out of her Chicago comfort zone in pursuit of a faded missing actress and young filmmaker in FALLOUT, legendary V. I. Warshawski is as dogged and ferocious as ever. So is Sara Paretsky, who is at the top of the crime novel game'
C.J. Box

'FALLOU is exactly what it promises: proof that so much of the pain in ur present is from mistakes in our past. This book h a soul. Come see a master at work'
Brad Meltzer

Also by Sara Paretsky

Brush Back
Critical Mass
Breakdown
Body Work
Hardball
Bleeding Kansas
Fire Sale
Blacklist
Total Recall
Hard Time
Ghost Country
Windy City Blues
Tunnel Vision
Guardian Angel
Burn Marks
Blood Shot
Bitter Medicine
Killing Orders
Deadlock
Indemnity Only

Sara Paretsky

FALLOUT

HODDER

First published in the United States of America in 2017 by HarperCollins

First published in Great Britain in 2017 by Hodder & Stoughton
An Hachette UK company

First published in paperback in 2017

1

A CIP catalogue record for this title is available from the British Library

A format ISBN 978 1 473 62437 5
B format ISBN 978 1 473 62436 8

Printed and bound in Great Britain by Clays Ltd, St Ives plc

Hodder & Stoughton policy is to use papers that are natural, renewable and recyclable products and made from wood grown in sustainable forests. The logging and manufacturing processes are expected to conform to the environmental regulations of the country of origin.

Hodder & Stoughton Ltd
Carmelite House
50 Victoria Embankment
London EC4Y 0DZ

www.hodder.co.u

FOR SUE BOWKER

With thanks for many things,
including your support for this book

1

PLAYING THE SAP—AGAIN

THE POLICE SAY it was drug-related, ma'am. They think August was stealing to deal." Angela Creedy spoke so softly I had to lean forward to hear her.

"That is a *bêtise*—a . . . a lie, a stupidity." Bernadine Fouchard stomped her foot for emphasis.

"Bernie, my little volcano, you could be right, but I have no idea what, or even who, you're talking about. Can you start at the beginning?"

Angela had been looking at her clasped hands, her face tight with worry, but that made her give a brief smile. "You *are* a little volcano, Bernie. Maybe that's what we'll start calling you at the training table. The thing is, August is missing, and when this break-in happened—"

"They had to pick on someone," Bernie interrupted. "And because he is black—"

Angela put a hand over Bernie's mouth. "August is my cousin, ma'am. I don't really know him—I'm from Shreveport, and he grew up in Chicago. We don't have the kind of family that stages big reunions. I haven't seen him since he was about eight or nine and came down with his mama to visit. Anyway, when I connected with him, after I moved up here, it turned out he's trying to be a filmmaker, but he works as a personal trainer to support himself. He also videos parties—weddings, kids' birthdays, things like that. It just seemed like the perfect combo."

The southern lilt in her soft voice made it hard for me to understand her. "Perfect for what?" I asked.

Bernie flung up her hands. "But to help us train and video us when we play, *naturellement,* so we can see where we must improve!"

Bernadine Fouchard was a rising hockey player. Her father had been my cousin Boom-Boom's closest friend on the Blackhawks, and he'd asked Boom-Boom to be Bernie's godfather. Now that she was a first-year student and athletic star at Northwestern, I had sort of inherited her.

"Angela is also an athlete?" I asked.

"Can't you tell? She is like a . . . a giraffe. She plays basketball and plays very well."

Angela looked at her in annoyance but went back to her narrative. "Anyway, Bernie and I, we're both freshmen, we have a lot to prove before we can be starters, so we started going to the Six-Points Gym, because that's where my cousin works and it's not far from campus."

"When this gym was broken into two nights ago, the police, at first they thought it was a prank, because of Halloween, but then today they said it must have been August, which is a *scandale,*" Bernie put in. "So I told Angela about you, and we agreed you are the exact person for proving he never did this thing."

Bernie favored me with a brilliant smile, as if she were the queen bestowing an important medal on me. I felt more as though the queen's horse was kicking me in the stomach.

"What does August say about it?"

"He's disappeared," Bernie said. "I think he's hiding—"

"Bernie, I'm going to call you a volcanic kangaroo, you jump around so much." Angela warned, her voice rising in exasperation. "The gym manager says August told her he was going away for a week but he didn't say where, just that it was a confidential project. He's a contract employee, so he doesn't get vacation time—he takes unpaid leave if he wants to go."

"He didn't tell you?" I asked.

Angela shook her head. "We're not that close, ma'am. I mean, I like him, but, you know how it is when you play college ball—Bernie told me you played basketball for the University of Chicago—you're training, you're practicing, you're fitting in your classes. Girls' ball isn't like boys': we *have* to graduate, we have to take our courses seriously. Not that I don't want to—I love everything I'm studying—but there isn't time left over for family. And August is pretty private anyway. He's never even invited me to his home."

"You have his phone number?" I said.

Angela nodded. "He's not answering it, or texts, or anything. No updates on his Facebook page or Twitter feed."

"The police must have something to go on," I objected. "Other than saying that nobody knows where your cousin is."

"It wasn't really a break-in." Angela picked at her cuticles. "Someone with a key opened all the doors, and August is the only person with a key they can't find."

"How long has he been out of touch?" I asked, cutting short another harangue by Bernie.

Angela hunched a shoulder. "I can't even tell you that, ma'am. It wasn't until today that I knew he was missing, and that's because the police came to talk to me, to see if I knew where he was."

I got up to turn on more lights. The only windows in the warehouse where I lease my office are at the top of the fourteen-foot walls. I've filled the place with floor and ceiling lamps, and at five on a November day I needed all of them to break the gloom.

Neither of my visitors seemed able to tell her story in a straightforward way, but what it boiled down to was that Six-Points Gym's medical-supplies closet had been ransacked during the break-in. The gym worked with a lot of athletes, from weekend warriors to some of the city's pro teams, along with many of the university's athletes. They had a doctor on call who could hand out drugs. Neither Angela nor Bernie knew what had been in the ransacked closet.

"We don't take drugs," Bernie snapped when I asked. "Why would we know?"

I sighed, loudly. "It's the kind of question you might have asked the police when they talked to you. Or they might have asked you. Six-Points must have controlled substances, or the cops wouldn't care."

"They didn't say." Angela was talking to her hands again. "They asked me how well I know August and did I know if he took drugs, sold drugs—all those things. I told them no, of course."

"Even though you don't know him well?" I prodded.

Angela looked up at that, her eyes hot. "I know when someone is on drugs. *Ma'am*. It's true I don't know him well—I was only two the one time he came to see us—but my mother told me he brought a toy farm with him that I kept messing with. She says August was so cute, how he put the animals to bed for the night, all the little lambs together, all the cows, how the dog got to sleep on the farmer's bed. A boy like that wouldn't be stealing drugs."

I didn't suggest that every drug dealer had once been a little child who played with toys.

Bernie nodded vigorously. "*Exactement!* So we need you to find August. Find him before the police do, or they will just arrest him and never listen to the truth."

"Which is?"

"That someone else did this break-in, this sabotage." Bernie cried, exasperated with my thickness.

"This is potentially a huge inquiry, Bernie. You need to fingerprint the premises, talk to everyone on the gym's staff, talk to customers. The police have the manpower and the technical resources for an investigation like this. I don't have the equipment or the staff to work a crime scene, even if the Evanston cops would let me look at it."

"But, Vic! You can at least talk to people. When you start asking questions, they will be squirming and saying things they thought they could keep secret. I know you can do this—I have seen you making it happen. Maybe even the manager of the gym, maybe she is doing this crime and trying to blame August."

I opened and shut my mouth a few times. Whether it was the flattery or the supplication in both their faces, I wrote down the address of Six-Points, the name of the manager, August's home address. When I asked Angela for August's mother's name, though, she said that "Auntie Jacquelyn" had died six years ago.

"I honestly don't think August has any other family in Chicago. Not on my side anyway. His daddy was killed in Iraq, years ago. If he has other relatives here, I don't know about them."

Of course she didn't know his friends either, or lovers, or whether he had debts he needed to pay off. At least she could provide his last name—Veriden. Even though I knew that neither woman could afford my fees, I still found myself saying I would call at the gym tomorrow and ask some questions.

Bernie leaped up to hug me. "Vic, I knew you would say yes! I knew we could count on you."

I thought of Sam Spade telling Brigid O'Shaughnessy he wouldn't play the sap for her. Why wasn't I as tough as Sam?

2

FIT FOR LIFE

THE NEXT DAY I had an early meeting in the Loop with my favorite kind of client, the kind who pays bills regularly and has well-focused inquiries, so it wasn't until late afternoon that I made it up to the Six-Points Gym. Which meant I had about a dozen texts from Bernie, demanding to know what I'd found out, before I even started north.

I'd made an appointment with the day manager, Denise LaPorte, and had phoned to let the Evanston police know I was on the case. The detective in charge didn't sound as though the break-in was high on his own to-do list. No one had been killed or even injured, and property damage was minimal.

"You want to look for this guy—what's his name? August Veriden?—knock yourself out. Just let me know when you find him."

"You're liking him for the break-in?"

The cop said, "We'd like to talk to him. He's the only employee with a key that we can't locate, so we've put out a bulletin for him."

I asked what drugs were missing. I whistled under my breath: the gym's medical closet had quite a cocktail on hand—Oxy, Toradol, Vicodin, along with stuff I'd never heard of.

"Were the quantities enough to make them worth stealing?"

The detective snorted derisively. "You ever been around a junkie, PI? Street value doesn't mean shit. Ease of access—you'll see when you get there. It ain't exactly Fort Knox."

Duly chastened, I promised I would let him know if I discovered anything helpful. Neither of us was optimistic when I hung up.

When I got to Six-Points Gym: Fitness for Life, it was just after five. The building was a kind of outsize warehouse. A signboard at the entrance advertised an Olympic-size pool, a dozen basketball courts, yoga rooms, weight rooms, five restaurants, and a separate spa wing. The sign urged me to join and become fit for life. Special rates for college and high-school students, 30 percent off for everyone who joined today. There must have been a lot of cancellations after the break-in.

The sign also explained the Six Points: USE YOUR HEAD AND HEART TO POWER YOUR FOUR LIMBS TO FITNESS.

A security camera videoed the main entrance, but the eye had been covered with a piece of chewing gum. Inside, a guard the size of a football tackle was dealing with a woman who demanded he let her into the locker room right now! He looked at me humorlessly and asked for my membership card and a photo ID.

"You were here during the break-in?" I said while the woman shouted that she'd been here before me and I couldn't butt in like I owned the place.

"And you get to ask questions because . . . ?" the guard said.

"Because I'm a detective who's been hired to help with the investigation. Denise LaPorte is expecting me."

The guard looked as though he'd like to pick me up and break me in half, just for someone to vent his frustration on, but he picked up the desk phone instead and called for permission to let me in.

"Down the hall to the back staircase and up to the second floor. You'll find her—just follow the noise."

"And *were* you here during the break-in?"

"What kind of asshole question is that? Of course not. We're closed from midnight to five A.M.—that's when it happened."

By the time I left, the angry woman had been joined by a couple of men also demanding answers.

I passed locker rooms. Police tape had been crisscrossed over the entrances, but someone had torn it down.

You know the footage that TV loves to show after a tornado or an earthquake, with homes and furniture flung across the landscape? That's what I saw when I stepped over the tape: every locker in the women's room had been pried open. Gym bags and backpacks had been dumped. Bras, tampons, water bottles, swimsuits, candy wrappers, makeup kits—all scattered over the benches and floor. Fingerprint dust had settled on the clothes, making them look like the tired remains of a dust storm.

I backed out and peered into the men's room. The damage was just as appalling, except for the absence of makeup. No one looking for drugs would have looted the locker rooms, although I suppose a serious addict might have been hunting jewelry or electronics. Could one person have done this on his own in five hours? The dumping maybe, but hundreds of lockers had been opened. It looked like a team effort.

I snapped some pictures and moved on to the back staircase. As I started up, I understood what the guard had meant by following the noise. The manager's office was a small space, and it was overflowing with screaming clients. A man in a purple Wildcats sweatshirt was pounding the desk demanding a refund, two women were shouting about something stolen, a third, weeping in fury, was waving a silver gym bag whose torn lining was hanging out.

"Two hundred twenty-five dollars! This is a Stella McCartney original. Are you going to reimburse me or not?"

"Take a number," LaPorte snapped at me when I squeezed through to her desk. "I can only deal with one person at a time."

"I'm V.I. Warshawski, the detective—we spoke earlier. Let me know when to come back."

LaPorte pressed her palms against her eyes. "There won't be a good time. There will never be a good time. This is going to go on all night."

"Damn right," the man said. "It's going to go on until you tell us when you're going to pay for the damages."

I climbed onto the desk and the room quieted. I looked down at the crowd. "Did the police take down the crime-scene tape, or was that you heroes?"

There was some grumbling and then another outburst from the Stella McCartney bag, wanting to know what difference that made and insisting it didn't get me off the hook from replacing her property.

I tried to school my face into a mix of sorrow and pity instead of annoyance and impatience. "If you removed the tape, there's no way to prove that your property was damaged by the vandals who broke into the locker room. Six-Points values you as a member and doesn't want a legal hassle, but their insurance carrier will be cranky because there's no way to prove you aren't bringing ruined property in from outside, hoping to cash in on the disaster. You can't file a police report, which you need when you're making a claim, because you tampered with a crime scene. Fresh prints on top of the fingerprint powder will be pretty easy to ID."

The people in the room seemed to contract, as if a freezing wind had blown through, except for the Stella McCartney woman. She was too outraged for logic, but a man whom I hadn't noticed—because he'd been quiet—took her arm and steered her out the door. The rest of the unhappy athletes followed.

Denise LaPorte slumped in her chair. She was young, probably early thirties, and on a normal day probably attractive—her buff arms an advertisement for the gym's fitness trainers, with that honey-colored hair that takes hours to hand-paint and keep glowing. Today her skin was the color of paste, and she had gray circles under her eyes.

"This is the first time the room has been quiet since I started my shift at noon. Is it true what you said about the insurance claims?"

I hopped off the desk and shut the door. "Depends on how generous your management and your insurers want to be with your customers, but insurance companies are used to train-wreck add-ons."

She looked at me blankly.

"When trains derail, you get more accident claims than the total number of passengers on board. Your carrier isn't likely to pay for damaged items people wave around, although the gym may want to take care of them as a goodwill gesture. The claims could turn into a nightmare, so for your own protection make this your legal department's problem."

LaPorte gave a wobbly smile. "Thanks. That's the first decent advice I've had for three days."

"You're beat and beaten up," I said, "but I need to ask you about August Veriden."

LaPorte shook her head. "I can't tell you much. He's a quiet guy, qualified trainer—he did a degree at Loyola, which has a great certification program, and he always met or exceeded our standards."

I blinked. "That sounds like one of those online questionnaires."

She flushed. "I memorized his employee chart when I was talking to the police and to corporate this morning. Some of the trainers like to chat, so I know about who they're dating or their dental bills or whatever, but August isn't a chatter. Everyone—I was going to say likes him, but maybe respects is more to the point. We all know that his dream is to be a filmmaker, and he does private jobs for people here—weddings or graduations. I've never worked with him, so I can't tell you how good his videos are."

"Any personal details in his file? Partner? Next of kin?"

LaPorte shook her head again. "When the cops asked to talk to him and he wasn't answering his phone, I looked him up, but he only put in this cousin, who's a freshman at Northwestern."

I grimaced. "She's the person who hired me to find him. She doesn't know other relatives."

LaPorte clasped her hands on the desk and looked at me earnestly. "I know his cousin and her friend, the little hockey player—"

"Bernadine Fouchard," I supplied.

"I know they think I gave the police his name because he's black, but honestly, three of our other trainers are black, one of them from Kenya. We have seventy-eight people working here, everything from janitors to trainers to PTs and massage therapists, and seven people on the management team, including me. August is the only one we can't locate. I don't want to finger him, but it does look suspicious."

"How long has it been since you last saw him?" I asked.

She made a face. "This morning I had to check that on my computer, but between talking to the police and to corporate, I know all this by heart. He left ten days ago, said he wanted personal time for a private project. That's all any of us here know."

I digested that: if he wanted to break in and steal the gym's drugs, he'd waited an awfully long time. "You have a doctor on staff, right?"

"Oh—you're thinking of the medical-supplies closet. We have two doctors who oversee any injury treatments that our PTs or exercise trainers do, but they're not employees."

I asked to see the medical closet. She got up readily—I'd saved her from assault, she wanted to help. As she opened her door, she even managed to joke that she wished she had a disguise.

A few people tried to stop her on our way down the hall, but she told them I was a detective, that she needed to show me part of the crime scene.

The door to the medical office was open, but the entrance was crisscrossed with more crime-scene tape, this time intact. I ducked underneath to inspect at the drugs cabinet.

"Should you be doing that?" LaPorte glanced around the hall.

"I'm not going to touch anything," I assured her.

The room held a desk and couple of exam tables. All the drawers—in the desk, under the tables, and in cabinets along the walls—were open. Some had been dumped on the floor with a rough hand, scattering latex gloves, swabs, test tubes across the room. I tiptoed through the detritus to the supply closet at the back, which also stood open. I squatted to shine my flashlight on the lock. It hadn't been forced, but whether someone had a key or was good with picks, I couldn't tell.

Floor-to-ceiling shelves had held everything from support tapes to plastic boxes of medicines. I shone my flash on the labels—over-the-counter painkillers along with an eye-popping collection of controlled substances. The rolls of stretchy tape had been unwound, leaving elastic coiled over the lips of shelves onto the floor like a nest of flesh-colored vipers.

I rejoined LaPorte in the hall.

"Do the trainers have keys to the medical supplies?"

"Only the doctors and the nurse who's on call. What do you think is going on?" LaPorte pulled nervously on her lank hair.

"I think your doctors are seriously overmedicating your clients."

Her mouth dropped open. "What does that have to do with the break-in?"

"I can't tell," I said. "You'd need the cops to look into it—they've got the bodies to question everyone the doctors ever treated, or athletes with a grudge, or parents who think their kids were damaged. Or the doctors could have nothing at all to do with it—it could be junkies helping themselves to a stash that's easy to get at. You have seventy-eight employees with keys, which means—"

"No, only about eighteen people have keys. August does because he opens once a week—the trainers all do because they take turns getting here for the five a.m. shift. And then there's me and the other—"

"Eighteen is a lot of keys," I interrupted. "Easy to pass around, even if they're not easy to duplicate. But unless the front-door key opens the medical closet, I'm voting against a junkie. Someone who's high or low, desperate for a fix, is more likely to break a lock than finesse it."

"What should I do?" LaPorte's voice was cracking with despair.

"Get police permission to go into the locker rooms. Photograph them so you have evidence for your insurance company, then hire a cleanup crew to tidy it up. The police don't seem excited by the crime, since no one was hurt, and the mess isn't very serious property damage. I don't think they'll object. Pity you don't know where August is—he could video it all for you."

3

AUTEUR DECONSTRUCTED

WHEN I FINISHED with Denise LaPorte at Six-Points, I was too tired to do anything except go home and collapse in the bath. I could hear the dings announcing incoming texts, but I lay comatose for half an hour, only stirring to add hot water to the tub when it cooled.

It was the two dogs I share with my downstairs neighbor that finally pushed me to my feet. They started scratching and whining outside the bathroom door. Mr. Contreras is over ninety, and although he'd rather root for the Cubs than admit he's not up to walking Mitch and Peppy, he must have let them into my place as a hint that they needed exercise.

"Okay, guys, okay," I muttered, toweling myself down.

I pulled on jeans and a heavy sweatshirt, running shoes, got the dogs leashed up, and took them for a quick jog to a nearby park. The tennis courts were empty but brightly lit, in case any enthusiast fancied a game on a cold autumn night. While the dogs ran off steam chasing balls around the court, I checked my texts. Five were from Bernie, anxious for word on August. She was about as subtle as Mitch, and equally insistent, scratching and whining at my in-box.

I tried August's phone number—I'd entered it in my speed-dial file and had been trying it periodically throughout the day. This time, as before, I got a tinny voice saying that he wasn't answering and that his mailbox was full.

THE POLICE AREN'T VERY INTERESTED, I texted Bernie and Angela. THE ODDS ARE THE BREAK-IN HAS NOTHING TO DO WITH AUGUST, BUT IT STILL WOULD BE GOOD IF HE TURNED UP.

Of course Bernie called almost at once and Angela about half an hour later, but I told them both I'd give them more details the next day, after I'd been to his apartment. "I want to see if I can find a friend or neighbor he might have talked to."

I changed into a silk shirt and a wool wrap and went down to the Golden Glow, the bar where I've been spending too much time lately. I needed the warmth of Sal Barthele's Tiffany lamps and the smoothness of her whisky, but mostly her acerbic friendship.

The next morning, when I got to August's place, I was long after the fair. My only consolation was knowing that if I'd gone last night, I would still have been too late.

August rented a one-bedroom in a courtyard building, six entrances, three stories, no doorman. I rang the bell, waited a minute, leaned on it for a good thirty seconds, waited again, but still had no response to my third ring.

There was a semiresident super—he had an apartment on the ground floor of one of the units opposite August's, but he also covered another building around the corner on Halsted. I knew this because my superior detecting skills had discovered the notice in the outer doorway about where to find Jorge Baros if he wasn't in the Buckingham Place building.

I called the number on the notice, saying I was a detective with some questions about August Veriden. Baros was in the middle of a plumbing repair.

"I am very worried about Mr. Veriden," Baros said, "but I have water leaking through two floors here. Wait for me and I will come as fast as I may."

I sat on the concrete slab outside the entrance. I was answering e-mails and texts but got to my feet when a young man emerged from August's doorway. He was in his twenties, dark hair hanging lankly over his forehead and a loosely knotted tie at the neck of a royal blue shirt. He was eating a bagel with one hand, clutching a travel cup in the other, a briefcase tucked under the coffee arm, manipulating the door with the bagel hand.

I held the door for him. "I'm a detective, looking for August Veriden. Do you know him?"

He swallowed, tried to speak, had to gulp down some coffee and said, "Not really," in a thick voice.

"When did you last see him?"

"Can this wait? I'm late for work."

"Yep, so is August. He hasn't shown up for over a week. We're trying to find him."

"You and about twenty other people."

"How so?"

He finished the bagel, licked cream cheese from his fingers, and switched the briefcase to the bagel hand. "He lives above me, so I can hear when someone else is there. He's a nice enough guy but a loner. Last few days he's had more visitors than the rest of the building put together. I've got to run."

He took off down the street, his tie flapping over his shoulder.

I ran after him. "I'll see you to your train or car or whatever. This is important. Over how many days? Last night? Night before?"

He stopped at the corner of Broadway, holding out his arm for a cab. One appeared almost magically, which calmed him enough that he paused, hand on the open door.

"I thought this might be serious. I told—well, the other person in my apartment—that we should have called the police, only you can't start complaining about other people's loud parties or they'll report you next, and August is usually the quietest person on earth."

"But when was it?" I tried not to shriek. "Last night? Night before?"

He thought for a moment. "Three nights ago. Yesterday I was at work, but another guy in the building said some cops showed up."

He climbed into the cab and shut the door on my demand for the name of the guy who'd told him about the cops.

I ran back up Buckingham. Jorge Baros hadn't arrived yet. When I phoned again, he said he was still drowning but would get there as quickly as possible.

I'd brought my picks with me on the principle that it's better to carry more than you need than to curse yourself for leaving vital tools behind. I didn't have to work the street door—I'd kept it from latching when I shut it behind the bagel eater—and August's front door was worryingly easy because it wasn't locked at all.

Three days ago his apartment had probably been a charming place, sparely furnished with a few good pieces, at least as nearly as I could make them out under the upended plants, CD and DVD covers, and dishes that had been dumped from a wooden hutch onto the floor.

The destruction felt like a shock wave. Angela's description of her cousin came to me: the little boy who'd carefully put his farm animals to bed at night. Not nice, not nice at all.

I tiptoed around the mess to peer into his kitchen alcove. The same violent hands had dumped canisters of rice and pasta onto the countertop. Ants were rooting around in the food, which had spilled onto the floor.

In the small bedroom, the mattress had been pulled from the bed, the bedding itself wadded into a ball and flung to the doorway. French windows led from the bed to a narrow balcony, where planters with baby sunflowers and late tomatoes had been emptied. The flowers were still alive, growing in the dirt that had landed around them, but the tomatoes looked feeble.

I tried to search for anything that might tell me where or when August had gone. I snapped pictures with my phone, close-ups of individual pieces of damage, wider shots of the general disarray. I started in the bedroom, then worked my way around the balcony and back to the main room.

When I'd taken a few hundred shots, I returned to the bedroom and unfurled the bedclothes, laying them across the slit mattress. I didn't see any bloodstains, either there or on the floor or furniture.

Not that I travel with luminol and a UV light, but these weren't subtle fingers at work, here or in Evanston.

Bernie and Angela had said August wanted to make movies. I didn't see any cameras or laptops, but that didn't mean anything: the wreckers could have taken them, August could have left with them, even the cops might have lifted them, since the bagel eater said they'd been here yesterday.

Looking around, I wondered if the police had really come. There wasn't any crime-scene tape, nor the telltale silver dust of a fingerprint search.

I sat back on my heels. There had to be something here that would give me a starting point. August owned books as well as CDs and DVDs. It seemed beside the point to worry about disturbing evidence; I just didn't want to leave my own prints here. Using my coat sleeve, I picked up books, shook them to see if any useful notes slipped out, then closed them and put them back on their shelves. He had a solid collection of black writers: James Baldwin, Lorraine Hansberry, Malcolm X, Ta-Nehisi Coates, Angela Davis.

My phone rang. I jumped up, hoping it was the building super, but it was only Bernie. I let it go to voice mail, but the call reminded me to check whether August was old-fashioned enough for a landline and voice mail.

I didn't find any jacks or dismembered phones: like his peers, he did everything via cell towers. I came upon an artist's sketchbook. I didn't touch it with my hands but lifted some of the pages with a kitchen knife. The book seemed to be a kind of artist's diary, where August wrote down story ideas and made rough drawings of sets.

I found a garbage bag in one of the open kitchen drawers and slipped the book inside. I also took some of the unlabeled DVDs, hoping they might include August's own film efforts. Perhaps he'd been filming something dangerous and the perpetrators had come hunting him, first at the gym and then in his own apartment. Perhaps it would be exciting footage of weddings and bar mitzvahs. Maybe I'd offload them onto Bernie and Angela—it would keep them occupied, keep them from buzzing around me demanding to know what I was doing.

As I made a last circuit of the rooms, I stopped to study the outsize film posters on the walls. Oscar Micheaux held pride of place over the bed, with a poster for *Within Our Gates*. Facing him was Ousmane Sembène's *Black Girl*.

I squinted to study the paper through the glare on the glass covers—the posters looked like originals, but along with luminol I lacked paper-authenticating equipment. And expertise.

Kasi Lemmons and Gordon Parks were in the main room. Emerald Ferring, in *Pride of Place,* faced the entryway. Her portrait, the expression aloof, filled most of the poster, with a small inset of her in prison garb, presumably a scene from the movie. It was different from the others because it was signed.

"August, I believe in you: believe in yourself," she'd written in small, neat letters along the right side and then signed her name with a flourish that covered most of the bottom of the frame. I'd never heard of Emerald Ferring or *Pride of Place,* but that didn't mean anything: I'm not a pop-culture maven like Alan Banks or Rebus.

The ruined apartment seemed to be draining my self-confidence—no luminol, no paper expertise, ignorant of pop culture. There must be something I was good at.

Jorge Baros, the building super, came up the walk as I was leaving the building. He was a tall, lean man, with the noble face of an Afghan hound. Incongruously, he was followed by a small white terrier, who sniffed at my jeans legs but sat at a hand sign from Baros.

The super knew about the wreck of August's apartment—he'd been the person who called the police. "And that was yesterday. Why is only today a detective coming?"

"I'm private, not with the police."

"Ah, private. Someone has hired you to solve this crime?"

"Someone has asked me to find Mr. Veriden. I didn't know about the break-in until I got here this morning. It doesn't look as though the police did much yesterday."

Baros spit. "The police did nothing. They asked was Mr. Veriden often fighting with his lovers, and I said he was always quiet, not a fighting kind of man. And always very neat. Whenever I go into his apartment—which is only when there is a problem, I am not spying, believe me, but sometimes I must fix a radiator or a refrigerator—everything is clean, orderly. The flowers—those broke my heart. He cares for his flowers, and they bring cheer to the apartment. He knows my wife is not well, and often he gives me flowers for her. What has happened to him? They did not harm him, did they?"

I spread my hands, universal sign of bafflement. "The night before Halloween, there was a major act of vandalism at a big Evanston gym where he works. Police think he was stealing their drug supply, but his apartment looks as though someone was trying to find something."

"He would not be stealing drugs. He is so honest." Baros pronounced the *h,* as my mother used to—Latin speakers uncertain about when it is silent in English, when it is aspirated.

"He took off about ten days ago without saying where he was going," I said. "Does he have a lover, or friends in the building or the neighborhood, he would talk to?"

Baros shook his head. "I don't know everything about the tenants—there are thirty-six apartments here, after all. But we live opposite, my wife and I, so we see this entrance more than the others, and my wife, she worries about August, that he is too lonely. He is so polite, so kindhearted, one of the few who even knows she is having radiation treatments. He has taken care of Rosquilla for us sometimes."

He pointed at the little terrier, who barked at his name.

"Can I talk to your wife? Maybe August confided in her."

Baros's wife was at work, despite her cancer treatments, but he promised to consult her and call me.

"You didn't see who broke in?" I asked.

"We are in bed at ten, so it has taken place after that. After seeing the destruction in Mr. Veriden's home, I am telling the owners they must put in better security, cameras, alarms, but it is too late to protect Mr. Veriden."

I shook hands and left him on that melancholy note. His phone was ringing as I went down the walk, and he called out to me to wait—it was his wife, on her break.

He spoke in Spanish, explaining that a *detective* was here asking about Señor Veriden. After that, I lost track of the conversation, except for the *"sí, sí, sí"* that Baros interjected at intervals.

When he hung up, Baros shook his head sadly. "She didn't know he was going away. He is a nice young man. We would not like to think of any harm coming to him."

4

LONG SHOT

EVEN THOUGH I'D never met August, I wouldn't want any harm to come to him either. I had gone to his place partly to quiet Bernie, partly because I'd been baffled by what I'd seen at the gym yesterday.

Now I was not only baffled but worried. In fiction it's the cliché of the serial killer or drug dealer that he's quiet, keeps himself to himself: *Such a good boy, so attentive to my wife, you'd never suspect him of dismembering and burying a dozen people. We never believed he was head of a cartel that stole drugs from college locker rooms.*

In fiction August would be that person—quiet, thoughtful, tidy on the outside, a raging psychopath within. This being real life, or at least as close as I could get to such a thing, I found it highly unlikely. Call it impossible.

A cold drizzle began to fall, forcing me to sprint the last quarter mile home—parking is at such a premium in August's neck of the woods that I'd walked the two miles from my own place. There's nothing like physical discomfort to clear the mind. When I'd changed into dry clothes and made myself an espresso, I phoned a detective I know at Area Six.

Terry Finchley and I have a long history. We respect each other and don't quite trust each other. In his case it's part general cop dislike of PIs complicated by his being close to a cop I used to date: Terry thinks I behaved badly to Conrad Rawlings, because Conrad got shot when he involved himself in a case I was working. However, Terry is one of the most senior officers I know whom I trust. He's also African-American and might be more empathetic with August's situation.

I left a précis of the situation on his voice mail. "Right now your buddies in Evanston aren't treating it like much of anything, but I don't want August in the cross hairs if they suddenly decide it's a major event. I'd love it if your techies printed the ruins in August's apartment and compared notes with Evanston over the break-in at the gym."

The dogs had come upstairs while I was on the phone, delighted to have me back in the middle of the day. I petted them absentmindedly.

I needed to talk to someone who knew August better than Bernie and Angela did. I'd run a search on him through my subscription utilities, which give me access to a lot of law-enforcement and financial data that ought not to be available to people like me.

Neither LifeStory nor DataMonitor had turned up much beyond what Angela had told me: August had studied exercise therapy and film at Loyola, he worked for Six-Points as a contract employee, he was an orphan whose father had died in the First Gulf War, and his only relatives were Angela's branch of the family down in Louisiana. His bank account was modest, but twelve days ago he'd cashed a check for four thousand dollars.

I whistled softly. Even though it didn't go as far today as it used to, that was a respectable wad to be carrying around. No sign of where it came from either. Maybe he'd done an exceptional job filming a middle reliever's trapezius movement.

Both search engines mentioned August's film work and his website: Spectral Vision, with the tagline "Turning ghosts of ideas from reel to real." I clicked on the link and found clips of some of his work—weddings, mostly of gay or lesbian couples; First Communions and bar mitzvahs; forays into art shorts of the kind that are popular today, featuring ominous unseeable presences with people running from horrors too terrible to make concrete. Nothing that suggested a four-thousand-dollar check.

His publicity photo on the website was an artfully arranged shot of him staring at himself in a sequence of mirrors. It showed him in standard young-auteur dress: black turtleneck, black leather jacket, blue jeans. His face was round, with full cheeks and deep-set, serious eyes. I copied the picture to my photo album.

"August, I believe in you," Emerald Ferring had written on his poster. I asked my phone if it knew anything about Ferring or *Pride of Place.* The movie had been made in 1967 by Jarvis Nilsson, a black male director I'd also never heard of. *Pride of Place* had been screened at only a handful of theaters in Harlem, Bronzeville, and other black neighborhoods around the country before it disappeared without a trace.

I scrolled through the plot summary. Ferring played a young woman raised in a wealthy black enclave on Cape Cod. It's 1964, Freedom Summer, and she's a freshman at Vassar who volunteers to go to Mississippi, against the wishes of her parents. She is arrested during a voter-registration drive. Her parents bail her out and try to bring her home, but she insists on staying in prison with the other detainees. After her release she gets involved with a sharecropper and witnesses his murder at the hands of the Klan. At the end of the movie, she withdraws from Vassar, following a hot altercation with the college president along with her parents, and returns to Mississippi to help run a Freedom School.

Wikipedia didn't offer much about Ferring. Neither did my databases, but they told me she'd been born in Fort Riley, Kansas, in 1944. The account of how she'd met Nilsson was sketchy, but she'd made two other films with him after *Pride of Place,* both of which had also disappeared after a minimal release.

Her current home was in Chicago, where she'd settled while filming *Lakeview,* a series that sounded like a thinly disguised remake of *The Jeffersons:* the show's theme song was "Moving On Up to the North Side." I wondered how much litigation that had spawned.

Ferring had given August her autograph and a personal message; maybe she'd also let him confide his dreams and plans. Maybe he'd even told her where he was going. It was a long shot, but I didn't have any close ones.

Ferring lived down on Ninety-sixth Street, in the Washington Heights neighborhood, a few blocks from the church where Barack used to worship when he was a state senator.

My calendar was clear until midafternoon, when I needed to be in court to testify in a warehouse-supply scam I'd helped uncover. I could get down to Ninety-sixth Street and still make my court date, if I hustled to my office for my case files. I changed quickly into my courtroom costume, a severely cut suit in superfine wool, but as I was stuffing keys and laptop into my briefcase, I recalled the aloof, regal face in August's poster. That photo was almost fifty years old, but Ms. Ferring didn't look like the kind of person a stray detective could just barge in on.

My databases had given me Ferring's unlisted number. A man with a deep, soft voice answered on the fifth ring.

When I announced myself and asked if I could speak with Ms. Ferring, the deep voice became cold. "What are you selling?"

"Nothing," I said. "I'm a private investigator—"

He hung up on me. A son or a butler whose job was to protect Ferring's privacy?

I tried phoning again. This time my call went straight to voice mail. Announcement only, no way to leave a message.

I gritted my teeth. If the traffic gods had any sense of decency, I could get down to Ninety-sixth and Halsted, have an hour with Ms. Ferring or her bulldog, and still make my court date. I made sure my makeup go-bag was in my briefcase, drove to my office for my files, and covered the fifteen miles to Ferring's house in a breathtaking forty-seven minutes. Speed record on the Ryan this time of day.

Ferring lived on a street of small ranch houses and tidy yards. The trees had dropped their leaves, but most people had raked their lawns. Halloween decorations still dripped ghostly fingers from the bushes, but Ferring's walk, like her neighbor's, was lined with potted mums. Her house was a bit bigger than the others on the block, but not ostentatiously so.

No one answered, and anyway, the house felt empty behind the shrouded windows. Empty buildings seem remote somehow, as if without people inside they were withholding themselves from the world.

Across the street an older woman was out with a dachshund. The dog was barking at a squirrel taunting it from a nearby tree, but the woman was staring at me in frank curiosity. White woman in a black neighborhood, what could I possibly be doing here?

I walked over and introduced myself. "I'm hoping to talk to Ms. Ferring. You wouldn't know if she's due back soon, would you?"

The woman curled her lip. "Are you expecting to sell her something, like sandy cement for her driveway?"

"A lot of scam artists trolling around here?" I asked. It's an infuriating part of modern life, bogus contractors preying on the elderly. That might explain the coldness of the young man who'd answered Ferring's phone.

"And you're not one of them." Her mouth twisted more derisively.

"I'm a private detective." I handed her one of my cards. "A young man, a wannabe filmmaker, has disappeared. He's a loner, without much family, and I can't find anyone who knows where he is. I know he made a good impression on Ms. Ferring, and I'm hoping he might have told her where he was going."

"Would this young filmmaker have a name?"

I pulled out my cell phone and showed her August's picture. "August Veriden."

"And what is it you think he's doing with Ms. Emerald? Stealing from her?" The contemptuous twist of her lips became more pronounced.

First the guy with the deep voice hung up on me, and now this. I began to wonder if August was actually hiding inside Ferring's house and the neighborhood was protecting him from authorities, or just from a nosy white woman. But that would mean he'd been involved in something that predated the break-ins at the gym and his home.

The dog kept whining and growling, pulling on its leash while the squirrel made that *chuck-chuck-chuck* sound: I'm up a tree and you're stuck. My sympathies were completely with the dog.

I shook my head. "I can't tell you more than I have already: I've been hired to find him, and I can't find anyone who knows him. Speaking to Ms. Ferring is my last hope. Is she ill or out of town that she isn't answering her phone herself?"

"Don't we all deserve some privacy, away from prying questions?" the woman burst out.

"Is that what this sounds like? I'm not trying to pry into Ms. Ferring's life and business, but young August Veriden may well get framed for a crime I don't think he committed. The police have issued a bulletin asking for anyone who spots him to turn him in. I'd like to find him first. If you can't help me, I'll ring every bell on the street. Someone will tell me something."

The woman looked down at her dog, yanked at its leash, snapped at "Poppy" to be quiet. Poppy grinned up at her and resumed barking.

"You'd better talk to Troy," she said to me, her lips tight with bitterness at having given in to me. "Troy Hempel."

She pointed at the house just south of Ferring's. "He ran errands for Ms. Emerald when he was a boy, and he's the person she trusts with her power of attorney and what-have-you. He's at work now—his mother's the only person home. He's at a downtown bank, technology director."

5

DESIGNER BEER

TROY HEMPEL ARRIVED at the Golden Glow about half an hour late, but I didn't mind. It had been a long day; I was glad of the chance to unwind, sip a little whisky, chat with Sal. She nudged me when Hempel came into the room—good bar owner that she was, even though she was in the middle of an amusing story about her grandmother's 103rd birthday, she could track the whole room.

My own computer consultant has the soft face and body of a cherub, or at least someone whose only workout involves moving from the desk to the coffee machine and back. Troy Hempel looked as though he could break Ukrainian hackers into his soup, like crackers: his navy superfine pullover stretched across traps that made Sal cock a wicked eye at me.

"Is this Jake's competition? Boy never got those muscles playing a bass."

Jake Thibaut, my lover. I think. At any rate he's a bass player, currently in Switzerland with his early-music group.

I shadowboxed Sal and got up to greet Hempel. I'd tracked him down while I was waiting in the hall at the Daley Center for my testimony to be called.

Court cases never work to a reliable timetable, which is fine with lawyers and judges who get paid for being there, but not so much fun for witnesses like me. At least during the hour I swung my heels,

I managed to dig up Hempel's phone numbers, both his cell and his office at the Fort Dearborn Trust.

Instead of trying to explain myself over the phone, I sent him a text. I composed it carefully, writing it out beforehand: I wanted to give him enough information to persuade him to meet me, without trying to second-guess why Ferring's neighbor had been so cagey or why Hempel himself had hung up on me—assuming it was he who'd answered my call to Ferring this morning. My formal, stilted approach proved effective: Hempel's response wasn't enthusiastic, but he agreed to meet me at the Glow at six.

After setting that up, I found the court still arguing over whether my evidence was admissible. I also found three new incoming messages from Bernie. NO NEWS, I wrote back. I'LL LET YOU KNOW WHEN I'VE LEARNED ANYTHING, SO PLEASE STOP SLAPPING YOUR STICK AT MY KNEES.

Netflix had all three feature films that Jarvis Nilsson had made with Emerald Ferring. I streamed *Pride of Place.* Ferring made an ardent activist, but the dialogue was heavy-handed.

The bailiff finally called me at four, just as Ferring was sitting by the sharecropper's grave with her baby boy. She was making a stirring speech to her parents about how one day a boy like him would be president, but until then, "We have work to do here, Mother. I can't leave Elton's side in death any more than I would in life."

Yes! Cue "The Star-Spangled Banner."

Court adjourned half an hour later, with my testimony still incomplete. I took the L north, changed out of court clothes to give the dog a quick run, then put on clean jeans and a bronze wool jacket and hiked back to the Glow. I was starting to feel like Peter Sellers, playing six characters in the same movie, racing from one costume to the next. I was late getting to the Glow, but still twenty minutes ahead of Hempel.

When I explained to Sal who I was meeting and why, she gripped my shoulder in an iron hand and pushed me onto a barstool.

"Emerald Ferring?" she said. "You've arranged a meeting with Emerald Ferring?"

"You know her?" I asked, prying her fingers out of my shoulder.

"I watched everything she was in when I was growing up, even that lame rip-off of *The Jeffersons*. She was such a model for me—if you meet her, you do it here."

"It all depends on this minder of hers," I said, "assuming he shows up. You'll be glad to know that her neighbors protect her privacy as if she were the head of the CIA."

Sal pelted me with questions—about the neighbors, Ferring's house, and how August Veriden had wormed his way into Ferring's confidence.

"You're like a teenage girl with a crush," I grumbled.

Sal nodded. "Where Emerald Ferring is concerned, I *am* a teenage girl with a crush."

I decided not to mention I'd never heard of Ferring until this morning: that might create a chasm that would be difficult to bridge. Instead I showed her Troy Hempel's entry on LinkedIn, and we bet on what he was likely to drink.

"Bourbon," I said. "He's young, he's hip, he's proving he's smooth."

"You might as well pay up now, girlfriend. Young, hip—beer, local brew."

Hempel came in about ten minutes later. He had the impassive face of a discreet butler, but his eyes widened as he took in Sal's famous bar, a mahogany horseshoe, and the Tiffany lamps that make her insurance too high for me to count even if I use my toes along with my fingers.

"I work five blocks away and never knew this place existed. How long has it been here?" he said.

"Since you were teething," Sal said, flashing her thousand-watt smile to take the sting out of the words. "What can I pour you?"

He wanted beer, which made Sal smirk. Hempel asked for something called Hophazardly. I thought maybe he was challenging Sal for making fun of his youth, but she just called over to Erica, her head bartender, who trotted down the stairs and came back with a case to stick under the bar.

Sal had reserved a table for me in the far corner of the room, away from the televisions, which were giving us news on one screen and the Bulls on the other.

"Okay," Hempel said. "Now tell me what you want with Ms. Emerald."

"August Veriden." I brought out my cell phone and showed him a couple of the shots I'd taken this morning in August's apartment. "I have no idea what's going on, but there's similar wreckage in the gym where he works."

I went through my spiel: August's cousin hiring me to find him before the police did, my various theories about what had led to the destruction, and my wondering how well August knew Emerald Ferring. "Is she someone he might have confided in?"

Hempel had drunk his Hophazardly in two swallows and was rolling the bottle between his palms. Erica, who scans the room almost as skillfully as Sal, appeared with a fresh bottle and a lifted eyebrow. Hempel nodded but asked for a word with Sal. In private.

I made a face as Erica took him over to the bar and interrupted Sal's conversation with one of her regulars, a trader who sits at the end every night, drinking four double bourbons whether the market is up or down. Sal is African-American: Hempel apparently needed her opinion on whether a white woman like me was trustworthy.

He came back to the table a few minutes later, Sal laughing at me behind his back. "Ms. Emerald left town ten days ago with August," he said without preamble. "She might have told me what she was doing if I'd been here, but I was attending an advanced training institute in Tel Aviv. I only got home five days after she left. She told my mother she'd forwarded her phone to mine, and she expected me to take care of her affairs while she was gone."

He gave a half smile. "I've been running errands for her since she moved onto our street twenty-five years ago. I think she still imagines I'm seven: 'Troy, I need my lawn cut today' or 'Troy, I need a ride to the hairdresser,' that kind of thing."

"She didn't tell your mother where she was going?"

"Oh, yes. She said August was a gifted young filmmaker who was going to put together a documentary of her life. They were driving down to Kansas so he could film her roots."

I digested that. "Was it supposed to be a big secret? I don't understand why August isn't answering his phone."

Hempel shook his head. "That has me worried, too. My mother wondered if August was taking advantage of Ms. Emerald. She never was a superstar, but she still gets royalties from a couple of TV shows she was in. She does better than most old black women, and we all—everyone on the street—try to keep an eye out for hustlers."

"Is she able to manage her own affairs?" I asked.

"Oh, her mind is fine, but she never had much business sense even when she was young. She's given me a power of attorney so I can handle her affairs. Anyway, my mother says she had a long talk with Veriden before they took off, and she thought he was on the level."

"Right before he disappeared, Veriden cashed a biggish check. I'm wondering if Ferring gave it to him, and if so—did he con her out of it, or did she offer it?"

"Is that where that money went?" Hempel said. "I'm a signer on her accounts. I saw she'd pulled out four thousand, but she did it as a cashier's check. Damn."

He smacked a wide palm on the table. "This all happened while I was out of the country, but my mother says it was Ms. Emerald's idea and that she talked August into going with her to film her, to make what they call an origin story these days. She's wanted to find a way to revive her career, or at least generate interest in those feature films of Nilsson's, so I believed it, believed it was Ms. Emerald driving the train, in a manner of speaking."

"Maybe August pitched it to her, but in such a way that she thought it was her own idea," I suggested.

"Yeah, that's what I've started to think, especially since neither of them is answering their phones. We—my mother and I—have been trying to decide what to do. I hate to involve the cops, especially when I don't know where Ms. Emerald is. They could be on the road in any of four different states or in some dinky Kansas town."

"They drove?" I asked.

"Yes, in Veriden's car, a Prius. Ms. Emerald hardly ever drives anymore, so he'd be doing it all. I've been worrying since I got back from Israel, but now I'm seriously disturbed. Look, I'd have to talk this over with my mother and one or two other people—but if they agree, would you try to find them?"

6

CROSSING THE RIVER

"ONE DAY MY grandfather walked across the Kansas River when a drought had shrunk it down to three feet," Gertrude Perec said. "He left behind a wife, eleven children, and all his recipes for curing everything from warts to cancer."

"You never told me that before, Gram. I mean about the cancer recipes," Cady Perec said. "Did you ever try any of them? Or show them to Dr. Kiel?"

Gertrude laughed. "I only remember one, for stomach cancer: you soaked rose petals in port for seventy-two hours. Probably made all those good church ladies who signed the Pledge feel better even if it didn't make them well. No, I never thought to mention it to Dr. Kiel, but maybe that lay behind my wanting to work for a scientist. Show up my grandfather for the charlatan he was."

"Who is Dr. Kiel?" I asked.

"He's a big disease authority—at least he was," Cady said. "He's retired now, but they still talk to him sometimes, like last year when there was a salmonella outbreak in Eudora—that's a town east of here—he tracked it down to someone who was handling food at a burger joint. Gram used to be his secretary."

She turned back to Gertrude. "I know that your grandfather never came home, everybody knows that, but did he ever write your granny, or your mom, or anyone?"

"If she did, she never let on," Gertrude said. "I always wondered if he had another family on the other side of the river or if he just kept walking north until he got to Canada. My grandmother was a terrifying woman—the only time I asked her about my grandfather, she beat me until my legs bled, with a switch she pulled from that bush."

Gertrude waved a hand toward the porch stairs, where a thick bush, stripped of most of its leaves by the fall storms, overhung the railing. The branches were about an inch around. Getting struck with one of those would hurt.

Cady Perec turned to me. "Disappearing grandfathers is a family theme. If I ever have kids, they'll never know what happened to their grandfather, because I never knew what became of him—my own father, I mean. Gram never hit me with anything, but she doesn't like to talk about him."

Gertrude stretched out a hand to press Cady's shoulder. "I've told you all I know, punkin."

"Which is nothing." Cady said.

"Even if I knew more about him, it's nothing a stranger wants to hear."

It was a warning signal, delivered with all the subtlety of a switch across the legs, but I ignored the hint.

"I want to hear things," I said. "It's how I sift out what I need so I can get where I want to be. And I never wantonly use the chaff."

"Listen to you," Gertrude Perec scoffed. "Sifting wheat from chaff. No one would ever guess you grew up in a big city instead of a farm."

My cheeks burned, but I said in a tone of innocent inquiry, "I knew this was a university town, so I didn't realize people who lived in it still farmed. Did the town grow up around houses like yours?"

Gertrude Perec's brick house would have qualified as a mansion in the South Chicago of my childhood. I hadn't been invited inside—we were sitting on a screened porch that faced northeast, toward the river that Gertrude's grandfather had waded across—but it was a big Victorian, with maybe a dozen rooms on two stories. The sun had set, but the streetlamps shone across a few dead sunflowers, not wheat fields.

Cady laughed softly. "Gram grew up in this house, but we all know a little about wheat and corn, it's so close to us. Everyone knows someone who works at the grain elevators or the fertilizer plant, especially us, because Grandpa Perec's family used to farm south of town."

It had been five days since my first meeting with Troy Hempel; I'd been in Kansas for two of them. It had taken Hempel, his mother, and six other neighbors several days to agree to hire me—after a fierce discussion on my abilities, whether I could be trusted to take Ms. Ferring's disappearance seriously, and whether my fees constituted price gouging. Troy and his mother called me to a neighborhood conference; Troy had invited Sal as a character witness.

I brought Bernie and Angela, putting them under strict orders not to speak. Both young women were furious when I weighed in on the side of "No, this private detective doesn't know or care enough about Emerald to waste our money on."

I shut them up and continued to explain that Chicago was my briar patch. "I know how to get things done here, who the players are, and what games they cheat at. It's where my friends are, so if I fall on my face, as we all sometimes do, the people are here who will glue me back together. Kansas—I might as well try to solve a crime in Milan. In fact, I'd probably feel more at home in Milan—at least it's an industrial hub with an identifiable group of thugs. There are local agencies in Kansas who know all the players. It makes more sense for you to work with one of them."

"None of us can go down there to evaluate an agency, except maybe Troy, and even then we wouldn't know if they could be trusted to do the right thing," Troy's mother said. "Believe me, Ms. Warshawski, we talked about that, we talked about calling the Kansas state police. And Missouri and Iowa, depending which route August and Emerald took. It's hard to involve an investigator in your private business, but at least we've met you and we've talked to people who think highly of you. Sal Barthele here says you are honest and reliable. We can pay you for a week's work down there."

Bernie interrupted to applaud vigorously. Angela said, "Another three days have gone by, and we don't know where August is, or Ms. Ferring either. You really have to do this, Vic."

I tried to suppress my visceral, two-year-old's objection to people telling me what I really have to do, especially when Sal weighed in on that theme as well, saying she'd go herself if I didn't.

"Ferring could be lost in some Iowa cornfield. Or this young moviemaker could have been hauled off to jail or shot by some small-town cop. Didn't you say the police put out one of those reports on him because of the break-in at the gym?"

"A BOLO," I said. "Yes. But I've checked with law enforcement in the four states where Veriden and Ferring might have been stopped and can't find any record that he's in custody."

"But would you get a report from every rinky-dink town between here and Kansas City?" Sal demanded.

I'd worried about that myself, but even if Veriden had been picked up somewhere along the route, I couldn't possibly check every small town along the interstates between Chicago and Kansas.

Sal's urging wasn't what sent me southwest. I'm not sure what my real reason was. It's true none of my big-money clients needed me right now and most of the cases I was working on could be handled online. Any essential surveillance in Chicago could be offloaded onto the Streeter brothers, a trio whose core business had never been clear to me—they did woodworking, piano moving, bodyguarding, and surveillance, all with the same patient attention to detail.

Mr. Contreras was going to the Caribbean for three weeks to stay with a niece who had a winter place in St. Croix. While he's able to look after himself, I don't like leaving him on his own for long stretches now that he's in his nineties. If he was going to be gone anyway, it removed one reason for my staying in Chicago.

And then there was Jake Thibaut, my bass player. A bass player.

We'd been dating, or whatever people our age do, ever since the night he smuggled me past a group of thugs in a bass case.

Jake plays both modern and early music; his early-music group, High Plainsong, had won an important competition whose prize was a year's residency in Switzerland. Jake had flown out in September, after six weeks of maniacal activity: renting his condo, working out logistics with venues where he already had commitments, helping his students find other teachers.

Long before he left, his head had been in the Alps, dreaming of music and musicians. Jake tried to talk me into going with him, which led to a major quarrel. "You're in a rut, Vic. You do the same thing over and over. Why not jump off the high board with me, see what the future would hold if you risked everything?"

"You're not risking anything," I'd replied, annoyed. "You have a paid-for fellowship. What would I do? Quickly master German so I could start investigating Swiss banks for defrauding Holocaust survivors?"

"That's what I mean," he responded, annoyed in turn. "You're bright, you're creative—why does your mind automatically go to banks and fraud instead of something bigger, more challenging?"

"Can't think of a bigger challenge than taking down a Swiss bank," I couldn't help saying.

"You take chances with your body all the time in your work, but you never take the big chances, life-changing chances," he argued. "Fly to Basel with me, see what will unfold for you. There's so much music there! It would inspire you in ways you can't predict."

"Listening to music and loving it, or loving you playing it, isn't the same as making music," I objected. "I can see myself in my life in Chicago. I love my work, and I don't know what kind of work I could find in Basel that would bring me as much satisfaction."

"Take a chance, see what opens up," Jake urged. "If you spend the rest of your life chasing con artists and corporate maniacs, they'll destroy your soul in the end."

He flushed as soon as the words left his mouth.

"That's what you think of my work?" I said after a stunned silence. "Soul-destroying? I thought I was helping people who'd lost all other options gain a measure of dignity."

We'd kissed and made up, sort of, but in the two months since he'd left, our Skype sessions had become shorter, less intimate, and a few days before Bernie and Angela had come to me, Jake had sent me an e-mail saying he wouldn't be back at Thanksgiving, as he'd originally planned.

"That's the only week that Galina Yakovna can come to Basel before our Christmas concert, so it's imperative that I stay here. Why don't you fly out to join me?"

Yakovna was a Belarusian cellist whose name cropped up more and more frequently in Jake's more and more infrequent messages. Maybe that's why my message back was a terse, single sentence:

AND DEVELOP A SOUL?

A trip out of town, even to Kansas, began to seem like a good way to keep my mind off my troubles.

At the end of the meeting with Troy Hempel and Emerald Ferring's other neighbors, I drove over to Max Loewenthal's house. He lives on one of the quiet streets fronting Lake Michigan, and I knew Lotty Herschel was there that evening.

Lotty is a doctor who's mended the breaks and tears my investigations have inflicted on my body; I've helped her navigate the painful journey through her murdered family's history. It's not a contest, no one's keeping score, it's just that despite the difference in age and background, we each keep the other going.

"The choice is between Kansas and Switzerland, and you choose Kansas?" Lotty's mouth twisted in affectionate mockery.

"Mountains versus prairies, artisanal chocolate versus wheat, cuckoo clocks versus cuckoo politicians—who wouldn't make the same choice?" I said. "Besides, even though I miss Jake, I don't want to be a third wheel with his Belarusian cellist. Eighth wheel, since High Plainsong has seven members already."

I could picture trying to find ways to amuse myself while Jake and his cohort practiced ten hours a day.

"You realize, Victoria, that something serious has perhaps already happened to Emerald Ferring and August Veriden," Max said quietly. "I won't tell you your duty, because you are the most duty-driven person I have ever known, but it would be a mitzvah to go in person, not rely on an unknown outsider."

When I got up to leave, he stood on tiptoe to kiss my forehead. "You know, you have quite a fine soul. I wouldn't tamper with it."

I suppose it was the kiss, the compliment, that pushed me the final wavering steps across the line. The next day I organized the Streeter brothers' support, mapped my route to Fort Riley, and rechecked law-enforcement databases for any dead or injured John and Jane Does who might match August's or Ferring's description.

I was bringing Peppy with me. A dog might be a hindrance in a strange place, but I felt as though I were setting off on a voyage to Mars, untethered from every place and person I knew and loved: I needed the dog's companionship. Mitch, her half-black-Lab son, I sent to Dr. Dan's, a boarding farm in Wisconsin—one companion on the road was all I could comfortably handle.

I packed a bag with my main physical tools: picklocks, extra clips for my Smith & Wesson, night-vision binoculars, evidence bags. A fifth of Johnnie Walker Black. My laptop, iPad, charging cables. Peppy's bed, a bag of dog food. For me, hiking boots, a suitcase with three pairs of jeans, T-shirts, sweaters, slickers for the rain in the forecast, underwear, dress boots, my red Bruno Magli pumps—after all, I was going to Kansas—and a good outfit, because you never know.

Midafternoon I drove Mr. Contreras to O'Hare to catch his flight to St. Croix. Home to Skype with Jake. It was 5:00 P.M. in Chicago, midnight in Basel; he had just returned from a post-concert dinner. In the past when he's been on the road, he's played for me across the ether. We'd been too unhappy with each other lately for either of us to get comfort from his music, but tonight I asked for "Non più andrai," from *The Marriage of Figaro*—a martial air to send me to battle in good spirits.

Jake got out his early-music bass and played the melody, then improvised on it for some minutes, finishing in a minor key. When the music faded, we hung up without speaking and I drove the first leg of the trip, spending the night on the Iowa border near the Mississippi River.

7

A HAPPENING PLACE

CHICAGO SITS ON flat land, but skyscrapers and Lake Michigan make us think we live near mountains and oceans. South and west of the city lie the prairies. A lot of them.

As I drove through Iowa, I began to understand how pioneers from the east went mad in the vast landscape. Field follows identical field: brown cornstalks, limp and rotting in the rain; straw stubble standing in rough-plowed soil; farmhouse, outbuildings, a clump of trees; cornstalks, stubble, farmhouse. An occasional horse or cow or tractor.

I began imagining I was driving in circles. The sameness, the unchanging distance from a remote perimeter, the low gray sky glued to the horizon, made me feel like a tiny fish on a large salver, choking for air, longing for a hand to remove the platter cover. It was hard to stay alert; more than once I found myself swerving over the lane dividers, brought back to myself by the goose honk of a passing semi.

I stopped periodically to slog through fields around the rest stops with Peppy. A thin, cold rain had been falling since we left the Quad Cities, turning the ground muddy. After the first stop, I changed my socks and jeans and then had to do it again at our next break. I should have packed more clothes, another pair of boots, newspapers to wrap them in, my espresso machine, a fireplace, my mother's piano, a case of Barolo, a ticket to Basel.

I drove through eastern Nebraska and took old US 77 south. Late afternoon we reached the Flint Hills in central Kansas. Even though the drizzle continued, at least the rolling hills made the horizon less oppressive. I found a dog-friendly motel on the outskirts of Fort Riley. It didn't have an espresso machine or a fireplace, but it did have a washer and dryer, and after supper I was able to clean the clothes I'd dirtied during the day.

When I woke early Tuesday morning, the air had cleared; I drove to a nearby national park with Peppy. On a rocky outcropping above a creek, I watched the sun rise over the hills while the dog splashed in the water. It was strange, urban dweller that I am, to be the sole human presence in a landscape. Birds were hard at work, hawks were circling in the vast sky, the dog flushed a rabbit and took off in furious chase, but I was the lone person. I stood still, letting the silence close in on me. At first it felt soothing, but after a time it began to seem ominous. I jumped down, called the dog, and ran along the trail.

At ten, in clean jeans and my good jacket, I presented myself to the base commandant. He proved surprisingly helpful, or at least his secretary did. A brisk woman in khaki whose insignia I was too ignorant to interpret, she was startled by my mission.

"Emerald Ferring? How funny—I never heard of her until she showed up last month, and now here you are, looking for her."

It was hard to believe the trail was so easy to pick up: I could have done this by phone from Chicago, saved myself a long drive and the client several hundred dollars. "When was she here, exactly?"

The secretary consulted her computer. "Thirteen days ago."

"Was there a young man with her?" I pulled out my phone and showed her August's website photo.

"Yes, that's the man. Ms. Ferring said he was going to film her childhood home, but all those units were torn down decades ago. The whole fort is configured differently now. The general asked Colonel Baggetto to show Ms. Ferring the location. He took them around, then gave them a pass to the base library so that Ms. Ferring could look at the archives and see maps of the fort from when her father served here."

"How much time did they spend here? Did they give you any idea where they were planning to go next?"

The secretary didn't know, but she phoned Colonel Baggetto. "I didn't see them again, but they might have told him where they were going from here."

Baggetto was in a meeting but could see me in an hour. While I waited, the secretary printed out some maps of the base, a current one and one from 1943, when Ferring's father had been stationed here before shipping out to Europe.

"I looked that one up for Ms. Ferring when she got here. We don't have a record of housing by resident going back that far, but Private Ferring would have been living in this general area." The secretary blushed as she pointed to a place on the map marked as housing for Negro soldiers. "We've come a long way since then, thank goodness, but it was an embarrassing thing to have to show Ms. Ferring. We did turn up a record of her birth at the base hospital, though, and that was a help."

While I waited for Baggetto, I took the maps and walked around the fort. Cul-de-sacs lined with houses set in immaculate yards, cul-de-sacs with barracks in immaculate grounds, swing sets, schools, shops. And soldiers, many soldiers, moving from Point A to Point B with an alert bearing that said they were on important business, although a number stopped to pet Peppy. ("Ma'am, may I greet your dog?") Maybe I'd move here—long runs in the Flint Hills and then home to streets without any litter, where bright-faced young men and women spoke to me politely.

The Negro barracks had disappeared into a small nature preserve. I walked through it with Peppy, who followed mysterious tracks in the undergrowth while I kicked aside rotting leaves, looking for some sign of the soldiers who'd been housed there. Not even a foundation stone remained.

On our way back to the commandant's office, we passed a coffee shop, where I took a chance on the espresso: thin, watery, essentially undrinkable, except that I was starting to have a caffeine-withdrawal headache. If I'd gone to Basel, I'd be drinking rich European coffee with hand-knit chocolates, walking along the banks of the Rhine. Alone, without even my dog for company.

Colonel Baggetto reached the commandant's office just as I did. Like the secretary, he was in khaki, with medals and insignia. Unlike her, he had the kind of heavy beard that needed shaving twice a day.

"Captain Arrieta tells me that Emerald Ferring's disappeared and you're looking for her?"

So the two bars on the secretary's collar meant she was a captain. I guess a general couldn't have just any Tom, Dick, or Harriet book his dinner reservations for him. Colonel Baggetto sported silver oak leaves and something that looked like lightning bolts from a Wonder Woman cartoon.

I repeated my spiel. "This is the first trace I've found of Ferring or Veriden, so I'm hoping you can tell me what they did here and where they were heading next."

Baggetto's cell phone rang. He looked at the screen, took the call, made a few cryptic remarks, and turned back to me. "I'd never heard of Ms. Ferring before, but we've ordered copies of the films she starred in. We'll be showing them at the base cinema next month. While she was here, I got the library to look up her father's service record for her. He died at the Battle of the Bulge."

He coughed self-consciously. "He should have been recommended for a Bronze Star, but the times being what they were . . . Anyway, we had a small private ceremony here for Ms. Ferring and awarded the star posthumously to Private Ferring."

While he was speaking, his phone rang twice more. Both times he took the call and then picked up what he'd been saying to me in midsentence. Field training must focus the brain in a special way.

"I assume August Veriden filmed the ceremony," I said. "And

then what? She said, 'Thanks, and I'm heading back to Chicago, or Hollywood'?"

Baggetto looked at Arrieta. "Jackie, call over to the library, will you, and see if Ferring or her escort said anything about their next stop."

Captain Arrieta touched a speed-dial number and asked for the librarian. We could hear her end of the conversation, but apparently she had to speak to someone else and then yet another someone.

I said to Baggetto, "The Chicago and Evanston police departments have a BOLO out for August Veriden. You wouldn't be holding him here in your fort's jail or stockade or whatever it's called, would you?"

Baggetto's eyes widened. "Jesus, I don't think so, but—" He touched a number on his phone. "Pluto? . . . Yeah, Baggetto. Have you picked up a civilian male, African-American, twenty-five, in the last two weeks? . . . Seen a BOLO? . . . Know anything?"

"We're not holding him," Baggetto reported after a pause for Pluto to consult his computer or perhaps a crystal ball. "And our MPs haven't heard anything about him."

Arrieta, who'd finished with the library, turned to me. "One of the spouses who volunteers there took Ms. Ferring and her escort to supper at the canteen when they'd finished for the day. He said Ms. Ferring told him they were spending the night at a motel in Manhattan and then driving on to Lawrence. She told him she'd grown up and gone to the university there.

"Lawrence is about eighty-five miles to the east," she added helpfully. "Just an hour or two on I-70, but I can recommend some motels in Manhattan for you if you'd like—the Flint Hills are beautiful this time of year. Your dog would love them."

My brows went up: I'd left Peppy in the car both times I'd been in her office.

Arrieta and Baggetto laughed. "The base telegraph is way better than any Internet system ever devised," Arrieta said. "Even before you came in here, I knew that a civilian with a golden was in the fort."

File for future reference: in a small town, you cannot be invisible. I thanked the officers, gave them my card, and promised Arrieta I'd let her know when I found Emerald and August.

I stopped for lunch at a diner on the outskirts of the fort, gave the dog one last run in the hills, and then headed out. The traffic was thicker than we'd seen yesterday—we were going toward the big cities of the eastern part of the state, Topeka, Lawrence, Eudora.

We passed a sign for a Wizard of Oz museum, everyone's idea of what Kansas is about: tornadoes and no place like home. Even after we left the Flint Hills, the countryside remained hillier than I'd expected. I guess I thought Kansas would be a long, flat land, like the country I'd driven through yesterday.

"Were they telling me the truth?" I asked Peppy. She had her head out the window, checking the strange smellscape, and didn't appear interested in the question.

"It seemed odd that the colonel didn't want to know why there was a BOLO on August," I told her. "I would: I'd worry that I'd let an ax murderer into my fort. That makes me wonder if they actually did arrest August but didn't want to tell me. In that case, though, what did they do with Ms. Ferring?"

Peppy pulled her head in long enough to lick the back of my ear. I took it as a sign she was listening and wanted me to go on, but the chances were it was a plea for food.

Even with the thicker traffic, we reached Lawrence before sundown. After I found a B and B that accepted dogs, we walked around the town, getting a feel for the layout. It was warmer here than in Chicago; I needed only a light windbreaker.

The University of Kansas seemed to be the center of the town's universe: statues of its Jayhawk mascot were everywhere—in store windows, restaurants, on bank lawns. The university itself loomed overhead on top of a big hill. I'd go there in the morning to see what records they had of Emerald Ferring's student years.

My big discovery of the afternoon was that downtown Lawrence was awash in coffee bars and cafés. I wandered into four, sampling the espresso, and decided I liked a place called the Decadent Hippo best. The baristas doubled as bartenders, making my cortado in between orders for Moscow Mules and Bruised Elbows.

"We could be happy here," I said to Peppy. She agreed: everyone wanted to pet her and offer her bits of muffins.

My other discovery was the number of homeless people on the streets. I'm used to the sight in Chicago—inured, not a good thing—but it seemed startling in a college town, one that looked affluent, at least on the surface. The street people were young, compared to Chicago's homeless, and most were white, with the hard, crusty look of people who drink too much and sleep too little.

In the morning, over the first cortado of the day, I looked up Emerald Ferring. She didn't have family here, at least not relatives named Ferring. I couldn't find a history of anyone with that name, but of course most pre-1995 public data didn't exist online. I phoned the local library, but they hadn't kept old phone books.

Before doing anything else, I went to the police station, which shared space in the Judicial and Law Enforcement Center with the county sheriff and municipal and county courts. In theory a private eye is supposed to check in with the local law before tailing or surveilling anyone. In practice, in Chicago, I figure why bother an overworked force, but in a place where I was a foreigner, it seemed prudent to go to them before they came to me.

Oddly enough, the station was the first place I'd felt at home since leaving Chicago. The jurisdiction might be different, but the desk sergeant, the wanted posters, the anxious mom seeking news about her boy—they were what I'd known since the first time I went to work with my dad, who'd been a Chicago patrol officer for thirty years. I could remember him lifting me onto the high counter when I was four and old Sergeant Reardon pinning a star on my jacket. I've never felt so important since.

I showed my credentials to the Lawrence desk sergeant. I repeated my story, which sounded increasingly threadbare with each repetition. The sergeant looked at Emerald's and August's pictures and smiled pityingly.

"This is a college town, miss. Look out the window, or at least go over to Ninth and Massachusetts, and you'll see dozens of kids just like him. We don't pay attention to them unless they're drunk and disorderly or beating each other up, and even then, unless we need an ambulance, we just tell them to go home and sleep it off."

I wondered how true that was, especially with a black youth, but all I'd get if I pressed him would be a boatload of bad will. Not the way to start off in a new place.

"Ms. Ferring, the older woman he's traveling with, supposedly hired him to make a documentary about her life and work. She went to school here back in the sixties, so I'd like to find where she lived, check if they've been to her dorm or apartment or whatever to film. They don't have old phone books at the library—where else can I look?"

The sergeant shrugged, but an older officer who'd stopped to listen said, "The city has a historical society just a couple of blocks away. You might try there."

There was something to be said for a small city: the library, the police station, the historical society, and bars and restaurants were all within about a six-block area along Massachusetts, the main north-south street. The historical society was in a massive Victorian building at Tenth and Massachusetts. It had been built as a bank, apparently, with all the opulent fittings that nineteenth-century financiers liked in their temples of mammon. Funny that today's moguls, whose real net worth is about seventy-five times the Morgans' and Carnegies', operate inside minimalist glass-and-steel walls.

The woman at the entrance told me that while I was free to look around the three floors of the museum, I needed an appointment to use the archives. She gave me a form to fill out, but I persuaded her to let me talk to the archivist. I followed her to a back room, where we ducked around an antique wedding dress hung just inside the door.

The archivist was an elfin woman, barely big enough to appear above the stacks of documents on the desk in front of her. She nodded briskly as I explained what I wanted to know, told me to fill out my forms and she'd make sure that one of her research associates would get back to me as soon as possible. I couldn't persuade her to let me look at their old phone books right now, while I was in the room.

"If I let everyone come back here without an appointment, I'd never get any work done. Melvin or Cady will get back to you, I promise."

Short of lying on the dusty floor and holding my breath until my face turned blue, I couldn't think of any argument to budge her. I left with as much grace as possible—if I argued every point with every obstructor, I, too, would never get anything done. At the gift shop by the front desk, I bought maps of the town and the surrounding county: I always do better in a strange place when I can see the whole place laid out, instead of the bits you get from computer apps.

I also picked up a history of Lawrence. Much of it dealt with the antislavery fights of the 1850s and the Civil War era, when many of the men in town were slaughtered in a raid by some pro-slavery guerrillas, but it covered a miscellany of other topics—chief crops (sorghum, alfalfa, wheat, corn) and other notable events in the town's history—such as the creation of basketball as a game and Wilt Chamberlain's arrival in the early fifties. A happening place indeed.

8

ON THE HILL

FRUSTRATED BY MY lack of progress downtown, I went up to the university. The police and the people I'd encountered in the coffee shops had talked of "going up the hill" or "being on the hill" when speaking about the campus. This had led me to believe that if I drove to the top of the hill, it would be easy to find the offices I wanted. Instead I arrived at a town within a town. A guard at the entrance told me I couldn't drive onto the campus, but he gave me a map and showed where the administration building was: they could direct me to other departments if I needed them. He also pointed out nearby streets with student apartments where I could leave my car.

Like Fort Riley, downtown Lawrence had been clean and well tended, but the area bordering the campus looked less like a storybook town, more like the dilapidated streets of my childhood—small houses whose foundations had settled at rakish angles, apartment buildings put together with the barest nod at building codes, trash mixing with weeds along the verge.

I hated leaving Peppy in the car in such a ratty area, especially since the day was unusually warm for November, which meant the windows had to stay open.

"Bite anyone who tries to grab you," I said.

When I walked past the guard station onto the campus, I saw Jayhawk statues sprouting everywhere, but it was a beautiful campus, with rolling hills and open spaces, a bell tower on one of the high points, overlooking a little pond.

Students flowed around me in a thick stream, texting, scowling, laughing. I'd gone to an urban university, where everyone, even the most affluent—or perhaps especially the most affluent—seemed to think grooming was for the little people. Kansas students looked so scrubbed, so wholesome, that I might have stumbled into a eugenics experiment.

In the administration office, the staff were friendly and polite. They became downright excited when they learned that a film star had been a student there fifty years ago. Ferring had never really been in the public eye, outside the African-American film world, and the young staff in the front office had never heard of her. As soon as I explained what I knew of her history, they were eager to help, but they came up empty. They found a record of her time on campus buried in an old microfiche, but no housing records went back that far. They polled all the offices in the building while I waited: no one had seen or spoken to her in the last few weeks.

The theater building was about half a mile from the administration offices. Perhaps that was what made the kids so wholesome—lots of running miles up and down the campus hills in the fresh air. I jogged over, half my mind worrying about the dog—it had been selfish to bring her with me. I should have sent her to board at Dr. Dan's with Mitch.

The theater people were like the administration staff: eager to help but unable to tell me anything. The departmental secretary called various faculty and staff and confirmed that no one had seen either August or Emerald. The department chair came out to talk to me personally.

"We'd love to reconnect with Ms. Ferring. She left without graduating when she went to Hollywood to make *Pride of Place.* We've tried writing her—we'd like to give her her degree, and we'd like to talk to her about possibly donating her papers here." The chair handed me her card. "If you find her, would you see if she'd meet with me?"

Back downtown, I returned to the historical society, but the research associate hadn't arrived yet. The woman at the front desk apologized.

"She teaches social studies at Central Middle School, and there's so little call for her here that she doesn't come in every day. If you want to e-mail her, it's Cady_Perec@LawrenceHistoricalSociety.org."

I thanked the woman as civilly as I could—why hadn't she given me the information this morning?—and sent an e-mail to Cady Perec.

Peppy, who'd been totally safe in the car, was getting restless. I drove her over to the Kansas River, which ran along the north edge of town. We spent a happy hour ambling along a river path, with Peppy running in and out of the muddy water, chasing seagulls and ducks, and me answering e-mails from clients in Chicago. One of them included a twenty-megabyte file, the discovery document for a fraud case where I would be a major prosecution witness.

I was so focused on the file that I didn't realize we'd reached open country. I called Peppy out of a plowed field, where she'd stirred up some gophers, and headed back toward town. It seemed disconcerting to have my head in Chicago and my body in a field, as if I were inhabiting two unconnected universes at the same time.

Yelp! directed me to an Internet-office-services café on a side street near the best of the coffee shops I'd visited. I found free parking in a lot. Chicago's mayor and city council would go berserk if they found out there were towns in America that offered free parking in the heart of their downtowns. How could they overlook such a perfect opportunity to gouge the citizenry?

In the Internet café, I Photoshopped August's picture together with Emerald Ferring's. I typed in my cell phone and e-mail, asking anyone who'd seen either August or Emerald to get in touch with me. I printed out several dozen copies, both of August alone and of him with Ferring.

While I wandered around the downtown streets, asking the myriad beer joints and little restaurants for permission to put the photos in their windows, I also showed the pictures to the homeless people squatting on the sidewalks. Life on the streets leaves most people inward-turned and listless: it's not just physically draining but also really boring, so the mind drifts. However, everyone who passed through the downtown went by the people on the streets—it was worth a chance.

"You get anything if you find 'em?" an older men asked.

"Like a reward, you mean? Absolutely. If the lead pans out, I'll pay twenty bucks."

"Twenty-five," he said.

"Did you see either of them?"

He scratched his head. "I might have. You give me the money, and then I'll tell you."

His blue eyes were sunk so deep in their sockets that I couldn't read his expression, but I was guessing the need for a drink predominated.

"If you might have seen them, when would that have been?"

"My memory would work better if it got some lubricating."

I knew I was being played, but I handed him a five. "When do you think you might have seem them?"

"He's a football player, am I right? And the coach wants you to find him and his ma."

"You're wasted out here on the street," I told him. "Go up to the university's theater department—they're looking for good screenwriters."

As I walked away, I heard him chortle, "Got her that time."

Let him have his triumph—life probably didn't afford him many. One of the coffee shops where I'd put my flyer told me I should check with the county sheriff—they had their own jail out east of town. The sheriff worked with the town forces, but they had their own forces, too.

The sheriff's department was in the same building where I'd talked to the police, in a park just south of the downtown business district. I walked over and spoke with one of the deputies. Like the town's police this morning, the deputy was civil and willing to help; she checked their list of inmates in custody, looked up anyone found dead or injured in the county in the last month, even called the hospitals in the area, but came up empty.

Cady Perec, the very part-time research associate, phoned as I returned to my car. She was breathless, apologetic: if she'd known someone wanted to look at the records, she would have come over straightaway.

"Not to worry," I assured her. "If this is a good time, I'm nearby."

This was perfect, she'd be right there, her school was only four blocks away, just give her a moment to organize her papers.

"Take it easy," I started to say, but she cut the connection.

Despite her protestations I waited another ten minutes in the museum lobby before Perec got there. She ran up the steps, dropping papers that she was trying to stuff into a backpack, and apologized again for her delay.

"One of my students, Dougie Mackelson—I didn't want to turn him away because he's never asked for help before and he needs it more than most, or I wouldn't have kept you waiting. Do you have time now, or do you need to come back?"

Cady Perec was a short woman in jeans and a corduroy jacket who hardly looked old enough to be out of junior high, let alone teaching there. Her copper-colored hair kept falling over her glasses as she spoke, and she dropped more papers as she tried to push strands away from her face.

I knelt to help collect the papers—student exams that seemed to be about Kansas in the 1850s. *"I think John Brown was a terorist,"* someone had written in large letters, *"because he wanted to blow people up. He didn't want to negoshate. He had extrem ideas just like ISIS."*

"Can we sit down, let you catch your breath while I explain what it is I'm looking for?"

"Sorry!" Perec pushed her hair behind her ears again. "Can you tell me your name? I'm afraid I didn't write it down when I saw your e-mail."

"V.I. Warshawski." I explained who I was, what I wanted.

Perec shook her head slowly as I went through my litany. "I know Ferring's name. We have old VHS tapes of the movies she made with Jarvis Nilsson here, but I don't think we have any personal papers or records."

"Old phone directories?" I asked. "I'm hoping to find where she lived."

Perec brightened: she could produce those. "Lawrence has two newspapers, the *Lawrence Journal-World* and the *Douglas County Herald*. I can go through the old indices while you look at the phone books, if you'd like—they didn't digitize anything before 1990, but we've got them on microfiche."

She sat me down with several boxes, covering 1945, the year Ferring's mother had left Fort Riley, to 1968, the year Ferring had gone to Hollywood with Nilsson. I found a Mrs. Steven Ferring on Sixth Street from 1945 to 1951, but no Ferrings after that. Frustrating and baffling.

Cady was still busy with the newspaper fiches, but she turned away from the fiche reader to pull a map up on her computer screen. She showed me where the Ferrings would have been living when Emerald was a little girl.

There was a thin sliver of town on the north side of the river, just beyond where Peppy and I had been walking earlier. I had seen a few houses from the river path, but the heavy undergrowth had blocked most of them from view. I'd go back over there in the morning, although I was beginning to think Ferring and August had never made it to Lawrence.

I was brooding over whether there was anyone else I could talk to when Cady Perec gave an excited squeak.

"I found her! At least I found her in 1983. She was at this protest, see: maybe she met my mother!"

I got up to peer over her shoulder at the fiche reader, but Cady printed out the article and handed it to me.

Douglas County Herald
July 5, 1983

We all believe in free speech: it's the cornerstone of our democracy. But when America is at war, we need to think before we speak. The demonstrations at the Kanwaka Missile Silo yesterday smack more of treachery than patriotism. Those missiles are there for a reason: to protect America from a nuclear attack by our deadliest enemies. Our President is trying to show the Russians that we are not afraid of anything Uncle Ivan wants to bring on. In our humble opinion, decorating a missile site with peace symbols made out of daisy chains, and doing it on the anniversary of our country's birth, comes perilously close to treason.

It pains us to label someone born and bred in Kansas as an outside agitator, but Emerald Ferring has become part of the flag-burning leftist establishment that runs Hollywood. Communist-sympathizing women in England have turned Greenham Common Air Base into a shameful collaboration with the Russians. That's what pinkos like Emerald Ferring want to do to Lawrence. It's bad enough for ABC to film an anti-nuke movie here. Uncle Ivan is going to think America is soft on nuclear war.

Ferring's presence at the missile silo drew a rowdy crowd from as far away as St. Louis and Omaha. The riot that broke out, thanks to rabble-rousing from her and her friends, was a shameful blot on our county and our city. She should stay in Hollywood with the other red rats who hate America.

9

RED MENACE

"WOW. STRONG MEDICINE." I folded the page and put it in my case. "Was Ferring arrested? What happened?"

Cady scrolled through the fiche. She tapped a finger on the screen to show me an article that had run the following day, but she gave me the highlights without looking at it—she'd been through this story more than once.

"The air force was in charge of the silo, so they could have arrested people under military law or something, but they didn't—they took them away forcibly. I guess they didn't want any more negative publicity than they already had."

> The Air Force escorted the demonstrators to buses, which drove them to Lawrence, where they were free to go about their business. At the request of U.S. Air Force Col. Malcolm Pavant, we are withholding photos of the protesters. We don't want people defacing a military installation to glorify themselves in public.

The article concluded with a comment from Colonel Pavant, who said the air force appreciated the support of the local law-enforcement agencies "and also of the many Kansans who understand that when you are facing an enemy like the Russians, you have to be prepared to make sacrifices." Pavant didn't spell out the sacrifices, but I suppose they included incineration in a nuclear holocaust.

Cady moved aside while I read through the next several days' worth of the paper, but she was right, there was no further mention of Emerald, or indeed of any other protesters, by name. The *Douglas County Herald* was doing its duty as diligent guardians of the First Amendment by keeping people who peaceably assembled out of the paper.

"Does the missile silo still exist?" I asked. "Where is it?"

"Out east of town about five miles. They took the missile out after the Cold War. We used to have thousands of them in the Midwest. There were a bunch of talks, and then treaties, between us and the Russians, and then the air force started taking missiles out. Anyway, the Kanwaka silo, out east of town, some developer wants to buy it from the air force and turn it into survivalist condos."

"That's a joke, right?"

Cady made a face. "You'd think, but it's happening around the country. Some people are buying them to live in right now, because they're cheap and they think it's cool, but some of the big ones, developers are turning them into hugely expensive shelters for surviving the worst."

She turned from the fiche reader to a computer, bringing up some sites of missile silos–turned–homes. A man in Texas had created the ultimate bachelor pad somewhere out in the bare, bleak stretches of the state, but the most eye-popping was one Cady showed me in Montana, labeled *"The Great Escape: Fifteen underground levels of peace of mind."* A subhead, with lightning bolts flashing off and on around it, screamed that *"Fortune Favors the Prepared."*

I bent over Cady's shoulder for a better view. The website showed a cutaway of the underground part of the missile silo, fifteen stories of condos, with five stories even deeper underground for the mechanicals, swimming pools, water and air filters, and so on. Units started at $1.5 million and came with a five-year supply of freeze-dried food. The silo had massive generators, updated from when they'd only had to power a Titan missile over the pole to Russia. There was also dedicated Wi-Fi—assuming the Internet would function post-Armageddon. Your choice of views from your windows—a computer would give you seascapes or mountains or amber fields of grain so you didn't have to stare at concrete walls.

I felt as though spiders were crawling up my arms: locked underground, no escape hatch, waiting for the end of the world with a few dozen other people, in units with the granite countertops, German dishwashers, under-the-counter refrigerators, and surround sound that all upscale buyers are looking for in their second home. The Great Escape had sold five units; thirteen more were available but going fast, so make an appointment today.

The slide show on the screen showed an artist's vision of the exterior, with trees and a heliport surrounded by rosebushes. I wondered if the real deal would include bunkers for snipers to shoot any of the 99 percent trying to flee nuclear winter.

"Is that what's happening to your silo, the— What is it called?"

"Kanwaka. It's from some Indian names," Cady said. "It's like everything else in Kansas. It used to be Indian land, and we took it and turned it into something bigger and better—namely, a huge bomb site. I haven't paid that much attention to what they're doing at Kanwaka, but last I heard, there was some question about the land. One of my grandmother's friends was trying to broker the conversion of Kanwaka into condos, but the deal fell apart."

"When Emerald and the others were protesting out there, there must have been pretty tight security," I said. "Did they camp out on the perimeter, or were there houses or trailers?"

"Tents in the field, is what I was always told," Cady said. "It's really hard to find anyone who remembers anything about it—details, I mean. You can talk to people in town, and they all remember the demonstrations. Depending on their politics, it was either a wonderful example of grass-roots activism or a horrendous display of mob violence. Of course, that was way before smartphones, so it's not like people were posting photos to Instagram or anything. And then the commune burned down about two months after the protest, so there's not anything left out there to look at."

"Burned down?" I echoed. "How?"

Cady hunched a shoulder. "They say one of the hippies was probably smoking—dope, they mean—and let a fire get out of control."

She turned back to the microform and found the story in the *Douglas County Herald*.

> After we and the rest of the Fourth Estate took the spotlight away from the demonstrators at the Kanwaka silo, the hippies evaporated, proving what Air Force Col. Malcolm Pavant suspected all along: these were bored publicity seekers. Apparently they didn't put out their campfires before they took off. Douglas County Sheriff Milt Julkis reports that about ten days ago a fire took out most of the tents and shacks the protesters left behind. The news was kept quiet until Col. Pavant was able to confirm that there was no damage to the silo and no radiation leakage as a result of the fire. He also confirms that there was no loss of life.

"It's really hopeless," Cady said. "The only person I know who really remembers the missile part is one of the math teachers at my school. She's about ten years older than me, and she grew up out near Kanwaka. She went to this two-room school out by the silo and said it totally spooked her and her friends, going past it every day in the school bus, knowing the U.S. thought we were expendable. Like, we could be a first-strike target because we didn't count."

I nodded absently, wanting to know more about Ferring's involvement. "What was the movie, the anti-nuke movie that they made here? Did Ferring star in that?"

"Oh, gosh, I don't think she had anything to do with it, but I'd have to look at the credits. *The Day After,* it's called. It was made for TV and showed the kind of radiation poisoning you could expect after a nuclear war, if you weren't killed right off, and how there wouldn't be food, that kind of thing. It was pretty controversial here in town, some people thinking the mayor should be thrown out of office for letting the Russians believe that Lawrence was scared of nuclear weapons. Of course, there was pretty strong support for disarmament here as well, but Reagan—he was president at the time—he tried to get ABC not to show it.

"The movie was released right after I was born, so of course I don't have personal knowledge about all the controversies, but I talk to everyone who was living here then about what they remember." She gave an embarrassed laugh. "I've watched the movie maybe fifty times. I keep hoping I'll see my mother."

"Was she an extra?"

"No. She was at the protest, though, at the missile silo, and then . . . she died."

She bit her lips, pushing back emotion, tears. I sat quietly, waiting until she felt like speaking again.

"No one knows what happened—I mean, how it happened. She drove her car off the road and drowned in the Wakarusa—that's a little river near the silo. I was six weeks old, and she'd taken off without me. She'd forgotten me—that's what hurts the most. One of the farmers found me and brought me to Gram. They say maybe she was smoking dope, which I guess could be true, or drunk—how would I know?"

I'd lost my mother when I was a teenager, and I still missed her. I could imagine the hole there'd be in the middle of my heart if I'd never known her at all.

"I started studying history—it's what I mostly teach, you know, although there's general social studies, politics, that kind of thing—and why I work here. I keep hoping I'll get some whiff of something that will explain my mother to me. Gram, she's so bitter about everything that went on around Kanwaka, she never talks about it. It wasn't until I got to high school that I even knew about the protests at the silo—all she ever would say was that my mom died when her car went off the road. First Grandpa—her husband—died in a car crash, then Jenny, my mom. Gram almost wouldn't let me learn how to drive, she's so sure there's some kind of curse. But you can't really get around in a town this size without a car."

"That sounds like a tough load for both of you."

Cady laughed self-consciously. "Some. You should have seen me when I took driver's ed—it was a month before I could figure out how to keep the car going in a straight line."

I waited a respectful moment before changing the subject. "Was the protest at the silo connected to the anti-nuke movie?"

"I don't think so. The protest was a part of the times, you know, people all over the country fed up with the arms race and wanting an end to it. *The Day After* was more like a reflection, see, of the public mood. My mother, from what I can dig up, she was part of this commune who wanted to try to re-create what the women in England were doing at that same time, protesting nuclear warheads in the middle of the country. At its height the English had almost a hundred thousand women at their air force base. Here in Lawrence they had maybe twenty. Kansas, you know!"

She fiddled with the reader dials, making the text jump in a sea-sickening way. "I've read all the local stories—including what the Kansas City and Topeka papers covered—a few dozen times, but I didn't know who Emerald Ferring was. I mean, that she was a movie star or African-American or anything. I didn't pay attention to her name all the times I read about the protests. I was just looking for any mention of my mom. Jenny, her name was. Jennifer Perec."

Cady whispered her name, talking more to herself than to me.

"What does your grandmother say about the commune and the protests?"

"I've never been able to get her to talk about it, beyond saying the only good that came out of it was me." She flushed and glanced up. "That's nice and all, but it's always felt to me like Gram is hugely angry with my mom, and I can't get her to talk about her. Or get any idea of who my father might have been. He wasn't in the car with my mom, and Gram doesn't know who he was, or at least she says she doesn't know."

I could imagine that deep wound as well: a teenage romance, the boy not wanting to be saddled with a baby when his girlfriend died. He'd had the option to disappear like smoke. "Did she—Jennifer—grow up here? She must have some childhood friends you could talk to."

Cady nodded. "I have, believe me. And I have her high-school yearbook. She was voted most likely to be the next Marie Curie because she was interested in science, but Gram won't even tell me if the physics classes she took were what turned her into a disarmament advocate. My mom was only nineteen when I was born, so it's hard to find people who can tell me much about her. She was good at math, she liked biology, she was an ace soccer player."

"Your grandmother didn't have other children?"

"My mom was three when my grandfather was killed. Gram had been putting him through law school, so they were waiting to have more children, I guess, and then she never married again."

So no aunts or uncles who could talk about the Kanwaka sit-in. I got Cady to let me look at the microfiches from both the *Douglas County Herald* and the *Lawrence Journal-World*.

Cady's focus had always been on a quest for her mother, but I wanted more coverage of Emerald Ferring's role in the protests. I couldn't find anything, except for photos that showed a heavy military presence around the missile silo. Any pictures of anti-nuke protesters were obscured by a huge banner that read GOD BLESS THE UNITED STATES OF AMERICA AIR FORCE, held aloft by people identified as Douglas County Freedom Lovers. It was decorated with pictures of fighter jets and the American flag.

Another story showed people playing softball and barbecuing near the half-moon dome covering the silo.

> Americans know the safety of our nation and her citizens is the number one priority of the U.S. Air Force. Douglas County citizens can picnic safely because the Air Force routinely checks radiation levels in the nearby land and water. And they know this missile is here to keep us all safe from the Russian menace.

I wondered how much radiation leakage there was around these old missiles, whether it was really safe to live in one of their silos—assuming your claustrophobia didn't put you at risk of a mental meltdown first.

I was turning the wheel faster when Emerald's name jumped out at me. I scrolled slowly back through the pages until I found the story. It didn't have anything to do with the missile or the Greenham wannabes: Lucinda Ferring, Emerald's mother, had died of pneumonia at age sixty-four, about six weeks after the protest. Emerald had returned for the funeral, held at St. Silas AME Church. There was a photograph: by 1983 an African-American actor was a celebrity. Emerald was wearing a hat with a veil that covered the top half of her face, so I couldn't what she'd looked like without stage makeup.

A cough from the doorway startled us both. The woman from the front desk gave an apologetic laugh. "I didn't mean to scare you, but it's six, Cady. I need to leave. Will you lock up?"

"Good grief, we've been talking our heads off in here, Melanie. I didn't even hear you come in. Sorry! You go on, but we're leaving now, too."

She leaned across me to pull the microfiche from the reader. She fiddled with the plastic sheet, waiting until we heard Melanie's footsteps heading down the hall, and then said shyly, "Maybe you could come over to the house with me, talk to Gram. She might say more to you than she does to me. Maybe she did know Emerald Ferring but didn't want to talk about her."

10

WHAT BIG TEETH YOU HAVE

AND SO I ended up on Gertrude Perec's front porch, watching moonlight shimmer on the slice of river we could see from her house. I don't know how Cady had advertised my visit or how her grandmother had reacted, since I'd been following in my own car, but the elder Perec didn't treat me like visiting royalty.

"Gram, it's dark and getting chilly. Shouldn't we go inside?" Cady had asked when her grandmother greeted me on the porch stairs.

Gertrude Perec said with a thin smile that it was a pleasant evening. "It will be winter soon enough, when we'll all be longing for an evening like this where we can sit outside without three sweaters and our down coats."

She hadn't been overtly rude—she told me to make myself comfortable in one of the wicker porch chairs—but she didn't offer anything to drink: I wasn't supposed to stay. And Peppy was to remain in the car, an edict that startled her granddaughter.

"Gram! You let Melanie bring in that terrier of hers, and it pees in the corners."

That was the first time in our conversation that Gertrude squeezed her granddaughter's shoulder in a kind of warning.

It was Cady who took a bowl of water out to Peppy; she also brought me a glass of white wine to go with the one she was drinking herself.

While Cady was inside dealing with Peppy's and my refreshments, Gertrude said, "Cady tells me you want to talk about that damned commune out by the Kanwaka silo."

"No, ma'am," I said, my voice neutral. "I'm trying to find Emerald Ferring. We came across a news story that Emerald was part of one of the protests out there, and I hoped you might have known her or her mother, since they'd lived here for quite a long time. As you have yourself."

"That commune, that's how I lost my daughter. Cady is obsessed with finding out what made Jenny take part or who she might have been dating, but I don't want those old scars cut open."

"I'm not looking for your daughter's lover," I said, although I wondered if it would cross Cady's mind to try to hire me and what I would say if she did. "Emerald Ferring set out on a road trip two weeks ago. She went to Fort Riley, where her father was stationed during the war, and she told people there she was coming to Lawrence. So far I haven't found anyone who's seen her here, although I plan to visit the church where her mother's funeral was held. Then, this afternoon, when Cady was going through records with me at the historical museum, I saw that Ferring had been at the same protest as your daughter, so I wondered if you knew her or her mother."

In the dim light of the porch's single weak bulb, I couldn't read Gertrude Perec's expression, but I could tell that her muscles tightened. "When Ferring came here in '83, she was famous, at least for Lawrence, Kansas, so of course I saw her. Anyway, she's black, and since that's such a small part of our town, she stood out. But I didn't know her when she was a child."

"She didn't live that far from here, just across that river, if I'm reading the maps correctly."

"Ah, that river." That was when Perec told me about her great-grandfather's vanishing act.

I waited patiently for the end of the anecdote and the end of the discussion on disappearing fathers.

"The listing in the phone book for Ferring's mother ends after

1951, when Emerald would have been about seven, so I guess they moved away, but still—"

"In 1951?" Gertrude interrupted. "They probably had to move, if they were living in North Lawrence."

"Oh. The flood," Cady said. "People still talk about it. We had a bad flood when I was eight, but everyone told me it was nothing compared to '51."

"And they were right, missy," Gertrude said. "I was twelve, and I still remember water lapping at the curve in the road there." She pointed toward the road, but it was too dark for me to see anything. "I had nightmares for months after, sure the water would get into my bedroom and sweep me away before my father could rescue me. During the day my brother Clarence and I would wade in the streets, which drove my mother wild—she was sure we would come home with cholera."

"North Lawrence," I prodded her. "The Ferrings were living on Sixth Street."

"I don't know the streets on that side of the river—not well, anyway—but many of those houses were completely underwater. The land is flatter on the north side and the houses a good deal closer to the river than we are here. And then many of them are built level with the ground. You drive over there in daylight and you'll see what I mean."

"So maybe the river forced Emerald and her mother out of town. Any thoughts on who might remember them, know where they went?"

Gertrude Perec finally seemed to give me her full attention. "It's such a long time ago. You need someone who was an adult then, who still is . . . well, mentally alert today, and someone who knew that part of town."

She paused, thinking it over. "The local Congregational church, Riverside—it's United Church now—they were doing service work in North Lawrence. I know I helped my mother make up care packages after Sunday school—clothes, canned goods, that kind of thing.

Check with the church secretary. She may be able to find someone who goes back that far."

Cady said, "What about Dr.—"

"Absolutely not." Gertrude's voice was a band saw, cutting her granddaughter's sentence in half. "That episode was as painful in his life as it is in mine. You brought this detective in here and let her pick at my scars. I will not have her doing it to anyone else."

She turned to me. "I've told you I know nothing about Emerald Ferring, and I've extended myself to give you a suggestion of people at a church who might help you. It's time you were on your way."

"Gram!" Cady expostulated. "I know you don't like talking about my mother, but honestly, this is —"

"She doesn't get to invade my privacy, however much you want her to invade yours, Miss Cady. I have dinner waiting in the oven, and it's likely a shriveled bit of casserole by this time."

"It's okay, Cady," I said as she stared openmouthed at her grandmother. "Your grandmother's right: she gets to protect her privacy. I'll check with the Riverside Church people, and drive over to North Lawrence to the church where Lucinda Ferring's funeral was held. If that doesn't lead anywhere, I'll head back along the interstate toward Fort Riley to see what I can figure out."

A statement that just went to prove that old bromide about the best-laid plans.

11

RABID FANS

IT WAS STARTING to mizzle again when I got back to the car. I put on my poncho and walked with Peppy toward the river. It wasn't as close as I'd thought, sitting on Gertrude Perec's porch, and it turned out there was a ravine between the river and the road. On the far side, a train's whistle hooted, a melancholy wail in the wet dark.

I drove back to the parks that bordered the center of town and let Peppy root around in the lamplight. She was annoyed at having been left in the car for too much of the afternoon and showed it by breaking away to greet other dogs and refusing to come when I called her.

I'd been sitting too long, too. I grabbed her leash and ran the length of the park five or six times, until Peppy was panting loudly. The rain was still falling, not hard, but we were both damp by the time I bundled Peppy back into the Mustang.

Although I saw some interesting restaurants, I didn't feel like changing into dry clothes, nor like leaving the dog in the car again. I went to a co-op grocer on the town's west side that had organic carry-out meals and took a salmon dinner back to the B and B with me. The owner provided a common room, an alcove, really, with a microwave and a small refrigerator.

"Who do you think the doctor is that Gertrude Perec was protecting from my scar picking?" I asked Peppy when we were in our room and dry again. "And what painful episode was she talking about? Do you think it has anything to do with Emerald Ferring?"

Peppy didn't look up from the peanut-butter bone I'd bought her, not for a question that could be answered only by consulting a medium. I tried texting Cady to ask if she'd tell me the doctor's name, but she said her grandmother would know I'd gotten it from her and she didn't want to cause any more domestic friction.

Was Cady afraid of her grandmother? Probably a little, but maybe she was protecting her, too. I didn't really need to know—I was grasping at straws, after all, looking for clues about Emerald Ferring at a protest camp that had disappeared almost thirty-five years ago. Anyway, it's impossible to persuade people via text to tell you something they want to keep to themselves.

Gertrude Perec didn't rate a Wikipedia entry. My subscription databases said she was seventy-eight, retired, owned her own home, had a modest pension, collected Social Security, and owned two apartment buildings on Louisiana Street. Cady had said her grandmother had lost her husband in a car crash; that had happened long before the digital age, so there was no mention of his death. Gertrude's brother, Clarence, who'd taken over the grandfather's farm, had died ten years earlier; he'd never married and the farm had been sold when he died.

I couldn't find any record of Gertrude's only child, Cady's mother, either. Nothing about Gertrude and a doctor. Had he been Gertrude's boss? Her lover?

Time I dealt with my in-box. Predictably, I had several urgent messages from Bernie, wanting to know why I hadn't been in touch and where was August??? Since she'd already texted me four times today, I wrote a snarky reply, then deleted it: no reason to take out my frustrations over my lack of progress on Bernie. I wrote jointly to her and Angela: *"It's a slow business, and I'm having trouble picking up a thread in a strange town, so hang tight for a few more days, okay?"*

One thing I'd like someone on the ground in Chicago to do was canvas August's neighbors in the evening, when people would be home from work, but that was a job for the Streeter brothers, not two impetuous young athletes. I sent Tim Streeter a long e-mail with the details of what I wanted and then turned to the hardest message, the no-progress report to the client.

For help with that, I poured myself a generous shot of Johnnie Walker while I explained to Troy Hempel what I'd done and who I would talk to in the morning.

"If the churches and her childhood home prove dead ends, I could retrace the road back to Fort Riley, to see if anything happened to Ferring and August on the way. It's eighty miles with a lot of small towns in between and might take several days to cover. My opinion—it's a needle in a haystack, but if you want me to do it, I'm game. Let me know."

When I'd finished that, I started working through my in-box—seventy-three new e-mails since this morning, including, of course, the piercing bleats from politicians and Nigerian princes, desperate for two hundred or even just five dollars, whatever I could spare, the situation is dire.

Two clients had problems I could solve long-distance. Mr. Contreras had written a chatty message from St. Croix, filled with goodwill and the endearing typos of a hunt-and-pecker. I wrote back, mostly highlights from my visit to Fort Riley, which a veteran of Anzio would care about, and included a photo that Dr. Dan had sent from Wisconsin of Mitch stalking a chipmunk.

I'd written Jake this morning before my visit to the Lawrence Police Department, when it had been 3:00 P.M. in Basel. It was 3:00 A.M. there now, and he hadn't had time to fit in a response.

No estés lejos de mí un solo día. The Neruda sonnet that Peter Lieberson had set to music for his wife came into my mind. *Do not be far from me for a single day.* Jake used to play the melody for me over Skype when he was on tour, and I had worked hard on the song so I could sing it to him when he'd been in Australia for six weeks last year. Now—not even an e-mail.

I got up and frowned at my reflection in a small mirror over the desk. More wiry threads of white in my dark hair, deeper crow's-feet around the eyes. *Silvered is the raven hair . . . Mottled the complexion fair.* Maybe Gilbert and Sullivan's Lady Jane was more suitable for me than Neruda's love sonnets.

Fortunately, I had my dog and my career: What more does a woman need? I settled down to the client queries, and after a time, deep in spreadsheets and a trail of strangely oscillating share prices, I forgot my bruised heart and my futile efforts to find August Veriden and Emerald Ferring.

I stretched out my hamstrings, did a half backbend in the doorway, took Peppy out to the small patio outside my room.

The rain had passed, bringing colder air behind it, cold air from the north, from home. We stood for a moment, looking at the night sky, at the North Star. I felt a longing for home deeper than my longing for Jake.

"Sniff the air, girl," I told Peppy. "Maybe you'll smell Mitch. I'll smell the Golden Glow and Lotty. Any luck and we'll be back there soon."

The bells on the university campanile were tolling midnight in the distance. I climbed into bed, the dog curled at my side, and fell deeply asleep. When my phone rang only two hours later, I woke disoriented, thinking I was in my Chicago bedroom, and floundered in the unfamiliar space, bumping into the couch where my phone was flashing its LEDs.

"Yes?" I grumbled, rubbing my sore shin.

"Did you put up those posters?" It was a woman's voice, hoarse from alcohol or cigarettes or maybe from screaming into phones in the middle of the night—the background noise sounded like a full-scale riot was in progress.

"What pos— Oh, looking for August Veriden and Emerald Ferring? Yes." I sucked in a breath.

"I saw them. I saw them out where my truelove is buried. They were walking on his grave."

Great. Another homeless drunk looking for a handout. "What did you see?" I demanded.

"A black kid was photographing the grave, and this black lady was egging him on! That ground is sacred, and they were taking pictures as if it was a football game."

"Where?" I shouted.

"I told you. At his burial place."

"But where is his burial place?"

"I tried to make him stop, but he wouldn't."

I was pulling on my jeans as she talked. "Where are you right now? I'll bring the reward down to you."

"The Lion's Pride."

I asked her name, but she'd hung up. I pulled boots on over my bare feet, hustled Peppy into the car, asked my phone to find the Lion's Pride. Eighth Street at Rhode Island, two blocks east of Massachusetts, the main downtown street. I hadn't gone that far with my posters.

Two-thirty in the morning; most places had closed, but the handful of bars still open had crowds of kids spilling into the streets, music blaring onto the sidewalks, roars of laughter, cars honking up and down Massachusetts. I found a parking space on a street of rickety bungalows and crooked brick sidewalks.

I thought living near Wrigley Field was a misery on game nights, but for the poor people near the bars it looked as though every night downtown might be game night.

The Lion's Pride was in the cellar of a building on the corner. When I got there, a young woman was being sick over the railing; two youths with her were laughing, one of them pulling on her cami straps.

I put an arm around the woman but looked at the young men. "You boys need to go home. Kindergarten starts early tomorrow, and you don't look adult enough for anything else."

One of the guys started to call me names, but when I demanded their IDs, they backed away—I might be a university cop. The woman stared at me with glassy, unseeing eyes. I didn't know what to do with her, so I kept an arm around her as I muscled my way down the stairs to the entrance.

As soon as I got there, I realized what a hopeless job it would be to find one person in this mob scene. I backed out again, set the young woman on the stairs, and called the number that had rung mine.

It rang about ten times before anyone answered: it was a bartender at the Lion's Pride. Great. My anonymous caller had used the bar's phone.

The young woman had passed out. I propped her against the edge of an iron staircase leading to the upper floors of the building. She had a purse dangling from her shoulder. I took it with me, just to keep it from being stolen while I went inside.

"I hope you're going to be okay out here, honey. I don't know how long this will take."

The elbows I'd developed growing up on Chicago's South Side got me past the thicket at the entrance and up to the bar, but the noise was so ferocious it was harder to take than the crowd. A balding man with a sizable paunch was filling beer steins without looking at them, putting them on the end where waitstaff picked them up and distributed them through the mob.

I waved, trying to get his attention, shouted, and finally worked my way around to his side of the bar.

"Five Moscow Mules!" one of the waitstaff screamed.

The balding man nodded, filled three more steins, and turned to plunk five copper mugs on the bar. I put my arm over them.

"Before you serve another underage drinker, I need to know who was using your phone half an hour ago."

He looked at me sourly. "Get your arm off the mugs. They have to be washed again if you get them dirty."

"Your phone. A woman called me from here. I'm a detective, she has information I need, and I want to know who she was."

He glared at me. "Some stupid homeless woman who I threw

out because she hassles the customers begging for booze. She helped herself to the phone just like you're helping yourself to my mule mugs. Now, get out of my bar before I throw you out after her."

"Don't make threats you can't back up," I said. "If she's a regular, you must know her name or where she lives—"

"I just told you she's homeless, which means she doesn't live anywhere."

The noise and my lack of sleep were making me light-headed. I saw a row of switches on the wall behind him. I shut down the three closest to me, and the bar went dark. People gasped and shrieked, but the noise decreased a few decibels. I counted five and turned the lights on again.

Before the roar could rebuild, I shouted, "Free Moscow Mule to the person who knows the homeless woman who was using the phone in here a little bit ago!"

The bartender shouted to one of the waitstaff to get Fred, time to throw me out and then call the cops.

"I'm a detective," I said loudly. "I need to find the woman who used your phone. If I do, when the cops arrive, I won't report you for serving alcohol to kids who are drunk and very likely had roofies fed to them at your bar while you were watching. Deal?"

He slapped an empty stein onto the counter so hard it broke. "Sonia. She comes around when she's scored enough change to buy a drink. She's a pain in the ass, but not as big a pain as you. Now, get out."

A muscly man in the ubiquitous Jayhawk T-shirt was waiting at the end of the bar for me. He grabbed my arm harder than was truly necessary and hustled me to the door, where I somehow tripped on the stoop and kicked his shin while I righted myself. Childish but satisfying.

The young woman was still slumped at the top of the stairs. The trio of youths was still there, carrying freshly filled mugs, speaking in disjointed sentences interspersed with loud laughter, when they pounded one another's shoulders.

I shone my phone flash inside the young woman's purse, where I found a student ID. It told me she was Naomi Wissenhurst but didn't reveal her address. I slapped her lightly, trying to wake her up.

"Naomi! Where do you live!"

The trio moved out to the sidewalk, not wanting to be part of Naomi's drama. It was then that I saw the bundle of clothes under the iron staircase. I shone my flash on it, but my gut twisted: the bundle had a shape of sorts, and in the light I could see a foot sticking out at an awkward angle.

12

UGLY DUCKLING

SHE WASN'T DEAD, but her pulse was so faint I could barely feel it. I called 911: two ODs at the Lion's Pride. I put my coat over the woman to keep her warm. I photographed her and Naomi Wissenhurst in situ. I didn't want any complaints coming back that I'd moved them, injured them, robbed them.

Just because the three guys were gawking and not helping, I took their pictures, too. They scowled and moved away from me.

The cops arrived first, blue-and-reds flashing. My one brief entertainment for the night—the male trio melting like snow as the squad cars arrived, dumping little bags filled with pills and powders into the gutter as they fled.

I stood as two officers reached to the staircase. "I was trying to get this woman to wake up when I saw the other one under the staircase."

They shone their flashlights, more powerful than my phone flash, and I saw the woman's face. Middle-aged, jowly, thick eyebrows, a trickle of vomit at the corner of her mouth.

The female officer called in the report, demanding two ambulances at once. A third squad car pulled up. The driver stayed put; he was ferrying a more senior officer, who joined us at the top of the stairs.

By now the police strobes had penetrated the bar. Eager patrons were trying to leave, or at least to gape at the action. The senior officer sent one of the uniforms down the stairs to keep everyone in place.

"What have we got here, Suze?"

Suze swung her light in my direction. "This person called it in, but that's Sonia Kiel, Sarge, you know—"

"Oh, yes, we all know Sonia." The senior man squatted and felt her wrist. "Sonia, what'd you take this time, huh? We gonna save your life for you one more time, or are you determined to let it go?"

He stood. "And the other one?"

I hesitated, not wanting to be closer to the center of attention than I already was, but when Suze didn't speak, I said the other one seemed to be a student who'd drunk too much, or swallowed roofies, or both.

"I was trying to get her to wake up enough to tell me where she lived when I saw the other woman lying there." I hesitated again, but there was no point in keeping my connection to Sonia quiet; everyone in the bar would report my dramatic effort to get her name. "I've never seen Sonia before, but she called me about forty-five minutes ago, asking me to come here to talk to her."

The ambulances arrived. The officers backed away as the EMTs jogged over with their equipment.

"Let's get our ladies to the hospital, and then you"—the sergeant nodded at me—"come over to the station and tell me all about it. You know where we are?"

I assured him I knew. When I started away from him toward my car, he said, "Other way."

"I know, Sergeant. My dog is in my car. I need to make sure she's okay."

"Officer Peabody will go with you. Suze, I'll drive your squad car back to the station."

As we walked to my car, I said, "Your sergeant said you all know Sonia Kiel. Does this happen often, her passing out near a bar?"

"Sergeant Everard can tell you more about her than I can," Suze said stiffly.

I ignored the rebuff. "I'd think if she needed hospitalizing very often, her health must be close to the breaking point."

"She isn't in good shape," Suze admitted, "but usually we just take her back to the group home. They don't want to keep her—" She broke off, remembering she was supposed to leave all those details to the sergeant.

We'd reached the Mustang. Peppy stuck an eager head over the backseat to inspect Suze, who patted her in return, a good sign, before strapping herself into her seat.

When we got to the station, I took Peppy out to stretch her legs. Suze said she thought it would be okay with the sergeant if I brought Peppy into the station. "If it isn't, I'll take her out and walk her while he talks to you."

Everard raised his eyebrows when we walked in. "That your lawyer?"

"More like my analyst," I said. "I don't have any secrets from her."

"I hope you don't have any from me. You want to start by telling me who you are?"

When I told him my name and started to pull out my PI license, he said, "Oh, right. We got a notice about you coming into town looking for two missing African-Americans. What took you to the Lion's Pride in the middle of the night, or is that all in the line of a big-city detective's life? They tell me you caused a bit of a disturbance."

"Hmm. More like I quieted the place down." I told him about getting Sonia's phone call and finding out that she'd used the bar's phone. "It was hard to get them to acknowledge that Sonia had been in there or that she'd used the phone. The place was pretty wild, even by big-city standards."

"Hawks won tonight, Sarge," Suze contributed.

I looked blank, thinking Chicago Blackhawks and wondering why Lawrence, Kansas, would care.

"Men's basketball," Sergeant Everard said sardonically. "If you're going to spend more than another twelve hours here, you'd better memorize the Hawks—Jayhawks—men's schedule so you know when you'll be able to get anyone to listen to what you're trying to say."

He asked me for chapter and verse on why I'd come to Lawrence to look for August and Emerald. I told him. He asked for proof that Sonia had phoned me from the bar. I showed him my call log. He asked what Sonia had to say. I gave him the gist.

"You really think she saw them?" Everard said. "She's quite a few filaments short of a bulb."

"She said a young man was taking pictures and an older black woman was encouraging him. I didn't include anything about Veriden being a videographer in the posters I put up."

Everard thought it over. "Maybe Sonia did see them. Just seems odd that no one else in town knows anything about them."

"Where's the cemetery that Sonia was talking about, where her truelove is buried?" I asked. "If I go there, maybe I can find someone who would have seen Ms. Ferring or August Veriden."

Everard shook his head. "That's all in Sonia's mind, a truelove and his burial ground."

"Who is she? Officer Peabody said you'd explain about the group home and who Sonia— What's her last name? Kiel, was it?"

Everard made a sour face. "Sonia Kiel. She grew up in this town. My older brother went to high school with her, and she was an oddball then. She's only turned odder with time."

I would have put Everard at about forty: the skin on his face was still taut, none of that sag under the chin where aging begins. Even if his brother were a lot older, Sonia had looked to be a tired fifty-something. Life on the streets does terrible things to the human body; a diet of alcohol and drugs isn't exactly a healing recipe.

"Oddball how?" I asked.

"Oh, it's all ancient history. Her old man was a big noise up on the Hill, scientist, knew all there was to know about what bugs got you sick. Anyway, Sonia, she's his youngest kid. Her two older brothers were academic all-stars, you know the kind. One was a math whiz, and the other could learn any language you put in front of him."

His cell phone rang. When he hung up, he told Suze that a fight had broken out over by the Cave. "Polanco is there. No shots fired yet, but you go help him sort it out. Call me if you need a bigger club to hit them with."

After Suze had taken off, he was interrupted by one of his patrols who'd found some kids slashing tires in a west-side mall lot, and then a holdup in a park on the south end of town. By the time he got back to me, he'd lost his train of thought.

"Sonia," I said helpfully. "Two whiz-kid brothers."

"Oh, yeah. Sonia was the ugly duckling, only she never turned into a swan. When she and Tyrone—my brother—were in school together, she used to spy on the kids who were dating. She was lonely, she was ugly, who knows what was driving her? She started making up stories about having a romance with some mystery man in her father's department. It was embarrassing to listen to.

"I don't know all the details, but there've been a lot of hospitalizations. When she was younger, she tried to make a go of it out east somewhere—thought she was an singer or an artist, I forget what—but it all fell apart, and she came toddling home. Kiel and his wife finally got fed up, turned to tough love. She's supposed to be living at St. Rafe's, only she keeps sneaking out and ending up drunk. They should boot her out, but I guess Dr. Kiel still has plenty of pull in the town."

"Dr. Kiel? He's a doctor?"

"Well, yeah, he's a professor up there, with all the degrees and everything." Everard stared at me, puzzled at my urgency.

Cady had started to ask about a doctor when Gertrude Perec cut her off. I'd assumed it was an M.D., because at the University of Chicago, where I'd done my degrees, there's a kind of inverted snobbery about the title "doctor": it's only for M.D.s. Ph.D.s are Mr. or Ms., and they call you out pretty sharply if you violate the code.

"Do you know Gertrude Perec?" I asked.

"I know who she is," he said cautiously.

"Do you know if she has a connection to Dr. Kiel?"

He shook his head. "It's a small town, but still, eighty thousand people give or take, we're not the KGB with the details of everyone's love life or whatever. Or the NSA, come to that. What's Ms. Perec got to do with this?"

I flung up my hands. "I have no idea. I have no idea about anything right now, except that I'm so bone tired I can't think. Can I leave? Do you need anything else from me?"

"Just the address where you're staying. And, you know, until we see what's going on with Sonia, I'd appreciate it if you stuck around town for another day or two. Give you a chance to look at the cemeteries. We have two."

"Five."

I jumped: an African-American officer, who'd been sitting so quietly in the corner that I hadn't noticed him, was speaking.

"There's that little Jewish cemetery out by Eudora and the Catholic Cemetery over on Sixth. And don't forget Maple Grove, Sarge."

Everard nodded slowly. "Right, Leonard. It's not used much anymore for new burials," he added to me, "but it's in the old part of town, north of the river. A lot of abolitionists and escaped slaves from when the town was first settled are buried there. If Sonia was going to imagine she had a lover who'd been buried, I bet that's where he'd be."

13

ONE SOBER MINUTE

I SLEPT UNTIL CLOSE to ten the next morning, but my dreams were unquiet, filled with moody, romantic girls wandering through old cemeteries. When I finally got up, I was as stiff and tired as if I'd never lain down.

I let Peppy out into the little patio outside my room. If I were home, I could make myself espresso and do my exercises until I felt human enough to face the day. In a strange place, I made do with a hot shower and a few stretches before driving down to the Decadent Hippo. This was my third morning, and the bartender/barista raised a brow and asked if I wanted my usual. There are compensations to small towns.

The day was overcast and crisply cool. I joined Peppy at the sidewalk tables and did a more strenuous set of stretches and squats. With a second cortado, I felt up to creating a to-do list.

It was hard to know where to start. Try to see Dr. Kiel, go to the cemeteries, find St. Raphael's group home, visit Riverside Church on the south side of the river and St. Silas AME on the north, drive out to the old missile silo in case Emerald Ferring had decided to revisit it.

At least I could do some basic research on people and places while I finished my coffee. Nathan Kiel, Ph.D., not M.D., had multiple listings, from the Society of American Microbiologists to Wikipedia and a whole bunch in between. He'd taught for decades at the

University of Kansas and was considered an authority on infectious diseases. I found 113 articles that he'd co-authored, but the titles might as well have been in Farsi for all the sense they made to me. Phosphorylation-dephosphorylation followed by chemical symbols and ending in *Y. enterocolitica*.

The *Douglas County Herald* had written about him several times, most recently over the food-poisoning event that Cady Perec had mentioned last night.

> Eighteen people were infected before the Kansas Department of Public Health called in Dr. Kiel. He's eighty and no longer teaches formally in the classroom, but he can still show younger people a thing or two.

The Internet produced a hundred or more images of him, dark-haired as a young man, white-haired now, with a square, serious face. Only a few showed him laughing, one a group photo taken in 1980, over this caption:

> KU Germ Expert Dr. Nathan Kiel with his lab team celebrating their first-place victory in the KU Charity Softball Series

He would have been about fifty at the time, but he looked younger. I enlarged the image. The team all wore T-shirts with a caricature of a Jayhawk and the slogan DR. K'S FIGHTING GERMS. There were four women on the squad, but unfortunately the *Douglas County Herald* hadn't included anyone else's name.

Kiel's two sons, Stuart and Larry, were around fifty. Larry the linguist worked for a think tank in Oregon. Stuart the math whiz was teaching high-school math in a private school near Bangor, Maine. Larry was married to a woman, with two children of his own. Stuart was married to a man and didn't have any children. Did it say something about Kiel that his two sons had moved as far from Kansas as possible, or was that just where their work had taken them?

I couldn't find any biographical information about Sonia, except her date of birth: she had recently turned forty-five. Nothing on going out east somewhere to make a career in the arts. Nothing about a truelove, real or imaginary.

Kiel's wife, Shirley, was two years younger than the scientist. She had worked only later in life, when she was in her fifties, for one of the downtown banks, and had retired three years ago. Roughly the same age as Gertrude Perec, although there was no mention of Perec in the Kiel dossier, as friend, lover, or relative.

I tapped my front teeth with my pen and finally texted Cady: DOES YOUR GRANNY KNOW DR. KIEL? I FOUND HIS DAUGHTER LAST NIGHT CLOSE TO DEATH OUTSIDE THE LION'S PRIDE.

Before heading out, I called the local hospital to check on Sonia. She was in the ICU. When the operator put me through to the charge nurse, I identified myself as a detective.

The nurse said Sonia was still unresponsive but was starting to breathe on her own for longer periods.

"Did you find drugs in her pockets when she came in? I'm wondering what she took—heroin, Rohypnol, or something I'm not imagining."

The charge nurse put me on hold and after a minute a physician came on the line. "Detective, did you say? What's your name?"

I spelled it, hoping the doctor didn't have a Lawrence PD directory in front of her. "And you are Dr. . . . ?"

"Cordley. We're doing a tox screen, Detective, but do you have a reason to suspect roofies or heroin?"

"I always think about roofies when I find comatose women outside bars," I said dryly. "There was a college student nearby who seemed to be in the same state. She may be in your unit, too—Naomi Wissenhurst? Did Ms. Kiel have any drugs on her when they brought her in?"

I could hear Cordley tapping on a tablet. "I don't think so. It's not listed here, but we'll double-check the clothes she was wearing."

"The department will send someone over when she's able to

make a statement," I promised, wondering if they would, hoping Cordley wouldn't mention my name if they did.

Before I hung up, I asked about the college student. Yes, Wissenhurst was in the ICU, but she was young and healthy; she was making a quick recovery.

Peppy gave me a few sharp barks: she is not a fan of sedentary detecting. "Right you are, girl."

We were only a few blocks from the downtown parks. I jogged over, and Peppy chased a tennis ball for half an hour, with a few breaks for treeing squirrels and running around with other dogs.

St. Raphael's, the group home where Sonia Kiel lived, was on the west side of town. According to their website, St. Rafe's was designed for people in recovery from addictions and people in transition from homelessness to permanent housing. The facility held twenty studio apartments, along with single rooms for sixty more people who shared kitchens and bathrooms. The photographs showed a three-story building made of native limestone. There were prairie grasses and a few deer in the background, while residents chatted in happy earnest groups around a small pond.

It wasn't easy to find St. Rafe's, not because of the wide prairie around it but because a strip mall had sprouted on the land. I finally discovered the entrance behind the back wall of an outsize Buy-Smart. A small sign, with the insignia of the Episcopal Church, announced that we were arriving at St. Raphael's House and to please turn down all noisemakers. Another sign begged shoppers not to block the driveway.

As I pulled into the drive, bulldozers were churning up the land west of the home. A parking lot held a handful of cars, most in spaces reserved for staff. Mine was the only car in the visitors' area. A woman with a small child whose hair was elaborately braided and decorated with plastic butterflies was sitting at a picnic table drinking from a Styrofoam cup while the girl bent over a handheld game, frowning in almost desperate concentration.

A receptionist at a desk just inside the entrance asked my business with a polite smile that didn't reach her eyes. I didn't blame her—I'd hate a job where I had to smile at everyone all day long. When I told her I was a detective from Chicago and why I was in Lawrence, her expression seemed to say that Chicago detectives hunting missing persons grew like ragweed in summer.

"I found Sonia Kiel last night—early this morning, really—after she had called to say she had information about the people I'm trying to find. She's in intensive care right now, so I'm hoping there's someone here who could talk to me about her."

The woman's plastic mask cracked into real feeling: annoyance. Yes, the police had been out first thing, they'd talked to Randy Marx, the facility manager. This was just one more way that Sonia Kiel showed why she had no business being at St. Raphael's.

"How long has she been living here?" I asked.

"Too long!" the receptionist snapped. "On and off for three years now. Everyone here has a story, everyone here is a diva one way or another, but most people understand that our rules are for the benefit of the whole community. And most people who violate them don't get ten chances to redeem themselves."

"I'm sure that's frustrating," I said with spurious sympathy. "Is there a therapist or social worker I could talk to about her? I'm hoping I can find someone to give me some context for what she said on the phone."

"I'll get Randy for you. He's a social worker besides being the day manager. Sorry to lose my cool." She forced another smile. "I guess I should sit in on the anger-management session."

The woman gestured at a whiteboard on the far wall, and I saw the day's schedule written in blue. R. Marx was currently leading an anger-management group in the Buffalo Grass Room. L. McCabe would conduct group art therapy at 1:20 in the Arrowfeather Room.

The receptionist phoned down to Marx. They'd be finishing in ten minutes; I was welcome to wait in the Sprangletop Room. She pointed toward a hall. Sprangletop was at the end; I was welcome to coffee from the kitchenette along the way. I poured a cup from the outsize urn, even though I knew it would be overboiled and bitter. Prediction confirmed and then some.

Slogans were taped on the walls, reminding us that RECOVERY IS A MARATHON, NOT A SPRINT; ONE DAY ONE MINUTE AT A TIME; EVERY RECOVERY BEGINS WITH ONE SOBER MINUTE. In between the slogans were photos of groups and of families, everyone smiling, even the receptionist. One set was labeled "Labor Day Picnic at Lake Clinton." I squinted at the volleyball players and barbecuers, trying to see if Sonia was in any of the shots.

"Are you the detective?" Randy Marx had come into the kitchenette behind me, his Birkenstocks noiseless on the linoleum floor.

I jumped, splashing some of the thin coffee onto the floor. Marx was a tall man in his thirties or early forties, wearing a blue T-shirt with the ubiquitous Jayhawk striding across the front. He was pale, so pale he looked ghostlike, his thick lips barely darker than his cheeks. He shook hands, smiling perfunctorily, but his eyes were watchful.

He refilled his coffee cup, which read GET OFF YOUR CROSS: WE NEED THE WOOD! and ushered me on down the hall to the Sprangletop Room. Its windows looked out at the bulldozers on one side but faced a small park on the other. The park held more playground equipment, a baseball diamond, and a garden where birds swooped among prairie grasses or pecked at the frost-burned remnants of sunflowers.

"That's all that's left of the land that St. Rafe's used to stand on." Marx nodded at the park. "We grow ten different varieties of native grasses there. The meeting rooms are named for them. That's sprangletop."

He pointed at a patch in the garden. I nodded respectfully, as if I knew which particular plant he was looking at.

"Anyway, St. Rafe's started as a retirement home about fifty years ago—of course, I wasn't here then—but we rethought our mission when addictions and homelessness became a bigger problem in Douglas County. About ten years ago, the board voted to change the building. They added more single rooms and treatment rooms and sold twenty acres to pay for it all. It gave St. Rafe's a respectable endowment, but the trade-off was to put us in the middle of big boxes and tract houses. So it goes. Life is full of trade-offs, we keep telling our residents."

"Sonia Kiel," I said. "The sergeant who came to the Lion's Pride when I called 911 said she'd done this before."

Marx ran a finger around the rim of his mug, not looking at me. "She knows she's not allowed to stay here if she's drinking, but sometimes that urge gets too strong for her. She'll leave, go out on the streets, stay in a church basement if the weather's bad—a lot of the downtown churches have a strong sense of community service. Then she'll be ready for another stint at sobriety and come back here. She's been hospitalized before, but it was for exposure, not an overdose."

"You must believe in her recovery if you let her keep coming back," I said.

He looked up briefly. "I don't know what I believe about Sonia. I— You don't live here, do you?"

I shook my head. "Chicago, where I sit on the board of a shelter for domestic-violence refugees. I confess to a big-city bias about how generous shelters can afford to be with limited resources."

His wide lips twisted in a bitter smile. "We have limited resources, too. Do you know the Kiels?"

"I'm only slowly meeting people in town." I explained my mission yet again. "I want to talk to Sonia, if she recovers, because she phoned me early this morning claiming she'd seen my missing persons. I haven't met Dr. or Ms. Kiel, but I do plan to talk to them after I leave here."

He started to speak, grimaced again, got up and shut the conference-room door. "Even when you think the halls are empty, someone manages to listen in on confidential conversations. Sonia Kiel is an odd duck by any standard. She shouldn't be here, shouldn't stay here—I mean, because she is often drunk, which is in violation of our rules. I make her leave when she's drunk, but I have to take her back."

He fiddled with his coffee cup again: he was pushing himself to reveal confidences. "The psychiatrist involved with our residents is a Dr. Chesnitz. Ernst Chesnitz. He's been treating Sonia for a lot of years, he's on our board, and he's close to Nathan Kiel. The Kiels made a substantial donation to St. Rafe's when we agreed to take Sonia. It was a condition of taking her. Tough love, which is possibly the only kind they know how to manifest."

His expression became bleaker, which I wouldn't have thought possible.

"You don't want her here, do you?" I asked.

"She doesn't belong here. It's true she's got an addiction problem, but we're only equipped to handle addicts or homeless people who are trying to stay sober. Sonia needs help that we can't provide, and the help she does need isn't available in Lawrence, at least not in my opinion."

"What's wrong with her?"

"Back when she was a teenager, Sonia had what Chesnitz considered a psychotic break. The Kiels called him in, and he prescribed lithium. He made a diagnosis of bipolar disorder with paranoid tendencies, and every time he examines her, which might be once a year or whenever Dr. Kiel can force her to see Chesnitz, he says there's no reason to change that diagnosis."

"She's forty-something now," I said. "Chesnitz has been her physician all this time?"

Marx hunched a shoulder. "I suppose he's seventy. Maybe it's strange, but it's not improbable."

"Is she still taking lithium?"

"Lithium requires a lot more patient cooperation than Sonia will provide. You can't drink, you have to have regular blood work, and it's dangerous to your whole body if you go off it cold turkey. Anyway, it's not used much these days. We have her on one of the new generation of atypical antipsychotics—Depakote, if you want to know. You shouldn't drink alcohol with Depakote either, but it doesn't stay in the system the way lithium does, and you can't go into shock the way you can when you stop lithium abruptly."

I described how I'd found Sonia, barely breathing under the iron staircase leading up to the floor above the Lion's Pride. "Would that be the interaction of Depakote with alcohol?"

He shrugged again. "It could be. She's not in good shape, and thirty years of antipsychotics, even with her going off them for five years when she went out east . . . it makes her more vulnerable to side effects. And her drinking, of course. When the police officer came this morning to tell me Sonia was hospitalized, I phoned the ward head and the on-call doctor, but there's not a lot they can do until they get the tox screen back, except see that she remains hydrated and breathing."

"You keep taking her back here because of Chesnitz and Kiel?" I ventured.

He nodded. "It's not fair to the other residents. We get complaints in group meetings, and I try to be honest, not to sugarcoat it. I'm not sure it's a bad thing for them to see that everyone with a job faces unpleasant choices. Or that's my rationalization."

We sat silent for a minute. I was watching the birds in the grasses, but Marx was staring at the bulldozers. His jaw worked in rhythm with their teeth, as if he'd like to chew something or someone up the way they were chewing the ground.

He roused himself at length. "I have another group-therapy session in five minutes. Do you have what you came for?"

"Sonia talked on the phone about seeing my missing pair at a cemetery where her truelove died. I need to know where that cemetery is. The cops told me there are five in town."

Marx drained his coffee cup and smacked it on the table. "Forget it: that's one of her persistent rants. Fantasies. A lover who was murdered by her father, or one of her father's colleagues, or the military, or the FBI. She journals about him, she talks about him—it gets none of us anywhere. You'd be a new audience for her, so she was probably trying to seduce you into listening to her by giving you what you want—a sighting of your runaways. I'm sure she made it up."

He started to stand, but I said, "The bartender took the phone away from her before Sonia said much, but she offered a detail that makes me think she truly did see Ferring and Veriden. Is she friendly with anyone here, any of the other therapists or residents who she might have confided in? I need to find the cemetery where this lover is buried."

Marx frowned. "First of all, I can't and won't violate the privacy of other residents by giving you access to them. And anyway, I thought I'd made clear that Sonia never had a lover, at least not as a fourteen-year-old."

I eyed him steadily. "I still want to find the graveyard where she saw Emerald Ferring. Even if the lover is a phantom, I presume the cemetery's real."

14

IT'S A MAD, MAD, MAD, MAD SCIENTIST

THE KIEL HOUSE was hidden from the street by a tangle of unkempt shrubs. When I pushed my way up the walk to the front door, I saw cracks in the redwood-shingled siding, while the walk itself could have used some rehab. A VW Passat, crusted in dirt, sat in the drive. Lights were on in the back of the house, but when I rang the doorbell, no one came.

The Kiels had a comfortable retirement income, at least according to LifeStory. Perhaps the bribes they paid St. Rafe's to keep their daughter made it hard for them to maintain their home.

They lived on Quivira Road, about three miles from the shelter, in a warren of short, curving streets and cul-de-sacs near the north side of campus. I'd gotten lost—humiliating for a Chicagoan supercilious about small-town life—but I kept finding myself at a fountain in the middle of a roundabout on the edge of campus. On my third circuit of the fountain, I finally found the right entrance to the maze.

"If the Kiels have anything helpful to say, let me know," Marx had said as he left me. "It would be a first, but our motto at St. Rafe's is 'Hope.'"

It was the closest he'd come to humor in our hour together, and it wasn't a comfortable sort of joke.

I checked my messages while I waited on the Kiels' doorstep. Still no answer from Cady Perec about whether her grandmother knew Dr. Kiel, but I suppose teachers set a bad example if they text while conducting classes.

I pinched my nose, trying to keep from falling asleep. Maybe Sonia *had* been playing me, hoping for a new audience, as Randy Marx thought. Maybe I was chasing a mirage. I rang the bell again and saw movement at the window next to the door. The watcher dropped the curtain and opened the inner door.

"We don't talk to Jehovah's Witnesses."

The woman who snapped at me had a bony face thrust forward on her neck like a turkey's. Pale blue eyes under hooded lids flicked from me to the walk behind me: she was ready to fly back into her tree if I made a sudden move.

"Have you ever seen a Jehovah's Witness?" I said. "They travel in groups. Besides, the women always wear stockings and long dresses." I had on jeans with a green wool blazer and a cream pullover. Not missionary wear.

"What do you want, then?"

"To talk to Shirley or Nathan Kiel. To let them know I'm the person who found their daughter early this morning and probably saved her life."

The lines around the woman's mouth deepened. She muttered something that I couldn't hear through the outer door, although it didn't seem like an expression of undying gratitude. After staring at me suspiciously for another few seconds, she flung the door open, so abruptly I barely had time to jump out of the way.

"Well, come on in, then, and get it over with. There's no reward, in case you were hoping."

I followed her into a room whose furniture was almost invisible under stacks of newspapers and magazines. The dust was so thick that I started to sneeze.

"Are you Shirley Kiel?" I asked, hoping she was an undertaker that I wouldn't have to talk to.

"Yes. Sonia's mother." I wouldn't have thought you could pack so much venom into those two words. It was hard to tell which she hated more—Sonia or being her mother.

Shirley led me to the back of the house, to a kind of sunporch next to the kitchen. I tripped on a Mixmaster set in the middle of the kitchen floor and just managed to keep from falling by grabbing the edge of the kitchen counter. My hand came away with some furry orange stuff on it.

My stomach turned. People have criticized my lackadaisical housekeeping, but compared to this I could have entered an America's Top Homemakers contest and come away with first prize. I turned on the sink tap, holding my fingers between the water and a crusty pot, while Shirley Kiel stared at me in growing impatience.

I hastily wiped my fingers on my jeans and joined her at the sunporch. A light baritone shouted from somewhere above us, demanding to know who was here.

"Sonia Bernhardt's been in a major play!" Shirley shouted back. "Her chief backer is here, wanting us to applaud her."

She didn't wait for a response but stumped out to the porch. It faced south and was glassed in, so that even on a cool day it felt almost too warm. Plants on a shelf along the south wall were on their last stalks, although a few showed a little greenery.

Shirley sat in an armchair whose end tables held open crossword-puzzle books. She picked up one and wrote in an entry. I shrugged and took all the books and magazines from a wicker chair, stacking them on another side table and pulling the chair up so I was facing her.

"I was told you weren't much interested in your daughter, and I can see that it's true, so I won't take a lot of your time."

Shirley Kiel sat back in the chair, jaw slack, as if I'd slapped her. The puzzle book fell to the floor. "You don't understand," she said feebly.

She was right: I didn't understand what it was like to have a child, let alone one who was grown and who was beyond my ability to help or cure. The pain would perhaps make you numb yourself with crossword puzzles. Make you apathetic to the dirt and debris around you. And maybe it would make you belittle your daughter's own pain by pretending it was melodrama: Sonia Bernhardt.

"What's she done this time to embarrass me?" The light baritone had swept into the room.

I turned to look. Nathan Kiel was a short man with a stocky body, but the force field of anger around him was so large that it seemed to push me against the back of the chair. His bio said he was eighty, but the brown eyes in his square face were alert, alive, even if the life was fueled by fury.

"I doubt she had you in mind," I said dryly. "Do you know that she's in a coma at the hospital?"

He grunted, affirmation I suppose. "And you are?"

"V.I. Warshawski. I'm a detective. I'm here from Chicago, trying—"

"You knew? You knew Sonia was in the hospital and you didn't tell me?" Shirley's pale eyes turned dark.

"What would *you* have done? Enacted one of your own dramas for me?" Kiel snorted. "Celia Cordley called me this morning—"

"Oh, *Cee-Cee.*" Shirley spoke with heavy sarcasm. "Another of Nate's groupies, anxious for the approval of the great doctor. She hasn't learned yet that his approval only comes if she spends the rest of her life following him around like an anxious puppy. You should tell her what happened to Ma—"

"Will you shut up?" Kiel bellowed. "I want to know what this detective is trying to stir up here in Lawrence. My daughter is seriously ill and very weak emotionally and morally. If you're preying on her, you could open yourself to major litigation."

"Dr. Kiel, you're supposedly an impressive scientist, but you and logic parted company some miles back down the road. Far from preying on your daughter, I saved her life."

"You knew there was a detective in town interested in Sonia and you didn't tell me?" Shirley blazed again.

Kiel scowled. "Gertrude called me this morning. Apparently this detective spoke to Cady yesterday, got her worked up all over again, and Gertrude was afraid she'd come here to harass me. As she has!"

"Gertrude Perec," I said. "Is she a family friend, a sister scientist—"

"She was Nate's secretary," Shirley spit at me. "She was that mirror that you hear about, the one who reflects men back at twice their normal size. Another one of Nate's female groupies who thought he walked on water. Men tend to see through him. If Gertrude had had to live with him—"

"No one could keep sane in the same house as you. No wonder your daughter—"

I've never learned to do that two-finger whistle, but when I have to, I can hit the A above high C. I stood and let it fly. Kiel and Shirley both stopped shouting and stared at me.

"You've answered one of my questions with this repulsive display. I don't know if you're entertaining each other or yourselves, but you're definitely making *me* sick to my stomach."

Kiel started to speak, but I shut him up. "My turn, then it's your turn. It's called conversation. I am a detective, from Chicago, looking for a missing woman who grew up in Lawrence in the 1950s and went to the University of Kansas. She came back here with a young man who is a videographer, to film her origin story. In trying to find where Ms. Ferring lived as a child and a young adult, I met Cady Perec at the historical society. She took me to meet her grandmother. I also put up flyers asking if anyone had seen Ms. Ferring and her videographer.

"Sonia called me at two this morning, saying she had seen them taking photographs on her dead lover's grave. By the time I got to Eighth and Rhode Island, where she'd phoned from, your daughter was in a coma, close to death. I called 911.

"All I want from you are answers to two questions. No, three. Who was Ms. Kiel's truelove? Where is he buried? And have you been to the hospital to see your daughter?"

Shirley had started to snarl something about Sonia's truelove, but my last question muted her.

"You're a stranger in a strange land," Kiel said. "You don't know me, or my wife, or our daughter, so don't sit in judgment on us."

A vein over his right eye was throbbing. I hoped he didn't have a stroke while I was talking to him.

"If you will tell me where your daughter's dead lover is buried, I will leave—I will get out of your hair, I promise." I'd started to say *leave you in peace* but realized in midsentence that wasn't a country either of them was like to inhabit.

Shirley darted a glance at her husband. He was frowning at her with more ferocity than ever.

"Sonia's belief that she had a lover was the start of all our troubles. She became infatuated with one of my graduate students when she was fourteen. She imagined it was reciprocated, and of course it wasn't. The whole episode was humiliating in the extreme."

"Sonia stalked him," Shirley said. "Of course he couldn't complain to Nate—Nate runs his lab like a medieval fiefdom. He owns his students, and if they divide their loyalty with a spouse or a sport, woe betide them. Besides, Matt—the student, Matt Chastain—was terrified that if he complained about one of Nate's children, Nate would take it out on him. Nate doesn't like being crossed." The last words came out in a childish, taunting tone.

Kiel made his swatting gesture again. "If I'd ever gotten a tenth of the respect in my own home that I got—"

"Sonia stalked Matt Chastain," I interrupted. "Is this who Ms. Kiel thought Dr. Cordley should know about?"

Shirley cawed raucously. "Everyone knows about Matt."

"Did your daughter kill him?"

The silence in the room became so absolute that I could hear the drip from a faucet down the hallway.

"Who have you been talking to?" Kiel finally asked, his voice little better than a whisper.

"No one, at least not about her killing Matt Chastain. Did she?"

Another silence stretched out. Finally Kiel said, "No. She didn't kill him. He . . . made a disastrous decision regarding an experiment

I was conducting. Helping conduct. He couldn't face the consequences, and he ran away. No one has heard from him since."

"Sonia refused to believe he disappeared," Shirley added. "She built a fantasy around him, that he was really in love with her but that Nate—or the government or maybe the Russians—murdered him to keep him from her."

"And whose fault was that?" Kiel snarled. "Who filled her head with those garbagey romance novels you gorge on—"

"Save it for when I've left," I snapped. "I can't tell you how vile you sound or how unpleasant it is to listen to you. Given that your daughter thought Matt Chastain had been murdered, where did she think that had happened?"

"Wherever it was she was spying on him at the time. Poor Chastain. He was one of the weakest students I ever had, both scientifically and morally, but he didn't deserve Sonia."

15

AND BESIDES, THE MENSCH IS DEAD

KIEL VANISHED ON his tagline. I could hear him stomping up a flight of stairs and then a door slamming. His man cave, perhaps, where he gnawed on raw alligator and brooded over how little recognition his wife and bipolar daughter gave him.

Shirley tracked him with her eyes, her expression malevolent. After he shut his door, she heaved herself to her feet and led me silently to the front of the house.

I handed her one of my cards, urging her to phone me if there was something else she could tell me about where Sonia might have last seen Matt Chastain. The graveyard Sonia was obsessed with could easily be a metaphor for her own buried hopes; perhaps Matt had talked to her there, kissed her, done something that made her feel that a particular spot was sacred.

"It was over thirty years ago, so I don't remember." Shirley pushed open the outer door. "Anyway, everyone was confused. What was real, what was imaginary, how could I know? I wasn't there."

"What happened?" I said. "What went so wrong with the experiment that Matt Chastain felt he had to run away?"

"Nate doesn't confide in me."

I would have believed her more readily if she hadn't swallowed a sly smile before answering.

"I don't know anything about this kind of work, but something going wrong with an experiment—was there an explosion? Were people hurt? Or did something your husband worked on make people sick?"

She looked startled, even alarmed. "I don't know, and anyway, I just told you, it was a long time ago."

"But your daughter must have seen something, if it terrified her so much that she had to cover the memory with the protective story that Chastain had died or been killed."

"My daughter," and she again invested a shocking amount of venom in the two syllables, "was sneaking out of the house and trailing around after poor Matt. Dr. Chesnitz says the most likely scenario is that she flung herself at Matt, who rejected her. She was fourteen, overweight, not the kind of girl anyone would respond to, let alone a young man in his twenties. Chesnitz says that in Sonia's mind Matt had to be punished by death. Thinking he was murdered helps her blot out the memory of the rejection and turn him into an idealized figure who was in love with her."

"It sounds like a convenient theory," I said.

"What's that supposed to mean?" She thrust her head forward in her signature turkey move.

"Keeps anyone from asking too many questions about what really happened, or where, or how."

She started to bristle, but I interrupted to ask if her sons kept in touch with Sonia.

Her expression darkened. "I wouldn't know. They couldn't take Nate, his bullying and his moods. Stuart went to school at Bowdoin, out in Maine, never came home after his sophomore year, and Larry, he went to college in Oregon and stayed out on the West Coast. If they talk to Sonia, that's something you'd have to ask them."

"It must be hard to have them so far away," I said, trying to infuse some sincerity into my voice.

"That's my business," she said roughly. "Don't you have to be someplace else?"

I suppose I did. I stepped outside but stopped to say, "If it wasn't Matt Chastain you thought Dr. Cordley should know about, who was it?"

Shirley smiled in a wolflike way that showed all her teeth, which were stained from coffee or cigarettes or maybe the fuzzy orange stuff on her kitchen counter. Even a fantasy lover would have brought more comfort to her daughter than that smile. She shut the door on me without speaking.

"I hope your dog mother never looked at you like that," I said to Peppy when I got back into the car.

Peppy licked my ear sympathetically. An hour with the Kiels made me feel as though I needed a bath in some kind of fumigation sink, the kind where they pummel your body with steam jets. As a substitute I spent an hour in the open air with my dog.

We left the car a block from Gertrude Perec's house and ran to a nearby park. This one had winding paths that led down to the south side of the river. Peppy flushed a rabbit and jumped in and out of the water. I ran along the river's edge, letting cool air and motion empty my mind. By the time we returned to the car, I was feeling easier, almost as though I'd had five hours of sleep instead of four, almost as though I'd spoken to my own mother instead of Sonia Kiel's.

"You stink," I told Peppy, who grinned at me happily, "but at least it's a good honest stench."

I climbed into the passenger seat to look up Matt Chastain, Kiel's errant graduate student, leaving the door open so I didn't have to breathe quite so much rotting dog. If Sonia had been fourteen when Chastain vanished, then he'd disappeared in the early eighties, before everyone's history had been digitized.

I searched news stories and law-enforcement databases but didn't find any reports of a public-health disaster involving Kiel or Chastain. Whatever had happened, I guess it had bruised Kiel's sensitive ego more than anything else.

I also couldn't find any trace of a Matt or Mathias or Matthew Chastain as a cell biologist, although there were dozens of men with that name scattered around the country. It would be a waste of my time and the client's money for me to start calling them just in the hopes of finding a person who could tell me where Sonia had seen Emerald Ferring a week ago: *Were you a graduate student in Kansas in the 1980s? Do you remember where Sonia Kiel saw you the last night you were in town?*

I'd left my cashmere blazer on the seat while Peppy and I ran. I put it back on, ran a comb through my hair, and walked up the road to Gertrude Perec's house. She might have been at the market or the hairdresser or serving in the Riverside Church soup kitchen, but this was my lucky day: lights were on in the back of the house, and she answered the bell within a minute of my ringing.

"Hello," I said before she could speak. "I've just come from Dr. Kiel's. I know you know that Sonia is in the hospital, since you called to tell him the news. Perhaps you even know that I found her last night in time to get her emergency help."

"Yes." Her voice came out in an uncertain whisper. She cleared her throat and tried to speak more firmly. "Dr. Kiel told me."

"You called him to tell him—warn him—that I had visited you but that you had protected his identity from me. So he returned the favor by calling you just now to tell you I'd found him anyway?"

She nodded. "Because of Sonia."

"Sonia is such a convenient whipping boy, or girl, isn't she?"

"What's that supposed to mean?" Perec's tone became belligerent.

"Whatever goes wrong, from Matt Chastain's dying, or disappearing, or whatever he did, to the grotesque relations between Shirley and Nathan Kiel, can be offloaded onto Sonia, who's not able to fight back."

"Fight back? That's all she's been doing her whole life. If she could behave herself—"

"When she was fourteen, someone not only diagnosed her with a mental illness but started medicating her so heavily that I doubt she could remember her own name in a well-lit room on a sunny day. Thirty years down the road, I have no idea how much or how little she can possibly remember or know from that time. That's why I need your help."

I hadn't meant to get off on such a confrontational foot. Of course Gertrude Perec didn't want to help me—she wanted to protect Dr. Kiel. I was an enemy; I'd saved the wicked Sonia's life.

Gertrude started to close the door on me, so I said quickly, "Sonia told me she'd seen Emerald Ferring and August Veriden—you remember, those are the people I'm trying to find—walking on Matt Chastain's grave."

"You spoke to her?" Gertrude poised the door between open and shut.

"Only very briefly. I'm trying to find out where Matt Chastain is buried. Or where Sonia thinks he's buried."

"What . . . what did Nate—Dr. Kiel—say?"

"Tell me about the experiment that went so badly that Chastain ran away. Do you know where he ran to?"

"I . . . I was Dr. Kiel's secretary, not part of his experimental team."

"Yes, of course. But he clearly relied on you. I'm sure you knew at least the outline of what was going on." I was almost leering with the effort to seem warm and fuzzy. It was keeping the door open but not making Gertrude more forthcoming.

"It was a long time ago, more than thirty years. I've forgotten the details."

This was so nearly identical to what Shirley Kiel had said that my mouth had opened with a sarcastic comment at the ready when the kaleidoscope turned in my brain and two pieces of glass lined up over each other: 1983, when so much happened—the protest at the silo, the death of Jennifer Perec, the birth of Cady Perec, the disappearance of Matt Chastain.

"Your daughter, Jennifer. Is Matt Chastain Cady's father? If he is, why don't you want Cady to know? Surely not because of some long-forgotten science—"

"You know nothing." Her face shriveled and turned white, transparent, like a petal from a dying narcissus. "You come from up north, you think you're smarter than us small-town folk, but you know nothing."

She shut the door on me. I lingered on the stoop, wondering if I should go in to make sure she hadn't collapsed. After a moment, though, I saw a light come on in the room behind the porch where I'd sat yesterday. The house was too stoutly built for me to hear anything—such as the phone call I assumed she was making to Nathan Kiel—but she was probably okay.

I walked slowly back to the car, trying to make sense of the story. Shirley Kiel said Sonia had stalked Matt. Say Sonia had seen him with Jennifer Perec, seen her own romantic daydreams ripped apart. What would she have done? Had the psychotic break her parents claimed? And then had she attacked Matt? No, more likely she attacked Jennifer. I felt something cold in my stomach, like a large glacier—had she killed Jennifer? Was the car in the Wakarusa a cover-up for that?

And where had Chastain been when Jennifer died? Was he glad not to be saddled with a baby? No one knew he was Cady's father, so he could slide out of town, away from Nathan Kiel's wrath, away from fatherhood. Maybe he'd changed his name and become CEO of a pharmaceutical company. Or he'd dropped off the grid and was living under a viaduct with a bottle of Mad Dog 20/20 to keep him warm.

Nothing I could imagine made any sense. It wasn't really my business either. My business was to find Emerald Ferring and August Veriden. I repeated that to myself about a dozen times as I drove over to the Hippo for another nourishing cortado.

16

DOWN BY THE RIVERSIDE

I'D PASSED RIVERSIDE United Church of Christ, tucked into the northeast corner of the park, when I'd been running with Peppy. You couldn't see it from the road, so they'd put up a sign on Sixth Street: HALF MILE ON YOUR RIGHT, ALL WELCOME. A bigger, brighter sign stood at the entrance to their drive, where you could see the building, made of local limestone that had aged to a golden gray. Some half-dozen cars were parked in a lot that could easily hold a hundred; it must be a big church.

I stopped to read a historical marker on the front lawn. Gathered in 1855 by antislavery emigrants from the Boston area, destroyed by the great flood of 1893, rebuilt in 1896 farther from the river. Up until the end of the Civil War, Riverside had harbored fugitive slaves in a cellar underneath the altar. Today they were a nuclear-free zone and "an inclusive, new-light community who welcome all to join us, wherever you are on your life's journey."

I followed directions on the church door to the office entrance. Laughter and chatter led me to a big meeting room, where some ten women, most in their sixties or seventies, were emptying black leaf bags filled with clothes.

One of them saw me standing at the entrance and bustled over, hand out. "Have you come to help? That's splendid. I'm Joy Helmsley."

I shook hands automatically. "V.I. Warshawski, but I'm afraid I'm here to get help, not give it."

"Oh?" She cocked her head, birdlike, to one side. "If you want to see Pastor Weld, he's out right now, but Lisa Carmody is here. She's the associate pastor."

At the sound of her name, a second woman came over. She was younger than the others, wearing jeans and a pullover turned shapeless from much washing.

"Lisa Carmody. Why don't we go into the office, have a little more privacy."

I felt a bit embarrassed. "Not that kind of help—I'm looking for information, something maybe one of you knows, or at least knows someone who knows."

The group abandoned the pretext of sorting clothes for what was definitely going to be more interesting.

"Ancient history," I said. "You may have heard that I'm a detective from Chicago, looking for Emerald Ferring."

"Oh, yes." Lisa Carmody nodded. "I saw the posters you put up downtown. Ferring and a young man, right? Ferring is one of our local stars, except we didn't give her star treatment when she lived here, but everyone knows who she is."

There was a murmur from the rest of the group, hard to decipher, but it sounded as though not all agreed with Carmody.

"I haven't found any trace of them. I was going to go back to Chicago today, but early this morning someone called to say that she'd seen them in the same place where another person disappeared thirty-some years ago."

"Sonia Kiel." A woman in a severely tailored navy blazer spoke. "She was picked up from in front of the Lion's Pride—that bar at Eighth and Rhode Island—we've been trying to get them shut down, or at least to close at eleven so that people unfortunate enough to live nearby can get a night's rest."

"Yes," I said. "She called me from the bar, but by the time I got there, she was in a coma. Someone had slipped her roofies."

"Poor Shirley," the tailored blazer said. "She's always worried about Sonia. If only she could have made a success out of Boston instead of coming back to Lawrence."

"This morning Shirley seemed more bitter than worried," I said.

"You're a stranger, and Shirley is awkward around strangers," the blazer said. "I worked with her for twenty years at Emigrant Bank and Savings. She was tireless, committed to the well-being of our clients and to her co-workers."

Joy Helmsley nodded emphatic agreement. "It's not easy having a child with the kind of problems Sonia does. Maybe it seems cruel to you, putting her in a group home, but she's forty-something. Shirley and Nate are eighty or so. How can they take care of an adult child!"

I held up my hands: stop sign. "I'm sure you're right. Ms. Kiel only presented one face to me, anger, but you all know her and I don't. I had about thirty seconds on the phone with Sonia at two this morning before the bartender took the phone from her. Sonia said she'd seen Ferring and August Veriden at the place, maybe a cemetery, where Matt Chastain was buried."

"Oh, she was making that up!" Helmsley burst out. "We all know she lives in a daydream about—"

"Sonia knew a detail I hadn't included in my flyer," I said. "That's why I believe her, despite any emotional problems she may have."

"What is it you want to know?" Lisa Carmody pulled the conversation back onto the main track.

"Does everyone know who Matt Chastain is?"

Most of the women shook their heads, so I gave the thumbnail of what I knew, or at least what I'd been told, leaving out my guess that Chastain was Cady Perec's father.

"Oh, yes. That was about the time that they had the big demonstration out by the missile silo," a woman who hadn't spoken before said. "Jenny Perec was marching with the anti-nuke people. I know Gertrude agreed with her in principle, but she hated it when Jenny started camping out with them on the missile site."

"That's right, Barbara," Joy said. "I remember Gertrude thought you encouraged her to take part in the protests."

"I never camped out there," Barbara said. "Too chicken, I suppose, but it's true she came to me when Gertrude was giving her grief over the commune."

"Did Dr. Kiel's experiment have something to do with the missile?" I asked.

"No, no," Barbara said. "It's just that's the last I can remember of talking to Jenny. Until she died, I was . . . quite close . . . to her mother. After that it . . . well, we're cordial at coffee hour."

"It turned out Jenny'd had a baby, little Cady," Joy said. "Someone actually left Cady on Gertrude's doorstep, as if it was a movie, with a note saying, 'This is Jenny's little girl. Please look after her.'"

"It didn't happen like that," Barbara said. "Jenny drove off without the baby. One of the local farmers rescued her and turned her over to Gertrude."

The room was quiet as we all imagined the scene. What had led Jenny to take off in that dramatic way, abandoning her baby? She'd been nineteen; was she racing after her baby's father? If I'd been looking for Matt Chastain instead of Emerald Ferring, I would have asked those questions.

"It sounds as though I need to go out to the missile silo, see the remains of the commune," I said.

"There's nothing out there," the woman in the blazer said. "Really nothing. It's in the middle of farmland. The air force compelled the sale of land from farmers, not just at Kanwaka but all over the Midwest. Then, when the commune burned down, the air force found that the land was contaminated and they seized about fifteen more acres so farmers wouldn't plant where there was a radiation danger. It was hard on the farmers. I can't remember whose land they took—"

"Doris McKinnon's," Barbara supplied.

"Anyway, the air force took the missile away after the disarmament agreements," the blazer continued. "Someone came into the bank wanting to borrow money to turn it into a condo, but there were too many issues with the site. It couldn't be done."

"Pity," Barbara said. "My niece clerks for the federal judges in Topeka. She says a lot of those abandoned silos have been taken over by meth makers, and God knows we have enough meth in the county already."

"You think meth contaminated the land around the silo?" I asked.

"Barbara always imagines the worst," the blazer said.

"Maybe because the worst happens so often," Barbara said dryly.

Lisa Carmody tried to change the subject before the fight got out of control. I helped by asking about Emerald Ferring.

"Her father was in the army," I said, "killed at the Battle of the Bulge, and her mother moved here with Emerald after that. They lived across the river until the big flood drove them away, although I think they stayed in the area: Emerald went to the university here but didn't live on campus, and there's no record in the old phone books. Who would know where the family moved?"

Lisa Carmody, the associate pastor, said, "They weren't part of the church, so I don't think anyone here could help you."

I looked at her in astonishment. "How do you know?"

She flushed. "It came up. Someone mentioned it, I think when they saw your flyer. Someone asked Pastor Weld. Our secretary checked."

She was like an inexpert gambler, covering a mistake by playing card after card on top of the first bad one.

"We weren't very welcoming to people across the river," Barbara said dryly, "at least not in those days."

"You can't be accountable for how your grandparents behaved in the past," Joy Helmsley said bracingly. "You were only a child."

"I was ten. I remember the language," Barbara said. "I don't know where Ferring's family moved after the flood, but there's an old woman who still lives over there. I got to know her when we were doing joint worship services with St. Silas a few years back—that's where she worships, St. Silas AME."

I'd forgotten St. Silas, where Lucinda Ferring's funeral had taken place. I told Barbara I'd head over there next.

"It's a small congregation. There may not be anyone in the church office on a weekday," Barbara said. "But the woman I met is named Nell Albritten. She's African-American herself, and she knew most of the black families that used to live in North Lawrence or on the old east side. Back when we thought indoor plumbing was a luxury a black schoolteacher didn't need to have. I think Emigrant Savings was the mortgage lender who tried to make that point."

"Barbara, there are many forms of ministry, and they don't all involve beating our breasts over race," the blazer said. "I'm only a few years younger than you, and my memories of this church and its outreach are very different."

"They would be, wouldn't they?" Barbara said. The words were mild, but the delivery sounded perilously close to contempt.

"Ministry is always a balancing act." The associate pastor hurriedly tried to end the conflict. "We all have to be careful not to think we have the only right answer or the only right understanding of God's call."

Barbara pursed up her mouth in an ironic smile. "True enough, Lisa. The teen reading group is arriving in a few minutes. I'm called right now to get the library set up."

The associate pastor put a hand on my sleeve, as if to keep me from following Barbara. "I don't think it's a good idea for you to visit Nell Albritten. You're a detective, which is often alarming, especially to an African-American. Mrs. Albritten is old, she's frail. It would be kinder to leave her alone."

"That's right," the blazer said. "Barbara has a good heart, and she means well, but she has a distorted sense of race relations. She caused a lot of friction, both here and at St. Silas when we were trying to worship together."

"That's unfair!" a woman who hadn't spoken before cried out. "Barbara did a lot to smooth out decades, maybe *centuries* of ill will between Riverside and the African-American community."

The blazer turned stony-faced. "We haven't been here for *centuries,* Alison. Speaking for myself, I have to be back at work in half an hour, so I'm going to do the job I came here to do." She marched over to the row of tables again and upended another plastic bag.

I headed for the exit, but Carmody stopped me again at the door. "You can see there are a lot of different views here on our history in Lawrence and on race. You should stay away from Nell Albritten. You're a stranger, and you could undo years of bridge building by going to talk to her."

"I'll keep that in mind," I said politely.

A buzz, like swarming bees, rose behind me as I left. Was Barbara sanctimonious, always thinking she was more righteous than the world around her? Did Riverside have a responsibility for some of the violence of the seventies? It was a challenging discussion, one that I lacked the history or theology to take part in. Conflict always interests me, however, and I would have liked to hear more.

17

JUNKYARD DOGS

St. Silas was a small church at Third and Lincoln, made of wood, which had weathered as the Riverside Church had done, but not as happily. The paint was peeling, and two of the high, narrow windows had cracks in their panes. As the woman from Riverside had foretold, the building was locked up tight.

A faded sign gave the times for Sunday school and Christian worship. A placard in front designated the building as a National Historic Landmark and mentioned its role as a place of hiding for free blacks during the Civil War. Perhaps Emerald and August were hiding in a secret basement, but the building had a desolate, unused feel to it.

The church didn't have a parking lot, but wheel marks in the wide grass verge along Lincoln showed where people parked. I left the car there and walked the few blocks to Sixth Street, where Nell Albritten lived, two doors down from the house where Emerald Ferring had spent part of her childhood.

I took Peppy with me: the chilly day was starting to get dark, a time when melancholy and loneliness can tighten their grip. Every time I logged on to my server, I checked for messages from Jake: e-mail, Skype, Facebook. Silence from Switzerland. I'd stopped sending my own messages—it made me feel too much like some forlorn figure in a fifties romance, waiting by the phone.

We passed the Amtrak station, a snug-looking little limestone building. A plaque on the station wall at about waist level commemorated the high-water mark from the 1951 flood. As I stopped to read the history, a dark SUV pulled up behind us and barely slowed before taking off with a great revving of its engine. I jerked Peppy's leash to pull her close to me: I didn't want to lose her to some would-be NASCAR racer.

Giant grain elevators blocked my view up the tracks. As we were crossing, a freight train rounded a curve, hooting mournfully. We jumped out of the way in time, but my heart was beating uncomfortably. Race-car drivers, fast trains, excitement I never experienced in Chicago.

We were about half a mile from the riverbank here. I imagined the muddy waters rushing in, taking away cars and houses, rotting the grain in the elevators. I shivered with something more than cold.

We skirted a dumping operation and a scrapyard whose sign proclaimed, LOU & ED: BREATHING NEW LIFE INTO OLD METAL. It was as though I were looking at a microcosm of my South Chicago childhood. Instead of steel mills and the CID landfill, North Lawrence held grain elevators and scrapyards.

When we reached the residential stretch of Sixth Street, the houses looked old and feeble, not strong enough to survive a wild wind, let alone floodwaters that would have covered their roofs. Industry, salvage, dumping, and housing for the poor—they always go hand in hand.

As we trudged along Sixth Street, I saw what Gertrude Perec had meant about the houses being built next to the ground. They didn't sit on foundations; doors opened level with the walkways. I would have guessed a Kansas house wouldn't be built without a basement against tornadoes, but these little bungalows couldn't run to anything more than a crawl space under the floor. Mud, spiders, snakes—I'd rather take my chance on the winds.

The Ferring house was still standing, or at least a house at that address was still there. With its peeling paint and sagging eaves, it looked as though it could have dated back to the Civil War.

The driveway was filled with detritus: bits of appliances, chunks of Styrofoam, old plastic bags. When I stopped to stare, trying to imagine what it might have looked like sixty-five years ago, a dog charged around from the back of the house, letting out a deep-throated bellow, hurling itself along the length of a heavy chain. Peppy growled softly, the fur on her back ruffing up. She was ready to go to war, very uncharacteristic.

A young woman came to the front door to see what the commotion was. I waved and started to move on but then thought I'd ask if she knew or had heard anything about Ferring. Perhaps old school records or a change-of-address card had survived the deluge.

I tied Peppy to a lamppost, where she and the house dog started a salvo. A dark blue Buick Enclave slowed to watch me. I frowned at it. Was this the SUV that had pulled up behind me at the train station? When the driver saw me looking, he gunned the engine and took off. Same driving technique anyway. I made Peppy quiet her threats back to throat rumbles before going up the walk.

The young woman was still in the doorway, watching me with active hostility. "You try to set one foot in this house and Peeta will eat your throat right out of your neck."

I heard a whimper and realized that she had an infant on her hip. She barely looked into her teens herself, her dirty blond hair pulled back from a narrow face with feather-covered clips.

"I'm not from a collection agency, and I'm not going to challenge your dog," I said. "I have a funny kind of errand. I'm guessing you're too young to help me, but I'm trying to find someone who might be old enough to remember the family that lived here sixty years ago."

Her small rosebud of a mouth opened in surprise. "You mean that black lady?"

I held my breath. "Yes, the black lady. Did she come here?"

"She was here with a man who was taking pictures. I came out with Peeta to drive them off—I thought they were trying some funny business with the house. Peeta chased them back to the car, and the man, he called out that she was a famous actress who grew up here. My boyfriend, when I told him, he said they were probably escaped convicts."

The homeless man yesterday had guessed August was a runaway football player. Lawrence seemed to breed highly active imaginations in its citizens. I showed the young woman Emerald's and August's photos.

"She really is a famous actress," I said. "Emerald Ferring. Look her up on Wikipedia."

"And she really lived *here*?" The young woman looked around in incredulity at the junk-filled drive and the peeling paint, then ran her finger over her baby's nose. "Hear that, Katniss? You could grow up to be someone famous, just breathing this moldy air."

The baby turned her head, revealing the same rosebud mouth and round blue eyes of her mother. A little trail of spit dribbled from the corner of her mouth.

"When were they here?" I asked.

"I don't really remember. Last week maybe, or the week before?"

"Did she say anything, like where she was going next?"

The young woman shook her head mournfully. "I thought they were robbers, so I didn't want to talk to them. If she comes back, though, I can get her autograph and ask her to call you."

I pushed one of my cards toward her through a tear in the screen door. "What about Nell Albritten? Do you know her?"

She nodded, warily.

"Did Emerald Ferring go on to see her after she left here?"

The young woman hunched a shoulder. "Can't see that house from here. Kyle doesn't like me talking to her anyway. He says let the neighbors mind their own business."

The baby began to cry, and Peeta renewed his invective. It seemed like a good time to leave, but partway down the walk I turned to ask if her boyfriend had been in the Buick that drove past when I was tying up Peppy: I was wondering if he was a drug dealer, checking to see who was visiting his lair.

"In a Buick?" Her mouth curled in scorn. "Kyle can barely keep his old Dodge pickup going."

I stepped carefully around the broken cement in the walk and knelt to unhook Peppy. I had to hold tightly to her collar while I did it—she wanted to make sure Peeta knew she might look like a chocolate-box illustration, but she could take him with three paws tied behind her.

"You realize we really are on the trail, girl? First Sonia, now the waif with the feathers in her hair have both seen our fugitives. I know you're all wound up, but try not to be too aggressive with Ms. Albritten."

When we passed the mountain of debris in Peeta's family's drive and saw Albritten's house, it came as a complete surprise. It belonged to a different universe, to the part of my childhood where my mother and the neighbors tried to keep the grime of the mills at bay. Gabriella and I had scoured the soot and sulfur from the front step every morning, calling greetings to Louisa Djiak and other women doing the same work. We'd washed the windows and curtains once a month, and my mother had tended an olive tree in our Kleenex-size garden to lessen her homesickness for her Umbrian childhood.

Ms. Albritten's front garden was similarly groomed, with bushes whose names I didn't know sporting red leaves against the November gray. The little house was painted mauve, with deep purple trim around the windows. An old hitching post stood at the curb; I tied Peppy's leash to it.

As I rang the bell, I could hear a television loudly proclaiming the virtues of a drug to help bladder control. I waited for the nanosecond pause between commercial's end and program's resumption before ringing again.

After another longish moment, the sound was muted and I could hear Ms. Albritten's slow step to the door. She was perhaps ninety, stooped only slightly from age, wearing a heavy sweater over a navy-figured dress. She frowned at me but didn't speak.

"My name is V.I. Warshawski," I said. "I'm from Chicago, and

I'm trying to find Emerald Ferring. A woman named Barbara at Riverside Church said you might know her."

Ms. Albritten peered at me through thick lenses for a long moment, as if comparing my face to a wanted poster. "I don't think I can help you, Miss V.I. whoever from Chicago. I never heard of an Emerald Ferring."

I started to remind her who Ferring was, that I was sure she'd been here with August Veriden a week or so ago, but I saw her jaw set in a stubborn line: she knew all this, and she wasn't going to talk to me.

I stared at a broken television in the driveway next door, thinking it through. I wondered if Lisa Carmody, the Riverside associate pastor, had called her, warning her that I would probably come round, urging her not to talk to me. Did Carmody and Albritten herself know where Emerald and August were, or was this a more basic matter—a white stranger poking her nose in where it didn't belong?

"Ma'am, would you talk to Ms. Ferring's friends in Chicago, the people who asked me to come down here to find her?"

Before she could say no, I brought up Troy Hempel's phone number, calling him on FaceTime so that Albritten could see that he was also African-American. Fortunately, he answered immediately.

"V.I. Warshawski! What is it? Have you found Ms. Emerald?"

I put him on speaker and held the phone so that Ms. Albritten could see the screen—and be seen—through the crack in the door. "I'm on the street where Emerald Ferring lived until she was seven. She was here about ten days ago with August Veriden, looking at her childhood home, and now I'm with a neighbor who needs you to vouch for me before she'll tell me anything. This is Ms. Nell Albritten."

Albritten took the phone but stepped back into the house to talk. "Who are you, young man, and why should I trust you?"

She shut the door as he started to explain how he knew Ferring. I could hear the faint rumble of his voice and Albritten's own slow cadences in reply, but I couldn't make out any of the words. They spoke for almost five minutes, and then I heard her unsteady gait going farther into her house, her voice on the phone, again with the words indistinguishable. Finally she returned to the front door.

"I hope I'm not making a mistake," she sighed, handing me back my phone, "but I guess you can come on in."

She peered down the sidewalk at Peppy. "Is that your dog out there? You might as well bring her in. There's a couple of rough boys who fight with dogs over on Ninth Street. I wouldn't leave her tied where they could pick her up."

I'd wondered if the Buick had belonged to a drug dealer, checking out strangers in the neighborhood, but maybe it was a fighting ring eyeing how easy it would be to steal Peppy.

"She's dirty," I said doubtfully. "Maybe we could talk out here where I can watch her."

"I need to sit. You bring her in and let her lay on a towel."

18

THOSE GOOD OLD DAYS

THE ROOM WHERE Ms. Albritten talked to me was cared for as meticulously as her garden. The floral-upholstered couch and armchair were recently vacuumed, and she used starched white antimacassars to protect the headrests. The towel she'd laid down for Peppy was as brightly yellow as if it had just come from the store. I cringed at the thought of how it would look when we left, but Peppy obediently took her place on it, despite her obvious wish to explore the room. She held up a paw to Ms. Albritten, who gave a faint twitch of a smile.

"Hmmpf. I have biscuits I give that dog Peeta. He's a little faker—barks for show, but that poor girl is deluding herself if she thinks he can protect her and her baby. Be best if he bit her worthless boyfriend in the ass and sent him about his business, but you can't talk to young girls about love. They think women like me never knew what it was like."

She gestured me to the couch before disappearing into the back of the house, her steps careful: her ankles were badly swollen under her support stockings. I heard the clink of ice against glass, the pouring of liquid, the fumbling with a canister, at which Peppy looked up alertly. Pictures were still flashing on the muted television—*Judge Judy,* it might have been.

Albritten had a gallery of framed photos on the walls: a solemn-faced man at different stages of life—in high school and college graduation robes, in an army uniform, and then older, with a wife and two teenage children. The children had their own array, chubby babies to Eagle Scouts. A recent picture on top of the TV showed Albritten with a group of other women in front of St. Silas. Albritten was by far the oldest; the youngest might have been in her forties. They were all smiling joyously, holding a banner that celebrated St. Silas's 150th anniversary: 1864–2014.

Albritten presently reappeared with a silver tray holding two glasses, a plate of cookies, and a handful of dog biscuits. I decided she might find it insulting if I tried to help, so I watched while she arranged the tray on a polished coffee table. She handed a glass to me. Iced tea, which I don't care much for in July and definitely not in November, but I've suffered worse in the line of duty.

"Your dog is well behaved," Albritten said. Peppy was looking at the biscuits but not standing or making begging noises. "Here you go, good girl."

She handed the biscuits to Peppy one at a time before sitting heavily in the armchair. "Emerald Ferring. Yes."

She arranged her skirt over her knees. "Her mother, Lucinda, she came here after her man was killed in the war. There was a big munitions plant here, you see, the Sunflower plant, and they were looking for workers. Lucinda rented the house you were just at, where Peeta and Tiffany and the baby live. It was a long bus ride every day out to Sunflower. My man was off in the war himself, and I had a baby boy. He was three then, Jordan." She nodded at the photos on the wall. "I was cleaning houses for white families over across the river, and my mother was here, looking after Jordan. It was good company for him to have little Emerald around."

She gave a surprised laugh. "Her name wasn't Emerald, it was Esmeralda, but Jordan couldn't say that. He said 'Emerald,' and we—Lucinda and I and my mother—loved it: she was a jewel of a child. I'd forgotten that. She was such a smart little girl, knew her letters when she was three, always asking the deepest questions, about God and life and where was her daddy, and how she was going to be a ballerina or a pilot when she grew up."

Albritten sipped her tea, the smile fading as she looked into a bitter distance. "You have to understand, this was a hard town to be black in. They fancied themselves, the white folks did, they fancied themselves because they were descended from the people who made Kansas a free state back in 1861, but they weren't descended from John Brown, no, ma'am. They wanted a town that was all white, and so they kept black folk over here in the river bottom. Black children drowned in that river every summer—they weren't allowed in the pools in town.

"Restaurants, only five restaurants in town would serve a meal to a black person. We sat in a corner of the balcony in the movie theaters. They had a Ku Klux Klan chapter up at the university, and the basketball coach—he's like a saint or a hero in this town—he was a big Klan booster. When Wilt Chamberlain showed up, he made them change some of their ways, but it went on for a long, long time. Ferguson, all these black boys being killed today, it's just another chapter in a long book."

She looked at me again, the same measuring look she'd given in the doorway. "I worried about Jordan over at the high school. They wouldn't let him into the college-prep classes, you see. One of the women I cleaned house for, she was on the school board, I tried to talk to her about it: my Jordan was as smart as any boy in that school. She fired me on the spot. Uppity, I was. When he organized a protest among the black students, I was afraid for what would happen to him. Soon as he graduated, off he went to Vietnam, no college deferment for him. Although he made it through Howard when he finally came safe home again."

A sense of shame made me hold myself completely still, the glass of iced tea freezing my fingers. Peppy looked worriedly from me to Ms. Albritten but fortunately didn't move.

She gave a heavy sigh. "This part of town, in the river bottom, this was where we were supposed to live and get over to the main town as best we could to do the dirty work, the heavy lifting. The house where Emerald and Lucinda lived, where little Katniss is now, it was like most of the houses over here—no real floor, just plywood over the dirt. When the flood came, that plywood was no more cover than an umbrella in a blizzard. Water pushed up—it happened so fast we were lucky we got away with our lives. We lost everything. Lucinda, her wedding pictures, her man in uniform on his way to the fighting, all that disappeared like dishwater down a drain. I managed to save my grandmother's silver spoons and the family Bible, but that was all.

"And then the waters receded and we had mud and mold and disease, but would those white landlords lift a finger to help? We had to clean and fumigate on our own. Those flimsy plywood floors, they came to put those back in but wouldn't clean up the dirt first."

She began describing the process in numbing detail: the effort to salvage blinds and carpets that were beyond hope, the terrible chest ailments children suffered the winter after the flood, the handouts from the white churches. "Canned food that no one had used that Thanksgiving and clothes with moth holes in them."

She stopped speaking. I sat silent for a few moments, not sure where her mind was, not sure what I felt able to ask, but finally I said, "What happened to Lucinda Ferring?"

Albritten didn't look at me. I wasn't even sure she'd heard me. The silence stretched as if it were a living thing, pushing into me, keeping me from moving or talking. The only motion in the room came from the silent images flickering across the television screen.

The phone rang, and Albritten jumped on it. A man was on the other end, deep voice but soft. Albritten only contributed "Yes" several times, and then, "God's will. Not always easy to accept."

When she hung up, she put her hands on her knees and took a breath, bracing herself. The caller had told her to put all her money on Stewball, and she wasn't sure it was good advice. I tried to put on a Kansas face: honest and empathetic.

"The plywood was the last straw for Lucinda. She demanded a real floor, concrete over the dirt, and the landlord evicted her! So Lucinda took little Emerald and moved out to the country, east of town.

"There was a woman there had a farm, widowed like Lucinda. Even though she was white, she rented rooms to black students up at the university, because the university wouldn't let them live in student housing. Lucinda had grown up on a farm up north someplace—Minnesota, maybe, or South Dakota.

"When she heard about Miz McKinnon, Lucinda went out to see about exchanging room and board for helping on the farm. Address wasn't in Lawrence but the little town next door, Eudora, so Emerald could go to school there. It wasn't perfect by any means, but they'd never gone in for segregation in Eudora the way they did in Lawrence."

That explained why the Ferring name had disappeared from the phone books. A blot on the detective's record—she should have thought of looking at other towns nearby.

"McKinnon?" I interrupted. "They mentioned her over at Riverside, a Doris McKinnon whose farmland the government seized for the missile silo. Is that the same one?"

Albritten's lower jaw moved, the way it sometimes does in the old, but in the pause that followed, it looked as though she were chewing her words, trying to decide which ones to keep, which to spit out.

"Yes, the McKinnon farm is out there near the silo. I don't have a car, so I didn't go there often, even before Lucinda passed."

"Emerald went to the University of Kansas, right?" I said. "But she kept living on the farm?"

"The student housing was still segregated when Emerald started at college," Albritten said. "So she kept out at the farm, until the week Jarvis Nilsson showed up and discovered her. Lucinda was a technician up in one of the science labs at the university. Sounds fancy, but it was a lot of dirty work. Still, it paid better than housecleaning, with regular hours and benefits, health insurance."

"Nathan Kiel's lab," I said slowly.

"Might have been. I didn't pay attention to the name. Even after Emerald went to Hollywood, Lucinda kept working. Emerald was making a good living, but nothing like what a white star made back then. Lucinda knew better than to think her daughter was riding on a gravy train."

Her jaw worked again as she thought about the past. "Two women together, one black, one white, it caused a lot of talk at the time. Even I—my old minister was very old-school. . . . Well, you didn't come to hear about that. And when Lucinda died, he didn't fuss about holding her funeral at St. Silas. Of course, Emerald had given him money for a new roof, so that softened his theology some. Our new pastor, he's a different generation, different views."

"Where was Lucinda buried?" I was thinking again of Sonia and her lover's grave. If Lucinda had worked for Dr. Kiel . . . Although Kiel and his wife both denied ever hearing Ferring's name—but that could be for a lot of reasons, including that they didn't want to think about their daughter and the old anti-nuke commune.

"Over here, in Maple Grove," the old woman was saying, meaning that perhaps tomorrow, when it was light, I should go look at the cemetery. Although what would it tell me? I could hardly sweep the ground looking for Sonia's DNA.

"Does Ms. McKinnon still live on the farm?" I asked

"She had to stop farming, too old, rents the land—" Albritten tried to drink some tea, but her hand was shaking, and she spilled what was left in the glass on her sweater.

I started to go to her, but she growled at me to sit. "I'll fix it when you leave. Last I heard, Ms. McKinnon was still out there. Someone would have told me if . . . if . . ."

Albritten's face turned gray, and the glass fell from her hands. I whipped out my phone and typed in 911.

"No," she whispered. "No ambulance, no hospital."

She tried to push me away, but her gesture was feeble. I found the side zipper to her dress and thrust my hands inside, unhooking her bra, pushing on her chest, phone tucked under my ear. When the dispatcher came on, I gave her Albritten's address, with a command to come at once.

19

DEAD END

IT WAS LONG past sunset when Peppy and I drove east of town, looking for Doris McKinnon's farm. I'd spent a tense two hours at the hospital but had finally received a reassuring report on Ms. Albritten.

I'd followed her into the emergency room, making sure she was getting priority attention, before checking in at the front desk. The ambulance driver was standing there. It turned out he was the same person who'd come for Sonia Kiel twelve hours earlier—he was working double shifts this week.

"Are you with some kind of Guardian Angels organization?" he demanded with heavy humor. "You go through the streets of Lawrence looking for ladies who've keeled over?"

"Hard to know what you would do without me," I said, trying to get into the spirit of the exchange.

Actually, I was tense. Say, scared. I was in a strange town with a woman who had a bitter history with the place. If she or her son claimed that something I'd done had pushed her over the brink, I would be in a lonely spot.

Albritten had never completely lost consciousness. She'd thrust her pocketbook and phone at me as she was wheeled out of her house, making the crew stop to watch me lock the door before she let them put her in the ambulance.

"Better you than them. At least I'll know who stole my money if it disappears," she said to me.

At the hospital, while I was filling out forms for them, I went into Albritten's phone. Her son's number was fortunately one of seven numbers in her favorites screen. It unnerved me when he answered the call with "Yes, Mother?" but of course her name had shown up on his own phone.

He lived in a town called Warrensburg, about ninety miles east of Lawrence, he said, when we'd sorted out who I was and why I was calling.

"Just who are you, and what were you doing with Mother?" he demanded.

"Do you remember Emerald Ferring?" I didn't say I was a detective, just that I had come from Chicago looking for her and a neighbor had directed me to Ms. Albritten.

"She was in the middle of telling me about Doris McKinnon, who owned the farm where the Ferrings moved back in 1951, when she suddenly collapsed."

"Mother's never had heart trouble," he said. "Nothing wrong with her health. What else went on? Was she agitated? Did you try to get her to do something she didn't want, like sign over the title to the house? It's in my name, so you'd be out of luck."

"No, Mr. Albritten." My lips were stiff: this was the kind of accusation I'd been afraid of. "When you talk to the doctors, see if they'll let you speak to her."

When he'd finished worrying and accusing, I turned him over to the doctors. While I waited to see if the ER team needed me for anything further, I called Lotty Herschel in Chicago. Although it was late afternoon, when she's usually at her busiest, she let her clinic nurse put me through to her. I'd texted her a few times from the road, but we hadn't actually spoken since I'd left Chicago.

"You did the right thing, Victoria," she said. "Get the doctor's name. I'll call him this evening. Try not to worry. You couldn't do more than what you've done."

I sat in the waiting area, trying not to worry. I made an effort to occupy my mind with reports for clients in Chicago, but the city, and my life there, seemed to belong to some movie I'd watched years ago, one whose details I couldn't remember or why they should matter to me.

I had several texts from Troy Hempel. DID YOU FIND MS. EMERALD? WHAT DID THE WOMAN YOU WERE SPEAKING TO TELL YOU?

SHE COLLAPSED WHILE WE WERE SPEAKING. WE'RE AT THE HOSPITAL. I'LL LET YOU KNOW IF SHE'S ABLE TO TELL ME ANYTHING. DID SHE SAY ANYTHING HELPFUL WHEN YOU SPOKE EARLIER?

SHE SAID SHE'D SEEN MS. EMERALD IN LAWRENCE, BUT SHE DIDN'T KNOW WHERE SHE IS NOW, AND IS WORRIED ABOUT HER SAFETY, HERS AND YOUNG VERIDEN'S.

I leaned back in the uncomfortable chair and tried to concentrate on my breathing and not on the yammer of the television. One of the torments of modern medicine, besides incomprehensible bills, endless sessions on phones or in waiting rooms, and outrageous drug prices, is the constant blare of a television in every room.

At length one of the interns came out to give me good news about Ms. Albritten: All her cardiac signs were stable. They would keep her for twenty-four hours to monitor her, but she should be fine. Yes, I could go back for five minutes to give her her phone and handbag in person.

Albritten was dozing. Even the strongest-hearted old woman gets worn out by an ambulance ride and an hour of poking and X-raying. They'd given her a mild sedative, so that when I gently touched her arm, she stared at me with puzzled eyes.

I reminded her that we'd been speaking about Emerald Ferring, that I was in from Chicago looking for Ferring.

Albritten tried to struggle upright. I pressed the buttons on the bed, but a nurse who'd been hovering outside the cubicle came in.

"No disturbance for you, Ms. Albritten."

"One thing," Albritten said through narcotic-thickened lips. "What I say 'bout Em'ral'?"

"That she and Lucinda had moved out to Doris McKinnon's farm east of town."

"I say 'bout McKi . . . Kin?"

"No more," the nurse said, taking me by the arm.

"Need know," Albritten insisted.

"You said she was a white woman who rented to black students. You said you hadn't seen her for years. And then you collapsed."

Albritten relaxed into the bed and shut her eyes. "S'right. Not see. Long time."

The nurse nodded significantly toward the exit. I bent to assure Albritten that her son would be arriving soon, and a corner of her mouth twitched into a smile.

Before leaving the hospital, I made my way to the intensive-care unit. I identified myself to the charge nurse as the detective responsible for getting Sonia Kiel and Naomi Wissenhurst to the ER. Had that really been early this morning? I felt as though I'd already spent months in Kansas, as if finding Sonia belonged to an earlier age, when I was jumping double Dutch with my friends, not jumping through flaming hoops for my clients.

"Oh, yes, Detective. We were able to release Naomi. She needs medical attention but can get that at home. She's taking a leave of absence from the university for the rest of the term. Sonia is still unresponsive, but of course she was in worse shape before she took the drugs, and at least she's able to breathe on her own. The next twenty-four hours will be important."

"Have Sonia's parents been here?" I asked, curious. "Or anyone from St. Rafe's?"

"A man phoned around noon. I think he said he was one of her brothers, but you're the first person who's actually come here. Would you like to see her?"

She led me into the back, where Sonia seemed like an appendage to the computers surrounding her. Her breathing was slow and shuddery. At the end of each exhalation, there was a dreadful pause, as if she weren't sure she should start up again.

They'd bathed her, of course, and put her into a clean gown. Her face was slack, so it wasn't easy to imagine what she would look like if she were awake and animated. She had her father's square face and dark coloring, not her mother's pale skin. Her wiry black curls were also like her father's, at least in the pictures of him as a young man that I'd seen online yesterday.

Drugs and street life had coarsened Sonia's skin. She had some old bruises on her arms, but I didn't think they were track marks, more like the residue of blows. Someone at St. Rafe's or someone on the street?

I picked up one of her flaccid hands between my own and knelt to talk to her. "It's V.I. Warshawski, Sonia. You called me this morning, to say you'd seen Emerald Ferring. You saw her on Matt Chastain's grave, you said. Matt Chastain."

She might have twitched when I repeated his name, but it was probably wishful thinking on my part.

"If you wake up—*when* you wake up—you call and tell me where he's buried. I want to see Matt's grave, okay?"

I held her hand a bit longer, massaging it lightly. Her fingers were rough, the nails cracked. An obscure impulse made me brush the curls away from her forehead.

The nurse gave me an approving nod as I left. "You're the officer the police should send when they need to question a patient. You have a good touch."

I smiled in embarrassment. "I'll talk to Sergeant Everard about that."

The sky and land were so dark as I drove out of town that I lost all sense of direction. Pinpricks of light shone from farmhouse windows, but once I left the main highway, I was alone—whatever farmers do in the fall must take place indoors.

Away from the highway, I found myself on gravel roads that didn't have streetlamps. I drove slowly, headlights up, staying in the center, trying to avoid the ditches on either side, trying not to hit the foxes and other animals who claimed the night for their own.

At one point someone showed up on my tail, a dark SUV, maybe a Buick Enclave. I thought I'd seen it as I got on the highway, but the traffic was heavy enough that I couldn't be sure. Here on the county roads, we were alone. The hair on the back of my neck prickled. Peppy, sensing my unease, stood, growling softly.

At the junction between East 1900 and North 2800 Roads, the SUV turned south, where a sign pointed to the Kanwaka missile silo. I went north, my shoulder muscles relaxing, my breathing easing back to normal.

After following North 2800 Road for a quarter of a mile, I came to a turnoff with a mailbox labeled McKinnon. My map app had been accurate, always a relief.

The drive ended in a turning circle about a hundred yards from the road. I pulled up behind an elderly Subaru and looked at the house. It was a square building, two stories and an attic. No lights showed.

I got out, releasing Peppy from her leash. The dog tore off into the night, after who knows what creature: I hoped not a skunk. I shone my flash over the ground and the outbuildings—two barns, some sheds.

If Emerald Ferring and August Veriden had come to see Doris McKinnon, they must have turned back and driven on. This was a complete dead end.

Peppy had raced back from her hunting adventure but had started nosing around the house, snuffling at the foundation. She disappeared again, this time at the back of the house. I called to her, but she started barking and whining.

"Come!" I said in my sharpest voice.

She came partway toward me, her eyes glittering in my flashlight, but barked and whined again and turned back to the house. I followed her, my legs stiff, the tingling on my neck moving down my spine.

The back door was shut but not locked. Peppy can smell ten thousand, or maybe it's ten million, times better than I do, but when I pushed the door open, even my inferior nose picked up what she had noticed from across the field—the sickly-sweet smell of rotting flesh, the metallic odor of blood.

20

THE SHORT-TEMPERED ARM OF THE LAW

IF THE HOUSE was dark when you got there, why did you go in? You have some kind of message that the owner had been killed?"

We were in the Douglas County sheriff's office. The questioning was sort of informal, but when we left the McKinnon farm, squad cars had flanked my Mustang fore and aft. While we rode, I'd called my lawyer in Chicago to see if he knew someone in Lawrence or one of the nearby bigger cities.

"My dog," I said now. "She smelled death and was so insistent that I went in to see what was troubling her."

In Cook County the sheriff shows up at a crime scene only if it's an important photo op, so I'd been surprised when the Douglas County sheriff arrived at the farm in person. He also headed the interrogation back at the Judicial and Law Enforcement Center in town. In a jurisdiction without a lot of violent crime, maybe he wanted the excitement of a murder investigation.

I'd called 911 from Doris McKinnon's back porch—I'd retreated there as soon as I saw the body. Her body, I guessed, but it was impossible to tell the race or sex with the bloating and the destruction. It looked as though her head had been battered, but even that was hard to be sure of.

"Are you cause or effect, Warshawski?" That had been Sergeant Everard, who picked up the call from the emergency dispatcher. "In sixteen hours you've been Joanie-on-the-spot for four women in crisis and we don't usually have even one murder in the county each year."

"It's a grim crime scene, Sergeant. This person has been dead for some time, and little animals have been eating the lips and eyes and probably the brains and so on. After you get the body to your medical examiner, you can deploy all the sarcasm you want against me."

"Oh . . . right. I'll let the sheriff know—you're in his jurisdiction. And then you and I will have our chat, sarcasm and all, about what you're really doing here in Lawrence and how come bodies are stacking up around you. Ken Gisborne, he's the sheriff, been in office a lot of years, was a deputy first, so he knows his way around a crime scene."

Even someone who knew all the roads in the county couldn't travel them in the dark at the speed of light. While I waited for Gisborne, I went back inside for a circumspect tour of the house, keeping Peppy on a tight leash. Crime-scene protocol meant I should have left her outside—dog hair and paw prints would contaminate the evidence. Only a really chicken detective would need the comfort of her dog to go through a house with a dead body in it. I couldn't possibly be a chicken, so I must have felt I needed her expert tracking skills.

Although the victim had been dead for some time, at least a week, I returned to the car for my gun first. Leaving my running shoes by the back door to minimize the dirt I was bringing in, I tiptoed around the edge of the kitchen, flipping on an overhead light with my gunstock. Peppy was on hyperalert, her ears cocked at the sounds of critters scurrying from the body—roaches, slithery animals. I tried not to look, but my gorge rose anyway.

I stood with my hands on my knees, breathing hard, risked messing up evidence by running my face under the kitchen tap and gulping down water with my cupped hands.

"Okay, girl?" I chirped at Peppy.

She was whining and straining on the leash, wanting to go after the rats and roaches, but I forced her to stay with me. I turned on lamps and overhead fixtures in the rooms as I came to them but didn't find anyone. No more bodies, no lurking assailants.

The place had been searched—drawers were open and papers and books scattered about—but it wasn't like August's apartment in Chicago since no furniture had been destroyed. Whatever they wanted, the invaders must have found it. Jewelry to feed a local meth habit? The women at the church had suggested that the nearby missile silo might have been taken over by meth heads.

As I went through the house, it didn't strike me as the home of a woman with valuables, but maybe there'd been family silver or something of that nature. An addict with a craving to feed would take pretty much anything that could be turned into cash.

The ground floor included a powder room off the kitchen and a full bath built awkwardly into an alcove by the front door. A room beyond the powder room seemed to be Doris McKinnon's bedroom—it held a small TV, a number of pill bottles for the conditions that beset aging bodies, and a stack of library books. She wasn't a novel reader. These were tomes on the Second World War, especially the Eastern Front, and on contemporary weapons of mass destruction. She might have been ninety-something, but her brain had stayed active. Brain. That thought brought the insects crawling out of what was left of her eyes—if those *were* McKinnon's eyes—unwelcome to my mind. I pulled on Peppy's collar so hard that the dog whimpered.

Beyond the dining room were two parlors, which looked like shrines to Emerald Ferring. Photos of her covered the walls: as a tap-dancing little girl, in her high-school graduation robes, stills of her from *Pride of Place* and the rest of her Hollywood oeuvre. Ferring had won two Emmys for *Lakeview,* the *Jeffersons* look-alike series she'd starred in. She'd been photographed at one White House gala with President Clinton and another with Michelle Obama.

The most interesting photo was next to McKinnon's bed. It showed Ferring at the Kanwaka missile protest back in 1983. It was a black-and-white shot of her at the gates, looking over her shoulder at the crowd behind her while a young man was using bolt cutters on the lock. Soldiers in riot gear were approaching the pair; whoever had taken the picture had chosen exactly the right moment, when everyone was poised on the brink of action. Ferring's expression was intense, Joan of Arc trying to raise the Siege of Orléans, not an actress trying to boost her career. Or maybe she'd been a gifted actress channeling Joan of Arc.

The photo was signed to *"Aunt Doris, I owe you much. This comes to you with love, not obligation. Emerald."*

A strange inscription. I frowned over it, until Peppy jerked against me again, reminding me to keep moving. I glanced at pictures of what I assumed had been Lucinda Ferring, some with Emerald, one of her on a tractor, mugging for the camera, another of her with McKinnon, the two women in floral-print dresses on the porch, martini glasses in hand. Nell Albritten said there'd been gossip, but you couldn't tell from the photo if they'd been lovers or comfortable companions.

We went up the front-hall stairs to the second floor, which held six bedrooms, three on either side of a long hall, with another full bath at the back, the end that overlooked the fields to the north. The only sign of use in the bathroom was a bottle of All Ways shampoo in the walk-in shower.

The rooms were presumably the ones McKinnon had rented to the Ferrings and other African-Americans back in the fifties and sixties. Four stood vacant now of everything but their narrow bedsteads, chenille spreads laid over bare mattresses, empty deal chests lined with shelf paper.

The two bedrooms at the front of the house were the biggest, and they'd been used recently: the beds were fully made up, the radiators were on, and towels hung on racks by the doors.

I took off my windbreaker and wrapped my hand in it to pull open the bureau drawers. In the east room, the most carefully decorated room in the house, with sunflower-bedecked wallpaper and curtains, I found a bra and two pairs of panties in one drawer. La

Perla. The owner—Emerald?—must have taken off in a hurry. Each wisp of Italian lace sets you back a few hundred dollars. I ran them my fingers across the delicate fabric, then on impulse stuck them into my pack.

Nothing had been left in the room across the hall, but the sloppily made bed showed that someone had been in here recently. I flipped the covers back. Nothing except rumpled sheets. I shone my flash under the bed and in the corners but came up empty.

The room overlooked North 2800 Road. I could see the flashes of strobes heralding the arrival of the sheriff's police. Peppy and I trotted back along the hall, turning off the lights behind us. I went slowly down the stairs so that I didn't inadvertently touch the railings. Peppy growled as the squad cars reached the drive. I wished there'd been time to explore the attic and the basement, but you can't have everything.

The flashlight on my cell phone picked up something at the bottom of the stairs, a black shadow. I froze for a second, thinking of the roaches in the kitchen, but when I made myself look, I saw that it was a thumb drive. I slipped it into my jeans pocket and went outside to greet the sheriff.

"So the dog persuaded you to enter," the sheriff said when we were back in town, in his office. "And you turned on the lights, even at the risk of tampering with the crime scene."

I had my temper on a lead as tight as the one I'd kept on Peppy. "A rat about as big as your size-thirteens was nibbling on the victim's nose. It seemed respectful to keep the lights on, not to let the vermin do any more damage than they already had."

"You didn't find anything you took away with you or buried in the grounds or something, did you?"

"Your crew patted me down, Sheriff, and they could search my car—assuming they had a warrant, of course."

The pat-down had been part of the confusion around the law's arrival on the scene: when there's a dead body and a live person, the first impulse is to connect the two. It's usually a correct impulse, so

I didn't hold it against them. The thumb drive I'd picked up was wedged deep in my jeans and they'd missed it. They must have assumed the La Perla belonged to me.

"Yep. The judge figured we might want to take a look."

I got up, forgetting I was controlling my anger: he'd consulted a judge, gotten a warrant. "Then I'd better check on my dog."

There was a uniformed deputy in the room who looked as though he wanted to block my exit. It was just as well that the sheriff nodded at him to step aside—my self-control was in shreds, and I would have slugged him if he'd tried to stop me.

They hadn't forced the locks—they apparently had one of those devices that can open cars electronically—but they hadn't relocked the car either. Peppy wasn't happy: strangers in the car made her uneasy. I put my arms around her, petted her, calmed her and myself.

The deputy tapped my shoulder through the open door. "Sheriff Gisborne has a couple more questions."

I leashed up Peppy and took her in with me. The sheriff's questions were time markers, just to show he was in charge, but he didn't try to challenge my having my dog with me.

Why was I in Kansas? Why had I gone to the McKinnon farm? Why had I gone into the house? Nothing else was relevant, but Gisborne also wanted to know why it was I who'd found Sonia Kiel, what I'd said to Randy Marx at St. Rafe's—

"Sheriff," I interrupted. "Do you or any of your team drive a Buick Enclave?"

He compressed his lips in annoyance. "I want to know what you and Randy Marx were talking about."

I smiled—not to be conciliatory, just to remind myself I was too far from my support systems to bait someone who could put me in jail. "A Buick Enclave has been showing up around me off and on today. I wondered how you knew I'd been to see Mr. Marx, so I thought perhaps you were following me."

"I'm not, but maybe I should, the way you're stirring the waters," Gisborne said. "Marx called me. You're in a small town now,

Warshawski, not the big city. We all know each other, we all look out for each other. You may think you're moving around stealthily, but everyone knows where you are and what you eat for breakfast."

"That's good. If you decide to lock me up, you'll know just what to bring me." I'd forgotten I wasn't going to bait him. "Since you're on me like my underwear, you know I was at the hospital. Did you also know that neither Nathan nor Shirley Kiel has been to see their near-dead daughter? Randy Marx either."

"That's just what I mean, Warshawski," Gisborne said heavily. "You don't know jack shit about these people. Sonia forfeited her right to parental regard a long time ago."

I nodded slowly, as if he'd said something particularly meaningful. "Before she passed out, Sonia said she'd seen Emerald Ferring in the place where Matt Chastain lies buried. Where is that?"

Gisborne's eyes darted around the interrogation room, as if a good answer might be posted on one of the walls, next to the DON'T SPIT OR SMOKE IN HERE signs. "If these friends of yours were staying out at Doris McKinnon's farm, you need to get them in here to answer questions about her murder."

"Sheriff," I said gently. "Number one: I've never met them, they're not my friends, I'm here in your county hoping to find them. Number two: this means you've identified the body and the means of death already, which is massively impressive. I'm going to get Nick Vishnikov from the Cook County ME's office to phone your pathologist so he can find out how you did this in three hours. I'll put it out on my Twitter feed."

"That's not for public consumption," he growled. His phone rang just then, sparing us both further escalation. He picked it up, snapped his name into the mouthpiece but put it against his chest while he told me not to leave his jurisdiction.

Must not bait the sheriff, must not bait the sheriff, I chanted to myself. "I wouldn't dream of it, Sheriff. I'm having way too much fun."

21

VOICES FROM HOME

IT WAS CLOSE to nine when the law decided they'd spent enough time with me for one evening. Before I could get out of the Judicial and Law Enforcement Center, Sergeant Everard and his superior, a Lieutenant Lowdham, had scooped me up to ask the same questions as Gisborne. I guess cops don't feel they've earned their pay if they can't drag a simple inquiry out for most of a shift.

Although the cops, like the sheriff, wanted to accuse Ferring and Veriden of murdering McKinnon, they were more willing to answer my questions about the dead person and the crime scene.

The lieutenant explained that violent crime wasn't significant enough in Douglas County for them to have their own crime lab or medical examiner, although they had a team of crime-scene techs—EMT crews trained in how to gather evidence. They'd sent the body to the state lab in Topeka, which would perform the autopsy.

"Everyone's stretched to the limit here with budget cuts, so they can't give us an autopsy date, and the state can't help local forces with crime-scene techs, which means we don't have DNA or prints to make an ID. The guess is it's Doris McKinnon, but . . . well, you were there, you saw. There was a fair amount of damage to the face and tissues."

Yes, I'd seen. Every time I shut my eyes, roaches ran underneath my lids.

"Right now your friends are the people of interest here, and the sooner you can produce them, the sooner we can get all this cleared up," the lieutenant said.

I spoke slowly and clearly to the recording device. "Lieutenant, once a lie becomes an accepted truth, it's almost impossible to refute, so let's not allow that to happen here." I repeated the same message I'd just given the sheriff, about not knowing Ferring or Veriden nor whether they'd been at McKinnon's house.

Both men shifted uneasily in their chairs, but neither spoke.

"I'm going to give you the phone numbers of Lieutenant Terry Finchley, Captain Bobby Mallory, and Lieutenant Conrad Rawlings with the Chicago Police Department. You can call them to discuss my reputation."

I helped myself to a piece of paper from a pad on the table—one put there so that suspects could write out their confessions—and copied the numbers from my cell phone.

This seemed like a good exit line, but as I was leaving, the lieutenant asked, "You being a trained investigator from the big city and all, what did you make of the crime scene?"

I spread my hands: ignorance. "I don't have enough evidence to make an informed guess. Meth addicts surprising the owner?"

"And the people who'd been staying there?"

"Again, not enough information. I wondered—hoped—it was the woman I came down here to find—but if that's the case, where is she now? People keep telling me what a small town this is and how you all know everything about one another, so I'd think if Ms. Ferring and Mr. Veriden were here, you'd know."

I took Peppy's leash and walked out without looking back, but I could hear Everard and his lieutenant murmuring to each other.

"This town is festering with secrets," I explained to Peppy once we were alone: golden retrievers are so honest and trusting that you have to tell them when you've been ironic. "There's the whole business of Sonia and Dr. Kiel's dead or missing graduate student. Gertrude Perec's dead daughter. The identity of Cady's father. And no one on this side of the river knows anything about the lives of people on the other side."

Peppy gave a little bark: she understood.

Even though I would not have found Doris McKinnon—or whoever the dead person turned out to be—without Peppy, I would have to find doggy day care for her tomorrow. It wasn't fair to keep her in my car for such long stretches. As it was, I was going to tuck her back into the Mustang while I ate dinner: the Oregon Trail Hotel downtown, which advertised itself as a meeting place for the original Free State settlers, had a restaurant that was open late.

It wasn't until I was leaning back in my booth, head against the padded upholstery, that I realized how tired I was. I'd been up a good chunk of the previous night. I'd spent the day with people ranging from Sonia Kiel's raging parents to the sheriff of Douglas County. I'd interviewed an old woman who'd had to be rushed to the hospital, before driving out to the middle of nowhere to find vermin nibbling on a dead person.

I took off my muddy hiking boots and sat cross-legged, surreptitiously massaging my sore toes under cover of the tablecloth. A glass of zinfandel gave me an illusion of warmth and home. I couldn't remember if you were supposed to load carbs or eat lean fish when you were too tired to function, so I compromised: pasta with squid, vodka-tomato sauce, extra mushrooms, romaine salad.

Nell Albritten's anxiety when I left her had been nudging the back of my mind since I'd found the dead body. When she was semiconscious, she wanted to know what she'd said to me about Doris McKinnon. She'd been relieved to hear she'd said only that McKinnon was a white woman she didn't often see.

When Albritten had started to say, "Someone would have told me if—" she'd fainted in midsentence. *If McKinnon had died,* was how I'd have completed the sentence. Albritten struck me as the kind of woman with a rigorous honesty: she'd fainted rather than tell a lie.

Albritten's story of the flood, its massive devastation followed by the brutal indifference of the landlords, had made me acutely uncomfortable. I shut my eyes, trying to re-create not just what Albritten had said but her body language.

I was holding the cold glass of tea. Peppy was whimpering, aware of the tension in the room. I was feeling shame, but also impatience: I wanted to know what had happened to Lucinda and Emerald Ferring after the flood, and Albritten kept circling the question, giving more details about the flood and the town's response.

And then she'd received a phone call. That's what I'd forgotten. She'd made a phone call before she let me into the house. My guess—she'd been asking for advice. She'd told someone—Lisa Carmody?—I was there. After she talked to my Chicago client, she wanted to know how much information she could safely give me.

Albritten hadn't mentioned Doris McKinnon until after she hung up. The person who phoned her had given her permission to tell me, which meant that Albritten and at least one other person in Lawrence already knew that McKinnon was dead. How did they know? From Ferring and Veriden? If Albritten was hiding them, they couldn't be in her basement; the house didn't have one. An attic crawl space? The little locked-up church?

I didn't think I could stake out St. Silas without the police or the sheriff hearing about it, but maybe Nell Albritten would open up to me now that I'd looked after her, maybe saved her life. Maybe I'd threatened her life with my questions, though.

I drank wine and pushed that ugly thought away.

Albritten's son, Jordan, had played with Emerald when they were toddlers: she would do what she could to protect Emerald, from the sheriff and the Lawrence police. As she should: Sergeant Everard had said Emerald and August were the persons of interest in the murder. Even if the Lawrence PD were more enlightened than Staten Island or Ferguson—or Chicago—forces, it would still be mighty convenient to have a young black man from Chicago around to take the rap.

I dismissed the possibility that August was guilty. I'd never met him, of course, but I didn't believe that the quiet, methodical young man who brought flowers to his janitor's sick wife could bash in the head of an old woman. He might strike someone in self-defense or even to defend Emerald, but not "Aunt Doris," to whom Emerald "owed much."

In the warm glow of food and wine, I had grandiose fantasies: tomorrow morning I would imagine a way to get Nell Albritten to confide in me. I would similarly persuade the Perec women, Cady and her doughty grandmother, to tell me what secrets they were keeping.

My food came as I was reading e-mails and texts. I had highly punctuated messages from Bernie: WHAT ARE YOU DOING???? I'M TAKING A LEAVE OF ABSENCE SO I CAN COME DOWN TO KANSAS BECAUSE YOU AREN'T MAKING PROGRESS!!!!

I wrote Troy a detailed message about Doris McKinnon's relationship with Emerald and her mother, about going out to the farm and finding a dead body but discovering only a putative connection to Ferring and August. IF SHE AND AUGUST WERE HERE, THEY'VE DISAPPEARED. I'M WONDERING IF THEY RETURNED TO CHICAGO. IF THEY'RE HIDING, DO YOU KNOW WHO THEY'D TURN TO?

I was curter with Bernie. DO NOT COME HERE. IF YOU SHOW UP, YOUR DAD WILL BE ON THE FIRST FLIGHT OUT OF MONTREAL TO COLLECT YOU. NO ARGUMENTS. Not that anything short of a crowbar over the skull had much effect on Bernie.

Lotty called as I was signaling for the bill, to check on me and to tell me she'd talked to the doctors at the Lawrence hospital. Nell Albritten was doing well; she'd be released in the morning. The news was less promising for Sonia Kiel. The hospital had shared the toxicology report with Lotty.

"Your guess about flunitrazepam—roofies—was correct. Sonia still had Depakote in her bloodstream and a terrifying blood-alcohol level, point two-six. She didn't seem to have other recreational drugs in her, but the alcohol with the roofies and her depleted immune system have left her seriously compromised. The only hopeful news is that they do have positive readings on the EEGs."

It warmed me more than wine and food, hearing from Lotty and knowing she'd made these calls out of love for me. We chatted longer, on general topics. She tactfully avoided Jake's name but hoped I would return home soon.

I signed my credit-card receipt and pushed my sore feet back into my boots. As I gathered up my belongings, I saw I'd dribbled vodka sauce onto my phone. If I was not a clever enough detective to eat and text at the same time, how could I possibly find Emerald Ferring before the law did?

22

BARFLIES

THE HOTEL BAR was on my left as I headed to the front door. I glanced in idly, the way one does. The bartender was watching an NBA game on the TV, desultorily wiping glasses, as bartenders everywhere do when trade is slow. The only customers were a quartet of men deep in conversation in the corner. They looked up as I peered in, and their faces congealed, as if I'd brought an arctic wind with me.

I wouldn't have stopped to stare if they hadn't looked so furtive, but after a second I realized that the oldest man in the group was Nathan Kiel. This morning he'd been wearing a sweat suit and slippers, but here he was all decked out in a shirt and tie. It took a moment longer, but I also recognized the man on his left. When I'd seen Col. Baggetto at Fort Riley four days ago, he'd had on khaki with lots of medals and ribbons, but tonight, like Kiel, he was in civvies.

When I started toward the table, the colonel got to his feet, frost melted, smiling as if I were his long-lost sister. "Ms. Warshawski. I thought I recognized you. We met a few days ago—"

"At Fort Riley." I smiled but couldn't emulate his warmth. "I didn't recognize you at first without your birds and medals and stuff."

"Even colonels get to take nights off, which means shedding the plumage. Come and have a drink."

He placed a hand on the small of my back, propelling me toward the table. The touch was light, but there was muscle behind it. He pulled a chair over for me, but I didn't sit, just nodded to his drinking buddies. One of the strangers was perhaps my age or a bit older, with the leathery skin of someone who spent a lot of time outside. The other was young, young enough to be Kiel's grandson. I had a fleeting thought that I'd seen him before, but I couldn't place him.

"Dr. Kiel. And . . . ?"

Baggetto performed introductions. The leathery face was Bram Roswell. "He does something important at Sea-2-Sea, so important that I can never figure out what it is. And this is Marlon Pinsen, who's a student here. Gentlemen, this is Ms. Warshawski—sorry, I've forgotten your first name. She visited me at the fort a couple of days ago."

Roswell nodded at me, not interested, but young Pinsen half stood, with a respectful "How do you do, ma'am?"

"I've been in so many places in Lawrence this week that I can't remember whom I've seen where," I said to Pinsen. "But we've met, haven't we?"

"I don't think so, miss . . . ma'am," he said, after a pause that lasted a hair too long.

"Best not to admit it if you have met her," Kiel said. "She'll start imagining she has a right to tell you how to live your life. Whose business have you been interfering with this evening?"

"Someone who was past any advice, good or bad," I said. "I discovered Doris McKinnon's dead body on her kitchen floor. I didn't realize that you knew her."

"I? You're badly mistaken. Which seems habitual with you."

I put my chin in my hand, exaggerated Rodin *Thinker.* "You're right. This morning when I mentioned that I'm in town looking for Emerald Ferring, you didn't react. You must not have realized that Lucinda Ferring was her mother. Not a common name, but perhaps you didn't know your lab tech's surname."

"You came to me with wild questions about my daughter. Forgive me if those seemed more important than someone who worked for me decades ago." Kiel's voice dripped heavy sarcasm.

I nodded judicially: good point. “Did you stop at the hospital to see your daughter on your way here? I know it’s hard for you and Ms. Kiel to get over there, but I visited her at the end of the afternoon.”

“How is she doing?” the young man, Pinsen, asked.

Again the nagging thought crossed my mind that I’d seen him before, but it came and went so quickly I couldn’t hold it.

“Not well. She’s breathing on her own. That’s the best the ICU nurse could tell me.”

“The dead woman at the farm,” Roswell said. “How did you know to look for her?”

I stared at him, astonished. “Why do you care?”

His leathery skin darkened. He didn’t answer immediately but seemed to be fishing for words. “Her land abuts one of our experimental farms. If a killer is running loose, I want my farmhands to be on the lookout. The sheriff tells me it was the black kid from Chicago who killed McKinnon.”

“You’re sure you don’t want a drink?” the colonel interjected.

“I’m over my limit, and my dog is waiting for me,” I said. “*The* black kid from Chicago, Sheriff Gisborne said? There’s a specific youth he knows about?”

“Don’t play games, Warshawski,” Kiel said. “You’ve broadcast all over town and university that you’re here hunting for a fugitive couple.”

“People tell me you’re a careful and knowledgeable scientist,” I said. “So you know how important it is not to use language carelessly. The people I’m looking for have disappeared. They are fugitives, but not from justice. Their friends believe they are in danger, either from a trigger-happy lawman or from the people who killed Ms. McKinnon.”

I turned to Roswell. “Why did the sheriff report Ms. McKinnon’s murder to you? As far as I can tell, the story hasn’t even made the local news. Are you some kind of special deputy or Gisborne’s nephew?”

Roswell swirled what was left of his drink and drank it down. "Dr. Kiel has already said you like to butt into other people's business, and I see what he means. Why the sheriff chose to call me has nothing to do with you, but if you know where your missing *friends* are, you'd do well to produce them."

I laughed. "You sound like someone out of one of those old westerns where the town bully tells the sheriff to 'String 'em up. They're half-breeds, no better than savages, and they belong on the end of a rope.'"

Baggetto held up a hand. "Whoa, let's put away the heavy artillery and the drones and so on. Bram, we're concerned at the fort because the woman Warshawski is trying to find is the daughter of one of our own. He died at the Battle of the Bulge, so we want to make sure no harm comes to his daughter. We're here to give Ms. Warshawski any help she needs.

"Ms. Warshawski, Bram has an interest in what happens at the McKinnon farm because there are patents involved in the crops they're experimenting with. They want to know of any criminal activity in the area, so the sheriff's office sends them security alerts."

"Then he's got the right person's ear."

I headed for the door, but Baggetto got up to walk out to the street with me.

"Sorry if Roswell was a bit heavy-handed there. Sea-2-Sea execs get goofy about security because their corporate history includes hippies running amok in their operations back in the Vietnam era. Not to mention bomb threats from people who are opposed to genetically modified food."

"Yep. As a nation we get hysterical over anticorporate protesters, but if a state government pollutes a city's drinking water, the law-and-order brigades are strangely quiet."

Baggetto shook his head. "I'm not going to debate politics with you, Ms. Warshawski. I just want to assure you that if the army can do anything to help you locate Emerald Ferring, all you have to do is call me." He handed me a card with his cell-phone number on it.

I stuffed it into my jeans pocket and opened my car door. Peppy stuck her head out. "Is that why you drove over to Lawrence? I gave your CO's secretary—the captain, Arata is it?"

"Arrieta," he corrected.

"Right. I gave Captain Arrieta my contact information. You could have texted or e-mailed me."

He laughed. "I came here to help out young Pinsen—he's the senior cadet in the Army ROTC up on the hill. I'm giving a lecture there tomorrow, the Signal Corps and modern intelligence intercepts. You're welcome to sit in."

"That's your specialty? Modern intelligence? I ought to sit in. The modern detective is probably like the modern army officer: these days we do most of our work at computers, not out on the ground."

Baggetto bent to scratch Peppy's ears. "You seem to be covering a fair amount of ground, Ms.— What can I call you? My name is Dante."

I thought of all the names I've been called during my life, from the "Iffy-Genius" taunts of my childhood to "Pit-Dog," "Donna Quixote," or "Interfering Bitch." I said, "Vic will do. . . . My mother used to quote Dante to me. She was Italian."

He shook his head again, this time with regret. "I'm third-generation. I can order five different kinds of pasta, but that's about it."

I climbed into the car. Baggetto shut the door for me. "Good night, Vic." He sketched a salute.

"Night, Dante."

I drove off, thinking of the pet names my mother used for me. My father called both of us his pepper pots, because we were so hot-tempered. My mother used to quote Dante only to me, saying that her love for me was *l'amor che move il sole e l'altre stelle*—the love that moves the sun and all the other stars.

I felt a spurt of anger toward the Kiels: they were both living into old age, they still had their daughter. Didn't either of them know what they were squandering?

23

PICTURE PERFECT

THE THUMB DRIVE I'd found at the bottom of Doris McKinnon's stairs fell out of my jeans when I tossed them at the little room's armchair—my long evening had pushed it from my mind. I put the drive on top of my phone, so I'd see it first thing, and slid under the covers, Peppy curled around my feet. I'd taken her into the bathroom shower with me, scrubbing the day's grime from us both, and we lay under the covers smelling sweetly of lavender.

Despite a fatigue that seemed to dig into my bone marrow, I couldn't relax into sleep. I finally got out of bed and powered up my laptop. Peppy opened an eye, wondering if I was stupid enough to be on the move again, and gave a sigh of relief when she saw me sit at the corner table. Perhaps in some future life I'd come back as a golden retriever, able to sleep the sleep of the just and good.

For a mercy, the drive wasn't password-protected. It also wasn't labeled, but my heart beat a little faster when I saw it held a series of photo and video files—it must have been August's, something he dropped as he fled the house.

When I started opening the file, though, my spirits sank: I was looking at blank frames. Apparently even pros like August can act like the rest of us, pressing the camera button a zillion times without knowing it. I scrolled through to the end of the file just to make sure and finally realized I actually was looking at photos. They'd been taken in a field at night, without a flash. About halfway through the series, predawn light began clarifying a picture of dead plants and overturned earth.

I turned to the videos. There were seven clips in all. The sound was muffled, but I was pretty sure I could make out three voices—one male, two female.

"How much do you need?" The first woman spoke in a rich contralto; she'd had serious vocal training. Emerald Ferring, I presumed.

"Not much, I just want to collect a good cross section. Hold the bag for me." The other woman's voice was thin with age. Doris.

"Just a second." August, in an urgent undertone. "I heard something."

Emerald whispered, "Where?"

"In the field, right behind you."

A brief silence, then a soft chuckle from Doris. "That's a badger, city boy. They have a burrow around here. You got this?"

The question seemed directed at August, because he held the camera for a few seconds over what I'd first thought was empty air but now saw was a black plastic bag, held by gloved hands while someone else dumped soil into it.

"How will you know where you took your samples from?" August asked.

"Just like a sailor," Doris said. "Latitude and longitude readings. Put this first tag on this first bag. I worked out where to dig before we came out, you know. We'll move on here, about fifteen steps to the left. Let me check my little GPS doohickey."

The camera shut off while someone wrapped the tag around the bag and Doris checked her GPS. The next two video clips looked the same, no real conversation except murmured directions between August and Doris. At the fourth, though, Doris asked for a light.

"It's a risk, but I want to see what I've found."

A narrow beam shone on crumbly dirt in the palm of Doris's hand. She brushed the top of it with gentle fingers to expose what looked like tiny twigs. I paused the video, tried to enhance it, but the flashlight hadn't carried enough wattage.

"What is it?" Emerald asked.

"Bones," Doris said. "Raccoon, maybe, or badger. I'll just slip them into their own bag, see if they have a story to tell about what's in this dirt."

As she sealed the bag, her trowel fell, hitting something with a thud. She handed the bag to Emerald and grunted, straining to heft whatever it was from the ground. August turned off the camera—I was guessing to lend her a hand. I held my breath, wondering, until the camera came back on. Doris was shining her flash on some large object—metal, from its dull gleam, so something that didn't corrode.

Maybe it was a solid-gold samovar that a Russian immigrant had buried to keep out of the hands of the pro-slavery forces during the Civil War. He'd died at Antietam, and his widow hadn't known where to look for it.

"This reminds me of something," Doris said. "I can't place it, and it's stuck in here pretty good. We'll make a note where it is and see if we can come back in the daytime. Emerald, it's next to where we tagged the fourth sample."

The clip ended there. The next segment started about ten minutes after Doris had demanded a light. We were still in the field, but the camera was focused on a distant point. The predawn light was making it possible to see in the distance; I could tell that a person was there, someone whose pale skin was faintly visible.

It wasn't possible to discern the person's sex, let alone age, creed, or place of national origin. The camera followed as the figure raised and lowered its arms, moving about in a clumsy mimicry of a ballet dancer. It looked as though the dancer was flinging things, but in the miserable light I couldn't be sure. August must have worked some magic with his mike, because the distant voice came hoarsely to life.

"'Rosemary, that's for remembrance, and pansies for thoughts, and columbines and rue, that's for memory. I remember you, I do, I do, you will not come again, no, no, he is dead.'"

"Ophelia," Emerald muttered. "Sort of Ophelia. She's left out a section. 'There's rosemary, that's for remembrance; pray, love, remember. There is pansies—'"

Doris urged her to keep her voice lowered. The clip ended there.

Ophelia? I looked up Ophelia's lament over Hamlet, right before she drowns herself. She's strewing herbs around, rosemary and fennel and rue—whatever that might be.

Sonia Kiel, it had to be, dancing where she believed her truelove was buried. Perhaps this was an old cemetery, where wheat or corn or just weeds had grown up around grave markers too old to be visible in the grainy footage.

The camera shifted. Sonia was on the ground, rocking back and forth, crooning, "Hey, nonny, nonny, hey, daddy, daddy."

My skin crawled. She hadn't known she was being filmed, poor thing. It was physically painful to watch her expose herself.

Headlights suddenly swept the field, the light breaking into halos in the camera lens. A pickup or an SUV.

The headlights picked up Sonia, who cried out and started running away from them, straight at the camera, yelling, "Fire, fire!" and then, as she caught sight of the photographer and his entourage, "What are *you* doing here? This land is sacred! Get off, go away, go away, go away!"

The drive didn't hold anything else. The date stamp on the videos meant August must have shot it two days after he and Ferring had been at Fort Riley.

I went through all the stills, hoping for shots of the bag tags showing the latitude and longitude of the digging, but couldn't see any. It was maddening: I was looking at the place where Sonia thought Matt Chastain was buried, but I still had no idea where it was.

The more I thought about it, the less I believed it could be a cemetery, at least not one in current use. Headstones would have stood out, paler stone against darker soil, even in the poor light. The arrival of the SUV or truck, coupled with the fact that they were working in the dark, made it pretty clear that Doris and her guests were trespassers.

I stood, stretching the kinks in my neck and hamstrings, pressing my palms together to straighten my fingers. I wandered to the patio door. It was satisfying to find evidence that August and Emerald had been here. Satisfying to find evidence that Sonia really had seen them. I toyed with sending the video of her to her parents or Randy Marx, to show she had in fact seen August and Emerald. Bad idea, I finally decided: they would only pay attention to her crude dance as an excuse to mock her further.

I pulled on the blind cord over the patio door, jamming the slats. I'd gotten so focused on Sonia, along with all the other oddly behaving people in Lawrence, that I'd lost track of the problem that had sent me to Kansas in the first place: the wanton destruction in August's home and at the Six-Points Gym.

Was this thumb drive what the thugs had been looking for? The search at the McKinnon farm hadn't been as destructive as the damage in Chicago—except, of course, for the murder of Doris McKinnon.

They would have searched Doris's home first and not found what they wanted. They thought August must have it; when he and Emerald disappeared, the creeps thought they'd gone back to Chicago. They became increasingly enraged, so they'd ripped apart August's home and then the gym. Why hadn't they torn up Emerald Ferring's house as well? Maybe Ferring's watchful neighbors kept invaders at bay. If vandals had been prowling around, it would help explain the neighbors' hypervigilance toward me.

I wondered about the SUV that had arrived in the field. Was it the Buick Enclave that had followed me yesterday? The sheriff claimed he wasn't tailing me. I believed him, if only because I'd checked on him in my databases. His personal SUV was a Ford Explorer, and the county budget definitely didn't run to Enclaves. Maybe I'd imagined yesterday's tail: no one had followed me to the McKinnon place after all.

I fiddled with the blinds cord but only made the tangle worse. I thought about the quartet I'd encountered in the Oregon Trail's bar this evening: Army, Academy, and Agribusiness huddling together. Colonel Baggetto said he was lecturing on campus in the morning, but he might have arranged that simply as an excuse to come to Lawrence when he learned about Doris McKinnon's dead body.

We're worried about hippies, Bram Roswell had said. Nobody talked about hippies these days, but Roswell certainly didn't want trespassers on Sea-2-Sea land.

The soil samples were the crux. Doris wanted evidence about what contaminants were in the soil. The bags she'd collected hadn't been in her house when Peppy and I got there this evening. Either the killers had found the samples or she'd gotten rid of them before she died.

I was forgetting the metal container McKinnon had found. Doris had said she was going back for it the next day. I hadn't seen any metal object in her home big enough to be the samovar or whatever they'd stumbled on—maybe that was what her killer had snatched.

It was maddening that I couldn't talk to Sonia—she'd know who had driven onto the field in the middle of August's video. She might even know about the soil samples.

I didn't believe that the vandals who'd turned August's home and the Six-Points Gym upside down were looking for dirt. The thumb drive was a real possibility. I needed to get it to a safe place. Cheviot, the private forensics lab I use, has the equipment and the expertise to bring the photos into better focus. They could analyze the drive itself for prints or DNA. They might even be able to bring up a license plate or a make and model number on the vehicle. They could perform a miracle and identify the samovar.

I copied the file to Dropbox and stored it in that mythic cloud. It sounds like a fluffy bit of white floating overhead, but of course it's really a massive data farm, some big power grid that's polluting some other person's river.

In the morning I'd do a property search for the boundaries of Doris McKinnon's land, check the boundaries of Sea-2-Sea's experimental farm.

I climbed back into bed, moving Peppy so that I could lie in the place she'd made warm. The handful of little bones that Doris had found floated through the cloud of my own mind. Those bones, we all come to those dusty remains. Even Jake's beautiful fingers, touching his bass strings, touching me, would one day be gray bones in a piece of soil.

24

TRESPASSERS W

IT TOOK ME a long time to relax into sleep. I felt vulnerable in this rented room, with its flimsy set of locks. I finally drifted into feverish dreams: The earth had swallowed me. Jake sat on the ground overhead, playing his bass for a twenty-year-old cellist whose golden hair flowed below her waist.

I was able to sleep only long enough to take the edge off my weariness. When I woke a little after seven, I hotfooted it downtown to a FedEx store, where I sent the original thumb drive to Cheviot. I used a store computer, not my own, to type the cover letter explaining what I wanted them to do. I even paid cash for the shipment, instead of billing it through to my credit-card account.

I felt foolish being so cautious, but I had no idea what direction violence was coming from and had no secure place to store either my own electronics or any evidence I came upon. If I lost my computer, I didn't want anyone to be able to trace my actions. Colonel Baggetto came to mind: a guy like him, with his training and access to government resources, could break into a computer like mine one-handed.

When I finished, my T-shirt was damp with sweat, clinging clammily to my skin. I zipped up my windbreaker and ran Peppy down to the river, where the morning wind off the water cut through my jacket to freeze my damp shirt. I ducked behind a scruffy bush and undressed, pulling off the shirt and shoving it into a pocket. Still cold, but not so bitter.

We ran back into the town, to the Decadent Hippo: when you're alone and forlorn, little routines become sources of comfort. The bartender/barista cocked an eye at her bean grinder. I nodded, and she made me a cortado. They sold long-sleeved T-shirts, which showed a pink hippo lounging in a hot tub drinking a cappuccino. Twenty-five dollars bought me a coffee and something warm for my cold back.

I took my coffee to a stool in the window, where Peppy and I could see each other through the glass, and started answering e-mails. Freeman Carter, my lawyer in Chicago, had found a good criminal-defense lawyer about twenty-five miles away, in a suburb of Kansas City. He'd written Luella Baumgart-Grams about me; she'd be happy to help if the need arose. I sent her a follow-up message with a few details about the job that had brought me to Kansas and added her to my speed dial, because you never know. When I'd caught up on queries from Chicago clients, I tried to plan my day.

First stop: day care for Peppy. There were a number of day boarders in town, but the one that got the best reviews was Free State Dogs: Where Dogs Run in a Free State. They had space if I could get my vet to fax them her health record and if her temperament passed muster.

"And if your environment works for her," I said sharply.

After I finished with my vet, I called Lawrence's hospital for humans. Sonia was no worse, still breathing on her own but no better. The ward head told me briskly that one shouldn't give up hope, as if I were her sister, which made me think I was the only person concerned enough about her health to call the hospital. How sad, especially since my chief concern wasn't her well-being but whether she would ever recover any memory of whom she'd encountered in the bar or of the field where she'd spotted August filming her.

The hospital also told me that Nell Albritten had been discharged; her son Jordan had escorted her home. This afternoon, after I'd inspected Sea-2-Sea's experimental farm, I could pay a neighborly visit to check up on her.

This meant identifying the property lines both for Doris McKinnon and for Sea-2-Sea. I was only two blocks from the Lawrence Public Library, so I went there first, before dropping off Peppy.

A reference librarian helped me find Doris McKinnon's farm and stepped me through decades of records, with their changing property lines. I had always imagined farms as static, land handed down unchanging across the centuries. Instead pieces were always being bought and sold, not all of them contiguous.

Most of McKinnon's land was a substantial chunk around the farmhouse where I'd found her body yesterday. In 1967 the U.S. government had seized three acres from her through the right of eminent domain for the Kanwaka Missile Silo. As I inspected the maps over the next several years, it looked as though special roads had been constructed, one from the west and one from the south, to connect the silo to existing county roads.

In 1967 Emerald Ferring was in Hollywood, just starting her career with Jarvis Nilsson. Her mother was probably still pipetting specimens for Dr. Kiel—I doubted that Emerald was making enough money at that point to support Lucinda. Doris McKinnon herself would have been in her thirties, fully capable of working her land on her own.

Over the next sixteen years, Doris bought and sold smallish parcels that lay in other parts of the county. Then, in September 1983, the United States took another fifteen acres from her, to the south and east of the silo. The southern edge now abutted one of the east-west county roads.

That was 1983—the year of the abortive effort to reenact Greenham Common, the year of Matt Chastain's disappearance (his death?), Jenny Perec's death, Cady Perec's birth.

Correlation does not mean causation, I know that in my head, but in my gut, that famous residence of detective intuition, I couldn't help wondering if all these things were tied together.

While I tried to find Sea-2-Sea's experimental farm, the helpful librarian printed out the most current map for McKinnon's holdings.

I would start my search at the fields near the silo and hope I didn't have to go riding all over Douglas County looking at her other land.

Sea-2-Sea's farms weren't listed under their name, but Emigrant Bank and Savings was the trustee for 160 acres along McKinnon's southern border, at the edge of the Kanwaka silo. Good bet that they were acting for Sea-2-Sea. The reference librarian printed out that map for me as well.

She was gathering them all into a folder when we were joined by a third woman, an African-American whose name badge identified her as PHYLLIS BARRIER, HEAD LIBRARIAN.

"What are we working on here, Agnes?" Barrier asked the reference librarian.

Her tone was genial, but the look she gave me was searching—not unfriendly exactly, but the kind of expression my mother took on when she was sure I'd been doing something dangerous with my cousin.

"I'm V.I. Warshawski," I said. "Ms. Chercavi has been helping me understand some property documents out near the Kanwaka silo."

"May I?" Barrier held out her hand; the reference librarian perforce gave her the folder.

Barrier thumbed through the pages, then smiled at me. "We love to have people use our library, and we consider our patrons' needs private, but I confess I'm curious. You're visiting from Chicago, as I understand. Why are you interested in these property maps?"

The smile signaled that we weren't in a hostile encounter, but it didn't reach her eyes.

"If you know I'm from Chicago, then you know I'm the person who found Doris McKinnon's body yesterday. Before she died, she was worried about activity on the land that abuts the silo, and I wanted to see where her property ended, whether the piece she was concerned about was actually hers. The Kanwaka silo sits on land that McKinnon used to own, but the rest of it now seems to belong either to Sea-2-Sea or to the air force."

Barrier studied me again, flipped through the pages again, before handing them to me and telling me to enjoy my time in Lawrence. As I walked away, I wondered if I'd seen her before. Her face seemed familiar, but I couldn't place it. Maybe she'd been at the hospital yesterday when I went there with Nell Albritten.

Lawrence was getting to be full of specters for me—first Marlon Pinsen and now the head librarian. I didn't have any familiar faces around me—maybe my unconscious was creating phantom friends.

Before I drove Peppy to her day-care appointment, I circled the downtown but didn't see any obvious signs of a tail. Yesterday's Buick Enclave wasn't parked nearby either. Another phantom?

Free State Dogs was the kind of place you could get only in a small town with a lot of open space—huge runs where the staff could sort dogs into compatible packs for play and rest. The staff seemed to know how to work with the animals, but I still felt a wrenching as I finally let Peppy trot off with one of their crew.

I guessed she'd be okay. I hoped she'd be okay. The third time I checked that they had my cell-phone number and would text me if anything went wrong, the manager patted me on the shoulder.

"Every parent feels like this the first time they leave their baby alone. She's a sweetheart; we'll take good care of her."

Free State was on the main east-west artery that led from Lawrence out to the McKinnon farm and the Kanwaka silo. I unfolded my paper maps and checked the roads against the property lines on the documents the library had printed for me. Folded them up, cast a last longing look at Free State Dogs, and put the car into gear, singing, *"Hey, said I, for the open road and the open camp beside it."*

Traffic was heavy on the highway, but as soon as I turned onto the county roads, I was alone. One good thing about the country, I guess, is that it's easy to spot a tail. Unless you counted the circling hawks, I was on my own. I didn't even see tractors in the fields I was passing, just the occasional herd of morose-looking cows.

At a crossroads near the McKinnon farm, I pulled over and took out my tablet, bringing up the stills that August had shot in the dark. I tried to compare them with the land around me. The ditches on either side of the road were filled with wild grass, brown now at winter's approach. A heavy wind blew through the grasses, creating waves that looked like Lake Michigan in a storm. The wind buffeted the Mustang, increasing my sense of vulnerability. I turned on the radio just to hear the sound of a human voice.

"And God said, the unclean shall you cast from you. When Jesus told us he brought not peace, but a sword—"

I turned off the radio: I'd risk going mad on the prairies.

All the land around me resembled the photos: the ground plowed or harrowed or whatever they did after they'd harvested the crops, leaving behind little hillocks with tufts sticking up. I wasn't looking for a needle in a haystack but a haystack in a land of hayfields. Impossible.

I'd start with the one place I could identify, the missile silo. I'd had vague *Dr. Strangelove* images in mind, so the actual site was a letdown: no giant Atlas rockets thrust their noses skyward, no heavily armed soldiers patrolled the perimeter. In fact, I almost missed the turnoff, it was so unobtrusively marked—just an old metal sign on a fence post, with the U.S. Air Force logo and faded letters announcing the Kanwaka Missile Silo.

THE COUNTY ROAD wasn't paved, just had a coating of gravel on it that had been dinging my car as I bumped along, but the access road to the silo was covered in tarmac. Newly surfaced, by the look of it, although the installation itself seemed run-down—everyone was tired of nuclear weapons, even the land around the old missile. A twelve-foot-high cyclone fence enclosed the land, but sections had fallen over.

Cady Perec had said how vulnerable it made kids feel when they saw it every day on their way to school. In my childhood we'd grown up with a vague fear of nuclear war, but a fully loaded Minuteman right by your school bus—that was the stuff of permanent nightmare.

I pulled over onto the verge and started to walk the perimeter.

Although the fence had collapsed in places that would make it easy to enter the site, the front gates still stood padlocked.

The odd thing about the layout, at least to my urban mind, was the way the property was cut up. The missile had sat in a triangle, with the apex pointing at Doris McKinnon's house. A barbed-wire fence ran along the same parallel as the triangle's base, smack in the middle of a field. If I had worked out the maps properly, the land beyond the fence belonged to the fifteen acres the air force had seized from McKinnon back in 1983. The conveyancing reports didn't show it as being redeeded to Sea-2-Sea.

When I walked along McKinnon's side of the barbed wire, I saw medallions every twenty feet or so, labeling the land beyond as private property, no trespassing. The medallions were stamped with the Sea-2-Sea logo—wheat sheaves crossing a stylized map of the United States.

I wondered if McKinnon had marked her own land on the opposite side. When I bent over to look, my skin tingled and I jumped back: the fence was electrified. Curiouser and curiouser.

I returned to the silo and slipped inside through a place where the fence had come unmoored from its post, taking care not to touch the metal, in case Sea-2-Sea's electrical circuits ran through the Kanwaka fence as well.

The resurfacing of the tarmac continued beyond the padlocked gates. The road, big enough for a double-wide, ended in the concrete wings of a loading bay. A narrower track branched out from there and led to an enormous concrete circle.

Broken antennas—what used to be radar, I supposed—stood in the corners of the triangle. An assortment of smaller manhole covers and what looked like fuel or water tanks were spread in a circle around the missile bay itself. The tanks were filled with dirt and weeds that had blown in since the missile was taken away.

I watched a snake glide past. Were the fields of Kansas home to poisonous snakes? Maybe this was the kind we were supposed to love because they ate rodents, but my toes curled and tingled inside my running shoes. The snake slid onto the oblong lid to some part of the complex, where two other snakes were already resting—perhaps the cover was made of a material that amplified the sun's weak late-autumn heat.

I tried singing, to boost my spirits, but the wind swallowed my voice. It ripped through my windbreaker and the thin Hippo shirt underneath. I jogged around the perimeter, trying to warm up, snapping pictures of the different empty tanks, of the snakes, of the loading bay. I didn't see any place that looked as though Doris and her team had been digging here.

On the far side of the enclosure I found what looked like a ranch house, wooden, with a concrete step up to the door. The windows had been painted black. At first I thought meth makers had taken over the place, but then I saw a small plaque next to the door: WHEN THE KANWAKA SILO WAS ACTIVE, THIS WAS THE LAUNCH CONTROL SUPPORT BUILDING, WHERE CREW MEMBERS OFF DUTY COULD SLEEP. WINDOWS WERE PAINTED BLACK SO THE OWL SHIFT COULD SLEEP DURING THE DAY.

The door had a new lock, I noticed, a sophisticated one. Maybe meth makers really had moved in. In which case the SUV that had chased Sonia and Doris's team across the fields belonged to a drug enterprise with major resources. Good people to stay away from. I sniffed the air and thought I picked up a tangy chemical smell, but not the sulfurous stench that comes with a big drug operation.

Before leaving the enclosure, I went to look at the high doors to the loading bay. Drops of oil on the tarmac showed that a truck or car had parked here fairly recently, but the doors themselves didn't look as though they'd been opened in some time. They were too heavy to manage without special winches, and I didn't see any shiny places in the hinges or massive handles that would show that someone had been operating them recently.

No one had gone in through that door for some time. So someone was parking here, using this out-of-the-way spot for . . . what? The only thing I could think of continued to be drugs.

I slid back through the opening in the silo fence and started into the fields, looking either for some sign of tire tracks or Doris McKinnon's digging or even, vain idea, some remnant of the thirty-five-year-old hippie camp.

It was hopeless. The rain of the past week had turned the fields into mud baths. Maybe one of those Indian or Bedouin trackers beloved of crime writers could sense where Doris had been digging, but I couldn't.

Mud was encasing my running shoes, making them so heavy that I felt as though I were walking through congealed molasses. My socks were soaked through, turning my toes into frozen lumps. I trudged back to my car, stopping again outside the perimeter gates. This is where Emerald Ferring had been photographed in 1983: *"Aunt Doris, I owe you much."*

I was just getting into my car when I saw a dust cloud rolling toward me, the telltale strobes of the law flashing through it. I shut the door quickly, locked it, turned on the engine, and got ready to move. A squad car pulled up alongside me.

Sheriff Gisborne rolled down his window and signaled me to open mine. "I might have guessed that if there was trouble in Douglas County today, you'd be behind it."

25

TROUBLE IN DOUGLAS COUNTY

WHAT'S TROUBLING YOU today in Douglas County, Sheriff?" I kept my voice neutral.

"You, Warshawski. Douglas County was a pretty calm place until you arrived."

"You mean until I arrived, no one would have found Ms. McKinnon's dead body or tried to rescue Sonia Kiel and the young student, who were overdosing outside that bar?"

He shifted his gaze. "I mean none of that happened until you showed up."

I laughed. "Come on, Sheriff. Horrible as Ms. McKinnon's death was, it happened long before I came to town."

"And now here you are, trespassing on private property."

"This road?" I said. "This road is private property? It looked to me like it was posted as a county road, but you're right: I'm a stranger."

His upper lip curled in a snarl. "We got a call that someone was trespassing on Sea-2-Sea land, and I decided to look for myself, because I had this hunch, this intuition, the kind of thing a lady or a private eye might have, that I'd find you were the perp."

"Good thing you're a guy and a law-enforcement pro who doesn't have to depend on his hunches, because they'd have misled you: I haven't been on Sea-2-Sea land."

He grinned in an ugly way. "Someone triggered an alarm at this location, and I don't see anyone else around here, do you?"

"Sheriff, to the best of my knowledge, I have only been on Doris McKinnon's land and on my own property. I did not cross that fence, the only one I've seen marked as Sea-2-Sea land." I pointed toward the fence on the south side of the silo.

"*Your* property? What the hell are you talking about?"

I smiled blandly. "I'm a citizen and a taxpayer, and that enclosure is labeled property of the air force, which is part of the U.S. government. Which means I own a one-three-hundred-millionth share in it."

"Like fuck you do. Like fuck you do." He swung open the door to the squad car.

If he was going to arrest me or beat me up, I wished I'd had time to change out of my wet socks and mud-laden shoes. My feet were acutely uncomfortable. My options were limited: If I took off, he'd flag me down. If I stayed, I was a sitting duck. If I reached for my phone to call Luella Baumgart-Grams, the Kansas City lawyer, Gisborne would enjoy shooting me, with the righteous claim that he thought I was pulling a gun.

I kept my hands on the steering wheel, looking grimly ahead. Another cloud of dust was rolling toward us. Reinforcements. Great.

The car rolled to a stop behind Gisborne; the dust settled. It was a dark SUV, not a squad car. Squinting in my side mirror, I couldn't see the emblem, couldn't tell if it was a Buick or some other make, but when the door opened, I knew the driver: Colonel Baggetto, back in military dress. The ribbons and medals on his left breast would have sprained a weaker man's traps.

When Gisborne turned to look at him, I took my hands from the steering wheel. My fingers were stiff—fear making me clench my muscles—and it was hard for me to open the car door.

"Colonel Baggetto—I thought you were addressing KU's soldiers-in-training today." I'm always grateful when my voice is steady at times like this, my mother's vocal lessons paying off.

"We finished about an hour ago. I was on my way back to the fort when I heard there was some kind of fracas at the silo." He smiled easily at the sheriff and me.

"It's posted U.S. Air Force. I thought you were army," I said.

"Nearest air base is a hundred and eighty miles away. Someone called someone who knew someone who knew I was in the area, asked me to check on it for them."

"It's under control," the sheriff said. "You don't need to stick around."

"What happened?" Baggetto asked him. "Don't tell me Warshawski vandalized the silo—it was decommissioned decades ago, and I'd think she'd have better things to do with her time than spray-paint old concrete."

"Decommissioned but still dangerous." Gisborne pointed at a sign on the locked gates with its familiar tan fan blades on a yellow background, cautioning us against radioactive material. "Or do Chicago dicks have radioactive shields in their panties?"

I ignored the gratuitous vulgarity. Vulgarities. "I saw the sign but assumed it dated to when the missile was housed here."

"It does," Gisborne said, impatient, "but there'd been leakage in the missile cradle. That's why the air force couldn't sell it to a developer the way they have with a lot of other sites."

I didn't think Gisborne would be standing here if we were in danger, but I shifted my legs uneasily, as if fallout could fall upward, through the hundreds of feet between the cradle and the ground.

"In that case, why is Sea-2-Sea using adjacent land for their experimental farm?" I demanded. "Are they testing whether some kind of sorghum will grow fat and bushy if it's got a lot of strontium 90 in it?"

Baggetto laughed, but Gisborne frowned. "How did you know they're growing sorghum there?"

"Are they? I don't know one crop from another: just a lucky guess from the list of 'Most Common Plants Under Cultivation in

Eastern Kansas.' I read it in a book at the Lawrence Historical Society," I added, seeing his scowl deepen.

"You say."

"I can show you the book," I said earnestly. "You know where the historical society is, right? That old bank building two blocks from your Law and Justice center—red stone, I think it is, or brick—"

"I know where the damned historical society is," Gisborne said. "I'm the one who grew up in this town—county—not you."

"Someone's been using the missile site," I said. "There's fresh transmission fluid in the loading bay. If you've got vandals out here, or meth heads, they must have a key to the lock on the front gates, and they don't seem scared of the gamma rays or whatever they are." I should have paid more attention in Professor Wright's Physics 101 class all those years ago.

"It's easy to walk onto the site," I added, "but you'd need to open the gates to drive in." I gestured at the place I'd climbed through.

Baggetto walked over to the front gates and shook them, as I had, and, as I had, inspected the lock. I went over to join him, looking again at the radiation warning sign. The yellows and blacks had faded to tans and grays. Someone had taken a potshot at it, missed a bull's-eye by a couple of inches.

"When did they discover that the site was still contaminated?" I asked the sheriff.

"Why do you care?"

I could almost see the hairs on the back of his neck bristle. He didn't like being challenged, but it felt like more than that.

"The sign is old," I said, spelling it out. "If it happened recently, why didn't they put up a bright new yellow sign that would catch people's attention? You can see empty bottles and condoms and so on here—local people are using the land. If it's dangerous, doesn't the county have some duty to warn them?"

"I'm warning *you,*" Gisborne growled. "Locals are smart enough to stay off the site."

"So it's those dreaded outside agitators who've been littering the silo." I nodded as if he'd made an important point. "It was good of you to drive all the way out here to alert me to the radiation."

"I was already out here," the sheriff said. "When the call came in from Sea-2-Sea, I said I'd take it myself because I was sure it'd be you, sticking your nose in other people's business. And don't give me crap about air-force bases belonging to you."

It would have been juvenile to whine that as a taxpayer it was hard to pay for things I never got to see or touch, like drones and warheads and so on.

"You were at the murder scene?" Baggetto asked Gisborne.

"Yep. We're not as well supported as city forces, maybe. We don't get to put sixteen bullets in a suspect, then take a hike, the way they can where this lady comes from, but we do slowly figure out how to walk and chew gum at the same time."

The sheriff was trying to goad me, but Baggetto's knowing the geography out here was what really had my attention. He was in the army, he lived a hundred miles away, but he knew about McKinnon's murder and knew where her farm was relative to the silo.

"Did you?" the sheriff said.

"Did I what?" I'd missed his question.

"Go into the barn when you were out here yesterday."

I shook my head, my stomach clenching: What had I missed? Emerald Ferring's body?

"Someone was keeping a car in there. McKinnon had an old pickup and an older Subaru. Subaru's there, but the pickup's gone. My techs say the tire tracks indicate a Prius. What do you know about that, Warshawski?"

"Prius is a hybrid, right? That's pretty much all I know about them, but a good mechanic could tell you how they work." I kept forgetting I wasn't going to bait the sheriff.

He jammed his hands in the pockets of his football jacket: he wasn't going to slug me, at least not with Baggetto watching, but the impulse was strong. "You know anyone who drives one?"

"I don't think so." I knew August Veriden owned a Prius, but I didn't actually know him, and I couldn't think of anyone in my own circle who did.

"We checked with Illinois, and this kid you say you're looking for, this August, he has one registered to his name."

"You could be right," I said politely. "I've never met him, so I know less about him than you seem to. Does Illinois believe those are his car's tire tracks?"

"I know you think you're the cleverest person to appear in Kansas since Dorothy and Toto came home, but we aren't total idiots in law enforcement here. We've caught a lot of murderers who think they're too smart for the law to get them."

I hung my head, duly chastened. "Has your pathologist given you a cause of death for Ms. McKinnon yet?"

"Last I heard, you were not on any need-to-know list. Just because you discovered her the first time doesn't give you—"

"The first time?" I interrupted. "Has there been a second time?"

"I meant in the first place. And basically you get to mind your own business, which has nothing to do with the cause of death."

"What about the truck?" I asked. "Ms. McKinnon's pickup?"

He was starting to shout me down when Baggetto repeated the question. "Do you have her truck?"

Gisborne hated having to answer while I was listening, but he snarled, "That's missing, as well. We've put out an APB. If it's in the county, it'll turn up."

"What are we looking for?" Baggetto asked.

"A 2002 Dodge Ram. Came from the manufacturer in red, but neighbors tell me the paint was pretty much worn off by now. Of course, Warshawski here, she might just trip on it taking her dog for a walk down by the river."

I didn't like anything about this story. Gisborne knew I'd been walking Peppy along the river. Maybe it was a lucky guess—as he himself said, he wasn't a lady or a PI who could rely on his hunches. But maybe he'd had a deputy in the Buick that was following me around yesterday.

Why would the Prius and the pickup both be missing? That didn't make sense, unless Emerald and August had thought they could ditch the Prius and make a more anonymous escape from the county in McKinnon's old truck. I refused to believe that Emerald or August could have attacked Doris McKinnon. I also didn't like to think they'd stood idly by while someone else killed her. Maybe they'd been out, come back and seen her body, and realized that August would be the prime suspect.

Sonia Kiel had been on the land. Could she have had some kind of psychotic break and attacked McKinnon, thinking that the old woman had been responsible for her supposed lover's death?

I shook my head, annoyed with myself: I'd lectured Sergeant Everard for profiling August, but here I was, profiling Sonia—last night I'd wondered if she'd killed Cady Perec's mother, and now I wanted to frame her for Doris McKinnon's death. It would be more to the point if I could find out who had fed her roofies at the Lion's Pride the other night—someone had tried to silence her, and it could well be the person who'd actually killed McKinnon.

26

PATRIOTS CARE

NEITHER GISBORNE NOR Baggetto tried to stop me from getting into my car. As I bounced down the gravel road to the highway, I kept checking my rearview mirror, but neither of them was following. I got off at the first exit and doubled back, pulling onto the shoulder on top of an overpass, watching the silo through my binoculars.

Baggetto was just leaving. I watched the dust cloud he stirred up until he reached the paved road and turned westbound onto the highway, where I lost him in the mass of cars. He might be going to Fort Riley or Lawrence, or taking the long way around to circle back on me.

Gisborne stood by his squad car, talking on his phone, then went into the missile site. If he had a key to the gate, he didn't use it—like me, he sidled through a gap in the fence. Once inside, he walked over to the loading bay, but the concrete wings blocked my view, so I couldn't tell what he did there. After a few minutes, he wandered around to the side, to the surface where the snakes had been resting, and tapped it with his boot. My binoculars weren't strong enough to see whether the snakes scampered off. He walked around to the annex with its black-painted windows and tried the door, which didn't open.

As if he could feel my eyes on him, he scanned the landscape before sidling through the gap in the fence and returning to his car.

I watched him drive down the county road and turn south, past the silo, toward the highway entrance. I thought maybe he'd spotted me, but he continued south, turning into a building complex at the limit of my vision's range.

Local offices for Sea-2-Sea, my map app told me, where Bram the hippie hater hung out. I didn't need to gate-crash—I could picture what I'd find, Gisborne and Bram powwowing over what I'd been doing at the silo. They'd look at me with guilty or aggressive or guiltily aggressive faces. All I'd learn was that they didn't want me in Douglas County.

I got back into the Mustang, trying to figure out what I could do or who I could do it to. My most pressing thought as I drove to town was how bad my shoes smelled and how much my feet hurt. Underneath that discomfort I wondered how Gisborne had known I was at the silo. My best guess was that when I touched the Sea-2-Sea fence, besides zapping me it sent a message to the company's computers. They might have cameras in the fence posts—I'd been so startled that I hadn't taken the time to check for surveillance.

Back at the B and B, I bundled all my filthy clothes into the washing machine the owner provided her guests, scraped the mud off my shoes, then took a long, hot shower. After that it seemed like a good idea to draw the curtains and lie down. I was dozing off when I started thinking about Colonel Baggetto: What had really brought him to Lawrence, and then to the missile silo?

Lying in the darkened room, I called the university's military office, identifying myself as a freelance writer for the *Douglas County Herald*.

"We heard that a colonel from Fort Riley gave a guest lecture to the cadets this morning. Is he still on campus? His name is . . ." I pretended to be looking at notes. "Baggetto. Dante Baggetto. We'd love to do an interview with him, find out what he thinks about—"

The secretary who'd answered cut me off. "We didn't have any special lectures here this morning. Maybe the colonel was meeting privately with the staff. If you'll hold for a minute, I'll check. What did you say your name was?"

"Martha Gellhorn." It was the first journalist's name to pop into my head. Fortunately, the secretary didn't seem to be a student of women's history.

I drowsed while she checked. "Sorry, Martha, but none of the girls report any visiting birds in their logbooks today. Who told you he was here?"

"One of the cadets." I burrowed deep in my mind for the kid who'd been with Baggetto at the hotel last night. "Marlon. Marlon Pinsen."

I could hear the woman typing at the other end, and then she said sharply, "Martha, you need to start double-checking your sources. We don't have anyone enrolled in the ROTC program named that, and I don't even find him in the university's student database. This is sloppy journalism, and it doesn't help either of us."

"And you should always call back a paper before volunteering information to strangers." I hung up.

I sat up, no longer sleepy, and turned on my bedside lamp. Colonel Baggetto had gone out of his way to lie to me last night. He could have let me walk away with nothing but a smile—last night I hadn't cared who he had drinks with or what had brought him to Lawrence.

I logged on to my subscription search engines, but they couldn't tell me much about Baggetto. He'd been born in Providence, Rhode Island, attended a science-and-math academy, and gone from there to West Point. He'd graduated nineteenth in his class, done three tours in Iraq and Afghanistan as part of army intelligence.

After the third tour, he'd undergone advanced training at the Army Command and General Staff College in Fort Leavenworth—only forty miles from Lawrence—and completed a master's in computer engineering at Columbia in New York. He'd been sent to Fort Riley three months ago, right after his promotion to colonel. That was it. Nothing personal, other than that he'd never married anyone of any sex.

I'm bone ignorant about the military, but it looked like Baggetto was being groomed for great things. Which meant he wouldn't be in Lawrence, or talking to me, if it was trivial. Or if it might hurt his career.

Which meant it was somehow tied to Sea-2-Sea, because he'd been at the hotel with Bram somebody along with the bogus cadet. I couldn't remember Bram's last name—I kept thinking Stoker, naturally—but the Net found it for me. Bram Roswell, head of R&D. M.B.A. from Wharton, undergraduate degree in agricultural science from Kansas State University, which happened to be near Fort Riley. I wondered if that was significant, if Roswell returned to his alma mater to root for football games and then got together with army intelligence officers at night to plan . . . what?

A search of news stories reported Roswell's appearance at various charity functions in Lawrence, Kansas City, and Dallas. Another story revealed that Roswell was active in Patriots CARE-NOW—Concerned Americans for Rearmament Now. He was shown with a former undersecretary of defense for nuclear arms getting a medal at their annual dinner.

Was whatever brought Baggetto and Roswell together somehow connected to Doris McKinnon and the digging she'd been doing? Had McKinnon's decision to dig brought Emerald Ferring to Kansas so hastily? Ferring had relied on Troy Hempel since he was seven and began cutting her lawn for her, but she turned to August Veriden, a stranger, because she couldn't wait five extra days for Troy Hempel to come home.

True, August was filming her origin story: they'd stopped at Fort Riley and taken pictures, they'd gone to her childhood home in North Lawrence, but the real reason they'd come to Kansas was to help Doris McKinnon. I felt sure of it, but I'd love to have confirmation. Especially an e-mail or tree-mail that laid out what had worried Doris so much she'd turned to her old friend's daughter for help.

I called Free State Dogs to check on Peppy, who was having way more fun than I was, and got dressed again—wool slacks instead of jeans, a cashmere knit top in my favorite rose, and the one good jacket I'd brought with me. All I needed was lunch and a burner phone and I'd be ready for action.

I found the phone store first. Three disposable phones, which I could rotate, each with six hundred minutes. I drove on into town and stopped at one of the zillion student cafés downtown for a sandwich. Hummus on homemade bread, delicious. Coffee, mediocre. I poured it out and walked over to the Hippo.

A handful of what looked like regulars were chatting with the bartender. I took my coffee into a corner and called Troy's mother.

"Ms. Hempel, I don't know how much Troy has told you about what I've encountered in Lawrence, but it's a worrying situation," I said when we'd covered the preliminaries—Troy was at work, I knew; it was she I was looking for. "Did Ms. Ferring ever talk to you about a woman named Doris McKinnon?"

"Troy told me you found her—found her dead yesterday."

"Did he also tell you the police think young August Veriden is the likely culprit?"

"Oh, yes." She didn't try to keep bitterness out of her voice. "And you, what do you think?"

"I don't think anything. I don't have any facts. I hope I find August before some trigger-happy local LEOs do. Have you heard from Ms. Ferring? I think you are one person she might consult."

"I don't know. God's truth." Ms. Hempel sighed heavily. "She's known me for twenty years, and I think she trusts me, so it scares me that I haven't heard from her."

"Could she have gone back home, back to Chicago?"

There was a pause on Hempel's end before she said, "If Ms. Emerald came home, she's kept it quiet. There aren't any lights on in the house."

I wished I were face-to-face with her: interrogations by phone leave out the cues of truth and lies and the shaded areas in between.

Ms. Hempel could be telling the literal truth—no lights in Emerald's basement—all the while shielding her neighbor in her own home.

"What about the real reason she decided to go to Kansas?" I asked.

"To make a documentary about her life. We told you that when Troy decided you were the best person to look for her." Her voice was still bitter, the subtext demanding what I could possibly do to merit Troy's confidence.

"I'm sure Ms. Ferring and August have been in Lawrence, as recently as last week, but I haven't found any trace of them since. It looks as though Ms. McKinnon took them out with her to dig up a field in the middle of the night. Something troubled Ms. McKinnon, something important enough that she wanted August to film it. In the middle of filming, an SUV drove into their midst. I don't know if they were chased away or captured."

There was a longer pause, and then Hempel burst out, "I wondered why Emerald was in such a rush to go down there. Troy would have taken her as soon as he got back from Israel, I told her that. He'd make sure she traveled in comfort. She didn't need to go off with some stranger who couldn't look after her. But all she'd say was she had the urge to go now, that she wasn't going to impose on Troy, make him drive all over the country when he had an important job to do."

There was a history buried in the long comment, hurt feelings, perhaps injured pride that Emerald hadn't confided in her, but I didn't try to sort that out, just asked if the Hempels had a key to Ferring's house. "Can you go in and see if you can find anything, a letter, an e-mail, from Doris McKinnon?"

Hempel was taken aback: What kind of person did I think she was, breaking into a neighbor's house and going through her things?

"You're the kind of person who would do a great deal if you feared for a friend's life," I said quietly. "And I'm afraid for Ms. Ferring's life."

That changed her attitude at once. If Emerald's life were in danger . . . well, why hadn't I said so? She'd call around to some of the other people in the neighborhood, see if they'd heard from her.

"Do it in person, okay? I don't know who or what we're dealing with, but they went up to Chicago and trashed August Veriden's workplace and apartment, looking for something they think he has. For all I know, they may be tapping your phone, although I hope not. I'm going to leave a message on Troy's office line, with a number you can send a text to if you learn anything."

I was feeling panicky. Not good. I wanted to be in Chicago, to check on Emerald's acquaintances myself, but I needed to stay here until I got some inkling of what Baggetto and Sea-2-Sea and Sheriff Gisborne were doing.

27

SPIRITUAL ADVISER

AS I PUT the burner phones in my day pack, I realized that if Baggetto cared enough about me to track me through my smartphone's GPS, I should ditch it. Come to think of it, the car also had a GPS tracker. As did my tablet. For all I knew, so did my dressy boots. After all, Samsung sells refrigerators with computer chips embedded in their skins.

If the bartender was surprised at my request for aluminum foil, he didn't show it. I took the roll into the toilet with me and lined the inside of my day pack with four layers of foil for a kind of DIY Faraday cage. I hoped it would work: if I locked my phone or computer in the car, it would be a cinch for Gisborne or Baggetto to get into the car and retrieve every detail of my private and business lives from my devices.

Assuming they were interested. Assuming I wasn't being paranoid. Lining the pack reminded me uncomfortably of Stan Wolinsky, who'd lived across the street from us when I was a child. He drove a garbage truck for the city and covered his head in foil every morning before he went to work to block signals from outer space. Kids at school were merciless with his son, Stanley Jr.—"Tinhead" was only the most printable insult they used. Still, as Yossarian or Satchel Paige or someone said, just because you're paranoid doesn't mean they aren't gaining on you.

It was about a mile from the Hippo to Nell Albritten's house.

Another outing in the cold November air would do me good, I firmly told my calves and hamstrings: they were a bit wobbly from hiking through the muddy ground around the silo. Paved roads all the way, so there wouldn't be a risk to my treasured Lario boots.

I parked in the free lot attached to the library and headed for the river. Halfway across the bridge, I stopped to look down at the water and covertly glance behind me. I was alone on the footbridge. Someone was fishing on the far side—perhaps the same man who'd been there yesterday. On the town side, no one seemed to be lingering.

Below me the water tumbled brown and dirty over a dam. Gulls swooped in and out. Something moved on the top of a dead tree: an eagle. I'd never seen one in nature before and watched, fascinated, while it dove after a creature that wriggled helplessly in its claws. I shuddered, walked on across the bridge, over to Sixth Street, past the driveways laden with old furniture, and up to Nell Albritten's house. A Nissan sat in front, old, but well cared for. Maybe the son's, not the kind of car that drug dealers or dogfighters drove.

When I rang the bell, a curtain twitched in the front-room window, I heard indistinct voices, and then the door was opened by a man of perhaps fifty, wearing a clerical collar over a magenta clerical shirt. He smiled, but his eyes were wary.

"I'm V.I. Warshawski. I was with Ms. Albritten yesterday when she collapsed. I wanted to see how she's doing."

"Yes, Ms. V.I. Detective, you may come in." Albritten's voice came from the living room, quavery but decisive.

The minister held the door open, but I paused to ask whether Albritten knew that I'd found Doris McKinnon's dead body.

"Oh, yes," he murmured. "It's been very hard for her, but it's why she wants to talk to you."

Nell Albritten was in the easy chair where she'd sat yesterday afternoon. Her face was drawn, a lock of gray hair hanging loose from the severely scraped bun. Yesterday's ordeal had taken a toll.

"Where's your friend?" she asked.

It took a moment to realize she meant Peppy. "Day care. It wasn't fair to drag her all over the county. Although she did help yesterday: she knew something was wrong when we were at Doris McKinnon's farm. It was the dog who insisted that I go into the house."

Albritten bowed her head, her eyes briefly closing. "Doris wasn't a Christian. We used to argue about it, back when Lucinda first moved in with her. I was so righteous when I was young! I was sure Doris and her atheism would corrupt young Emerald. It shames me now, all that time wasted on a quarrel with a woman who was decent clear down to her bones. Whatever she did or didn't believe, whatever she and Lucinda did or didn't do, I know Doris is with Jesus now."

"That's right." The minister bent over to take her hand. "Hold that thought, Sister Albritten. It will carry you through a time of trouble."

I shifted in my chair, uncomfortable with the religious conversation.

The minister straightened and pulled a stool over next to Albritten. "Now you've seen that she's doing well, you can let her rest."

"I'd like to tell her something that I would hate anyone else overhearing. Ms. Albritten apparently knows you and trusts you, but I don't even know your name or who you are."

"Of course." The minister kept his hand cupped over Albritten's. "I'm Bayard Clements, Sister Albritten's pastor at St. Silas AME Church. I hear you went over to look at the church, so I won't waste time telling you where it is."

I looked at him squarely. "I went there because I wondered if Emerald Ferring and August Veriden might be hiding in the church, but it was locked up tight."

Clements laughed as if in delight, but again the amusement touched only his mouth. "It's a small building, as you saw: sanctuary, minute office, a vestry room the size of a hall closet. Not a lot of places to hide. And much as I love my parishioners, I wouldn't want them to carry the burden of a secret like that."

"Historically important," I said, my tone dreamy, musing on the past. "A refuge for free African-Americans during the Civil War. Those crypts or underground rooms, they'd be at high risk during the floods, I'm guessing."

Clements's eyes narrowed. "Good point, Detective Warshawski. We have a job preserving those historic spaces. Much too damp for anyone to hide in today, but I'll be glad to show them to you when you've finished talking to Sister Albritten."

I bowed my head, half ironic, and told him I would enjoy a tour. "I'm about to tell Ms. Albritten something that amounts to evidence tampering. I could be arrested, so if you don't want another burden to carry on your own, you might step outside."

"Unless you're going to confess to a murder or something of that nature, I won't call the *Douglas County Herald,*" Clements said. "Since you're speaking in confidence to one of my parishioners, I'm even willing to extend my pastoral exemption to you."

I turned to Albritten. "Ma'am, when I went out to the farm yesterday, I found a thumb drive—a piece of computer equipment—that contains photos and videos that August took in the middle of the night. He was out in a field with Ms. McKinnon and Ms. Ferring. They apparently didn't want anyone to know what they were doing, so he filmed without using a light. Ms. McKinnon was digging up soil samples. Do you know which field she might have been in?"

"I told you yesterday, I hadn't seen Doris McKinnon in some time," she said fretfully.

"Yes, ma'am. Forgive my putting it this way, but . . . I used to practice law before I became an investigator. That's a 'letter of the law' response. I believe you hadn't seen her, but did she phone you? Or you her? Or did Emerald—Ms. Ferring—talk to you about what they'd been doing?"

There was a long silence, during which she took her hand away from her pastor's and clasped it with the other in her lap.

When she didn't speak, I said as gently as I could, "Yesterday, when you collapsed, it was while you were trying to say that someone would have told you if Ms. McKinnon had died. I think you are such a truthful woman that you fainted rather than speak a lie: you already knew she was dead."

"Detective! That is completely out of line." Clements moved so that his whole body was between me and Albritten.

Albritten plucked at his sleeve. "Let it be, Bayard, let it be. She's right, after all. I did hear, not from Emerald but from the young man. Doris had sent them away. He went back, maybe to collect that piece of computer. The thumb piece. He saw her body on the kitchen floor and ran. I told him to make himself scarce, him and Emerald, too. I didn't want him turning up dead in the middle of Massachusetts Street, shot by the first white deputy to see him. I wanted to let them hide at St. Silas, but Bayard was right: those old cellar rooms, they're full of mold and who knows what all."

"Where did they go?" I put every ounce of pleading I possessed into my voice.

Albritten shook her head. "I wish I could tell you, but I can't."

"Can't? Or won't?" I asked.

"Over the line," Clements repeated, but Albritten said, "She's not asking out of spite, Bayard. She wants to help. Can't, Detective. I can't tell you. I don't know."

I had to be content with that. I asked if August had said anything about the dirt they'd been digging up.

"No." Her lower jaw worked. "We didn't have a conversation. August was frightened, and I was frightened for him and for my girl; neither of us was thinking clearly. But one of the women from Riverside Church, over across the bridge, Barbara Rutledge, I ran into her at the farmers' market, oh, maybe a month ago. She told me I'd just missed Doris. And Doris was upset because someone was planting on her land. So I called her at the farm, and Doris said she rented out all the land now, that she couldn't look after it herself, but she'd driven over there in her pickup, looking to make sure the fences and all were being kept up. She thought someone was planting on her land, where they shouldn't have been."

“Would she have brought Emerald down from Chicago just for that?” I asked doubtfully. “Isn’t that something her lawyer could handle for her?”

Albritten gave a ghost of a smile. “You don’t know us old Kansas women, city girl. We’d rather dig our own graves than pay the undertaker to do it for us.”

28

DISAPPEARING ACT

I DIDN'T NEED BAYARD Clements' prodding to get to my feet: Albritten was clearly at the end of her strength. I waited in the front room while he escorted her to her bedroom. The pictures on the television had been rearranged, I noticed idly; the one of the women joyously celebrating St. Silas's 150th anniversary had been removed. Curious.

Clements reappeared. He said he'd walk to St. Silas with me, show me the church's undercroft so I could see for myself it didn't harbor any fugitives.

We made the usual small talk while we walked to the church—how long had he been here, what did he know about the town. He'd grown up in Atlanta; his mother had worked for Bayard Rustin, which was how he'd gotten his name. Lawrence was an adjustment, small town, small African-American community, but he loved the spirit in the place and loved bringing the university students into the St. Silas family.

"You weren't here for the St. Silas hundred-fiftieth anniversary?" I asked.

He stiffened. "What do you know about that?"

"Just making conversation. I saw the photo in Ms. Albritten's living room yesterday," I said. "It wasn't there today."

"I came here the following year," he said. "Sister Albritten wanted the picture next to her bed. I moved it for her this morning."

"When you saw me coming up the walk?"

He gave another social laugh. "Chicago manners are more unceremonious than I'm used to, Detective. I always thought coming to Kansas meant moving north, but manners here are much more southern."

I nodded, acknowledging the rebuke but still wondering about the picture. Our conversation had brought us to the church door, which meant an easy change of topic.

"God's house ought to be open to anyone needing a sanctuary," Clements said, "but we can't afford to employ anyone to look after the place, and it's sad but true that people help themselves to what they see sitting around, even in a church."

The sanctuary had a musty smell, not unpleasant, but I could see the warping in the floorboards from the river damps. I asked him about floods, and he said they'd done the best they could with foundation protection. After the 1951 flood, the Corps of Engineers had put in dams along the river, which helped as well.

"Lately Kansas has been more plagued by drought than flood, so we forget the menace the river can offer."

He led me into the cellars. I was worried about my precious Italian boots, but the floors were cemented over. Even so, water had pooled in the uneven surface and the walls felt clammy when I ran my hand over them. Clements turned on the lights—naked bulbs strung across low-hanging ceilings—and stood in a corner, arms folded, watching me with an ironic smile while I looked for any signs that someone had been here recently. Not so much as a La Perla bra strap or a USB port.

It was also cold. Someone desperate—a runaway slave, a black youth scared of the cops—might tough it out, but I doubted that Emerald Ferring would want to. She might have come up the hard way, but that had been fifty years ago.

Clements was parked behind the church. When he realized I was on foot, he offered to drive me to my own car, but he seemed surprised that I'd parked at the library.

"I was using the collection this morning," I said. "It seemed easier to leave the car there."

I didn't feel like explaining my worries about being tracked. I wondered if the fact that the sheriff or the colonel or whoever could track me through my phone meant they no longer needed to use their SUV. I put a reflexive hand on my throat, which suddenly felt tight.

When Clements dropped me at the library, he brushed aside my thanks with a brusque comment. "I hope you won't go doubling back to trouble Sister Albritten again."

I smiled perfunctorily. "Could she stay with her son for a few weeks? I don't know what's going on or who's instigating it, but the violence at the McKinnon farm and at August's home in Chicago—if those thugs think that she knows something—"

"I know." He cut me off. "That's why I've organized people in the community to stay with her. I wanted her to go to her son Jordan, but she's a stubborn woman. Old, besides, and the old need to be in their own places. Jordan will come back tomorrow. He has to get his business organized so that someone can take care of things while he's away, and then he'll stay with her, or his oldest boy will. It's not perfect, but it will have to do."

I didn't offer to help with guard duty; I didn't know where my investigations might lead or when, but Albritten's safety was yet another worry.

Back in my own car, I took my electronics out of their foil casing. I had a raft of messages, some urgent, but my own first priority was to collect my dog.

Peppy was delighted to see me, although the manager assured me that everyone had fallen in love with her; I could bring her back anytime. Peppy had played fetch longer than they thought possible for any dog, had worked well with the rest of the animals, and so on. I felt as though I were reading a kindergarten report: *Your little Peppy is the ideal child, bright but caring about others*. Not that I disagreed with a word of it.

As we drove into town, I was thankful she'd had enough exercise that I didn't need to walk her tonight. We went back to the Hippo. It was five-thirty, sun over the yardarm, whatever that was.

The bartender/barista I usually saw in the mornings was on duty, so I brought Peppy inside with me.

I put two twenties on the counter and asked for a double Oban, neat. My usual drink, Johnnie Walker Black, is half the price, but I wanted pampering. "Do you need proof that she's my emotional-support dog, or can you take my word for it?"

"I can tell by looking at the two of you," the woman said, picking up one of the twenties and giving me back a five along with the second. "Keep your change. We all need emotional support around here."

I left the five on the counter and went to a corner table with my devices and my dog. Among the messages from my Chicago clients was one from Troy Hempel: he'd talked to his mother, and he'd get back to me when he could. I had seven texts from Bernie, telling me if I didn't find August by tomorrow, she was flying down, no matter what I or her coach or her parents had to say.

I replied to my most important clients, texted the Streeter brothers to ask them to do some legwork for me, and wrote an emphatic NO WAY, JOSÉ to Bernie. PEOPLE ARE KILLING EACH OTHER AND LEAVING THE BODIES FOR RATS TO EAT. STAY AWAY.

After that I looked up Barbara Rutledge, who'd talked to Doris McKinnon at the farmers' market a month ago. Although there are services that search for cell-phone numbers, they're slow and costly, so I was glad that Rutledge turned out to be old-fashioned enough to have a landline. She answered on the third ring, too, so I didn't have to waste time trading calls.

I introduced myself and asked if I were right in thinking I'd met her the day before at Riverside Church.

"Oh, yes. The detective who got everybody so agitated. Did you call on Nell Albritten?"

"Yes. I'm sure you've heard she collapsed when I was with her."

Barbara was astonished. "I didn't know— Has she seen a doctor? What did you do?"

"I made sure she went to the ER," I said. "She's home again, depleted, the way one is after an episode like that, especially someone who's in her nineties, but they say her heart is fine."

"Why did you think I already knew?"

"Everyone in Douglas County keeps stressing to me how you all know one another," I said. "That's been proved true to me so many times that I've started to think my job here is to phone people and have them tell me what I'm doing."

"We do all talk about one another all the time," Barbara agreed. "Probably no different from a big city, but so many of us grew up together or have worked together for such a long time that maybe we're in one another's business more than you'd be in Chicago."

She hesitated. "Me not knowing about Nell Albritten is typical of what I was trying to say yesterday at church. There's a divide in this town between black and white and between the people north of the river, North Lawrence, and the rest of the town. Only a handful of people at Riverside know Ms. Albritten, and unless they're connected to the hospital, they won't have heard a peep about her. If it had been Gertrude Perec or Joy Helmsley, we'd all have our casseroles baked by now."

"On the subject of casseroles, or at least food," I said, "Ms. Albritten told me this afternoon that Doris McKinnon talked to you at the farmers' market about a month ago. She was upset that someone was planting on her land?"

"No-o-o." Rutledge drew the word out, trying to remember. "She was upset, but she was talking about the land she'd had to sell to the air force. She said it looked as though they'd sold it to another farmer instead of giving her the chance to buy it back. 'They're growing something there, and I need to know why'—something like that."

"If she was digging up the ground in the middle of the night, trying to prove something, then it would be on that land?" That would be a wonderful break. I could ID the fifteen acres she'd had to cede and inspect them for signs of digging, instead of going all over the county.

"She was digging in the middle of the night?" Rutledge was startled. "She was always . . . I don't want to say eccentric—we're too fast to slap that label on any woman who marches to her own beat—but she was always more out there than most other people. She let the anti-nuke kids camp on her land, back in '83. That caused a lot of antagonism out in the county, hippies or Communists spoiling the landscape."

We'd hung up, and I was looking at the maps I'd used this morning, trying to work out where McKinnon's old fifteen acres overlapped with the Sea-2-Sea experimental farm, when Sergeant Everard came in.

He and the barista chatted for a minute—banter, it looked like—while she pulled a beer for him. He brought it over to my table.

"Just got off duty." He waved the beer stein. "So she's an emotional-support animal, huh?" He leaned over to scratch Peppy's ears. "I thought she was your analyst."

"She's an exceptional multitasker."

"They told me you usually come here in the mornings for coffee."

"Best in Lawrence, at least for my taste," I agreed.

"That doesn't look a lot like coffee," he said, "but I took a chance that you'd come in at night. It's how we LEOs catch perps: people like their routines."

"We perps do," I agreed, "but maybe you saw my GPS come back on stream."

He raised his brows, surprised. "Not tracking you, Warshawski, just looking for you."

"Okay," I said. "You found me."

"A friend of mine at the state lab called me a little bit ago, about Doris McKinnon, or at least the woman whose body we assume belonged to Doris."

I waited some more.

"Dr. Roque collapsed in the morgue this morning while he was starting the autopsy. He was there on his own: state can't afford full-time tech support anymore, so it wasn't until a guard saw him on a TV monitor that they called for help. He was airlifted to the med center in Kansas City, with some kind of acute flu."

"I'm sorry to hear that," I said formally. "Does this mean the autopsy is on hold?"

Everard grinned humorlessly. "We're not quite a hick place down here, Warshawski, despite what the *New York Times* says. We do have more than one pathologist in the state. No, the problem is that McKinnon's body is gone."

29

DATA SWAPPING

GONE?" I ECHOED stupidly.

"Disappeared, vanished. I can't think of any other synonyms."

I was too bewildered to say anything. Everard took my silence as criticism.

"We're not like Chicago, with thousands of homicides every year. We have security—guards, cameras, all the modern stuff—but we don't need to run our path lab as if national security depended on it. At least we never thought we did."

I shook my head. "Not that. Anyway, the Cook County Morgue has been a disgrace recently, with bodies stacked every which way, oozing their secretions into one another. No, I'm trying to remember what the sheriff said this morning."

I stared at the scarred counter through the whisky, which gave everything beneath it an amber glow. I'd asked Gisborne if they had a cause of death yet, and he'd slapped me down: I didn't have a right to ask even if I discovered the body "the first time." Yes, that was it, and then he made a good recovery, claimed he'd meant "in the first place."

When I repeated this to Everard, he frowned in a worried way. "You don't think Gisborne knew already, do you? He and I don't always see eye to eye, but I've known him practically my whole life."

"I grew up with people who are doing five to ten for fraud and arson, just to name a few counts."

"Gisborne is honest. I'd know if he wasn't," Everard shot back.

"Just harassing you," I said. "You know him, I don't. It struck me as odd. If you're so sure he's honest, why did you come looking for me to tell me about McKinnon's disappearance?"

Everard's mouth twisted in mockery. "People talk about you at the station, you know. They say they're bored with vandalism and drunk drivers, with the occasional armed robbery for spice, that if we want real crime, we should keep you around. 'Warshawski's like a crime divining rod—does she make 'em or find 'em?' Drugged women, murder victims, people faint when you show up. I wondered . . ."

"If I'd given Dr. Roque a bad disease and walked off with your body?" I said helpfully when his voice trailed off.

He grinned again, a real smile, relieved that I'd taken the kidding in good part. "That's what the scuttlebutt is. I have confidence in the Lawrence force, certainly in my lieutenant and most of the people in his command. The KBI—Kansas Bureau—has done some impressive work, solved murders that needed a lot of finesse. So I'm not going to say that we need your expertise. We don't, even though they're understaffed these days, given the state's financial crisis. But. Something's going on that's making me . . . I don't know what the word is. If I were your friend on the floor here, the hair on my neck would be standing up."

He rubbed the back of Peppy's head with his boot toe.

"What in particular?" I asked.

"The body disappearing, of course. What you said about Gisborne—I don't know what bug is crawling up his ass, but he's acting weird. I mean, county, city, we have our own crimes, our own investigations, but we know we're in it together, and we don't usually play turf wars with each other. When the word came in from the morgue, though, the sheriff went to Lieutenant Lowdham and told him this was a county matter and Lawrence should stay out of it."

"And the lieutenant?" I prompted when Everard fell silent again.

"Lieutenant said if any crimes committed in Lawrence tied into McKinnon's death, we'd have to take the lead, but for now we'd lay low."

"Sonia Kiel," I said. "Drugged and left to die outside the Lion's Pride."

"You're tying this to the McKinnon death? What, a drone hovered over your head and a little alien said, 'Warshawski, Sonia Kiel saw Doris McKinnon die'?"

"I knew it was a mistake to release another *Star Wars* flick," I said. "Maybe Sonia did see the murder. She saw something. Listen to the whole story—it's weird enough without needing to throw in aliens. Do you know a Colonel Baggetto?"

When he shook his head, I told him about running into Baggetto at the hotel last night with Bram from Sea-2-Sea and Dr. Kiel. "Gisborne is doing special favors for Sea-2-Sea. Is that normal for him?"

"What do you mean, normal?" Everard kept veering between hostile and conciliatory; the needle swung to the red again.

"I'm not judging." I kept my voice patient; I couldn't alienate the one local LEO who'd shown me some good will. "Can any company or citizen ask the sheriff to respond when an alarm goes off on their property?"

Everard shrugged. "If Sea-2-Sea had it set up to ring in the sheriff's office, sure. Why not?"

"I leaned over the fence, which is electrified. I guess that brought Gisborne running. Sea-2-Sea is awfully protective of a few cereal plants."

"City girl." The needle swung into the blue again. "Those plants could be a special hybrid potentially worth millions of dollars. Sea-2-Sea doesn't want anyone touching them—not a crime."

Everard waved his mug at the bartender. "Simone, bring me another, would you, pretty please?"

"Deke, you're not crippled, last I saw. You come on up here yourself. You can see I got a line waiting, and I'm on my own."

The crowd was building, but it was modest compared to the one at the Lion's Pride. Only a tiny TV in the far corner, so diehard Jayhawk fans would be at the bigger sports screens.

I shook my head when Everard offered me a refill. A double whisky after a long day was making me sleepy. Any more and I wouldn't be able to drive or, more important, stay tuned to what Everard was saying.

When he got back, I told him about Baggetto's arriving at the missile silo. "He said he was in Lawrence to lecture to the ROTC unit up on the hill, but when I called, they didn't have a record of his being there. On the other hand, he kept the sheriff from arresting me, or maybe shooting me while I tried to flee the scene."

Everard banged his stein on the counter, slopping some beer over the side. "See, that's what I mean. Gisborne, he's been sheriff here a million years, started as a deputy back in the eighties. He doesn't usually fly off the handle like that."

"I wondered about drugs," I said. "There's a building on the missile site with black windows and a new lock."

"Whatever Gisborne may or may not be doing, he will *not* be covering for a drug ring," Everard snapped. "Nor Dr. Kiel—he's Dr. Public Health around here. No way would he support a meth lab."

"I know they're not growing medical marijuana on that land," I said, trying to lower the temperature. "It's probably the one crop I could identify. But two different things could be happening out there—meth in the abandoned silo and something else on Doris McKinnon's old land."

Everard nodded grudgingly

"Not to light another fuse under you, but I'm wondering about Baggetto, too."

"You're safe, since I don't know the guy. What's he up to?"

"I have no idea, but Baggetto knows an awful lot about what's happening in the county for an army man with a big career behind and in front of him."

I put the maps I'd been using at Everard's right hand, away from the beer puddle. "See this outline? That's the fifteen acres the air force took from Doris McKinnon back in 1983, after the commune burned down. They said it was too contaminated to use, and a woman from the Emigrant Bank said that's why the silo hasn't been sold to a private developer, the way a lot of them have."

"Yeah?" Everard's phone rang; he said he was off duty, turn the call over to Officer Peabody.

"Why is Sea-2-Sea planting there? Unless I've got the map wrong."

Everard took the county map and the property conveyances from me and stared at them for a good ten minutes. I answered my own ever-growing queue of texts, checked for the nth time on whether Jake had been in touch.

"No, you've got it right. Good question. I'll see what the scuttlebutt is around the station." He grimaced. "Things are tense right now between the city and the county, so I have to walk softly—and definitely not wave a big stick around."

I grunted acknowledgment and added, "Doris McKinnon did a secret nighttime digging project. I'm guessing it was on the land the air force seized. I'm guessing she wanted to check the radiation level in the soil—that's the only explanation I can come up with. I don't think the samples were still in the house when I was there last night—I didn't know about her digging then, so I didn't look for them, but a whole bunch of bags with tags showing latitude and longitude—"

"How do you know this, Warshawski?" Everard cried. "Damn it, you're sitting on evidence—"

"An anonymous tip," I said coldly. "You're taking a risk talking to me, but I'm taking one as well, sharing my information with you."

Everard scowled at his beer but finally said, "Okay. Anonymous tip. And?"

"And Sonia Kiel showed up, dancing in the field, saw Doris, screamed 'Fire, go away, you're on sacred ground!' That's all I know. But a few nights later, someone slipped her enough roofies to damn near kill her. That connects Sonia to the McKinnon murder, at least in my book."

"I don't know. That's a pretty thin thread."

I looked at him seriously. "You're probably right, but what sent me out to McKinnon's farm in the first place was because that's where Emerald Ferring grew up. Sonia Kiel was out there the night McKinnon was digging her soil samples; in my fifteen seconds on the phone with her, as I told you at the time, she said she'd seen Ferring and August on her truelove's grave. According to her mother, Sonia thinks Matt Chastain was her truelove. He disappeared after the old nuclear protest campsite burned down, and Sonia thinks Matt died there. So my idea of looking for a cemetery was wrong; it was McKinnon's land."

"And that has something to do with the price of tomatoes in Topeka?" Everard said.

"Matt was Dr. Kiel's student, and Kiel says Matt was involved in an experiment that went bad. I wondered if that's what contaminated the land? People at Riverside Church said the land couldn't be used for development."

"Could be, but what's the point?"

"I don't know," I admitted. "Maybe because I only know three things about the land—Sea-2-Sea is cultivating it; it's where the protest site used to be; it's where Sonia thinks Matt disappeared or died—but those things make me connect what happened there in '83 to what's going on there now. Another thing is how hostile Gertrude Perec is to me. It made me wonder if Matt Chastain might be Cady Perec's father—he was on the land back then, and Gertrude's daughter was camping there. If she doesn't want Cady to know . . ." My voice trailed away.

Everard said, "Cady's always wanted to know who her father was, which is understandable, but it beats me why Gertrude would want to keep it hidden if she knew."

"She worked for Dr. Kiel. Chastain was Kiel's student. Sonia had a crush on Chastain and stalked him. Kiel threw Chastain out of the department for making a major blunder on an experiment. And now Kiel is drinking with the guy who's running an experimental farm on the site of the commune. And this colonel is showing up, flashing his medals, along with a sidekick who he told me was a cadet in the university's ROTC program. Only when I talked to them, they told me they didn't have a record of anyone by that name."

Everard's phone pinged. He looked at the screen and looked up, his expression bleak. "Dr. Roque died twenty minutes ago. He wasn't young, but . . . hell, he was a good, impartial pathologist. One of the few people in this damned state who had a job because he knew what the fuck he was doing, not because he buttered the right butt."

I offered the awkward condolences you make to someone you don't know well about someone you've never met.

His eyes were bright. "Catch you later, Warshawski. Catch you later."

30

VISITING BRASS

PEPPY JUMPED INTO the passenger seat. As I started to slide in next to her, someone got out of a car across the street and crossed to me. I stood back up, leaning against the doorframe.

"Colonel Baggetto. Don't they need you at the fort?"

"No one is indispensable, especially on a military base where colonels grow like tumbleweeds and captains do the heavy lifting."

"I didn't think tumbleweeds took much lifting," I said. "If you're looking for me, I'm going back to my room and resting. Alone. If you want the sheriff, I can't help you—the local LEO I was just talking to is with the police."

"I was hoping I could buy you dinner," Baggetto said.

"So you tracked my car down? Wouldn't it have been easier to phone?"

Under the streetlamps his teeth gleamed white. "I know your car but not your phone number."

"And you with your degrees in computer engineering and experience with army intelligence. *NCIS* makes it seem as though all anyone in military intelligence has to do is press a computer button to see every phone call I've made in the last ten years."

"I probably could," he said, still smiling, "but that wouldn't be ethical. Can I persuade you to talk to me inside someplace warm, instead of the middle of Eighth Street?"

In the end, because I wanted to talk to him and I wanted to be inside with Peppy, not in a restaurant with her in a car, I told him he could meet me at the B and B. I didn't feel like feeding him, but he told me he'd pick up a pizza on the way there, along with a bottle of wine.

In the B and B's laundry room, I changed out of my good clothes into jeans and a sweatshirt, fed Peppy, and settled in the easy chair, leaving the straight-backed chair at the small desk for Baggetto. I turned down the wine.

"I haven't put scopolamine in it," he said testily.

"'Drinking wine on top of scotch / Will a detective's thinking botch,'" I said. "They taught us that jingle when I was at the detective academy."

"You didn't go—"

"To a detective academy," I said when he stopped in midsentence. "I don't mind you looking me up—I tried to do the same to you, but your history is, of course, harder to penetrate. What you really did in Afghanistan, for instance. That's all deeply buried behind DoD fire-breathing dragons."

"Every teenage hacker can break into the Pentagon computers, so I don't think there's anything too secret there."

"If only I were a teenager. Maybe then I could find out what you're really doing in Lawrence. You weren't lecturing to the ROTC kids this morning, and there's no Marlon Pinsen enrolled at the university. Or on Facebook. I know he's a real person because I shook his hand and he called me 'ma'am' in that endearing way you army guys have, but I don't think 'Marlon Pinsen' is the name his mama calls him."

"Hmm." Baggetto poured wine into one of the coffee mugs on the desk and sniffed it. "It smells good. Sure you don't want some? No? I don't know what his mother calls him, but you're right, I wasn't lecturing on the hill. I don't know why I lied to you."

"Embarrassment over speaking the truth is sometimes the reason. Or hiding criminal activity—I find that often in my work."

My feet, my hips, my tibias—every bone from pelvis to toe ached.

I pulled my knees up so I could sit cross-legged and began massaging the balls of my feet. Baggetto looked and then made a determined effort to look away, busying himself with cutting the pizza. Peppy, who'd been lying flat next to me, got up to stare longingly at him. I called her to me.

"We don't beg, remember? Especially not from strangers who might feed us scopolamine."

Baggetto laughed, put a slice on a napkin, and handed it to me across the dog. "Embarrassment or criminal—those the only two choices? How about hunting in the dark and not knowing what I might trip over?"

"Is AKA Marlon hunting with you?" I asked.

Baggetto took a long time to reply, eating, wiping his fingers, pouring another mug of wine. "He's at the General Staff College in Fort Leavenworth, forty miles up the road, one of their young computer hotshots. He was assigned to work with me."

"On?"

"The silo. What were you doing there this morning?"

"I could lie or stonewall, since that's the name of tonight's game, but I was there out of simple curiosity. The investigation that brought me to Lawrence is exactly what I told you when I met you at Fort Riley a week ago. Emerald Ferring lived with Doris McKinnon when she was growing up and as a university student. She and August Veriden visited Ms. McKinnon, presumably spent at least one night with her—I'm sure your buddy Gisborne has told you that much. I was curious about her land. The air force commandeered eighteen acres from her.

"Various people have told me that the land is contaminated, too radioactive to farm, so I was especially curious about her property lines and whether Sea-2-Sea was farming on land that was contaminated. Your turn."

"You aren't eating. Are you a vegan?"

The slice of pizza was oozing cheese and red sauce through the flimsy napkin. I unfolded my legs and found a plate to put it on, wiped up the tabletop. "I know it's heresy for a Chicagoan, but I don't like deep dish. My mother was from Umbria. Thin crust, minimalist toppings. It's still your turn to explain why you showed up there right after the sheriff arrived. Give me a more entertaining story than a friend of a commanding officer's second cousin knew you were in the area."

"That part is true," Baggetto said. "Before Sea-2-Sea bought the land from the air force, they had it tested. Their crew didn't turn up any traces of radioactivity. That should have been the end of the story, but you know how it is—people talk. Bram Roswell got worried: if people started thinking that Sea-2-Sea was selling radioactive crops, the company could go toes-up.

"Roswell called the air force, who did a more thorough inspection, going through the silo inch by inch. They found a cylinder with spent fuel rods in it. Do not ask me what that was doing at an abandoned missile base. It didn't belong there to begin with: nukes aren't like reactors—they're not actively generating power, they don't require fuel rods. Dumping the rods there looked like malicious vandalism by someone who had access to a nuclear facility, either weapons manufacture or a power plant. Before we could analyze them to see where the rods came from, the cylinder disappeared. We're terrified, frankly."

"Disappeared from where?" I asked. "Surely the air force's technical experts didn't leave the cylinder lying where they found it."

Baggetto rubbed his neck, buying time: debating how much truth to reveal or what lie to tell.

"They found it on the base. They thought they could leave it inside the silo, which is essentially impregnable without a crane and three different keys. You know. You tried the door when you were there this morning."

"Without your special knowledge of the number of keys it would take to open," I said. "But back to the rods—they're spent, so why are they dangerous?"

"Oh, that." He made an impatient gesture—even though he

knew nothing about nukes, that was apparently a primitive level of knowledge that even kindergartners possess. "Spent rods are still radioactive. They don't generate enough power to build a big bomb or run a plant, but you could do a lot of damage with them. Just look at Fukushima."

"So you're here to find out who walked off with the rods?" I asked.

"My goal is twofold: to find the cylinder and to keep it quiet so we don't start a public panic," he warned.

"Okay, I won't put it on Facebook. I'll just get a Geiger counter for my next trip to McKinnon's farm."

"It's not a joke." His frown was formidable: forceful officer with a lot of military power to back him up.

"I don't think it is, Colonel, but I'd love to know if it's true. What does Dr. Kiel have to do with it, for instance? I thought he was a cell biologist, not a physicist."

"Love to know if it's true? I'm talking to you in confidence about matters of national security."

I studied my fingers. All this outdoor work was wreaking havoc with my nails. I'd noticed a half-dozen beauty spas downtown—maybe I should take a couple of hours off for a manicure in the morning.

"Are you listening to me?" His tone was somewhere between angry and petulant.

"Colonel, I'm a stranger in a strange land. I'm alone, except for my dog. You have a sheriff, a major scientist, an intelligence officer from some fancy army college, and the whole First Infantry if you need them. I'm listening to you, but that doesn't mean you're telling the truth. Back to Dr. Kiel, the non-physicist."

He eyed me narrowly but decided not to push back. "We talked to Kiel because he had a lot of involvement at the site during a big protest back in '83."

"Yes, I know about that. Not his involvement, but the protest. His daughter was there."

"We hoped he could give us a list of names of people to talk to who might have carried a grudge against the military all this time. He's a fierce guy, reminds me of one of my own colonels when I was at the Point, didn't have any use for sloppy thinkers or people who were late to anything. Parade, class, handing in assignments, even mess."

I turned it over in my mind. It could be true, but how could I possibly find out?

"I'm telling you this because you're talking to a lot of people, and some of them are people I wouldn't think of talking to, like that African-American lady you met yesterday, the one who went to the hospital."

I smiled sourly. "You *have* been doing a thorough job on me. When I get my Geiger counter, I'll be able to tell you if the rods are in her home."

He ignored the levity—and the sourness. "We can't help thinking the McKinnon woman's murder is tied to the rods. She was upset that the air force sold the land to Sea-2-Sea instead of back to her. She talked to her lawyer about it, but it was legal. Maybe not moral, but legal. And then Emerald Ferring, who took an active part in that '83 protest, she showed up, along with the youth. McKinnon wouldn't be strong enough to heft that cylinder, but the kid—young man—could have done it."

I leaned back in my chair, eyes shut, putting the narrative in order in my mind. "Someone ransacked August Veriden's home and place of work up in Chicago, but they seemed to be looking for something small. How big was this cylinder?"

Baggetto pulled out his phone and showed me a photograph. "The cylinder looks like this. If you see it, please don't open it or try to move it. Just call me."

I shook my head. "It looks kind of like the coffeepot they had on the counter at Riverside Church when I was there yesterday afternoon."

"Why do you turn everything I say into a joke?" Baggetto demanded, his parade-ground voice back. Private Warshawski, a hundred push-ups in the sun.

I pulled out my laptop and typed in a few search questions. When I'd finished, I showed the page to him. "Spent rods take up way more space than a coffee urn. What is this really?" I tapped on his phone screen.

He shook his head, his mouth a thin line. "You're showing your ignorance. One set of rods is only about three to four feet high. This is a container holding a couple of spent rods. It's vandalism or incipient terrorism, but it is not a joke."

"I'll just text the picture to my—"

He snatched the phone from me. "No. This is a top-secret item, and I don't want to find it out on Facebook."

I squinted at him. "I'm sure photos like this are all over the Web, unless there's some kind of code hidden in it that you're afraid I'll find."

Baggetto stood. "The stakes are very high, Warshawski. We'd like to believe that the cylinder is still in Douglas County, and we'd like to think you care enough about national security to help, not hinder us."

"Of course, Colonel." I stood as well. "I will do my very best."

He walked out, leaving the pizza carton and the half-drunk bottle of wine on the desk. Of course, at Fort Riley he had Captain Arrieta to clean up his mess. I poured the wine down the sink and took the remaining three slices of pizza out to the garbage.

Peppy followed me, looking wistfully at the vanishing pizza.

"It's okay. We'll go over to the organic grocery and get something tasty, like barbecue-flavored tofu, for supper."

Peppy curled her lip at me but jumped into the backseat.

31

ORIGIN STORIES

I WAS WANDERING GLOOMILY through the store, trying to summon enthusiasm for steamed broccolini with fish cakes, when Cady Perec called.

"Can I talk to you?"

I stopped in front of organic Cajun salmon with whipped organic sweet potatoes. "Sure. I don't have anything specific scheduled for tomorrow." Unless the sheriff or the army decided to detain me, of course.

"I know it's late, but I kind of meant tonight."

"I'm really beat, Cady, and I haven't had dinner yet."

"Oh, my goodness, I'm so sorry. Gram roasted a chicken—I'll bring you leftovers."

The fish cakes looked dried out and the broccolini limp, but was homemade chicken enough of a compensation for a late-night meeting? Still, I gave Cady the B and B address and bought a bottle of valpolicella.

Cady pulled up just as Peppy and I were getting out of the car. She bent to fondle the dog's ears, apologizing again for the lateness.

"It's Gram," she said, handing me a foil pan: chicken, green beans, and a salad.

I made encouraging noises while I poured wine and started eating. The green beans were as limp as the store's broccolini, but the chicken was good and the salad crisp.

"She was pretty witchy last night. She kept making sharp remarks about me not knowing when to keep my big mouth shut, and finally, tonight, I forced her to tell me what had her so wound up. She says you came around and said terrible, really hateful things and that it was my fault for letting you into the private part of our lives."

She blinked to hide her tears, fishing in her blazer pockets for a tissue. I handed her the box from the bedside table.

"What did you say to her?" Cady sniffled.

"We talked about Sonia Kiel."

I tried to reconstruct the conversation: so much had happened since I'd seen Gertrude Perec that I had a hard time remembering what we'd said. Sonia, her phantom lover, and yes.

"Every time I ask questions about your mother, or Sonia, or the graduate student who Dr. Kiel says ruined his experiment, people start barking at me. Not just your grandmother."

"But what did you say to Gram?" Cady insisted.

"I wanted to know more about Matt Chastain—he was Kiel's graduate student—he's the one Sonia had the crush on, the one she thinks died. I figured since your grandmother had worked for Dr. Kiel, she'd know about Chastain."

"She says you said something cruel," Cady said. "I need to know what it was."

I shook my head helplessly. "Cady, I wondered if Matt might have been your father. I don't know what made me say it to her, just that he was there, Jenny—your mother—was there, and then Matt disappeared. They might easily have met—your grandmother was Dr. Kiel's secretary and I imagine your mother going to Kiel's lab to see your granny."

She swallowed her mug of wine in a single gulp. "Ugh. That's strong."

I ate more of the chicken, sipped the wine, waited.

"Sonia," Cady said. "She used to babysit me, can you believe that? Why they tortured her, not to mention me, by making her do it, I have no idea. She used to go on about my mom, how she saw her with Matt at the Diamond Duck—that doesn't exist anymore. It used to be a bar on Massachusetts Street.

"'He looked *miserable,'* she'd say, '*trapped.* You could tell he didn't want to be with her, but he had such exquisite good manners, he wouldn't tell her to go away.' Finally, one day when I was about six or seven, Gram overheard her and told her never to come back. I asked who Sonia was talking about, and she said Sonia couldn't tell truth from imagination if it hit her with a two-by-four and Gram should never have let Dr. Kiel push her into hiring Sonia. I guess Sonia couldn't hold down any kind of job, and the Kiels wanted her out of the house.

"Of course, my whole life I've wondered. But whenever I'd ask Gram, she'd shut me up—pretty much like she was hitting *me* with a two-by-four. Well, you saw her the other night."

She poured herself another splash of wine. "'Why you would want the most incompetent student who ever walked into Dr. Kiel's lab to be your father is beyond me.' Then I'd ask who it really was and she'd say, 'I don't know, punkin,' and that would be the end of it. I wish you had real proof. Or do you, and you're just not telling me, like every other goddamn person in Lawrence old enough to know?"

"I really don't know," I said gently. "Unless we can find his DNA, or his family, or something about him, I don't think you'll ever prove it either."

Cady's mouth twisted in a guilty smile. "When I was a teenager, I snuck into the microbiology department office—Gram was still working for Dr. Kiel, and I'd sometimes go up there after school. Anyway, she was off doing something, so I went and looked at the microbiology-student files. I wanted to find Matt Chastain's home address. I had this plan where I was going to borrow the car and drive to wherever his family lived."

She blushed. "I saw the whole scene, me interrupting the family at dinner. 'Where's my daddy?' I'd cry, and then, while they were all flabbergasted, I'd announce who I was. I've never told this to a single soul, not even my best friends, because it sounds so crazy, something Sonia Kiel would do, not sober, reliable Cady Perec."

She laughed with embarrassment and turned her head aside.

"I take it you never went?" I asked.

"There wasn't any record of him," she said. "All the graduate-student files were there, people who I knew had been students even before him, but not one word about Matt Chastain. Then I began to wonder if he'd ever even existed. Maybe Dr. Kiel made him up to cover for a mistake he'd made himself."

I was as bewildered as Cady, but I shook my head. "Although Sonia could have imagined a lot of different things emotionally, she *saw* him with your mother. Whatever she imagined Chastain saying to your mom is a fantasy, but not his existence. Maybe he wasn't a student, though, maybe a lab tech or something."

"I don't think so. There'd have been some file on him, whether he was staff or student."

I couldn't fit a narrative over it. Whatever Chastain had done had been so outrageous that he had to be put down the memory hole. And that had happened long before Emerald Ferring and August Veriden—and I—showed up and rattled everyone.

"Tell me more about your mother's death," I said.

"I can't—I wasn't there."

"Tell me what you've been told about it."

Kansas, August 1983

It's always hot in Kansas in August, temperatures climbing to three digits, humidity high. The wheat harvest came in two months ago, but the corn was as high as an elephant's eye, the tasseling silky cream, everything as it should be, more or less.

Doris was doing her third alfalfa mowing for the season. She took the tractor down to the southeast edge of her land, where the missile silo dug an ugly gouge in the field.

She hated weapons of every kind, nukes most of all. Her older brother had served with the Army of Occupation in Japan after the Second World War. He'd written about the cancers the children had, the deformities of babies born in the fallout regions around Hiroshima and Nagasaki, and then he'd died of leukemia himself. Of course she'd said yes when Jenny Perec and the others had come and asked if they could camp out next to the silo.

Jenny was pregnant. Lucinda Ferring noticed it right away, even though she wasn't showing. "It's in the face, Dorrie," Lucinda had told her.

"Don't tell my mom," Jenny begged when Doris went to talk to her about it: she didn't want Jenny going into labor out here in a tent, miles from any medical help. "She's already having ten fits, me out here with the hippies."

The baby came a little after the big July 4 protest. One of the protesters was a nurse-midwife; the delivery went uneventfully. "I'm naming her Cady for Elizabeth Cady Stanton. She's going to grow up to be a strong woman, just look at her."

Jenny insisted on staying on the land, even after most of the other protesters went home. "My baby is going to grow up knowing she helped keep all the world's children safe from nuclear war."

Oh, Jenny, precious young idealist. Lucinda had driven her into town for postpartum medical care, and to show little Cady to her grandmother. Gertrude tried to keep the baby—it wasn't safe for a child to be camping out right next to a military installation—but Lucinda reswaddled her and helped Jenny back to the car.

That morning Doris had brought a care package with her on the tractor, as she did once or twice a week. Cheese for Jenny, who was nursing, fruit, things that wouldn't go bad without a refrigerator.

This morning she saw the signs posted on her land without word one to her about putting them up or what was going on. DANGER: HIGHLY TOXIC, HAZARDOUS WASTE, KEEP OUT. Skulls and crossbones, the familiar radiation-hazard trefoil. She jumped down from the tractor and ran to the side of the silo where the tents had been. They were still there, but as Doris opened the flaps, she saw they'd been abandoned, including Jenny's.

She marched to the silo's front gate and confronted the soldier standing guard. "Who posted these notices on my land? When did they go up?"

The soldier couldn't or wouldn't answer, but he did summon someone with more authority. "Routine tests, ma'am, confirmed a hazard here. I'm sorry you weren't notified. We were so concerned with getting the demonstrators out of harm's way that we forgot to let you know. I'll make sure Major Schreiber comes to see you as soon as he returns to the base. Just don't try to pick any crops inside the posted area."

She'd fought and railed and called them names: "pick crops," as if alfalfa were apples growing on trees? They were condescending, they were ignorant.

"Yes, ma'am," the junior officer said. "I'll make sure Major Schreiber comes to see you."

It was Lucinda who found Cady. When she came home from work that afternoon, home from injecting some bug into Dr. Kiel's mice, and Doris told her what had happened, she drove down to the silo herself.

"I heard the baby. She was tucked under a sleeping bag, dehydrated and worn out, poor little mite. Best get her to a doctor and try to find what's happened to Jenny."

After that, everything blurred together in Doris's mind. When they got to the car, Lucinda came over faint, a chill, she said, she'd be fine, just needed some water after running around in the hot sun. Doris drove Cady to the hospital, and while they were checking her into the pediatric unit, Lucinda fainted. She was dead by morning. Doris never left her side, lying next to her in the bed as she shivered and sweated her life away in the ICU.

"Did you see the cans, Dorrie?" she muttered once through her cracked lips. "Cans behind tents."

Sometime in the middle of the night, Dr. Kiel had looked in. He'd been distraught, a surprise, since he didn't seem like the kind of man to care about his technician. When the nurses took Lucinda out of Doris's arms, they gave Doris an injection, told her to come back at once if she started feeling sick, come back in a week for a recheck.

Doris hadn't bothered. What difference would it make? She didn't want to put one foot in front of another on a morning where Lucinda wasn't next to her in bed, waiting for her morning coffee. *You're up with the birds, farm girl. You can pamper me in the mornings. I'll take care of you at night.*

Sometime in that hard first week alone, alone except for Emerald coming back for the funeral, Doris had heard that Jenny Perec was dead. She'd driven off the road, off K-10 where it crossed the Wakarusa and landed in the river. People said she'd remembered she'd run away without her baby and was making a U-turn, going back to find Cady, and lost control of the car. And then the fire burned down the hippie tents. Probably set by Major Schreiber; he'd seemed like that kind of bully.

Doris didn't believe in Jesus or heaven or any of those things. Lucinda was ambivalent, but she went into town to worship at St. Silas most Sundays—the music refreshed her spirit even if the pastor was a narrow-minded old fool.

Doris had wanted cremation, to spread the ashes over the garden where they'd sat on summer evenings smelling the honeysuckle, but Emerald was Lucinda's daughter. She wanted a proper burial for her mother, and the daughter's wishes trump a friend's, every time. They did the whole thing, Doris in a hat that Emerald had chosen for her, the choir singing Lucinda's favorite hymns, "Take My Hand, Precious Lord" and "Amazing Grace," the pastor preaching about Jesus and how our sister was in his arms, in glory, today.

Doris thought life was like a high-speed train where you kept leaving friends and brothers and lovers at stations along the route.

Maybe when you died, you walked back down the tracks until you met each of the people you'd lost. You collected them all, brother Logan, mother, father, Lucinda, and you got to find a quiet garden where you sat and watched the sun go down, the huge red-gold Kansas sun sinking behind the waves of wheat, while you sipped a little bit of a martini that your beloved had mixed for you.

32

CARRYING THE CAN

THAT'S ALL I know," Cady said. "Doris was the only person who would ever talk about my mom, but she never paid attention to who my father might have been. Lucinda might have known if it was one of Dr. Kiel's students, Doris would say, but it wasn't something they talked about."

"I see," I said, a meaningless phrase, because I saw nothing.

I wondered how Doris McKinnon ever found a market for her crops if they came from soil contaminated with radioactivity. At the same time, I couldn't help wondering if the air force invented the contamination just to drive the remnants of the demonstrators away from the silo. Mid-August in 1983, people's attention had waned; there hadn't been any action since the Independence Day protest. The air force's action hadn't generated additional protests, at least not any covered by the *Douglas County Herald* or the *Journal-World*.

Dr. Kiel's arriving at the hospital in the middle of the night to look in at his technician, that was a surprise as well. Of course, thirty-five years ago he might have been a more active, engaged person than he was today. But why had he claimed not to remember the Ferrings? Protective amnesia? Maybe all the Kiels were given to high drama.

"How could my mother have forgotten me?" Cady was weeping openly now. "I would have died if Lucinda hadn't found me, you know. How could a woman race away from toxic dangers and leave her own baby to die?"

I shifted unhappily in my chair but tried to find a reassuring strand to follow. "The memories that Doris gave you tell me your mother was a lively and vibrant woman who loved you deeply. She wouldn't have left you if something hadn't gone badly wrong with her. Perhaps the air force released some dangerous gas that poisoned your mother. Something like that could have impaired her mind and judgment. She might have had chemicals on her body and didn't dare touch you for fear of injuring you, so she tucked you underneath the sleeping bag to protect you."

Cady brightened. "I never thought of that. Maybe she put me under the sleeping bag to save me and went to try to get help. Doris used to say the six weeks she was alive with me, she bragged to everyone how I was going to grow up to save the world. What would she think if she knew all I was doing was teaching social studies to twelve-year-olds?"

"She'd think you were saving the world. She'd know you were raising many children to think clearly about the serious issues we all face on this planet."

I leaned over to squeeze her hand, knocking the plate of chicken off my lap. Peppy bounded over: Cleanup in Aisle Five? I'm here, ready for work. This made us both laugh, breaking the tension. Cady squatted on the floor to help me pry chicken bones out of the dog's mouth.

When we'd gotten the mess cleared up and Peppy was sulking in the bathroom, I pulled out my maps and asked Cady to show me where her mother had gone off the road.

"This is another thing that doesn't make any sense," Cady said. "See, she was on the old highway, which is maybe a half mile north of K-10, the one you probably drove today when you went out to the silo. They'd just opened the new K-10, so I guess if she was panicking, she didn't think to go the extra distance."

Cady pointed to the Kanwaka silo, five miles east of town, and

Old K-10, which ran close to it. "But she was going east. If she thought she needed help, she should have driven the other way, back to Lawrence, to Gram or a hospital or something. Maybe you're right, maybe she had some kind of brain damage or a seizure and didn't know where she was or where she was going."

I imagined Jenny covered with chemical burns, racing to the river to bathe herself head to toe, so maddened by pain that it didn't occur to her to drive to Doris's house. Or she'd been running after her lover who'd run off without her. I could see that, too, but that vision I kept to myself.

The Wakarusa was a small stream, a tributary from the big Kansas River—the Kaw, Cady told me to call it.

"Only strangers and Google Maps call it the 'Kansas River,'" she explained. "When I was in my teens and trying to get at the truth—or at least more information than I can ever pry out of anyone in Lawrence, including my own grandmother—I went and asked the sheriff if I could see the file on my mom's death."

"Gisborne?" I asked.

"No, he was a deputy back then, when it was only a part-time job. He also sold insurance for the Reingold Agency. It was another deputy, a guy who knew my mom when they were in high school. Probably he had a crush on her. He went down to the basement where they store the old files and found the report on my mom. They had photos of the skid marks and a picture of her car, nose down, with water all the way over the top of the steering wheel. The Wakarusa looks small on the map, but it's big enough to drown in. You go look at it, you'll see."

"Did you get a copy of the report?" I asked. "I'd like to see the photos."

Cady hunched a shoulder. "Sure, yeah, I guess, but you know it was almost thirty-five years ago, so there isn't going to be any trace. That deputy, he copied the whole file for me. Then, when I got my own computer, one I wasn't sharing with Gram, I scanned it all into my machine. I don't know why. Every year on my birthday, I look at my mom's hair, floating over the steering wheel. If she'd taken me with her, maybe the picture would show me floating next to her."

"Send it to me, okay? The report and the photos and everything."

Cady collected her handbag and jacket, found her car keys on the floor under the desk. "Vic, I really appreciate your taking the time tonight. I feel better about my mom, my birth—everything—than I ever did before. You're so . . . so *sensible.* You don't jump on the first wild pony of an idea that gallops past you. Thank you."

"Sensible" wasn't a romantic word. Solid, sensible V.I.? I've been called worse, though.

"The cans that Doris mentioned, the ones Lucinda claimed she saw—did she ever say anything about them? Had she gone back to look for them?"

Cady shook her head. "I don't even know why I remember it, except it's a weird thing to say when you're dying. Why?"

"Just wondering."

I walked out with her so that Peppy could relieve herself one last time. The canister holding spent rods that Baggetto said he was looking for. The container that Doris had found when she was digging in the field. The cans that Lucinda saw lying around. Hard to believe they weren't all the same. Maybe there really was radiation poisoning out by the silo. Maybe that's what had killed Lucinda as well as Jenny Perec.

"Cady, I found photos that August Veriden took of Doris McKinnon digging in a field." I was startled to hear myself blurt this out.

Cady stopped in midstride and turned to face me. "August who? Oh, that black guy you're looking for along with Emerald Ferring. Right. What field? When was this?"

I explained as much as I knew. "I have to believe it's the field adjacent to the silo, the one Doris was forced to sell after your mother died, when the air force found such high levels of radioactivity in it. That's also the place where your mother and her friends camped out all those years ago. I want to inspect it, but I might need help."

Her teeth flashed white in the dark. "The Cady Perec Memorial Birthplace: I know it well. I can show you just where to look."

"They've built sophisticated security into the fences," I warned her. "If you come with me, it could mean you'd have to find some other way to save the world when you get out of prison. I'll take a look in the morning and see what we might need to bypass it. Of course, if they've buried cameras in their sorghum stubble, we're out of luck."

Cady laughed, then turned impulsively to hug me before getting into her car. I called to Peppy and walked slowly back into our rented room, feeling better myself for Cady's friendship.

I climbed into bed and started going through my photo album to look at pictures of the people I was missing. Sal, with her head thrown back, laughing, her four-inch feather earrings brushing her shoulders. Lotty, deep in conversation with Max. Mr. Contreras at the lake with Mitch and Peppy. Even Bernie, skates on, a look of ferocious concentration on her face.

And Jake. Playing onstage at Ravinia, at Symphony Center in the Logan Center for the Arts. In my apartment, his face alight with music and the joy of connecting to me through it.

Jake wasn't a coward or a grudge holder. If he wanted to break up with me, he'd tell me directly, not play a cruel game of silence. If he was out of touch, I was guessing he'd done something he was ashamed to report—sleeping with another woman came to mind first. It was a hurt but not a disaster.

I took a deep breath and tried to put Jake not out of my mind—I couldn't—but in a corner where that little wound beneath the diaphragm wouldn't keep me from working.

I came to the pictures I'd been taking since arriving in Kansas: Peppy running freely in the Flint Hills our first morning here. Had that been only last week? It felt like a lifetime ago. The copse at Fort Riley where the quarters for Negro soldiers used to stand. And on to Lawrence.

I had forgotten the pictures I'd taken at the Lion's Pride when

I was waiting for an ambulance to collect Sonia Kiel. I stopped to look at her, poor little bundle of rags under the iron staircase, and then at the frames of Naomi, the college student, comatose on the concrete stairs, her pink cami straps slipping from her shoulders.

I'd photographed a trio of young men who'd been gawking and making crude jokes about Naomi, taken a couple of shots of them emptying their little bags in the gutter when the cops arrived. I wondered now if their stash had included the roofies that knocked out Naomi and Sonia, but of course those pills would be long gone.

I was about to move forward to the pictures I'd taken at Riverside and St. Silas Churches when a face behind the trio of punks jumped out at me. It wasn't quite in focus, an observer behind them in the street who'd faded from sight when the EMTs showed up.

That was why I'd thought I'd met Marlon Pinsen when I met him at the hotel last night. First introduced to me as a student cadet up on the Hill, identity changed tonight by Colonel Baggetto to computer hotshot at the army college in Fort Leavenworth.

I put his name into every database I subscribe to, but none of them had ever heard of him.

33

PICKING THROUGH THE BONES

I CAME FULLY AWAKE, heart pounding. Someone was in the room, bumping into the furniture. I rolled off the bed onto the floor, fumbled until I found my phone on the nightstand. I crawled to the outside door, stuck up a hand to undo the chain lock, and yanked it open, backing outside before switching on my phone flashlight.

My light discovered Peppy, whose head was stuck underneath the low-hanging drawers of the corner desk. She inched out and looked at me sheepishly.

"Dog, what on earth? It's two-thirty in the morning."

I got to my feet, my teeth chattering as my muscles relaxed: I was nearly naked, and it was cold outside. I locked the door again and turned on a lamp before investigating the space where Peppy had been scrabbling. I shone my flash under the space where the drawers ended. One of the chicken bones that I'd dropped earlier had landed there.

"You are a merciless hunter, aren't you?" I said severely.

Peppy's eyes were bright; she started licking my face, delighted that I was helping her. I pushed her aside, lying on my back so I could stick my arm all the way underneath.

That was when I saw a tiny metal circle underneath the desktop. It was about the size and shape of those silvery gadgets that come in sewing kits to help you thread a needle, but this one had an orange circle in the middle and a minute piece of wire where the threading arm would be. I started to reach my free hand up for it, then lay back down.

Colonel Baggetto had been sitting at this desk eating his pizza. No wonder he'd been happy to talk to me in my room instead of at a restaurant. Of course, a guy with his skills could have broken in anytime, planted any number of devices in the room, but the homeowner might have come in on him, wondering why a stranger was in her house. So much easier to do it while asking if I was a vegan.

Peppy gave a short, angry bark: Was I going to get that chicken bone or not? I pulled it out and got to my feet but annoyed her no end by taking it outside to the trash—this time with a jacket over my nightshirt.

"You deserve a special reward, my mighty huntress," I said while we were still outside, out of mike range—I hoped. "Just not that bone."

Back inside I gave her some peanut butter, then cleaned chicken grease and floor dust from my arms and went back to bed. The mike made me feel vulnerable, overexposed, but I wanted to leave it in place. Better Baggetto not know I'd discovered it.

To my surprise I slept soundly, despite the ear underneath the desk. I should ask Baggetto if I snored. None of my lovers has ever complained, but chivalry might have been trumping annoyance. In the morning I put my iPad on the desktop and tuned in to WFMT radio in Chicago, high volume, while I did a full workout. Baggetto and his sidekick, AKA Marlon, deserved a chance to listen to Haydn.

I wondered if I had malware on my phone, perhaps in my computer and iPad as well. It would be prudent to assume the worst, which would mean Baggetto and his army computer sidekick had access to all my case notes, including the photos August had taken. Which meant anything new I learned, I needed to write by hand. They say writing by hand makes the brain expand, so this was a good thing. I should send the colonel a thank-you note—handwritten, of course.

I sat cross-legged on the floor, eyes shut, trying to remember last night's conversation with Cady Perec. We were inside when we discussed whether something like a radioactive gas leak had made her mother roar off without her. It wasn't until we were outside that we'd talked about trying to get into the Sea-2-Sea field. We were safe, sort of.

I'd go for a run, drop Peppy off at Free State Dogs, then leave a note for Cady at the junior high, giving her a burner phone number to text or call. I was pulling on my sweats when my phone rang, a local number, not one I recognized.

I wasn't sure how sensitive Baggetto's mike was, whether it could pick up voices on incoming calls. I took the phone into the bathroom and sat next to the shower with the water running. Of course, if there *was* malware on the phone, what difference did it make?

"Is this Detective Warshawski? It's Sandy Heinz at the hospital. I'm the ICU ward head you spoke to on Wednesday."

"Sonia Kiel." I turned off the water.

"She's regained consciousness. I don't know how much she can talk or tell you, but you can have a few minutes with her this morning."

"Does her family know?" I asked.

"Dr. Cordley—she's the attending, you may recall—phoned Dr. and Mrs. Kiel, but I don't think she spoke to them: I heard her leaving a message for them to call her."

"Ms. Heinz, as my investigation has progressed, I think it's possible someone deliberately harmed Sonia, hoping to kill her. I'll get to the hospital as soon as I can—in half an hour anyway—but can you make sure you or another nurse is with her if anyone comes to see her? Anyone besides me or Sergeant Everard?"

"Detective, the only person trying to hurt Sonia Kiel is Sonia Kiel herself, but we have a duty to her care. No one can harm her in the ICU."

From your lips to the NSA's ears, but that I said to myself. No point wasting time arguing, especially when it could get me labeled as a nutjob who shouldn't be allowed near a patient. I pulled off my sweats and dressed in jeans and my good jacket. My Italian dress boots, with a change of shoes, two pairs of socks, and my windbreaker for the car. And a change of shirt. A water bottle. Gun with an extra clip, which I locked in the trunk. Yes, today was going to be full of fun.

I didn't want to leave Peppy alone, in a car or in the B and B, so I took the time to drive over to Free State Dogs before heading into the heart of the downtown.

If Baggetto had bugged my room, chances were he was tracking my car. I parked in the library lot again and stuffed my phone and other electronics in my foil-wrapped day pack. "Tin-Butt" Warshawski, that's what my South Chicago classmates would be calling me.

One of the town parks was behind the library. I walked through it, slow pace, looking for cars that were dawdling, for bicyclists, anyone on foot. It was morning rush hour, and even a small town has a lot of rush-hour traffic, so it was hard to be a hundred-percent sure I was clean, but no one was on foot, and I didn't think I saw any Buick Enclaves, at least not twice.

When I got to the nurses' station at the ICU, a young woman at the counter texted Nurse Heinz for me. The charge nurse appeared a moment later and escorted me into the back.

Heinz paused outside the door to the unit. "Do you really think her life is in danger? It sounds extremely dramatic, like the kind of thing Sonia would make up, not something that could actually happen."

"You know her personally?" I asked.

"We were in high school together. She didn't have friends, so she'd say anything to get attention. And it was always something made up—about the Russian spies her father was outwitting or the lover who died a tragic death trying to reach her through a fire."

"I've never talked to her when she's been awake, so I don't think she's infected me with melodrama. A week or maybe ten days ago, Sonia was out in the country and encountered Doris McKinnon."

"Who's she?"

"A farmer, around ninety, who was murdered soon after Sonia saw her. Yesterday McKinnon's body disappeared from the state's morgue before the pathologist could perform an autopsy. It was all over the local news."

"I see so many hard things in here that I keep away from real life when I'm off duty," Heinz said.

"Who can blame you?" I said. "But here's what has me worried: Last night I was reexamining the pictures I took outside the bar where I found Sonia. I hadn't looked at them before, but I recognized someone in the background, a guy who supposedly is here in Lawrence from some army college—it has a fancy name—something something staff college."

"Oh, yes," Heinz said. "Over in Fort Leavenworth."

"I don't know if he's there or not. I get a different story about him every time I ask, and I'm not sure I've even been told his real name. I was photographing a trio of guys who'd been hanging around outside where I found Sonia and the young college student, and Mr. Staff College was in the background. Did he give her roofies? Or give them to this trio to give her?"

"Or he was a drinker who happened to be at a late-night bar at the same time," Heinz said sharply. "I would think a detective like you would have enough experience to know that coincidences do happen."

I nodded. "You could be right—maybe I *am* melodramatic. I don't want to take a chance, that's all. Sonia saw something odd at Doris McKinnon's farm last week. If anyone is afraid she'll start spreading it around . . ."

"No one would believe her." Heinz smiled sourly. "Everyone in Lawrence who knows her is so used to her theatrics that they don't pay attention to her."

"But the people who don't know her . . ."

Heinz thought about it. "Maybe. However, you're the only person who's been here for her the whole time she's been unconscious.

One of her brothers has called several times, but I don't think she's on anyone's radar, for good or bad. And in any event, it's most unlikely she'll remember anything from the Lion's Pride—she was extremely drunk before she took the roofies on board."

She let me into the room. Although Sonia was breathing on her own, she had an oxygen feed attached to her nose, a heart monitor, tubes dripping saline and sugar into her arms.

When I sat next to her and lightly clasped her hand, her eyes fluttered open. "Doctor?"

Her throat was dry, her speech slurred. Heinz pointed at a carton of lemon-glycerin swabs. I took one and put it in Sonia's mouth.

"I'm a detective, Sonia. I found you last Tuesday. You called me from the Lion's Pride because you'd seen the people I was trying to find. You'd seen Emerald Ferring and August Veriden."

She sucked on the swab, her eyes closed. "Em'ral'. Show-off."

I kept my fingers around her hand, pressed lightly, didn't speak.

"People at missile, muns, muns. Em'ral' comes July Fourth, picture in papers."

Months and months, I finally translated. "Were you there for months and months?"

Her slack mouth contorted in a frown. "No, Daddy shit fit. Always wrong. Get out bed, wrong. Wrong clothes. Fat, stupid. Matt, darling dear. Dad super mad, stupid boy, what he doing?"

"Matt didn't camp at the silo, did he?" I said, voice just loud enough to carry over the machines. "He went out to visit Jenny Perec. And the baby."

"Jenny, baby, try keep Matt. No good. She died. I saw her on the cartafalque."

The effort to speak wore her out, and she drifted off. *Cartafalque?* I supposed she meant catafalque, but it was an odd image.

I sat for a time, resisting the urge to pull out my computer and answer e-mails or to look up. The hardest thing in the world, just to sit. One of the nurses came in several times to check on Sonia, but she didn't try to make me leave.

After about fifteen minutes, Sonia opened her eyes again. "Doctor?"

I gave her another lemon swab. "Detective. Two weeks ago you went out to the silo, to the place where Matt is buried. Doris McKinnon was there. You ran to her when you saw her. What happened next? Did she take you home with her?"

"Doris." Sonia frowned. "You right. Doris, black people, digging Matt grave. Wrong, wrong, wrong. Black man grabbed arms, dragged me. Like soldiers drag Jenny."

"Drag Jenny?" I asked.

"Dragged me to truck. Truck, fuck, suck, luck." She giggled disconcertingly and passed into sleep again. This time she was breathing heavily and didn't seem likely to waken soon.

I released her hand and got up, wishing there were some way to unscramble Sonia's confused neurons. Soldiers had dragged Jenny? Maybe during the 1983 protest they'd dragged Jenny away from the silo gates. August had dragged Sonia out of harm's way, into Doris's truck—that was my guess anyway. And taken her . . . back to town? To the farmhouse?

"She will be stronger tomorrow." Heinz had appeared next to the bed. "You can come back then to talk to her again."

I nodded, thanked her for letting me come in at all. Don't whine about how little Sonia said. Be grateful she's regained consciousness and can speak, I lectured myself as I followed the nurse out of the room.

When we passed through the soundproofed ICU doors, we heard sharp shouts coming from the nurses' station. Heinz hurried over, me on her heels.

"You let a detective into talk to her before her own father saw her? How dare you? How *dare* you!" The telltale vein was throbbing over Dr. Kiel's right eye, and he was pounding on the countertop.

A man of about seventy, in a white shirt and tie, was standing next to him. "Calm down, Nate. I can handle this."

"Dr. Kiel," I said loudly. "I'm V.I. Warshawski. The detective.

Who has been to see your daughter while you and Shirley sulked at home."

"And you, young lady, don't get insolent with me."

Young lady? "Or what? You'll cut off my allowance and shoot me full of lithium?"

"Stop this now! This is a hospital, not a football stadium. If either of you starts up again, I will call security and have you both escorted from the building." Heinz's voice was full of authority; Kiel and I both shut up.

"Dr. Kiel is raising a legitimate question," the white shirt said. "Sonia Kiel is his daughter and my patient. Letting a detective question her without notifying us or allowing us to be present raises questions of malpractice."

"You must be Dr. Chesnitz," I said. "I've been hearing about you. Ms. Kiel is forty-five, and unless you have a legal mandate as guardian ad litem—"

Heinz cut me off. "Dr. Kiel, you had specifically told Dr. Cordley not to involve you in questions about Sonia's care when she talked to you on Wednesday. I have those orders in writing."

Kiel turned to me. "What did Sonia say to you?" His hands were shaking, but he was making an effort not to shout.

"She says she saw Doris McKinnon on the land where Matt Chastain is buried. And she saw Emerald Ferring and August Veriden there as well. This is one of the fields around the missile silo, right?"

"Sonia is delusional," Chesnitz put in. "I would discount almost anything she said, especially now, if she's been without her medication for a week or more."

"If I could undo one thing in my life, it would be to go back to the day I agreed to let him be a student in my lab," Kiel said, the pulse still throbbing. "No. I retract that. I'd go back to the day I met Shirley Wachter and I'd turn around and walk away from her. The tinkling bells of the harlots of Zion! My grandfather warned me."

I hadn't eaten today, and his wild speech was making me feel as though I were a rudderless ship in a heavy storm. Harlots of Zion, cartafalques. Dinner at the Kiel household must have been a rage-infused flying circus.

"Dr. Kiel, could we sit down and talk, quietly? Sonia's gone back to sleep. She won't wake again for a while."

"Talk about what?" he demanded.

"What Matt Chastain did that was so terrible. And why you won't believe your daughter when she says she saw him die."

For a moment I thought he was about to explode again, but he suddenly became very still. I thought perhaps he was having a stroke. Nurse Heinz went to his side, holding his arm. Then I saw that AKA Marlon, the man from the Fort Leavenworth army college, had appeared in the ICU lobby.

34

HARD WORDS

MARLON PINSEN!" I moved across the floor to him, hands outstretched, face wreathed in smiles. "Colonel Baggetto told me about your work, and of course your secret is safe with me."

Under the bright lights in the ICU atrium, I could see that he was older than I'd thought when I met him in the hotel three nights ago. He was young, but not college young.

He stepped away from my hands, but I kept smiling. "Army Staff College. Is that why you were at the Lion's Pride on Wednesday? I've been in Lawrence less than a week, but I know that men's basketball is the beating heart of this town. Were they playing the Army Staff College and you're such a fan you had to stay for the closing festivities?"

"The Army Command and General Staff College isn't that kind of school," he said stiffly.

"Of course not," I agreed, still jovial. "It's where you design all those important classes for people like Colonel Baggetto to keep them on their toes, with up-to-the-minute strategies on how to persuade ISIS to cough up their secrets. In your spare time, you protect America's farms from invasive species."

He'd been screwing the corners of his mouth down in annoyance, but at my last sentence his expression shifted. I couldn't quite decipher it. Alert? Worried?

"What did the colonel tell you?"

"Yes." Kiel and Chesnitz had joined us. "Just what did Baggetto say?"

"I don't think I should discuss it in an open space like this," I said, my tone provocative.

Actually, no one was paying attention to us. There were perhaps a dozen family members waiting in the atrium, along with the staff members who stopped periodically to talk to them, sympathetic hands on frightened shoulders. Life in the ICU was a constant round of intense drama; families screaming in anguish near the nurses' station probably happened so often that no one found our histrionics worth watching—except Nurse Heinz, frown lines deep between her eyes as she tried to assess whether Kiel or I was going to lose control again.

"The spent fuel rods," I whispered.

"Oh." Pinsen's face relaxed. "Yes. They've disappeared. I'm sure Dante—the colonel—told you not to touch them if you found them."

"My college library sat on top of the first nuclear chain reaction," I said. "We all knew better than to play with uranium rods."

"Good. Call the colonel at once if you come upon the canister. If you can't reach him, phone me." Pinsen pulled a card case from his jacket, extracted one, and gave it to me.

It didn't reveal anything—not a rank, not an address, just a cellphone number and an e-mail address. Maybe he had other cards with his real name, his actual organizational loyalty—CIA, NSA, NFL? I stuck it in my hip pocket.

"You were with Sonia Kiel just now," Pinsen stated. "Did she have anything interesting to contribute?"

"Depends on what you think is interesting. Her parents thought she was too fat as a teenager."

"And she's still fat," Kiel growled.

"But losing weight while she's laid up here," I said encouragingly. "How much does she need to lose before you can listen to what she's saying?"

"You've met Sonia once, but you think you understand her mind," Chesnitz said. "I've been treating her for thirty years and—"

"And we all see how much good that's done," I snapped.

"Did she talk about the missing material?" Pinsen cut off the start of a tirade from Chesnitz.

I shook my head. "She's only just regaining consciousness, and her speech is shaky. I doubt she remembers anything about the night outside the Lion's Pride. We did touch on the 1983 protest."

Kiel clenched and unclenched his right fist. "Sonia's forty, but her head is stuck at age fourteen. I need to see her. And Dr. Chesnitz will have to check on her."

"I'll discuss it with her medical team," Heinz said. "Right now the priority is building up her physical strength. We will need Ms. Kiel's consent for her to see Dr. Chesnitz. Unless, as Ms. Warshawski said, you or he is her legal guardian."

One of Heinz's nurses came to whisper something to her. Heinz nodded. "I have to leave to take care of another patient, but no one can talk to Ms. Kiel at the moment: Dr. Cordley gave her an injection of propofol a few minutes ago, and she'll be sleeping through most of the rest of the day."

Dr. Chesnitz sputtered that propofol on top of Depakote constituted dangerous misjudgment.

"Dr. Kiel, if you've changed your mind about involving yourself in your daughter's care, can you discuss it with Dr. Cordley? And of course if you wish to sit with your daughter and talk to her, it might be beneficial to her. People understand what's said to them under sedation. But you, Mr. . . . uh . . ."

"He says his name is Pinsen," I supplied helpfully.

"Because it is Pinsen," he said.

"Mr. Pinsen," Heinz said. "She can't have any people with her right now who are strangers to her."

"This detective," Pinsen began, in chorus with Chesnitz.

"This detective has visited Sonia almost every day while she's been unconscious. She also saved Sonia's life."

The head nurse swept away, back behind the soundproofed doors into the unit. Both she and the rest of her team were wearing comfortable street clothes, but you could almost hear the snap that a heavily starched uniform would have made.

I left, but the men remained near the nursing information counter. When my elevator arrived, I could see that Pinsen was talking urgently to Kiel, who continued to clench and unclench his hands. At least if he had a stroke here, he'd get instant help.

Despite my bravado with Pinsen and Chesnitz, I was feeling dizzy from the Kiel family's gyrations. There were a few cabs outside the hospital's main entrance; I got one to take me to the Hippo.

Simone was behind the bar again this morning. "Where's your emotional support?" she asked, starting to grind beans for me.

"She's receiving, not giving, this morning, alas!"

I glanced through the *Douglas County Herald* while I waited for my drink. The men's basketball team dominated the front page. Women's basketball got a couple of lines inside. The editorial page brayed happily about the recent election results but also issued a warning to the Lawrence Public Library.

> We've received numerous reports of lights showing in the library in the middle of the night. This town approved a bond issue to expand the library, but taxpayers did not give the board carte blanche to run up the electric bill.

What a lucky town, to care enough about their library to expand it when all over America, communities were closing facilities and cutting acquisitions—including in Chicago.

I drank the cortado in one swallow. Simone offered me a second, but I needed actual food now. At an upscale diner across the street, I ordered eggs, grits, and fruit. While I waited, I unloaded my computer from the cage and started checking mail.

A message from Jake led the pack.

I'm sorry I've been out of touch, but I've been angry that you would go to Kansas in response to pleas from Bernie Fouchard yet not fly to Switzerland in response to pleas from me. Perhaps you are similarly angry that I chose Switzerland over you. I can't put you ahead of my music. I try to understand that you can't put me ahead of your investigative work, but there will always be another crime to investigate; there won't always be another chance to study and perform in the heart of the early-music movement. This was a onetime opportunity. This is a conversation that would be better face-to-face, but I don't know when we will next be face-to-face. Are you still coming at Christmas? Or will crime win out? J.

The message left me feeling as though I'd been kicked in the diaphragm. My food arrived, but I'd lost my appetite. I wrote back and sent the message without editing it.

I read your message in a diner in Kansas. If I'd been in Basel, I'd have been sitting alone in a café while you rehearsed. I'm not Penelope. I have my own mission on the planet. It isn't as beautiful or ennobling as music, but I also heal people's lives. I'll think about Switzerland and Christmas when I'm back in Chicago, feeling less fragile than I do here on my own. V.I.

I tried reading reports from the Streeter brothers, queries from clients, but angry, hurt tears were blurring the screen. *You want to sit in your room feeling sorry for yourself?* my mother used to say. *That's all right, then, because no one else is feeling sorry for you.*

Buck up, Warshawski, get your head back in the game. I returned grimly to my mail, sorted out what I could handle myself remotely, what I needed to offload, all the time in the back of my mind wondering if Baggetto and Pinsen were shadowing my keystrokes. Wondering if Jake was playing Lieberson's setting of Neruda to a stranger.

I called Cheviot, my forensics lab, on one of my burners. I explained my concern and asked if they could do a sweep remotely from Chicago. It wouldn't be cheap, and they needed all my passwords and access codes. I put those into a text to them on the burner and went back to work.

The biggest file in my in-box came from Cady Perec, with the sheriff's report on her mother's death. The incident report was terse:

> Responded to a call from John and Jim Pendleton, who'd gone down to the Wakarusa to fish. Boys had found the half-submerged Toyota, had seen the body inside, tried unsuccessfully to open the doors.

The boys had run the better part of a mile up the road to a filling station, where the manager let them use the phone. Responding deputies Kenneth Gisborne and Lucas Gerstenberg had called for a tow truck with a winch. Once the car was out of the water, they'd been able to pull the victim from the driver's seat. They'd recognized Jennifer, or at least Gerstenberg had—he'd gone to school with her.

I scrolled through the file looking for an autopsy report but couldn't find one. I turned to the photos, which had transmitted with surprising clarity.

The county photographer had been thorough. I looked at the skid marks, where the Toyota had gone off the road, the trail of broken bushes and crushed weeds the car created as it careered down the bank to the Wakarusa.

There were a dozen shots of the Toyota nose-down in the river. Jennifer Perec's hair floated over the steering wheel, looking like river grasses, until the deputies opened the door and lifted her out and laid her on the verge.

Her face was swollen, with what looked like bruises around the ears and cheeks. Blows from the steering wheel? Distension from her time in the water? Or perhaps my comforting suggestion to Cady last night had been accurate and her mother had been hit with some kind of chemical or radioactive gas.

I pushed my uneaten food aside and paid the bill. The Law and Justice Center was only a couple of blocks away. I walked there and put in a request at the county information counter to look at an old file; yes, I had the file number. I copied it out of my computer and handed in the form.

While I sat waiting, Deke Everard strolled past. "Warshawski! I hear you caused quite the dustup at the hospital this morning."

I lifted my jean legs to stare at my ankles. "I don't see a tracking device."

Everard grinned. "I like to show the computer jockeys that old-fashioned gossip is quicker and more reliable than sifting through a quintillion text messages. What are you doing here?"

"Someone will tell you before you get to your office," I assured him.

The clerk at the information desk called my name. Everard walked over with me and leaned an elbow on the countertop.

"What's she after, Sharene?"

"An old file that's disappeared, Deke. I'm sorry, miss. We'll put in a message to the clerical staff to hunt around for it in case it got misfiled, but for now it's just plain missing."

Everard picked up my request form. "Jenny Perec's incident report? Why do you want that, Warshawski? You keep telling me and everyone else that the only reason you came down here was to find Emerald Ferring."

"You don't need to remind me that I'm failing miserably," I said. "So I'm grasping at straws. Ms. Ferring's life intersects with the Perec family in a lot of places. Did you know it was Ferring's mother who found Cady Perec, saved her life?"

"Before my time. Do you think looking at Jenny Perec's death certificate will tell you where to find Emerald Ferring?"

"Stranger things have happened. What I really wanted to see was the autopsy report. And I wouldn't mind knowing what Sheriff Gisborne found in the car when he pulled it out."

"Mud, that's what." Gisborne had appeared in the room: someone must have told him I was here, looking for the file. "Mud and stink. No one goes through a car that's been in the water, Warshawski."

"Not even to find any valuables? Or a hint as to who Cady Perec's father was?"

We were starting to draw a crowd. The foreign detective who attracted death like a blowfly was confronting the sheriff.

"You're looking for Cady's father now, Warshawski? Don't you have enough to do in Chicago?"

"You told me not to leave Douglas County. I'm making hay while the sun shines."

The homely farm metaphor didn't endear me to him. "Leave the Perec family alone. If Gertrude Perec wanted to find Cady's father, she'd have started that search while the trail was still hot."

"Right, Sheriff. We all know that Gertrude doesn't want to know. Maybe doesn't want Cady to find out would be a better way of putting it. If Cady were four, her grandmother could make a case for being her spokesperson, but Cady's *thirty*-four, so she gets to choose for herself."

The sheriff looked at the deputies and clerks hovering in earshot. "Don't you people have jobs to do? Or has Warshawski cleaned up all the crime in Douglas County, making your jobs unnecessary?"

The crowd melted, although Everard continued to lean against the counter. City employee—his promotions didn't depend on the sheriff.

Gisborne started to leave as well but stopped in midstride to look back at me. "You asked what *I* found in the car. The incident report is gone, so how did you know I caught that call?"

I smiled seraphically. "It's in the air, Sheriff. Everyone keeps telling me how everyone in the county knows each other's bra size and so on. I've been here a week, and I'm already catching on."

He eyed me measuringly, as if he were picturing us in the Old West with me in a noose on a makeshift gallows.

I stopped smiling, looked at him seriously. "I actually came here in the hopes I could read the autopsy report on Jenny Perec."

"Gertrude Perec didn't want her daughter cut open. Since it was clear that Jenny had drowned, we let her bury her daughter and get on with her life."

"Thirty-four years ago, and you still remember. No wonder they keep reelecting you."

35

KNEE-DEEP IN WATER

"YOU KNOW, WARSHAWSKI, Lieutenant Lowdham was curious enough about your real mission that he called a couple of people in Chicago to ask about you." Sergeant Everard walked out the side door with me.

Sharene's face dropped as we moved out of earshot: everyone would have liked to know what the Chicago cops said about me.

"The consensus seems to be that you're honest, you get results, you're reckless. And you're a pain in the ass."

"If I die down here in Kansas, make sure they chisel that on my tombstone," I said.

"It could happen." Everard looked at me seriously. "I don't know what is keeping you here, since no one has caught a whiff of Ferring or her cameraman. But something about the land around the silo is causing Gisborne to act more like the Sheriff of Nottingham than the guy we all love to reelect every four years. Besides which, the town is crawling with strangers who pop up in places you wouldn't think they belonged."

"That would be Colonel Baggetto and his odd-job man AKA Pinsen."

"Not to mention you," Everard said. "Why do you call him AKA?"

"There's no mention of him in any database I have access to, and I have access to quite a few." I told him about Pinsen's arrival at the hospital. "He showed up so patly you'd almost think he was listening in on someone's phone—mine, for instance."

I looked directly at Everard, who flung up his hands, surrender position. "Not guilty. But don't you think you're a little paranoid? Why would he tap your phone? Maybe he was listening in on Dr. Kiel's. Or maybe Kiel called Pinsen. If they're involved in something together, Kiel would make sure Pinsen was in the loop."

"Something that includes keeping tabs on Sonia? I don't buy it. What is Kiel's role in all this?"

Everard shrugged. "I don't see any role for him at all, except for maybe his daughter stumbling into the middle of the picture."

His lapel phone rang; I could hear a woman's scratchy voice on the other end.

"They need me to do my real job, not bird-dog you." He grinned. "The dispatcher's actual words. Before I go hunting some house-breakers, you want to tell me how you knew that Gisborne caught the call when Jenny Perec drowned?"

I studied him thoughtfully: trustable or a skilled cop knowing how to run a con? "Cady Perec told me. How she knows, that you'd have to ask her yourself."

"Fair enough." He squeezed my arm, a friendly farewell, not a warning. "Warshawski, you find yourself falling down some rabbit hole, call Officer Friendly. I don't want all the paperwork I'd have to fill out if you stopped a bullet in my jurisdiction."

I walked over to the FedEx store in a lighter mood than I would have thought possible half an hour earlier. I copied Jenny Perec's incident report onto a thumb drive and expressed it to the Cheviot lab. I printed the photos that showed the accident site itself, both the long shot, with the skid marks from Old K-10 down through the broken bushes, and the close-ups, then uploaded the pictures of Jenny's dead face in an e-mail to Lotty.

I explained who she was, the absence of an autopsy report, and asked if Lotty could show the pictures to a pathologist. *"I'd like some off-the-record speculation here. Water damage, radiation poisoning, weed killer?"*

Thanks to Jake's e-mail, I hadn't eaten breakfast. I found another diner, one where they baked their own bread in a stone oven you could see from the counter. While I ate, I made some rough calculations on the dimensions of the fifteen acres Doris McKinnon had been forced to cede and sketched those in on my county map, putting them relative to the missile silo a couple of different ways.

After homemade bean soup and four slices of bread with goat cheese, I wanted a nap. "No sleeping, Warshawski," I said sternly. "Woman up. You are now ready for whatever dangers the Kansas prairies may unleash."

The wind was blowing from the north, rain spitting in with it. It sliced through my wool jacket and knit top as if I were walking naked down the street. Maybe I wasn't ready for the prairies to unleash their fury.

When I got to the library lot, I placed some sheets of newspaper on the concrete and knelt to look under my car, taking off my good jacket and putting on my windbreaker first. The trackers that Baggetto and Pinsen had access to were so tiny they'd be hard to find. I looked under the wheel housings and inched my fingers around the exhaust system but didn't find anything except grease and mud.

Of course, that didn't really prove anything—they could have inserted an industrial tracker behind my dashboard or stuck a tiny button out of reach. I supposed I could do a serious Wolinsky and wrap my whole car in foil, but what's life without some risk?

In case they were relying on my devices to tell them my route, I put them all back in my Faraday pack. It would have to be protection enough.

I drove east once more, this time taking a side road, where it would be easier to spot a tail. Fifteenth Street went past the school where Cady Perec taught twelve-year-olds to be thoughtful citizens, then ran between two big cemeteries. Thank goodness I hadn't wasted months hunting Sonia Kiel's dead lover in an actual graveyard.

I crested a couple of hills, bumped across a set of train tracks, and was instantly in farmland again, my car bouncing along a pock-marked gravel road. I went by a place with boarded-up windows, possibly a meth house, something for Sheriff Gisborne to take care of once he'd finished looking after Sea-2-Sea's problems.

When I reached Doris McKinnon's farmhouse, I parked next to the barn, where Gisborne said they'd found the Prius and McKinnon's pickup's tire tracks. I put on my hiking boots and went inside.

A flex lamp hanging near the door held a powerful bulb; even inside the barn on a gray afternoon, I got a pretty good idea of the interior. I skirted the perimeter, not wanting to disturb the scene, if it was a crime scene, and not wanting to leave traces of my own presence.

Dust of all kinds—hay, dirt, seeds—billowed around as the wind gusted through the high open doors. I was sneezing heavily, so someone from *NCIS*, or Baggetto's entourage, definitely could pick up my DNA if they cared to swab the building. The dust made it easy to see the oil drippings and tire marks left by the pickup and the Prius; they'd been parked close to the wide door that opened onto the yard.

Two cats snarled and slunk away when I moved the light into the interior. Besides the dust, the barn was packed with old equipment. A rusty tractor, stacks of things with jagged teeth, giant rake heads. Rustling in the corners came from whatever the cats were hunting—I hoped mice, but probably rats.

I didn't see anything that looked like the canister in the photo Baggetto had shown me or the bags of dirt Doris had been digging up and tagging. Several sets of recent footprints showed where Gisborne and his team had been looking, so if Doris had left anything important, the sheriff's team would already have taken it.

I went into the house again, this time searching in a more concentrated fashion. The kitchen, which looked as though it might date to the pioneer era, had cupboards that stretched to the ceiling. I found a ladder, climbed up, discovered old glass dishes, a stash of gasoline rations from the Second World War, and what looked like a complete set of antique Delft, all thickly coated with dust.

Deep bins at the floor level might have been designed for flour when the house was built. Doris had stored boots and windbreakers in them, along with empty egg cartons. I spent an hour looking in drawers, even going to the basement, which had a dirt floor and a few snakes that were keeping warm on the hot-water heater. They stirred and lifted their heads, tongues flickering, when I turned on the lights. My guidebook to Kansas had assured me that benign snakes outnumbers the venomous five to one; the book told me to look for elliptical pupils, but I didn't want to get that close. If Doris let them live in her basement, they were surely benign, but it still took an effort to walk past them.

I finally gave up on it. I could spend weeks exploring the house and the grounds and still wonder if I was overlooking a hiding place in the outbuildings or in the fields themselves. Daylight would hold for only another hour, and I needed to look at the chunk of Doris's old land that Sea-2-Sea was farming.

I drove over to the silo, scanning the skies for surveillance drones. Twice I spotted something circling, and twice, when I pulled out my binoculars, it was a hawk riding the air currents.

I wished I had a drone myself that could survey the field to see if any of Doris's diggings remained. Instead I parked outside the silo gates and started walking through the field on Doris's side of the fence. She seemed to have been a methodical thinker: if she wanted to test for radiation levels, she would have dug up some of her own soil for comparison.

Out in the open fields, nothing blocked the north wind. My ears began to throb, and my hands turned numb, even though I jammed them deep into my jeans pockets. Periodically a burst of rain would sweep through, hitting my jacket like buckshot, but fortunately it never lingered long. My teeth chattered from cold; it was hard to conjure the hot August day when Lucinda Ferring had discovered Cady tucked under a sleeping bag in her mother's tent.

I paced McKinnon's side of the fence, keeping about six feet away to avoid any Sea-2-Sea motion detectors. Close to the eastern boundary of my sketch of McKinnon's land, I did find a hole. I squatted to study it. I had a plastic spoon and one of the plastic bags I keep on hand to clean up after Peppy. I dug up a few spoonfuls of dirt and tied a knot in the top of the bag. I counted off paces from the eastern end of the silo complex and made a note so I could find the spot again—I was hoping McKinnon had dug on the Sea-2-Sea side of the fence at the same longitude.

Next step involved taking my iPhone out of its Faraday cage to use an app that detects infrared rays. This meant revealing my location if anyone was tracking me. Maybe the bug in my room was the only surveillance they thought they needed. Maybe it wasn't even there for me—perhaps a previous tenant had been doing surveillance on an errant spouse or a disloyal dog.

If Baggetto or Gisborne *was* tracking me, though, I had about fifteen minutes before they showed up. I sprinted over to the fence to scan it.

The app found Sea-2-Sea's cameras easily: they were set in the tops of the fence posts and at the midpoint of each section of fencing, creating a cat's-cradle kind of pattern. It should be possible to circumvent, with a little careful planning. I shut off the phone and stuffed it back in my day pack, jogged down to the road and into the Mustang. I made a fast U-turn and floored the car, churning up gravel and dust as I rocketed south to Old K-10.

The road was empty. The fierce wind had blown away most of the clouds; in my rearview mirror, I could see a dull orange sunset outlining the university's buildings along the top of Mount Oread.

I was almost at the Wakarusa when I saw the flashing lights of a cop car in the mirror. It had exited from the main highway, I guessed, heading north at speed. I sucked in a breath, but the cop car—no, cars, there were three of them—continued past the Old K-10, turning toward the silo. That showed one thing, or three, I guess: my phone was being monitored, my Faraday cage was a success, and they hadn't put a bug in my car.

My hands were damp, sliding on the steering wheel. I braked near the low bridge over the Wakarusa and turned onto a county road that skirted the river. I pulled over to the edge but kept off the verge—the Mustang wasn't designed for mud. Maybe next time I totaled a car, I'd get an off-road vehicle, something sturdy, like a decommissioned tank.

I got out and peered down the ravine at the greeny-brown water. A few water birds were hunting in the middle; others were resting on the tiny gravel islands that dotted the river. "Knee-deep in mud," Cady had told me Wakarusa meant in the local Indian language. Knee-deep, but still deep enough to drown her mother.

I took out the photos of the accident scene that I'd printed and tried to match them to today's landscape. Of course the undergrowth had changed, and it was fall, not high summer, but I could guess the car's path pretty accurately from the pictures.

Also from new tire tracks through the broken bushes and marsh grasses on the steep hillside. I climbed down the ravine face, following the tracks, my feet dragging, fearing what I'd find at the end of the trail.

It wasn't the Prius but a Dodge Ram pickup. The cab and body were rusted: you could see only a few patches of the red it had been painted when it left the factory.

Like Jenny Perec's Toyota, it was pointing nose-down in the water, but the pickup sat too high to go all the way in. Water rose about half a foot above the running board. I could see the figure in the driver's seat, head against the steering wheel.

My legs felt like wooden stalks, too hard to bend enough to walk me over to the truck. I did not want this to be Emerald Ferring, perhaps with August in the seat next to her.

The autumn sunset provided only a thin afterglow of light, which barely reached the bottom of the ravine. My wooden legs needed to come to life before it grew completely dark. I stumbled back up the hillside to my car for my high-powered flashlight and used it to inspect the ground around the truck. My footprints, easy to see in the mud. Others that had almost disappeared in the soft ground.

I held my flash in my mouth and photographed the ground, hoping something might emerge, then pulled on my gloves and climbed onto the running board. The growing darkness made the windows reflect blackly back at me. Water oozed in over the tops of my boots. Rank, old.

I tugged on the door, which gave slightly—it wasn't locked, but pressure from the river water made it hard to open. Bad behavior at a crime scene: I was rubbing off prints, I was letting water into the cab.

I shone my flash around the interior. The dead person was alone at the steering wheel. It was neither Ferring nor August Veriden; the wispy gray-white curls had belonged to a white woman, an old one. The cool air had probably slowed decomposition, but her face was still bloated, the skin darkening as it decayed.

I tried to inspect the body without touching it. There was an ugly hole on the right side of the back of the neck. There wasn't much blood around it, but blood had seeped down through layers of clothes and pooled in the gearbox.

I took more pictures. I wondered if I could slip a hand into the victim's coat or pants pockets to look for an ID, but she was leaning against the steering wheel and I'd have to move her, effectively destroying all evidence around her death.

Her right hand was holding the steering wheel, but the left had fallen to the seat. When I shone my flash on it, I saw a scrap of paper in the cup made by her palm. She'd been clutching it when she died. As her muscles relaxed, the scrap had dropped free.

Bad detective, I admonished myself, removing evidence, but I took off my right glove and stuck two fingers in like tweezers to retrieve it. Held it carefully while I stepped away from the truck, away from the water, tucked it into a zip pocket of my windbreaker, and returned to the truck long enough to shut the door.

I was climbing back up the ravine side, my wet socks squelching inside my boots, when I saw the flashing lights. Idiot! In the stress and excitement of finding McKinnon's truck, I'd used my iPhone to take pictures. Damn and triple damn. I had a fleeting urge to shinny up the pillars and stop a car on the road above. Instead I used the time to text Luella Baumgart-Grams, the defense attorney my Chicago lawyer had found for me.

36

CASUAL DAY IN COURT

I'VE SPENT TIME in holding cells in Chicago. Compared to them, the Douglas County Jail was the Ritz. No bedbugs, no people suffering psychotic breaks at two in the morning, no stench from years of sweat and other bodily fluids thinly masked by bleach.

Luella Baumgart-Grams had driven to Lawrence from Overland Park, but she'd arrived after the end of business hours in the Douglas County courts. However, she promised to spend the night in Lawrence and escort me to the Law and Justice Center in the morning. More important, Luella took care of my biggest worry: looking after Peppy. Luella had Free State Dogs board the dog overnight, which meant I didn't go nuts with worry in my clean cell.

The lawyer also brought me fresh clothes and brushes for teeth and hair so that I could make a reasonable impression in public. Saturday-morning bond court held a mixed bag of bail applications—drunk drivers, public nuisances, bar fighters who'd fired weapons. And one arrest for murder. Since my case was the most complicated, Judge Thelma Katz saved me for last. She and my lawyer knew each other from the state women's bar association; that speeded things up, that and the fact that the DA didn't want to deny my bail request.

Sheriff Gisborne had to agree he had no real grounds for my arrest. He grudgingly admitted that I couldn't have driven Doris McKinnon's truck off the road.

"Is there anything to suggest that Ms. Warshawski shot the dead woman?" Thelma Katz asked.

"Warshawski showing up like that—" Gisborne began.

"Forensic evidence, Sheriff. Anything to connect the bullet to Warshawski? Anything to show she could have driven the truck there or forced the victim to drive the truck there before shooting her?"

"We haven't fully processed the scene," Gisborne grumbled.

"Then get to work on that. Ms. Warshawski, what made you go down to the river in the first place? Assuming you weren't checking to see if your murder victim was still there."

"I saw tire tracks and broken branches and wondered if someone was in trouble."

Thelma made a note on the pad of paper in front of her. "That was an admirable Good Samaritan act, but when you found the truck with a dead woman in it, why did you open the door instead of calling 911?"

"I didn't know she was dead, Your Honor. I hoped she might be alive and that I could help her."

"Thelma!" Gisborne interrupted. "This is a private investigator from Chicago. She's familiar with crime scenes, she's seen dead bodies. She's been interfering with investigations ever since she came to town."

"Ken, this is a courtroom, not the Rock Chalk Pub. Let's pretend you didn't play high-school football with my father and follow normal protocol."

Gisborne turned red but subsided. Luella stepped forward to sort out what I should or shouldn't have done; she said that far from interfering with investigations I had saved Sonia Kiel's and Naomi Wissenhurst's lives. Thelma got the DA to vacate the arrest. Somehow I ended up with a two-hundred-dollar fine—I think for stupidity, although that isn't what they wrote on the form.

When we finished, Luella stayed behind to chat with Thelma—it wasn't a courtroom anymore, apparently, even if it wasn't the Rock Chalk Pub. Gisborne didn't try to join them—one of his deputies came into the room and muttered something that made the sheriff stride to the exit, with nothing but a malevolent glance for me.

I brought my forms over to the cashier, wondering how big a bite Luella's bill would take from my budget. Standing in line behind people paying traffic fines, court-ordered child support, penalties for littering, tampering with crime scenes, I felt too tired to go on. One never sleeps well in jail, no matter how splendid the accommodations, but I was tired down to my bones.

I was tired of cleaning up the sad detritus of other people's lives, tired of arguing with government agents, tired of trying to imagine why decent lawmen, as Sheriff Gisborne reportedly was, suddenly began acting as shills for the army or big corporations. Money had changed hands, or threats had changed ears—it was always the same story, and I was tired of reading it. No wonder Jake was fed up with me: I was fed up with myself.

When I'd handed over my credit card and signed on all the appropriate lines, I collapsed onto the nearest bench. My hair felt filthy, and my good jacket needed cleaning. I could smell my own body, and it wasn't enticing.

One of the clerks tapped me on the shoulder. "You okay, miss?"

I jerked awake and managed a ghastly smile. I was fine—in which case there was no loitering.

I pushed myself upright and headed for the exit, where I stopped abruptly. Colonel Baggetto, AKA Pinsen, and the sheriff were having an intense conversation in the middle of the hall.

The woman behind me, with two toddlers in tow, ran into me and shouted angrily.

"Sorry," I said. "I wasn't expecting to see my ex here."

"You still need to watch where you're going," she said, but less belligerently: running into an ex is never pleasant.

The deputies and clerks were eyeing the sheriff and his cohort overtly, but the trio had picked a strategic spot where they could see anyone who was trying to eavesdrop and they were far enough away that only a skilled lip-reader could make out their words. One of the many skills TV detectives have that I lack.

I paused a moment, but I was no more successful than the clerks in deciphering the conversation. I walked over to the men and smiled sunnily, or at least tried to, despite my fatigue-fogged brain.

"Warshawski!" The colonel tried to act nonchalant. "What are you doing here?"

"Recovering from a night in the Douglas County Jail. Paying my fine so I can return to society without a blemish on my character. The sheriff here can tell you all about it. How about you? They must miss you over at Fort Riley."

Gisborne and Pinsen were giving me those glassy looks that tell you you were a topic of their conversation, but Baggetto had easier social skills; he smiled genially and said, "It's good for all relationships to have some space now and then."

"Any luck with your canister?" I asked.

"You had plenty of time to remove it from the truck before we found you," Gisborne said.

"People tell me you've been a good sheriff here," I said. "I can't believe you didn't inspect my car before my lawyer got there to demand a warrant. Which leads me to another question: How did you know I was at the riverbank?"

Gisborne scanned the lobby, as if it would give him an answer. "Someone phoned to report suspicious activity."

"Someone saw suspicious activity around a half-submerged truck hidden under shrubs? It's not visible from the road. You can do better than that, Sheriff."

"What's that supposed to mean?" His jaw jutted out at an ominous angle. "That's a working farm up above. Someone could have seen you."

"Someone could have, but that doesn't mean they did." I pulled my phone from my pocket. "You can all check your own smart devices and check me out at this very moment."

Gisborne and Pinson both reached for their phones, but Baggetto shook his head. "She's goading you, Marlon. Don't let it get to you."

"No one's told me you've been a good detective," Gisborne said to me. His voice was thick, as if someone had stuffed mashed potatoes against his tonsils. "You think you're funny, and you're not, so I don't see you making a living doing stand-up. In fact, I don't see you doing anything that jumps out as special. Unless you did shoot Doris McKinnon and figured out a clever way to cover it up."

"I'm hoping I can learn from you," I said earnestly. "Say, for instance, about Doris McKinnon. I thought her body disappeared from the morgue before Dr. Roque's backup could perform the autopsy. How do you know there was a bullet in her head? She was pretty badly damaged when I found her. I couldn't tell she'd been shot."

The three men stood as though a taxidermist had suddenly squirted them full of formaldehyde. Pinsen recovered fastest.

"The woman in McKinnon's truck, that's what he meant," Pinsen said quickly.

"Everyone here has been wondering what you guys had on your minds that was so secret." I gestured at the county employees, who'd been joined by a good half-dozen members of the public. "I'm betting you just realized it was Doris McKinnon in her truck, which raises a truly interesting question: Who was lying dead on her kitchen floor last week?"

Gisborne jumped on that like a flea on Peppy. If I knew it was McKinnon in the truck, then my protestations of stumbling on the truck by accident were exactly what he'd said all along, a smokescreen to cover up the fact that I'd killed her.

"I can take this to Thelma Katz and get her to reopen the inquiry," he threatened.

"My attorney is still talking to Ms. Katz." I made myself sound eager to assist, not confrontational. "She could help you and Ms. Katz sort out whether you have grounds for a warrant."

Pinsen quacked that national security wasn't something we should talk about, let alone joke about, in an open atrium. If it turned out that Homeland wanted to question me, they wouldn't need a warrant.

"Is that who you work for?" I asked. "I thought it was the army college."

"Look, Ms. Warshawski." Baggetto gave a sympathetic smile. "I can imagine how it must feel to you, our coming on so strong. But you know what's at stake. If you know something else about the woman in the truck—if you spotted something out of the ordinary yesterday—"

"A truck nose-down in a creek always seems unusual to me, but that's probably because I'm so ignorant about life in the country. Maybe drunk or methed-up drivers go into the Wakarusa every day of the week and twice on Sundays. But if there was anything else weird, the sheriff's people have had plenty of time to sort it out. You talk to Gisborne here, see what his deputies found at the scene and in my car. *Hasta la próxima,* Colonel, Sheriff, Mr. Homeland Army College."

I half expected one of them to stop me when I headed for the exit, but Gisborne only turned to his underlings, demanding once again to know what work wasn't getting done.

I was ravenous, and I badly wanted my dog. Also a shower, but I needed new clothes—I didn't want to have to put back on the things I'd worn in prison and in court. Everything back at the B and B needed washing or cleaning after slogging around the rain and mud of Douglas County this past week.

When I stopped for a coffee at the Hippo, Simone advised me on a place that would carry clothes women my age might wear—most of the shops in town catered to the college kids. After a detour for a cheese sandwich at the bakery where I'd had lunch yesterday, I went to a shop called On the Town, where I found a well-cut jacket, a new pair of jeans, and a few knit tops.

37

TWENTY-FOUR-KARAT SMILE

ON MY WAY to the B and B to shower, I dropped my travel-worn clothes at a dry cleaners. Going through the pockets to make sure I wasn't also leaving keys or earrings, I found the torn corner of an envelope.

> Francis Roque, M.
> Forensic Pathol
> 5026 Sunset
> Kansas Cit

I stared at it. Dr. Roque was the pathologist who'd died—was it two days ago?—of flu. Why was an envelope with his name in my— And then I remembered: I'd removed it from Doris McKinnon's hand yesterday afternoon. An oddity I definitely was not going to mention to the three musketeers.

"When do you want these back, honey?"

The "honey" was laced with impatience; it was the third time the woman at the counter had asked me that question. In the hope things might wind up quickly enough for me to leave Lawrence soon, I chose second-day service.

Back in my car, I continued to look at the envelope fragment while I ate my sandwich. Dr. Roque had written to Doris McKinnon. Why? That was easy: because she'd written him. Maybe her last cow had died and she wanted an autopsy, but I was betting she had soil samples she wanted tested.

I started to pull out my computer to look up Dr. Roque but remembered in time that nothing I did online was private right now, not until the Cheviot lab could confidently say they'd removed all the spyware from my devices. I drove over to the library to use their computers.

Francis Roque, M.D., had been the chief medical examiner at the Kansas Bureau of Investigation in Topeka, but he also taught pathology at the University of Kansas School of Medicine in Kansas City. He'd lived in Kansas City, close to the medical school, not in Topeka where the KBI offices were. A widower, he lived alone, his two grown children in Texas and Florida.

He'd been twenty years younger than Doris McKinnon, so they hadn't gone to school together, but she must have had some kind of personal connection to him: she was worried about what was happening on her land; she wouldn't have just pulled a name out of a phone book.

After thinking over my meager contacts in the area, I called Barbara Rutledge again, using one of my burner phones. Before I could ask about Roque, Rutledge thanked me for letting her know about Nell Albritten's collapse: it was a help to building bridges in Lawrence for Barbara and other Riverdale members to bring her casseroles as they would if someone at Riverside took sick.

Ms. Albritten had seemed in good spirits when Barbara visited. Albritten's son and daughter-in-law were staying with her until she was fully recovered. Her pastor, Reverend Clements, came regularly to sit with her, as did other members of the St. Silas family, along with Reverend Weld, Riverside's chief pastor.

I felt guilty—I'd forgotten Albritten in the rush of other activities, like going to jail—but when Rutledge came to a halt, I asked her if she knew of any connection between Doris McKinnon and Dr. Roque.

"Roque? Oh. The pathologist who died while he was doing

Doris's autopsy. I didn't know Doris well, but I could make a few calls."

I started to ask her to keep my query to herself but realized it was hopeless—everyone talked to everyone here, and I was a high-profile stranger. Of course she wouldn't keep it to herself. I gave Barbara the number of one of the burner phones and used another to call Dr. Roque's office in Kansas City. He'd written McKinnon from his home address, not the KBI, so I was guessing his KC staff would be more likely than the state people to know why he'd written her.

Although it was Saturday, Roque's secretary was in the office. Her voice was thick with weeping.

Dr. Roque had been a great man, a great doctor, charitable, witty but never cruel. She didn't know how they would go on without him. She recognized McKinnon's name—Dr. Roque had been about to start the autopsy when he was suddenly taken sick—but she didn't remember handling any correspondence with McKinnon. When I said all I had was an envelope addressed to McKinnon with his home address on it, she couldn't help me, but she was struck by the coincidence.

"That's so strange, him writing to her and then getting her body to work on. That's just bizarre, but he didn't say word one to me. Talk to his lab tech—if it was some weird question, he might have mentioned it to Aanya when they were in the lab together."

Like the secretary, Aanya Malik was grief-stricken. "I owe everything to Dr. Roque. He helped me get my green card, my education, everything. When my sister ran away from a forced marriage, he helped me bring her to Kansas City so she would not be shot by my uncles. I know we will go on, but I don't know how." Malik spoke idiomatic English, overlaid with a South Asian accent that was sometimes hard to understand.

I murmured those phrases we always use, even though they seem empty in the face of great loss. After a few minutes, Malik tried to pull herself together.

"You said you were a detective. I know the police have come from Lawrence and gone through Dr. Roque's files. Even someone from the army has come. Is that why you are calling? If you think he did anything wrong, I will tell you personally that—"

"No, no. I'm not with the police, I'm private." I repeated my story, which seemed to be getting as long as the *Odyssey.* I tried to keep it concise but included my conflicts with the sheriff and my fears about the colonel in the hopes that would make her feel she could trust me.

When she decided to risk talking to me, we had to do it through Skype, so she could see my face; she needed to be sure I was who I said I was, not someone in a government office with a soothing voice tricking her into talking about Dr. Roque.

I set up a temporary Skype account on the library server and let Malik see me against the background of the library's computer room. "Someone, either the sheriff or the army, has planted malware on my own computer, so I have to use public ones."

Malik herself was in her home, sitting on a couch in what I judged was her living room. She was young, perhaps thirty, hair cut short around a narrow face, dark eyes rimmed red from weeping.

"Of course I remember Doris McKinnon. That was the woman Dr. Roque was starting to work on when he collapsed. He dictated his preliminary notes, which came to me: the budget cuts in the state have left him—*had* left him," she corrected herself mournfully, "short-staffed at the KBI lab, so I often typed his autopsy notes for him."

"Were you there when the body disappeared?"

"Not with him: I am not—was not—allowed in the Topeka lab because I do not work for the state: my salary is paid by the doctor's research grants. However, his dictation came to me through a conferencing app, so I know exactly what he said.

"He was puzzled indeed by what he was seeing. He did not believe that the body could belong to Ms. McKinnon, because she was old, perhaps ninety. The woman he was examining was also old, but she was closer to his own age, around seventy. He also was puzzled by her teeth, so he sent me the X-rays—he took those before he started the actual autopsy, that and he took scrapings from the fingernails."

Malik fiddled with her computer and sent me a copy of the jaw X-rays. "He had to take those himself because there was no lab tech available in Topeka that day. The state budget cuts mean the techs can only work twenty hours a week. The dead woman's teeth were bad—she had not seen a dentist probably for many years. Another thing also was strange: some of the dental work Dr. Roque thought had been done in Eastern Europe or possibly Greece. When he sent me the X-rays, he asked if I could do some deeper research on them."

I looked at the X-rays, but they told me nothing, except that there were teeth involved. "What did you find?"

"I did not look," she said. "I heard Dr. Roque gasping for air, I heard his body fall. I was sixty-five miles away and terrified; I called the guard at the state lab and finally he looked at his monitor and saw the doctor on the floor. If only he had been more alert—! But in any event, Dr. Roque was hospitalized, the dead woman's body disappeared, I did not know if there was any point. However, I see she had two old gold teeth with a great deal of decay underneath." Malik pointed at two of the teeth, an upper molar and a bottom front tooth.

"These weren't American crowns, which are usually porcelain with gold inlays. They were gold that you see flashing when the person smiles. Dr. Roque said that was typically Eastern European."

My stomach twisted: I've seen gold teeth in Chicago—some South Side dentists used to make them. And someone closer to Roque's age than to McKinnon's—that description fit Emerald Ferring.

"The dead woman," I said, my throat tight. "Did Dr. Roque say what he thought her race was?"

"No, no. Dr. Roque was only starting the autopsy, and of course everything was going to take twice as long since he had to do all the tech support himself. Oh, why did I not say to hell with state regulations and go with him? I could have gotten him to a hospital as soon as he felt ill. By himself he would never leave the morgue if he felt unwell. His sense of duty was very keen. By the time he fainted, it was too late for medical help."

She started to weep again.

I let her cry into the computer a bit longer but finally asked if she'd told the sheriff's deputies anything about the dental X-rays.

"No. They were so rude. They wanted to take apart his office, look at his mail. Rhoda was crying, I was trying not to cry: I would not tell them anything."

"Splendid," I said. "Let's not tell them yet. They're being rather annoying, and I don't feel like helping them. I know you're tired, but I have one last question. Dr. Roque wrote a letter to McKinnon—at least I think he might have. All I have is the fragment of the envelope with his name on it."

I held up the torn scrap for her inspection. "Dr. Roque's secretary didn't know anything about it. Do you?"

Malik frowned in puzzlement for a moment, then said, "Oh, she must have written one of the mold letters!"

"Mold letters?" I echoed, bewildered.

She laughed slightly. "I know it sounds crazy. He was in the news about five years ago because one of his autopsies showed a man had killed his mother using toxic black mold. It was in Luray, a tiny town in the middle of the state . . . well, never mind all those details. The lady's death was called an accident, but a neighbor insisted the son had murdered his mother—he was in financial trouble, and he would inherit the farm when she died.

"The local sheriff decided to ask the state to perform an autopsy. It was like an episode out of *CSI* or *NCIS*—Dr. Roque discovered that the dead woman's lungs were filled with black mold. He sent KBI investigators to the home, and they discovered that the son had been coating her mattress with it. All the TV stations covered the story. Dr. Roque even was on *60 Minutes*.

"After that, people wrote him from all over the world. They wanted him to prove that this or that person had been poisoned. Sometimes they sent him horrible things, pieces of skin or jars with blood or sputum in them. Rhoda would return everything with a cover letter saying the doctor was a state employee who did not do private work. After a while the letters and things stopped coming."

"Doris McKinnon had collected soil samples, I think from land that had been declared contaminated by radiation. I don't know what happened to the samples, but I wonder if she thought Dr. Roque's mold experience would qualify him to test soil for radiation."

"Yes," Malik agreed, "but I do not know why she wrote him at home, which she must have done, since Rhoda did not see the letter. Or she e-mailed him. I suppose she could have done that—I can look at his e-mail account."

"Do you have a key to Dr. Roque's house?" I asked. "Could we go there, do you think, and see if we can find anything from McKinnon, maybe even her soil samples?"

Malik had a key—when the doctor traveled, as he often had, she looked after his houseplants and his cat. She said she'd go over and search. "It will give me something to do, something concrete. Otherwise I will sit here playing what Dr. Roque always said was a loser's game: 'should have, would have, could have, did not.'"

38

UPSCALE HOUSING

WHEN WE'D SAID our good-byes, I took a minute to look up the mold story and found the *60 Minutes* clip. Dr. Roque did well on television—he'd been a Marcus Welby kind of doctor, square-built, with a soothing professional manner that works well with juries. He would have made a good internist, too—his kind, calm manner was wasted on the dead. Or maybe not. The dead deserve kindness as well as the living.

I realized that someone was standing over me. When I looked up, I was startled to see the head librarian, Phyllis Barrier.

"Are you still researching property lines?" Barrier asked.

"Does the town ask you to monitor out-of-state users of your system?" I asked, puzzled by her attention.

"I like to keep track of *all* our users. What can we provide that they can't find on their own computers, I wonder?"

"My computer is out of commission." I smiled and got to my feet. "I'm grateful to the library for letting a stranger use one here."

She didn't smile back, but she didn't try to question me further, just watched me as I walked to the stairs. Perhaps Marlon Pinsen had sent her a National Security Letter, demanding to know what websites I visited. Librarians are not allowed to discuss the receipt of a National Security Letter with anyone, not even their counsel, let alone a Chicago private eye. The longer I stayed in Lawrence, the more beleaguered I felt.

I sat on a bench in the park across from the library to call Troy Hempel's mother—I hoped she could help determine whether the body that had disappeared from the morgue might have been Ferring's.

"The pathologist who died as he started the autopsy sent her dental X-rays to his technician. The dead woman had two gold teeth. Do you know, did Ms. Ferring—"

"No. Ms. Emerald had beautiful teeth. Perfect white teeth. What makes you think she'd go around looking like a pimp?"

"I don't," I said wearily. "I just need to make sure we didn't overlook the possibility that we'd misidentified the dead woman."

Ms. Hempel said sharply that my lack of progress in finding Emerald was making her son and all the neighbors—not to mention Ms. Hempel herself—doubt whether I could really do the job.

"We're meeting tonight to decide whether to keep you on the job."

"Fair enough," I said. "Get in touch when you've made up your minds."

"What's that supposed to mean?" she bristled.

"That I'm not going to try to argue with you if you decide to cut me loose. I'm more frustrated than you are, because *I'm* down here slogging around, finding whiffs of disturbing secrets without turning up any new traces of August Veriden or Ms. Ferring. I want to come home, but I can't, or won't, until I get things sorted out in Lawrence."

It was private on the park bench, but it was also cold. I drove back to the B and B to shower and then went to Free State Dogs to collect Peppy.

She'd been a model border, they'd be happy to continue to look after her, but I was feeling anxious and bereft. Peppy was gratifyingly happy to see me as well, twining herself around my legs and making little grunting sounds in the back of her throat. Who needs a bass player when you have a golden retriever? "So there, Jake Thibaut," I muttered, shepherding Peppy into the Mustang.

We had a leisurely evening together, a welcome change. I baked a piece of cod in the toaster oven in the B and B's common room, made a salad, was curled up in the bedroom with a glass of pinot grigio watching Jack Lemmon and Tony Curtis fleeing the Chicago mob in drag when one of my burner phones rang.

"Ms. Warshawski . . . I know it is late—I am sorry, but . . ."

"Aanya." I recognized her voice despite her agitation and muted the television. "What's up?"

A moment too late, I remembered the transmitter under the desk. Damn and double damn. Maybe the TV masked my saying her name. I took the phone out onto the patio.

"I'm at Dr. Roque's, only . . . it is terrible. Someone has broken in, the house, his beautiful orchids, his papers . . . Who would do this?"

"What were they looking for?" I asked. "Something big or something small?" Small was what intruders had hunted at August's home and gym. Big, that might mean they were looking for Doris's soil samples, or Colonel Baggetto's fuel rods.

"How can I know that? I only know that the door was locked when I got here. I switched off the burglar alarm, I turned on the lights, and I saw a disaster. And why does it matter, big, small? His computer is gone, that is the only thing I could notice."

"Have you called the police?"

"I called you first, but I will call them, yes, only I do not want to stay here waiting for them. What if these criminals are hiding in the house? What if they attack me?"

She was in her car, the doors locked. I told her to stay there, and I would meet her as fast as I could. As fast as I could make my tired body move through time and space. I didn't want to risk leading the sheriff, the colonel, or anyone else to Roque's house before I had a chance to look at it, which meant no downloading maps or using my phone app. I made Aanya step me through the directions, one exit at a time, read them back to her, and told her to call me if someone approached the house but otherwise to sit tight.

I was longing for home, but I sure didn't miss Chicago traffic: it was forty-five miles from the B and B to Roque's house, but fifty minutes after hanging up I was pulling in behind Aanya's hybrid. She was parked near a kind of tiny creek or maybe a drainage ditch that snaked through the neighborhood.

Even under the dim streetlights, it was clear that Roque had lived in a wealthy area—well-kept grounds, large houses set back from the road, most with those little signs announcing their alarm systems. When Peppy and I got out of the Mustang, Aanya opened the door and came toward us on shaky legs.

"Thank goodness you're here. And you brought a dog." She knelt to embrace Peppy, who obligingly sat and licked her nose. "I'm sorry to be a coward, but—"

"You're not a coward. You did what you were strong enough to do, which was a lot. I want to see the house for myself anyway, and we need to call the cops as fast as possible."

A couple of dogs out for late-night walks barked at Peppy. Their owners lifted a hand in greeting but didn't try to talk.

Aanya told me no one had come by to question why she'd been parked out front for an hour. "But the Plaza—it's a place with restaurants and shops just over there, so probably neighbors pay little attention to strangers as long as people are quiet."

She pointed at lights across a tiny creek—shops, restaurants, which I'd only vaguely noticed when I was driving in. As long as Roque's intruders hadn't been noisy, the neighbors would have ignored them.

Aanya didn't want to go back inside, but I told her I needed her to show me where Dr. Roque had kept his computer and let me see how extensive the disturbance had been.

Extensive. That would be the word for the damage. It looked like the same hands that had torn apart August's apartment. I'd asked about big or small, to try to gauge what they were looking for, but that had been an irrelevant question. Or maybe they'd been looking for both big *and* small.

I followed Aanya into the room Dr. Roque had used as his home office. It had been a lovely place, I imagined, before wild hands tore it apart. An étagère had held crystals, but these had been dumped, some shattered.

"Oh, he traveled the world looking for these. I can hardly bear it," Aanya mourned. "He had a friend in the geology department at the University of Kansas, Professor Hitchcock, who also liked geodes. They used to go to Utah together. They even went to Mongolia once, and to Australia."

She was on the floor, trying to put pieces of one back together.

"You said his computer was gone. What else?"

"I do not know, I cannot tell. I was never in his private rooms, of course, but you can see there's an expensive television still sitting, and his stereo." She put her hands over her eyes, not wanting to look. "And the geodes, they knocked them to the floor but did not take them."

There are housebreakers who read the obituaries and stake out houses of the recently dead, but I didn't imagine we were dealing with that kind of robber: the fact they'd left salable items behind wasn't a surprise.

I put a hand on her shoulder. "We can't do any good here. I'm going to call the cops from my car. You take off. You don't need to tell them you were here—your fingerprints would be here in any event, since you were the person who tended to things when he traveled."

I made one last survey of the room and realized I'd overlooked his phone—so usual an object, even these days with people going exclusively to cell phones, that I hadn't registered it. Covering my fingers with a tissue, I fiddled with the menu button until I got the registry of the last calls he'd made or received. Three were from the same number in Lawrence.

Aanya was peering over my shoulder. "That's from the university." She opened her own phone. "Yes, that is Dr. Hitchcock. He called me two days ago, when he heard about Dr. Roque."

Peppy startled us both with a sudden, sharp bark. Aanya clutched my arm, sucked in a harsh breath. A second later a black-and-white ball of fur streaked across the room and jumped onto the toppled étagère.

Aanya laughed weakly. “Dinah! How could I be forgetting her? If you take your dog out of the room, I will coax her to me and bring her home.”

39

SURPRISE, SURPRISE!

I'D DRIVEN OVER to the Plaza shopping center to call the Kansas City police—late on Saturday night, the bars and streets were crowded, so they wouldn't bother too much with tracking me down. The burner phone was becoming a liability, though—Aanya and Cady had both called it, and I'd used it with too many of my Chicago clients. I put it under my front tire and ran over it on my way out of town. I had two more, but I'd pick up another couple on Monday.

It was past midnight when I got back to the B and B, but any hopes I had of falling into bed were destroyed when I reached the walk at the back of the house where my suite was. Peppy gave a sharp, excited bark and raced forward; a small figure emerged from the shadows to embrace her.

"Vic! Where have you been? I have been calling and calling and calling, and getting only your voice mail."

"Bernadine Fouchard, what the *hell* are you doing here?"

"But I have come to help, of course. I took the bus, twelve hours—*horrible, ma foi,* crying babies, men imagining I want a career as a whore—but here I am. You are doing nothing to find August. You are only looking for old women who are dying in rivers."

"Tomorrow you will get on the bus to go back to Chicago, *horrible* or not. It's hard enough to conduct an investigation in a strange city with a hostile sheriff and a host of other obstacles, but you, my little tornado, will make things a thousand times worse."

Bernie's mouth set in a mulish line. "You are not my mother. You cannot make me do anything."

"Right you are. However, I'm sure Arlette agrees with me."

I opened the door to my room and took my phone out of its cage. Seven messages from Bernie popped up on the screen: she'd been here half an hour, or at least she'd been phoning me for half an hour.

It was almost two in the morning in Quebec, and it took Arlette a moment or two to understand what I was saying, but as soon as she did, she was furious. I handed the phone to Bernie

Her conversation with her mother was in French, which I don't understand; I could tell that Bernie was annoyed, waving her free arm angrily but able to speak only in fragments because her mother kept cutting her off. Finally Bernie handed the phone back to me.

Arlette said, "I will be buying an airplane ticket for her. The nearest airport is Kansas City? *Bien.* I will text you the details in the morning. This child is more trouble than a busful of hockey players. What Pierre will say . . . He is in California this week—the Canadiens are playing the Sharks. Maybe he will stop in Kansas City on his way home and put her in a . . . I don't know the English word. *Une camisole de force.*"

"Whatever it is, I hope he can," I said. "She can sleep on the foldout bed in my room tonight, and we'll deal with things in the morning."

Bernie was completely unchastened. "Since Mama is so strict, I will of course go back to Chicago, but until then I will make sure that you are doing everything possible to find August. By the way, I watched all those videos you gave Angela and me, the ones you found in August's apartment. There's one where he interviewed Emerald about her career. There's nothing on it about why she wanted to come here, just old stuff about Hollywood and being an African-American actor in the seventies and eighties. I brought a copy for you."

She fished a data stick from her backpack.

"This isn't a justification for your trip," I said. "You could have e-mailed it to me."

"It's not that interesting anyway. It doesn't say, 'We will go to Lawrence and hide beneath the football stadium.'"

I snatched it from her, angry but wanting to see it for myself. It didn't, in fact, reveal anything useful. Ferring had one of those classically trained actor's voices, recognizable from the video in the field but richer on this clip. She was acting for August, telling a dramatic tale of her childhood in Kansas. At the end she held out her hands in a pleading gesture, saying, "I know it's an imposition, but if you could drive me down, I'd like to go *soon*."

No wonder August had packed up and taken off with her. The tone, the emphasis, made her sound like Violetta or Mimi collapsing from consumption—just one last dance before the end.

"Where's Angela?" I asked Bernie when Ferring's interview had drawn to a close.

"She was afraid of the demerits for missing practice."

"And you're not?"

"We don't practice on Sunday. With my help we can find August before they miss me. You know Uncle Sal would say I should be here."

That being Mr. Contreras. At least he was in St. Croix, one small blessing.

I smiled grimly. "Instead you're going back to Chicago tomorrow. I will drive you to the airport, even if it means handcuffing you to the floorboards. But for now I've had a long, stressful day. It's my bedtime. You get the chair."

Bernie had brought a toothbrush and a nightshirt in her backpack. The armchair opened into a narrow bed. I found a set of sheets on a shelf in the closet and made it up.

Despite my anger and my worries, I fell deeply asleep. My dreams were turbulent, though: Bernie's arrival added to my worries.

My hopes that she'd be back in Chicago by Sunday night were

undone by her father's phone call Sunday morning. He spoke to us on a conference hookup—he wanted to make sure I knew exactly what he was saying to his daughter. He was as furious as Arlette that Bernie had down to Chicago without permission from her coach or from the school. He wanted to pick her up and take her back home himself to make sure she apologized to her professors and her coaches.

"Otherwise she will do what she has done since she was three years old: try to charm her way out of trouble. But I cannot be in Kansas before Tuesday, Vic, so I must ask you to shoulder this burden for another forty-eight hours. And Bernadine, you are in deep disgrace. You have known since you first put on skates that you do what your coach says, *hein?* If this happens a second time, you will leave university and return to Quebec. *Comprise?*"

Bernadine said, *"Oui, Papa,"* in a small voice, but when Pierre had hung up, she said, "Well, at least I have two days before I need to leave. What can we do?"

"Go to church."

Her mouth dropped ludicrously. "This is a joke, right? Since when have you ever gone to church? And if you think I need to attend Mass—"

"I need to go to church." Mindful of the mike under the desk, I didn't elaborate. "Did you bring anything respectable to wear?"

"I thought we would be detecting. I have only jeans and sweatshirts."

"Then that's what you'll wear to worship."

I put on my new jacket, a new superfine wool top in my favorite rose, my new jeans, and my Lario boots. Since Bernie was wearing jeans and her Northwestern Wildcats shirt, I had her run with Peppy up and down the hills on the university campus on our way into town.

When she was back in the car, I told her about the mike and explained why I wanted to attend worship: to see if there was any possibility that St. Silas or Riverside was harboring August and Ms. Ferring.

At that, of course, Bernie became animated, even excited, and was annoyed with me for stopping at the Hippo. We still made it to North Lawrence in good time for St. Silas's morning service, but the church doors were locked: a notice in a plastic sleeve reminded parishioners that they were worshipping this morning at Riverside United Church. Great. I'd be able to see everyone. I drove back across the river, Peppy leaning out the window, happily anticipating a swim, Bernie chattering brightly about the possibility of locating August in Riverside's basement.

The lot was full, with two buses labeled ST. SILAS AME parked near the entrance, alongside vans from several assisted-living facilities. There was even one from St. Raphael's. I managed to slide in between an SUV and the church's garbage cans.

The service started at ten. We were fifteen minutes late, but not the only stragglers: a family whose mother was shouting in a whisper at her bickering daughters blocked the entrance until an usher hurried over to move them on.

Another usher handed us programs and escorted us to stairs that led to a balcony. As we climbed, the joint choirs of the two churches were singing a prelude, the music so loud that my diaphragm vibrated.

We squeezed into a spot in the middle of the right side, which gave me a good view of most of the main floor. Nell Albritten was in a front pew, flanked by her son and a tall teen who I supposed must be a grandson, perhaps a great-grandson. Bayard Clements, her pastor, was in the chancel with a large number of other people.

Gertrude Perec, also near the front, was next to the banker I'd met on Thursday at the clothing drive. Cady wasn't with her. At first I thought she hadn't come, but I finally spotted her in the sea of choir members. The red robe didn't suit her copper hair and freckles, but she was talking happily with her seatmates.

Lisa Carmody, Riverside's associate pastor, was the only other person I recognized. When a short, stocky man with graying hair got up to start the service, the program told me he was the senior pastor at Riverside, Theo Weld.

It was a long service, as both choirs were offering anthems. Bernie was restless: we needed to be up and moving about, not sitting through some Protestant idea of worship. I hushed her so sternly that she actually subsided.

Bayard Clements preached on the prelude to Thanksgiving: We were suspended between the Day of the Dead and the offering of thanks, and what did we propose to do about it? He was a good preacher, but my attention wandered, especially during a detour through the wise and foolish virgins.

It gave me a chance to study the church windows. The stained glass seemed to be a combination of biblical stories and the Riverside Church's narrative—pioneers on the prairies, a hand holding a cup of water to a slave in chains, the same hand holding a cup of water to Jesus on the cross. It was almost noon when the service ended.

"Now do we question people?" Bernie demanded.

"Now we talk to people. No one is going to reveal anything to a stranger, especially not one whose idea of subtlety is to knock someone into the boards."

Bernie shrugged. "It often works."

"Do you want to wait in the car with Peppy? If not, show the manners that I know Arlette taught you. These are older people who should be treated with respect."

The tide of worshippers carried us to the parish hall, where coffee and snacks were laid out. I was thankful that they had cheese and hummus amid the requisite cakes and brownies—I hadn't had breakfast, and hunger was starting to be my dominant feeling.

Nell Albritten was sitting at one of the round tables that dotted the room, her grandson next to her. When I went to pay my respects, Bernie stayed at the table, helping herself to an astonishing number of muffins. Members of the St. Silas congregation moved closer to Albritten, protecting her. Among them I saw Phyllis Barrier, the head librarian. I almost didn't recognize her in her church clothes—at the library she wore casual trousers and knit vests or cardigans. Now I realized she'd been one of the women in Albritten's photo of St. Silas's 150th-anniversary celebration.

Barrier saw me staring at her and quickly turned, walking out of the church. I realized that Albritten had been speaking to me, and I knelt to ask her to repeat herself.

"You found Doris McKinnon, I see," Albritten said.

When I squatted next to her to hear her over the hubbub, her grandson put an arm around her waist.

"Yes, ma'am. It was a second shock to find her a second time."

"And they don't know who that woman was, laying on Doris's kitchen floor, hnn? Who you going to find next? I hope it's not me."

"Mother!" Jordan had appeared behind her with a plate of food and a glass of iced tea. "Please don't. And you, you're the detective, right? Don't come bothering my mother. You almost cost her her life last week. She doesn't need your kind of excitement."

There was a murmur of agreement from the St. Silesians behind him, but Albritten laid a hand on my knee. She had so little flesh around the bone that her tendons stood out, ropes between fingers and elbow.

"Ms. Chicago Detective is doing her best for Emerald, Jordan. Don't fault her for that."

Jordan folded his lips in disapproval; they'd probably had this argument a few hundred times over the last two days. I pushed myself up to standing and kissed her lightly on the cheek.

"Don't lose heart, Ms. Detective," Albritten said. "That isn't your own daughter paying you a visit, is it?"

"No, ma'am. She works with August in Chicago. She's the person who came with August's cousin and asked me to look for him."

That caused a new murmur, this time of interest, but none of them said anything, no volunteers of information about where August and Emerald were hiding.

Cady Perec had been hovering. When I moved away from Albritten, she demanded to know when we were going to break into Sea-2-Sea's experimental farm. I'd forgotten that part of my agenda, hunting for the places where McKinnon had been digging. I urged Cady not to bellow her felonious urges to the world, but she only laughed.

"If we tried to whisper, everyone would lean in to eavesdrop. Me shouting is just one more clanging gong among all these wagging tongues."

Bernie had moved up closer to us, unfortunately. "You are going to break into a farm?" Her eyes sparkled. "Why? Can I come?"

"No!" I cried. "And I'm not sure it's a useful idea."

"But we need to know what Doris thought was going on with Sea-2-Sea, and I can help you find the place where she might have been digging," Cady argued.

We changed the subject as Barbara Rutledge came over. I didn't want a relationship between Bernie and Cady to blossom—Cady's ardor, and her desire to explore the ground where she'd been born, would inevitably ignite a wildfire in Bernie.

Rutledge merely wanted to report that she hadn't found a connection between Doris McKinnon and Francis Roque, the dead pathologist. "I thought maybe they were cousins or in-laws or something, but he moved here from South Dakota when he finished medical school. He doesn't have any family in the area."

"His tech seems to think it was because he'd done high-profile work on a murder case some years ago that involved black mold," I said. "Ms. McKinnon wanted soil samples tested. Maybe she thought *her* soil had black mold in it." When the words came out, I wondered if that was the case: not radiation poison in her farm but something almost as toxic.

After that, it seemed as though everyone in the room wanted to talk to me, or at least about me. I could make out some of the comments, since most people weren't bothering to whisper:

That's who's hunting Emerald Ferring? She found Doris down by the

Kaw? No, the Wakarusa. Didn't Gisborne arrest her? Did she murder Doris? Who's the girl with her, her daughter? No, it's a student she's training to become a detective.

I claimed a need for a toilet. Barbara offered to escort me, but under cover of taking my dirty dishes to the kitchen I slid out through a rear exit. Bernie was still in conversation with Cady, but that couldn't be helped.

A door there led into the church proper. It was empty now, the white-painted pews and simple stained glass a respite for the spirit. I climbed the two shallow steps to the chancel. During the service the pastor and lectors had entered via a curtain behind the choir stalls. I went through it and found what I was looking for: a door that took me to a flight of stairs leading to the church basement.

Riverside had been rebuilt thirty years after Emancipation, but they were proud of their abolitionist heritage. In the basement they had re-created the rooms where fugitive slaves were harbored. One inner door was locked. I took out my picks and worked it open, holding my breath, but on the far side I found a strong room, not Emerald Ferring or August Veriden. There were shelves bearing silver and gold goblets and plates, some probably very valuable indeed. Labels in front of the items identified the families who'd donated them: a who's who of transplanted New England aristocracy—Cottons, Pearsons, Cabots, and so on.

"I assume you have a reason for being here?"

The hair stood up on the back of my neck, and my heart lurched. Theo Weld, the pastor, had followed me, and I'd been stupid enough not to keep watch.

"I was hoping you were sheltering Emerald Ferring and August Veriden. I'd like to know they're safe."

"They're not hiding inside Emerson Prence's Communion chalice," he said dryly. "You can leave now."

He stood with his hand on the doorknob, but I stopped when I passed him. "Ms. Ferring and Mr. Veriden might have seen something or someone out on Doris McKinnon's land that puts their lives at risk. I hope they're still alive. If you know where they are, please send a message to them. Please get them to tell you what they saw. If I can find that out, then maybe I can clear things up so that they can come out of hiding."

Weld wasn't any taller than me. Standing next to him, I could see he had the pale blue eyes of a Scandinavian sailor. They stared at me with all the coldness of the North Atlantic.

"I don't know where they are, Ms. Warshawski. I'm not sure I'd tell you if I did, but I don't know."

40

POLAR BEAR

I LEFT THE CHURCH, rather embarrassed, and was in a nearby field with Peppy and Bernie when my phone buzzed against my hip. I glanced at the screen and froze: the ICU nurses' station.

A woman was on the other end, rattled and not completely coherent. "Can you come? I didn't know who to call, but Sandy, Sandy Heinz, she said you were reliable and to call—"

"Can you start with who you are and what's happening?" My voice was sharp, a slap to settle her nerves.

"Tricia. Tricia Polanco, I'm the ward head at the ICU today. Sandy said to call you if something went wrong with Sonia Kiel, and it has. Her brother . . . I don't know which one—"

"Call Sergeant Everard at the police department. I'll be with you in five."

I grabbed Peppy's leash and told Bernie we had to leave. As we ran to the parking lot, I explained that I had to go to the hospital as fast as possible; she'd have to stay in the car with the dog or walk Peppy around the hospital perimeter.

Cady and Gertrude were leaving as we reached our car. They heard Bernie's piercing questions, including a demand as to why we had to go so instantly to the hospital.

"Sonia?" Cady asked.

I nodded. "I'm not sure what, but it sounds frightening."

Cady offered to take Bernie home to lunch, which made Gertrude's face tighten with annoyance. "Not the dog," she said.

"Right," I agreed. "Dog stays with me. Bernie, I'll call you as soon as I know when and where I'll be."

I bundled Peppy into the Mustang and took off with a great squealing of rubber. I tried phoning Everard, but my call went to voice mail. He was in church or on a golf course. Or lying in on Sunday with some woman or man I hadn't met.

At the hospital I sprinted across the lobby to the ICU elevators, skidding on my boot heels. Slow it down, take it easy: not good if I ended up in an emergency ward myself.

Tricia Polanco was waiting near the elevator when I got off. A woman in her late fifties, with hazel eyes, she was probably usually as calm and commanding as Heinz, but today she was frightened. Her face lightened when she saw me, which made me feel as though a yoke loaded down with steel buckets had been plopped onto my neck.

"What happened?"

"Sonia's brother—at least a man who *said* he was her brother—he's been calling every day. I recognized his voice from the phone. I took him back to see her. She's been waking up more, been more alert all weekend, but she's often belligerent, so when she said, 'Not my brother,' I thought she was . . . you know, the way she can get."

"And then?" I prodded.

"I left them together. In about one minute, she flatlined. We ran in at once—the emergency-response team is there now, and our security team, but the brother disappeared. Hospitals—so many exits and stairwells—people can vanish in a blink."

"What do you think he did—if he did do something?"

She shook her head. "Her IV lines are intact. We replaced all the bags, the saline and so on, just in case, you know, in case he . . ."

I nodded. "Good thinking."

"We've sent them to the path lab. But honestly, I think he put a pillow over her head and . . . and held it. The bedclothes are disturbed, as if she'd been thrashing her legs, trying to fight—her arms are in restraints—light ones, you understand—to keep her from pulling out her lines. The response team is using defibrillators now, and they don't need me for that, but I have to monitor how she's doing."

I trotted into the back with her, through the wide doors that hissed open and shut as we passed. When we got to Sonia's room, it was packed with the emergency crew. It was impermissible for me to join the throng, but what would I have done anyway, besides peer anxiously over the professionals' shoulders?

I stood in the hall listening to the sounds of controlled excitement. Not the shouts of a TV show, where someone is yelling "Clear!" and other characters are calling back, but urgent voices speaking too softly for me to understand.

While I waited, my own mind began to clear. A brother had come to visit. I had never gotten around to calling either of Sonia's brothers.

Cell phones were strictly prohibited in the ICU. I don't know if they really interfere with heart defibrillators, but I didn't want to be the person to conduct the experiment. I left a note for Nurse Polanco with the woman at the ICU information desk and went down to my car, where I could call up my case notes on my iPad; I'd entered the two brothers' phone numbers there.

Stuart, the math brother, was just about to set out for an afternoon's sailing with his husband—it was two o'clock in Maine; I'd caught him in the nick of time, right before they cast off. No one had told him Sonia was hospitalized, but when I explained who I was and gave him a précis of the week's events, he seemed more saddened than distressed.

"She was such an energetic little girl, whip smart, but our mother—she was drunk too much of the time to pay attention to her, and Sonia started acting out. I see now, now that I'm a teacher, that she was doing anything to get attention from Mom, but at the time I was six years older and I only thought of her as an annoying brat. She came to Boston for a few years—she had some real talent in the arts—sculpting, painting, even a bit of performance studies—but she couldn't stay focused. Kevin—my husband—Kevin and I tried to help her, but she couldn't or wouldn't accept any medical treatment, and finally, when she was broke and got arrested for disorderly conduct, she went back to Kansas."

"There's some issue with one of your dad's experiments that seems to lie behind your sister's first collapse back in the eighties—do you know anything about it? Matt Chastain, a student who she was infatuated with, disappeared after supposedly making some colossal mistake."

"I was already out here in Maine, at Bowdoin. My brother Larry, he's two years older than me, he was at Reed in Oregon. Neither of us wanted to spend our vacations at home, and we were young—we didn't care about anything except our own issues, so we didn't know what Sonia was going through. I got a garbled story from my mother: she was sure Sonia was making things up to grab attention, and she was angry about some woman my dad had invited to his lab from Europe—Barcelona, maybe—but she didn't talk about any of Dad's students."

When I told him about this morning's attack, he was shocked. "Will she survive? Should we come out?"

I said I didn't know, that I'd get back to him when I had more news.

"Poor little bear," he said. "Tell her I love her."

Larry, who was hiking outside Portland with his two children, knew even less about his sister's adolescent history than Stuart, but his description of their mother was similar.

"She was angry all the time after Sonia was born. Up to then she'd been normal some of the time. I mean, she sometimes had the interactions with Stu and me that I see my wife doing with our kids: Did you hurt yourself when you fell? What happened at school today? After Sonia was born, Mom checked out for good. She seemed to want us all to look after her, and she didn't pay much attention to the baby. I remember her screaming at Dad all through the pregnancy: What about her life? She wasn't dealing with any more kids. He could stay home from the lab a few nights a week to help out. I was eight, Stuart was six—you can imagine what that was like."

I grunted agreement. I'd met Shirley and Nate. I could picture it.

"Made me nervous as hell about having any kids of my own, put it off until I was almost fifty. Poor little polar bear, though. Tell her I love her."

"Polar bear?" I echoed. "Your brother called her 'little bear.'"

"It was our nickname," Larry said. "She had a white bear winter suit when she was three or four, and she loved wearing it. When we got home from school, she'd meet us at the door growling and beg for a raw seal. We'd cut up an apple and pretend it was a seal and let her hunt for it. Maybe it was the only time we were all happy together."

Like his brother, Larry asked me to tell him as soon as I knew Sonia's condition. Like his brother, Larry knew nothing about Matt Chastain or the experiment, but he did remember Shirley screaming at Kiel about the European woman.

"Bratislava, not Barcelona," he said. "Dad went to some conference in Czechoslovakia about his bug, not sure when. He was always jetting around the world—summer institutes in Aspen, meetings with the army at Fort Detrick, conferences in Europe. He was a big noise in his field, and he loved being the center of attention.

"Anyway, couple of years after he went to that particular jamboree, this woman showed up. I was counting the hours until I could leave for college, and I was spending as little time at home as possible, so I don't remember too much about it, just my mother's histrionics—drunk, sobbing, yelling, throwing things—and Dad screaming back at her."

He was silent, revisiting a place he hadn't liked to begin with.

"Looking back, I think Dad and this woman had slept together at the conference and she thought it was love, but he's tightly wound, and he didn't know what to do with her when she showed up. What a fuckup all that was. I was practically weeping with the need to get away from it. I haven't been back to Kansas since, but I'm sorry for the poor polar bear: Stu and I shouldn't have left her to fend for herself all those years."

He couldn't remember the woman's name or if she'd had gold teeth. When he finished, I curled up on the seat next to Peppy, letting her warmth comfort me. I finally uncoiled myself and returned to the ICU.

Tricia Polanco was still on the ward, but the ICU receptionist paged her for me. Polanco came out to tell me they'd been able to restart Sonia's heart but had once more put her into a protective coma until her systems became stable.

"That wasn't either of her brothers who did this," I said. "I spoke with both of them while you were in with Sonia."

I'd snapped a picture of AKA Pinsen with Baggetto, Kiel, and Bram when I saw them at the hotel bar last week. The lighting was poor, but you could make out the faces.

"Was the guy one of these?"

She squinted at my phone but shook her head. "Sonia's brothers are both around fifty, I knew that, and the man who came here was about that age. He did look a little like this one, though—"

She tapped Pinsen's face with a fingernail. "Bland, I mean, nothing special, but it wasn't this man. He made me think military—the muscles, the way he walked."

She fiddled with the edges of my phone, then finally said, "We found a fabric thread in her nose, so it definitely was someone trying to kill her."

Poor little polar bear indeed.

41

YOU'RE SO IGNORANT

BY THE TIME I finished with Tricia Polanco, I was longing for solitude—so much so that when I saw Sergeant Everard getting out of his car as I was leaving the hospital, I ducked back inside and left through a different exit. Just like Sonia's assailant.

Bernie's presence in town made my nerve endings vibrate with the intensity of the Riverside Church organ. I didn't think I could bear to spend an afternoon with her, but I couldn't leave her on her own. However, when I called, she said Cady was showing her around and she'd meet me at suppertime.

I didn't bother to ask if they were going out to look at the Sea-2-Sea experimental farm—I didn't want to know; I only wanted time alone. I changed into my running shoes, collected a picnic, and crossed the river on foot so that my long-suffering dog could have an energetic afternoon along the river bottom. The sun had come out, a pallid late-year sun, but it warmed the air and helped improve my mood.

While Peppy explored, I found a wide rock where I could go through my case notes and plan my next steps. And eat. Lentil soup, still warm in its lined carton, bread and goat cheese. I was, if not happy, at least content.

Before leaving the ICU, I'd asked Polanco if anyone had notified the Kiels about the attempt on their daughter. She said the nurses had agreed that that was the job of the ICU attending, Dr. Cordley, who'd been one of Kiel's students. *Not that we expect them to respond,* she'd added.

Nor did I, but I wanted to talk to them about the woman from Bratislava or Barcelona or wherever. Hers might be the body that had disappeared from the morgue after Dr. Roque collapsed on the autopsy-room floor—although it was funny that no one had mentioned her until now. Maybe not, though—I hadn't been talking to anyone in Kiel's lab. The separation between university and town could easily mean the populations didn't know each other.

What would get either Shirley or Nate Kiel to tell me Ms. Bratislava's name and where they'd last seen her?

I thought of Stuart and Larry Kiel telling me how furious their mother had been over Bratislava's appearance thirty years ago. I wondered if Shirley had come upon the woman unexpectedly and murdered her in a fit of fury. It was hard to imagine keeping rage at a white-hot pitch for so many years, but a sudden encounter might have startled Shirley into acting. Although what would have brought both women out to the McKinnon farm at the same time?

I decided to call Edward Hitchcock, the geologist who'd gone geode hunting with Dr. Roque: he'd tried phoning the pathologist several times right before his death. Maybe it was only to arrange another geode-hunting expedition, but perhaps Roque had consulted his old friend about Doris McKinnon's soil samples.

The phone rang unanswered, no voice mail or machine. I had only Hitchcock's office number, not his cell, and I didn't want to risk giving away his identity to whoever might be reading my files by going into my subscription databases.

I reclined on the rock, my backpack as a pillow, and watched the swallows swooping and rising among the gulls. It was twenty degrees warmer here than in Chicago, my weather app told me: not an inducement to move to Kansas, but enough to warm the rock and bring a few insects out.

Dr. Roque's death had been very convenient for whoever wanted Bratislava's body. A sudden collapse from a virulent flu—could that have been engineered? Would Colonel Baggetto, for instance, have sneaked into the lab and stabbed Roque with a needleful of a mysterious drug or bug?

I imagined them struggling, the needle dropping, Dr. Roque dying a hideous death while the colonel straightened his medals and gave a loud, sinister laugh. It was ludicrous: I could only see it as cartoon panels, Wonder Woman versus Cheetah, Superman against Lex Luthor. Anyway, Aanya Malik was listening to Dr. Roque's dictation. If he'd had his mike on, then she would have overheard a struggle.

On the other hand—had Roque been sick already when he drove to Topeka on Thursday morning? I used one of my remaining burner phones to call Malik.

She repeated her thanks for my making the drive to Kansas City in the middle of the night, assured me she was fine, as was Dinah the cat—"I cannot believe I forgot her and left her to starve for all those days!"—and that the Kansas City cops hadn't been in touch about the break-in. They probably hadn't printed his house—overworked, underfunded police departments don't process every crime scene.

The oddity was that the break-in hadn't made any of the news feeds. I would think anyone monitoring police frequencies would pick it up: Roque had that national reputation, even if it was five years old, and he was dead—two things that gave the break-in national interest. Either no one had seen the connection or the cops were playing this closer to their collective chest than I imagined. I didn't say so to Aanya—I didn't want her hyperventilating every time her phone rang.

"Dr. Roque's collapse at the start of an autopsy seems dramatic," I said. "Could someone have engineered his illness? They wanted to get rid of that body before he examined it more closely."

"During the famous flu epidemic of 1919, people left their houses in the morning feeling fine and were dead by noon, so a swift-growing and powerful virus, it could have killed him quickly, on its own. For the body stealers, Dr. Roque's collapse was perhaps merely a sign of fortune favoring their wishes, not them making it happen." Aanya objected.

"Fortune has certainly been favoring whoever is orchestrating this mayhem," I agreed. "Where is Dr. Roque's body? Can you get one of his colleagues to perform the autopsy?"

"I do not know," Aanya said doubtfully. "The budget crisis means not so many autopsies, and the state, they are saying he died of flu. The children, they are arriving tonight to conduct the funeral. I can ask them to authorize an examination by a private pathologist, but people are— I can't think of the word in English. It troubles people to have their family members cut upon. It would trouble me, I know."

"I can understand that." I tried to keep the impatience out of my voice. "But it's such a big coincidence, his collapse at the moment that someone wanted to steal the dead woman's body."

"I will try," Aanya said unhappily. "I understand what you are saying, but . . . well, I will try."

When she hung up, I called Peppy to me. The sun was starting to set, the air was getting cold, she'd had almost two hours of fun, which had left her coated in mud, with burs embedded in the feathers on her tail and haunches.

"You look like a role model for every golden who ever pined for a life in the open," I told her, trying to extract the worst of the burs. Since she kept squirming to bite at them herself, it was a frustrating business. Free State Dogs had advertised a grooming service. I called and was told that if I got her there in the next twenty minutes, they'd take care of her.

"Okay, *bellissima,* we're going to run like the wind and drive like Danica Patrick!"

I dropped her off at Free State one minute over the limit, but the woman at the desk had seen Peppy on her two days at the place and said she'd fit her in.

"We close at six on Sundays. If you're not back by then, we'll board her overnight and charge you for twenty-four hours."

I looked at the clock. One hour. Not enough time to go to the Kiels' and persuade them to talk, but I was close to St. Raphael's. While I drove, I texted Bernie on one of my burner phones. Cady had dropped her at the B and B; I would be glad to know she was working on an essay for her French-literature class.

I *was* glad to know. I was glad to believe it even if it wasn't true.

Sunday evening the receptionist at St. Rafe's was a bored youth playing a game on his phone. When I asked for Randy Marx, he pushed a button on the desk phone without taking his eyes from his screen.

"Randy? Some lady here to see you. . . . I didn't ask." He sighed and said, without looking at me, "Your name?"

"V.I. Warshawski."

"Like I can be expected to say that," he grumbled. "She's a foreigner," he added to the desk phone. "Viyai something."

"Warshawski!" I shouted. "Chicago detective. Sonia Kiel."

That surprised the receptionist enough that he actually looked at me. "Damn, now I lost my ranking!"

I supposed that referred to his game, not a contest for how long he could go without actually engaging with a visitor.

Marx appeared a few minutes later. I hadn't expected to find him on a Sunday evening. I'd been trying to imagine scenarios that would persuade his backup to let me into Sonia's room.

"I'm going out of town tomorrow," he explained, ushering me into the Arrowfeather Room. "I wanted to get all the rescheduled therapy sessions and so on squared away with my administrative assistant."

I turned down the offer of thin, overboiled coffee. "Did you know there was an attempt on Sonia Kiel's life today? Someone posing as a brother tried to suffocate her."

His pale face didn't register emotion easily, but his reaction seemed more one of fatigue than alarm or astonishment. "Are you sure about that? I was told she went into arrest, but that didn't surprise me. Her heart's taken a lot of abuse."

"Her drug use didn't lead her to hold a pillow over her own face until she stopped breathing."

At that he did flinch. "Are you sure?"

He pulled out his cell phone and started to text, but I took the phone from him.

"I *am* sure. If someone says otherwise, they're either protecting Sonia's assailant or keeping the news secret in hopes that the perp will think he got away with it. In which case it was wrong of me to tell you, but that's water over the Kaw River dam now. I came here because I want to see Sonia's writing."

I powered off the phone and handed it back to him.

"I can't do that. Resident records are confidential. Even if you had a warrant, we're covered by HIPAA. Our therapists are licensed—"

"I don't want to see what *you've* written about *her*," I interrupted sharply. "I want to see what she wrote about herself."

When he looked puzzled, puzzled and mulish both, I added, "You told me on Thursday that Sonia was always journaling about Matt Chastain and the protest out at the old missile silo. I want to see her journals, or computer files, or whatever she wrote on. She can't give me permission. They've put her back into a protective coma."

"I . . ." Marx fiddled with his phone, turned it back on, saw me eyeing him, and put it in his pocket. "I'll have to consult our lawyers. I'll be gone all this week. We can talk a week from Tuesday."

I resisted the urge to lift him by his T-shirt and shake him. "Mr. Marx, by a week from Tuesday, Sonia may be dead. Even if she recovers from today's assault, it's hard to guard someone in a hospital—there are too many ways in and out of the building, and no one is enthusiastic about protecting her.

"I know you've tried to work with her. I know she's a pain, but right now she's a living, breathing pain. If you won't let me see Sonia's papers tonight, my lawyer will be in court tomorrow to get me appointed Sonia's guardian ad interim. And if something happens to her between now and my getting that authority, I will sue you and St. Rafe's for causing harm to her by your failure to act tonight."

I know you catch more flies with honey, but I didn't want any more damned flies piling up around me. I wanted Sonia's writings.

Marx looked at me with as much loathing as his colorless face could summon and tapped a speed-dial number on his phone. "Hank—Marx here." He sketched the scenario I'd proposed, apparently was told I could make it happen, and turned to me to say sulkily that Chet would escort me up to Sonia's room and oversee anything I took away with me.

"I didn't think having Sonia here could get any worse, but you've certainly proved me wrong."

I bared my teeth. "Sonia never had an advocate before. You have a good trip, and comfort yourself with the hope that before you get back, I'll have sorted out this situation to the point that I can head for my own home."

Chet was the young man with the handheld device. He led me to Sonia's room on the second floor, expressing his ill humor at being asked to work by going as slowly as possible.

"Sorry to tear you away from your game," I said. "Why don't you give me the key so you can get back to your battle station?"

"Against regulations," he said huffily, but he picked up his pace. When he'd opened the door to Sonia's room, he left me alone to explore.

I was keeping an eye on the clock: I could spend only fifteen minutes here if I wanted to get back to Peppy by six. Fortunately, it was a small space, with a bed, an open closet that included shelves and drawers, and a table big enough to write at. Bathrooms were shared among the residents, but the room held a sink. No coffeemakers or hot plates; kitchens were also shared.

Sonia had lived here for three years, but she hadn't accumulated much. Her clothes were dumped willy-nilly in the closet. Most were shapeless, sweats and polyester probably pulled from a donation box. She had a few good pieces, a red sweater with navy piping and a well-known label in the neck. The drawers and shelves held an assortment of underwear, toiletries, and a dozen or so books.

She also had printouts of articles on weapons disasters of all kinds—biological, chemical, nuclear.

I gathered those up along with the books, which ran the gamut of conspiracy theories, from who killed JFK to reports of UFOs descending on Roswell. *Clouds Without Witnesses: Secret Weapons Tests on Human Populations* was a thick volume, but heavy even for a book. I opened it to find that Sonia had cut out the interior. A pint of vodka, almost empty, nestled inside. Sonia had written *"You're So Ignorant"* on the endpaper with a broad-tipped red Magic Marker, accompanied by an R. Crumb–like caricature of a man in a U.S. Army uniform.

I flipped through the rest of the books, but they were all just that, books. I lay on the floor to look under the bed and pulled out her two suitcases. One was empty, but the other held a jumble of legal pads and notebooks, covered with a sprawling hand.

I put the books and articles inside and sprinted down the hall and stairs. I made it back to Free State just as the receptionist was starting to lock the outer door.

42

SONIA, APRIL 1983

SUSTAIN ME WITH *raisin cakes, refresh me with apples, for I am faint with love."*

Hidden under her bedclothes, she murmured the words into the T-shirt. All the little hairs on her arms stood up, almost as if his hands were there, stroking her. The shirt smelled of ash and sweat, not myrrh and lilies, but she knew her beloved's sweat, and it was sweeter than wine.

One of the girls at school was born-again, and she thought it was her duty to convert Sonia. Apparently bringing a Jew to Jesus earned you buckets of brownie points in heaven. Gerri thought Sonia's family were doubly damned, because not only were they Jews but Sonia's father was a scientist who believed in evolution.

Gerri had left a Bible on Sonia's desk, with a letter that explained her mission: *"Read Genesis and you will know the truth about the creation of the world."*

Sonia thought the creation stories were ridiculous. They were followed by pages and pages of who was whose daddy. The rest of it looked equally dull—long lectures on how wicked everyone was, or page after page of genealogies. Still, she'd toyed with pretending to be converted—it would drive Daddy and Mother into a frenzy of shouting and door slamming and screaming at each other over whose fault it was that their only daughter was such a loser.

But then Sonia had stumbled on the Song of Solomon, buried in the middle of some incredibly boring proverbs. *"Upon my couch at night I sought the one I love—I sought but found him not. I must rise and roam the town."*

It was like the story of her life, or the story of her love, roaming through the town, looking for her beloved, peering into the windows of the bars downtown until she saw him at the Diamond Duck. It was eleven o'clock, and neither parent knew or cared that she wasn't home. Matt was having a beer with Jennifer Perec, of all people. Stupid Jennifer.

Sonia imagined sauntering in, feigning surprise at seeing him. "Just passing by, I'll join you for a minute if I may. Let me have a beer." The bartender would try to throw her out for being too young to drink, and Matt would get to his feet, fling a few bills on the table, and say curtly, "She looks too young to you because you can't see beneath the surface, to the quality of her soul."

She couldn't quite bring herself to do it. If she'd had a friend, someone to egg her on, double-dare her, maybe she would have, but she didn't have friends.

Lucinda, the lab tech, said to leave the poor boy alone, find someone her own age in high school, but the high-school boys were all acne and gross jokes, and anyway, what difference did it make when deep down Sonia knew the truth, that she was fat, lumbering, unlovable? Her life was working in Nate's lab, then home to do homework—that was pretty funny, everything at home was work. She washed the dinner dishes while Mother passed out in front of the TV and Daddy was at some seminar or his experiment was running late. Or he was pecking the Magpie, that was Mother's claim.

She'd taken Matt's T-shirt out of the trash. She was in the lab, wondering if she could filch one of the petri dishes Matt had put in the tub, when she smelled smoke and heard him swear. He'd bent too close to the Bunsen burner and his T-shirt had started to smolder. He ripped it off before it actually burst into flames and thrust it under the cold-water tap, but when he pulled it back, the front was full of blackened holes.

"Don't tell your dad," he'd said to Sonia, who was looking at his bare chest, wide-eyed. "He already thinks I'm the clumsiest SOB who's ever set foot in his lab."

She shook her head dumbly. She should have leaped on him and saved his life, but instead she'd stood stock-still, her hands in the soapy water. He tossed the shirt into the trash and buttoned his lab coat up to his neck, but later, when he went to collect something from the cold-storage locker, Sonia grabbed the shirt and stuck it into her book bag.

Later she took one of her brother Stuart's razors and cut the Song of Songs out of the Bible to keep, then put the book on Gerri's desk with a note that said, *"I must accept my fate of eternal damnation. You will do detention for thousands of years in the afterlife for failing to rescue my lost soul."*

Sonia 2007

Dickheads and Drunks I Have Known

1. Dan Bors, creep, probably not drunk. I go to collect my drugs and he says, *You back home, Sonia?*

No, dickhead, this is my doppelgänger. She goes out in public to talk to assholes like you.

So of course everyone in the place turns to stare. Oh, Sonia Kiel's back in town. Might have known that potty-mouth without looking. Couldn't make it in Boston, could she? Poor Shirley, poor Nathan, having their grown daughter back on their hands again.

Sonia could read the thought balloons over their heads. It was one of the side effects of her illness, or maybe her drugs. People smiled and said one thing, but the thought balloon said the opposite.

Therapists who tried to read Sonia's thought balloons only ever saw a cloud so dense they couldn't make out the words. They imagined anger when it was usually sadness or fragility.

2. My agent. Molly Pierrot. *I've tried every gallery in the Northeast, Sonia, but I warned you that the days of big abstract installations are over. And these pieces lack coherence. They're derivative of Louise Nevelson. Blah, blah, blah.*

Sonia couldn't remember with great clarity what happened next, but she'd been caught on a surveillance tape smashing the front window of the Zivany Sculpture Gallery on Newbury Street with a fire extinguisher and then posing in the show window naked except for a placard that read ABSTRACT EXPRESSIONIST GOING-OUT-OF-BUSINESS SALE, 50¢ OR BEST OFFER. Her arms and feet were bleeding from where she'd sliced them on the broken plate glass of the gallery window.

Sonia thought her exhibition was witty, but the cops thought it was criminal trespass. *Why is it art when Marina Abramović stands naked onstage and cuts herself but criminal trespass and indecent exposure when I do it?* Sonia had demanded, first of the arresting officer and then the assistant DA handling emergency warrants that night. No one answered, just a lot of eye-rolling.

She didn't have money for bail and found herself in a holding cell with five other women, one of them puking all night, two of them delusional. She'd been there . . . a day? A week? She wasn't sure.

And then Nathan suddenly appeared, explained to a judge that she had diminished responsibility. Waved around those papers that CheeseNuts, winner of first place in the dickhead competition, the dickiest head of all, signed when she was fourteen. *That was twenty years ago, ancient history,* she said, but the DA murmured sympathetically with Nathan. Balloon over head saying, *Didn't need a piece of paper to show me she's nuts.*

The Zivany Gallery said they wouldn't press charges if Sonia, meaning Nathan, replaced the window. The DA's office said they'd let everything go if Nathan took her back to Kansas. Back to Cheese-Nuts, DDH. Dr. Dickhead.

Molly called yesterday to say she'd sold three pieces, one to a private collector. And two to the Zivany Gallery, oh, irony of ironies. There's excitement attached to a piece by a certified crazy person. Molly acted as though she'd created the drama just to help my career. Maybe a woman can't be a dickhead, but she can show more sliminess than most of the male varieties. Bitch, wormhole, you get 35 percent and you want me to thank you for taking it. Fuck off.

Sonia didn't tell her parents about the sale. They would have taken the money in the name of protecting her from her impulsiveness. Or to cover the bills Nathan had paid in Boston.

3. Shirley Kiel. *Greatest drunk I've known.*

Sonia underlined her mother's name in her journal with such heavy strokes that the pen tore through the paper. Nathan was hard to live with. Okay, Nathan was impossible to live with, but when Shirley was younger, she hadn't wanted to leave him. She'd rather sit with a cup of vodka—sort of disguised as coffee—muttering under her breath, rehearsing all the insults she would slam him with when they sat down to a burned-up dinner.

Now that Shirley was almost eighty, she would never leave. Where would she go?

Sonia thought about putting fluoxetine in her mother's vodka bottles. Supposedly it diminished your desire for alcohol, even if you couldn't admit you had a drinking problem.

Fluoxetine, olanzapine, her own cocktails. Prescribed by Cheese-Nuts, hovered over by Dan Bors. Dan had been a creep in first grade, and he was still a creep when they graduated from high school twelve years later. He'd crept off to pharmaceutical school and now he was rubbing his sweaty palms against Sonia's pills, going home, telling his grinning bottle-blond wife— What was her name? It sounded like Jaundice. Jaundice did something or other at the university.

Of course, Nathan would have told everyone in his lab about his latest bout of martyrdom at the hands of his unstable daughter. He'd stopped teaching eight years ago, but he still kept his lab, still dabbled in experiments, still had a couple of graduate students, faithful unto death, Shirley put it. *They work with the lab mice but they don't understand they're lab rats themselves, clinging to your father like a piece of decaying driftwood far out to sea.*

Shirley had studied English and drama when she'd been an earnest undergraduate, and even after decades of vodka she could still quote reams of poetry. Most often Amy Lowell, ending with "Christ! What are patterns for?" so many times that Sonia and her older brothers used to chant it as a chorus to any complaint.

Like the night that Larry took the car without permission and drove to Kansas City with his buddies to watch the Smashing Pumpkins at the Starlight Theatre. Larry drove off the road on their way home. He'd been picked up by the sheriff for drunk driving, and the car had to be towed out of the drainage ditch. Somehow a branch had lanced the radiator.

Nathan was predictably furious, so Shirley took refuge in mordant laughter. When Nathan finished with his tirade, Larry and Sonia and Stu shouted, "Christ! What are patterns for?" which of course made Nathan and Shirley even more furious. It seemed strange that Nathan had lived to be eighty without popping a blood vessel.

And then there was the night that Sonia— That saga had ended not with Amy Lowell but CheeseNuts. Whose name was on the bottles she'd picked up from sweaty Dan Bors. Twenty years later and she was back where she'd started.

Sonia October 2016

I don't know what is real, I can't touch what I feel, And I hide behind the shield of my illusion

She'd been reading old copies of the *Douglas County Herald* on the group home's computer when she saw the report of the air force sale of the land east of the silo. It wasn't reported like that, not as a story: *United States Air Force sells sacred ground to greedy grubbing corporation.* It was a report in the legal notices: sale of 15 acres, lat: 38.946021, long: −95.120369, from a line extending from one-sixteenth mile north of North 1420 Road and so on.

Sonia knew those numbers, knew every inch of that land, every way of describing it. In his sympathetic moments, Randy tried to get her to admit how exhausting such knowledge must be: *It weighs you down, Sonia, keeps you from moving on.*

She didn't want to move on. She'd seen Nathan, she was sure she'd seen him, heard him yelling at Matt: *You subhuman specimen, how could you do this to me? Do you hate me that much?*

Matt had fallen over and hadn't gotten up. Had Nathan hit him? She thought it was the heavy blows from the words, not from her father's fists, that had sent him to the ground.

She'd been watching from behind one of the tents, the tent where Jennifer and her baby had lain, both of them pretending to sleep so they wouldn't have to face Nathan. Jennifer had even kept her eyes shut when the soldiers carried her to the car.

When Matt fell over, Sonia stood like the witless lump her father often called her. It was like the day in the lab all over again. The memory made her hot with shame and finally gave her strength to move over to him. *I will heal him, and he will be forever grateful. Jennifer isn't moving, she doesn't really care. How beautiful is my beloved.*

Her heavy legs, she walked like a polar bear, maybe she'd been half transformed when Stu and Larry played polar bear with her. She'd never grown fur or big protective claws and teeth, had only acquired the lumbering, uncertain gait of a bear on its hind legs.

She'd flung herself on Matt, hadn't she? Sonia rolled so that she blocked Jenny's view. The Magpie appeared from nowhere, and then Nathan, crazy with fury, came back. Fury with her or the Magpie or both of them? A baby was crying. Magda was telling Nathan he had to do something about the baby.

Sonia looked up from Matt's body. She found her polar-bear voice and growled, *Nathan doesn't have tits, you ignorant bitch! He can't nurse a baby, and he for sure never changed a diaper in his life, so don't expect him to look after a baby for you!*

She bent over Matt to give him mouth-to-mouth resuscitation, but the Magpie pulled her away, screaming in bird talk, and Nathan joined her, the two of them yanking on Sonia's arms, dragging her away from her beloved. She went limp, the way the protesters did at the silo, and Nathan let go of her. Dusted his hands: *I'm washing my hands of you.*

Nathan strode away, got back in his car, but the Magpie kept hopping around, looking for treasures. Sonia saw the movie, but the soldiers were arguing with the Magpie, so no one else was watching.

The soldiers left, the Magpie left, no one paid attention to Sonia, lying on the ground with her arms around Matt, his blood oozing onto her breasts—we are joined now for eternity, we are blood brother and sister. She heard a baby crying, but it seemed so far away and she was too heavy to move.

The fire came. Some man screamed—*She's alive!*—and they lifted her into a truck. Come along unless you want to be burned alive. *I want to be burned alive. I want you to burn me up with Matt.*

First she thought they had: burning, freezing, lungs aching for air, a sound like ocean waves. Only slowly did she realize that the ocean waves came from a machine making her breathe, in, out, until someone said, *She's going to make it, she's breathing on her own,* but then when she tried to sit up, her head had been stuffed full of cotton.

Gertrude Perec, Nathan's secretary, liked to tell about the time her mother filled banana skins with cotton and glued them together so carefully they looked untouched. Then she handed them out to people as a joke. *My head is a banana skin sewn full of cotton.*

That was CheeseNuts, but she didn't realize it until much later, of course. CheeseNuts had filled her head with lithium. He agreed with Nathan that she had dreamed up the whole scene at the silo. Vivid imagination turning into delusions. They'd all tut-tutted sadly, even Shirley, looking at her with a malevolent eye that said, *You lost. You didn't know you were in a race, and you're already so far behind you might as well give up.*

Why should I give you or Nathan or CheeseNuts the satisfaction of putting my obsession aside? she said to Randy. *No one tells you that memorizing every variety of grass in the Midwest is exhausting. No one tells CheeseNuts what an imbecile he sounds like when he starts talking about terroir and how 1883 was the best year for horse piss but 1992 was better for cow manure.*

When she read the legal notice—three years old by the time she saw it—that old itch came over her. She had to get out to the land, see that his grave was secure. She'd hitched a ride partway, walked the rest of the way. Not so bad when you didn't have a job you had to get up for, you could spend a night walking those country roads.

The sun was coming up when she finally got there, and Sonia could see that it was worse than she'd thought. A fence slicing through the graveyard, plants—corn or alfalfa or some stupid farm crop. And then like some nightmare, there was the Magpie, hopping along, stealing the seeds. She was older, and her hair was bleached so it looked like strings.

You shouldn't bleach your hair. The chemicals make it ropy, Sonia said, and the Magpie said, *Who the fuck are you?*

Some men were with the Magpie, of course—there were always men with her—and they laughed and said, *Who is that?*

One of her fans. I saw you at the movies, hopping along between the tents. When your hair was red and your tits were full of useless milk. Why are you despoiling Matt's grave?

The Magpie lunged at her, but Sonia backed away. The men said Sonia was a lunatic and leave her alone, and she hitched a ride back to town. After that, though, she couldn't stay away. She kept coming back, watching them desecrate the grave. Until the night she saw trolls digging it up! She'd tried to stop them, but the sheriff came just as he had thirty years ago, threw her into his truck, bad girl, Sonia, get off the land.

43

HAZMAT SITE

THE CARILLON HAD bonged midnight, and then one, before I finished sifting through the papers in the trunk. Bernie was heavily asleep, despite the lamps I had turned on and the clicking of my fingers on my keyboard. She'd been in a bright mood when I came in, which made me think she'd hatched a scheme with Cady, but I didn't have the energy to catechize her on it. I also prudently didn't ask to see her French essay.

Sonia's fury and pain with her parents made those parts of her journals almost incoherent, but she wrote about the staff and other residents at St. Rafe's with a compassion she apparently couldn't speak aloud. She seemed to have built a relationship with two of the children in St. Rafe's permanent housing units, although she colluded with their mother in hiding substance use: *Mindy let me have Lima and Autumn this afternoon. Hopscotch, swings, ice cream . . . Mindy passed out, I took L & A, walked out in garden, we painted until Mindy woke up.*

The suitcase included a number of drawings, most of them quick sketches, although Sonia had taken care with portraits of the little girls. She'd caught them in action, playing hopscotch, and had captured the intensity of children concentrating on a project. She'd drawn Randy Marx as part grasshopper, his wide lips exaggerated, while he counted grass seeds into piles.

I found a colored sketch of an adult Cady Perec looking at herself in a mirror, freckles prominent, copper hair done in ponytails that made her look like a child. *Who are you?* the mirror was asking her. A savage self-portrait of Sonia showed up in a corner of the mirror, leering down at Cady's reflection. Another self-portrait: Sonia's face in the body of a polar bear, swimming in a giant teacup whose liquid was labeled *"Lithium."* Underneath it Sonia had printed *"The Bi-Polar Bear."* My heart twisted with pain at her self-loathing.

Of most interest to me was a series of sketches of a man's face. He had dark hair that grew almost to his collar and fell over his forehead in unkempt bangs. There were at least thirty versions of the face, some seemingly dating to Sonia's adolescence, when the sketches were more immature.

I laid them out on the floor. When Peppy came over to inspect, I asked her opinion. "This is undoubtedly Matt Chastain, the clumsiest SOB who ever set foot in Nathan Kiel's lab. Which are the two best, do you think? Shall we launch them into the ether?"

Peppy wagged her tail, knocking one of the newer sketches askew. I took that one, and one of Sonia's juvenile efforts that held the clearest depiction of Chastain's eyes and mouth. I photographed them and posted them on Imgur, created a subreddit for Matt Chastain, put them on Facebook. *"Matt Chastain, graduate student at the University of Kansas in the 1980s, missing since 1983. Do you know him? Do you know his family? Please contact V.I. Warshawski."* I added my e-mail address, my cell number, and my Facebook and Twitter pages. There didn't seem much else to do tonight but go to bed.

I'd been in Lawrence less than a week, and I'd been hauled out of bed almost every night, but Sunday the natives seemed less restless and allowed me the sleep of the blessed. I didn't wake until nine, when Peppy licked my face, demanding to be let out. Bernie was still asleep, but she stirred when I opened the door for Peppy.

"You got it, girl. We're rested, we're awake, aware, alive, we're going to crack this case wide open today."

Several people had posted on my Facebook page, suggesting Matt Chastains that they knew in different parts of the country. When I dug up their details, two of them seemed to be about the right age. I sent them e-mails, then did my full workout, which I hadn't had time for in the last few mornings. Once I'd showered, Bernie was awake and fully ready to play detective.

I told her to take the dog for a run while I drove to the market for kefir and fruit. I also made phone calls, including to the hospital, where Sonia continued to breathe on her own in her medical coma.

When Bernie came back, she said she'd ride downtown with me, but she didn't want to watch me answer e-mails at the Hippo; she'd explore the town on her own.

I looked at her narrowly but couldn't imagine what mischief she could get up to in broad daylight without a car. I agreed to drop her at the Hippo and told her to stay in touch.

Bernie had given Peppy a good run, so the dog was content to lie at my feet while I drank coffee and answered messages. I had begun recognizing the regulars in the Hippo: a woman who owned an art gallery on Massachusetts Street, a graduate student in English lit who always came in with a stack of books but played a video game while his coffee grew cold. Only a few greeted me, but most stopped to scratch Peppy's ears.

My first e-mail of the day came from the Cheviot lab in suburban Chicago, to tell me they had cleared the mal- and spyware from my computer, phone, and tablet and added the most sophisticated encryption protocols possible, for a fee only slightly less than the national debt.

When I thought of the charges I was incurring every night I was away from home, my blood ran cold. I did the prudent thing and stopped thinking about them.

I wondered how much of Sonia's journal was reliable. There'd been a fire—at least the *Douglas County Herald* had reported one—but the chronology with Matt Chastain and the bad experiment was impossible to sort out from Sonia's writing. Her description of her symptoms sounded like a serious illness: she'd run a high fever, been attached to a ventilator. Could she have contracted polio? Is that what Matt Chastain, or the woman from Bratislava, or Kiel himself had spread around?

I shuddered. The Salk vaccine had been in place during my childhood, but there'd been a teen across the street from me, a girl who'd lived to dance. Polio left her walking only with an elaborately constructed set of braces.

I had a message from Cady, reinforcing the invitation to Bernie to visit her classroom and to ask what I'd decided to do about going to the Sea-2-Sea field at night. TOMORROW SHOULD BE CLEAR. I KNOW A PLACE TO ROLL UNDER THE FENCE WITHOUT SETTING OFF THE ALARMS. TEN O'CLOCK?

If I'd thought any trace of Emerald Ferring or August was in those fields, I would have cast prudence to the winds. But Baggetto and Pinsen had had plenty of time to scour them. The soil I'd taken on McKinnon's side of the fence should have the same toxins as the dirt eight feet away.

I wrote Cady back to say I'd reconsidered; it would be foolhardy, even dangerous, to go. She didn't reply. I hoped that meant she was sulking but wouldn't go without me.

I sighed, dispirited, and turned back to my to-do list, started with a phone call to the geology professor's office. A secretary answered.

I introduced myself as an investigator looking into circumstances around Dr. Roquc's death. "Since his last phone calls were from Professor Hitchcock, I'm hoping the professor would be willing to tell me what they were discussing."

"Who are you really?" the secretary said.

"Really, I am V.I. Warshawski, a private investigator." I repeated my message.

"I . . . I can't talk to you."

"What, did someone from the army tell you not to? Just put me through to Professor Hitchcock and you can safely say we never spoke."

"It's . . . that's not possible, I'm sorry." It sounded as though she was starting to cry.

"Ma'am, please tell me what the problem is."

She hung up. I stared baffled at my phone.

"How'd you get hold of that name, Warshawski?"

I looked up, startled: Sergeant Everard had come in without my noticing.

"I'll tell you if you'll explain why there's a lockdown on anyone letting me talk to him."

Everard eyed me measuringly, looked around to see who was in earshot. "Outside."

No one had seemed to be paying attention, but I suppose that's how the local network got its feed: people texted or worked the crossword while their ears pointed toward the most interesting conversation in the room.

Peppy followed us. We moved away from the smokers in the outdoor seats and leaned against an iron railing in front of the neighboring building.

"Dr. Hitchcock was hospitalized over the weekend, with acute pneumonia," Everard said. "They medevacked him to Cleveland last night, to the Cleveland Clinic, which apparently can do a better job than anything we have in Kansas."

"Pneumonia? Not flu?"

"What difference does it make?"

"Dr. Roque died of flu. He and Hitchcock were close friends, and . . . I don't know. It seems weird, too much of a coincidence, both men being so sick. Does flu cause pneumonia?"

"I don't know about that." Everard was impatient. "All I know is the army shut down Hitchcock's lab last night as a hazardous site that needs professional cleaning. His students, his staff, anyone who's been near him—they're all in quarantine."

"His secretary just answered the phone," I objected.

"I don't know about that," he repeated. "I'm giving you the scuttlebutt, and I only know that much because I have a cousin who works for the university's public-safety department. Now it's your turn. How do you know Hitchcock, or know enough to call him?"

"Doris McKinnon sent Dr. Roque some soil samples that she wanted tested."

"And you know this because . . . ?"

"Because I talked to Dr. Roque's chief tech, whom you are not to bother or harass. She told me about Dr. Roque and the black mold—remember that?"

"Oh, yes. It turned him into a local hero. I think Dr. Kiel's nose was out of joint because Roque got so much publicity from it. Kiel's usually the go-to guy around here for odd deaths." Everard flashed a brief grin. "Black mold. Then what?"

"The tech thinks maybe Doris sent Dr. Roque dirt samples to be tested because of the mold story."

When I stopped, Everard said coldly, "And then what?"

"And then I need your word of honor as a whatever you most honor that you will not feed the tech to the KC cops, Colonel Baggetto, Marlon Pinsen, Gisborne, or your own revered lieutenant."

"Not if you're concealing evidence of a crime," the sergeant growled.

"I'm not concealing any crimes. They're all right out in the open where anyone who cares can see them."

Everard rocked back and forth on his toes. It takes serious strength in the soleus muscle to do that in thick-soled shoes.

At length he said, "How can a stranger to these parts team up with an unknown lab tech in less than a week? I'll give you this: I'll let the tech go, but if you're covering up a crime, I'll feed you to the sheriff, the colonel, and all those other people. I'll even add salt so you go down more tasty."

My hands were freezing. I jammed them into my jeans pockets. "Someone broke into Roque's home, in between his leaving for Topeka on Thursday morning and Saturday night, which is when the tech discovered it. She went over to rescue his cat—she always fed it when he was out of town. She had a key. She'd forgotten the cat in her grief and misery. She called me."

"And?" Everard eyed me measuringly, testing my story in his

mind. All true, just not necessarily in that sequence, but it made me feel and therefore sound solid as a rock.

"I gather that the damage was impressive enough that she couldn't tell if anything was missing, except his home computer. But the last three incoming calls on his home phone were from Hitchcock. When I learned that, it made me think Roque consulted with Hitchcock—they shared a passion for collecting rocks, geodes, the tech said. I was hoping Hitchcock could tell me what Roque said, maybe even that he had Doris McKinnon's dirt. If the lab has been declared a hazmat site, it's a cinch that Roque sent the dirt to Hitchcock. Something's in it that Colonel Baggetto or AKA Pinsen knows is toxic. Let me stress that *I* have no idea if it is or isn't."

Everard spoke into his lapel phone. A voice squawked something back, and he pulled out his cell phone. After a minute I could see messages scrolling on his screen.

"KC confirms the break-in, says they got an anonymous tip. You know anything about that, Warshawski?"

"No, Sergeant." Liars are voluble; I kept my smart add-ons to myself.

"Kansas City sure as sin doesn't need any help from the Lawrence cops, who are overworked anyway, so I'll leave that dog lay."

His baleful glance fell on Peppy, who shrank closer to me. "Not you, girl. You keep giving emotional support." He bent to scratch her ears. "Since you know so much, Warshawski, tell me where McKinnon's dirt came from."

"I don't know, but I guess from her land, or what used to be her land. The churchwomen at St. Silas and Riverside tell me that back in September or October they saw Ms. McKinnon at the farmers' market. She was upset because people were planting on her land. They told me she didn't have the energy to farm anymore, that she'd been leasing the land to other farmers, and she hadn't been out on the perimeter for a while. The air force had seized another fifteen acres from her back in 1983 or '84. They let Sea-2-Sea buy it two or three years ago, I guess without her knowing. So Sea-2-Sea is planting on what used to be her land, which the air force had said was too contaminated with radiation to cultivate. In her place I would have been spitting mad and looked for confirmation."

Everard punched his left fist into his open palm. "I am so fucking goddamn sick of being shut out from every piece of this damned investigation."

I stared at him. "Sergeant—I'm not shutting you out. How can I? I don't have any official status. I talk to people, and if I'm lucky, they talk back to me."

His mouth set in a hard line. "Church ladies, army colonels, lab techs—hell, the nurses at the hospital called you before they called me yesterday when someone tried to suffocate Sonia Kiel!"

"It's my full-time job," I said lamely. "I'm not answering calls about home invasions or armed robberies on Iowa Street."

Everard walked away from me, made a little circle while he communed with himself, came back, squatted to pet the dog.

"Francis Roque was one of the good guys. Now, given what's happened to Dr. Hitchcock, it sounds as though Roque's death was engin— But that doesn't make sense. You don't give someone pneumonia and hope they'll die on you at just the right moment. I'm going to find out if there's an autopsy. If there isn't—I'll see if I can make it happen."

"And you'll sharc the results with me because . . . ?"

"Because if I don't, you'll do whatever magic dance you do that gets church ladies and nameless techs to confide their deepest secrets."

I squeezed his forearm. "If it's any comfort, Sergeant, you're one of the good guys, too."

44

SWABBING THE DECKS, OR SOMETHING

AFTER EVERARD LEFT, I went back into the Hippo, but I couldn't focus on any of the mail or messages needing my attention. Hitchcock and Roque, both with serious lung illnesses. Both exposed to dirt from Sea-2-Sea's experimental farm. I'd been walking that land; I wondered if I had some bug multiplying in me that would suddenly make me start to gasp and choke. I took a deep breath and heard myself wheezing.

I called Lotty, who was in surgery. I called her clinic and spoke to Jewel Kim, her advanced-practice nurse.

"Oh, yes, those photographs you sent Lotty," Jewel said. "She got them late on Saturday, you know. She sent them on to me, but I only saw them this morning. Her cover note said she couldn't tell anything from the pictures. She doubts that anyone could make a diagnosis of anything except drowning, but she asked me to pass them on to the Beth Israel pathology team. I've done that, but, Vic, you can't be impatient about it—they have a lot of work of their own, and they probably won't get back to me before Wednesday at the earliest."

I thanked her but explained I was calling about a different problem and told her about Hitchcock's illnesses. "I'm wondering if it's the same strain of flu that killed his good friend, Dr. Roque."

"I can't possibly guess at a diagnosis over the phone for two men I've never laid eyes on," Jewel said, exasperated. "I know Lotty would tell you the same."

"When you put it like that—"

"It *is* like that," Jewel said.

"Here's the problem: A local farmer—also now dead—sent soil samples to Dr. Roque, wanting to know if they were contaminated. I'm pretty sure Dr. Roque sent them to Dr. Hitchcock. So . . . what was in the soil that made both men sick? I wondered if the soil was contaminated by someone playing around with the 1919 flu—I keep hearing about a 1983 experiment that went awry and wondering if that has something to do with the murders and the illnesses and so on."

"I see," Jewel said slowly. "When you put it like *that* . . ."

She put me on hold but came back after five minutes to say that she'd texted the surgical secretary at Beth Israel. "If Lotty has a break in the afternoon, I've asked her to call the Cleveland Clinic and find out what they say about Dr. Hitchcock."

"I collected dirt from what I think is the place they got their samples. Could I be at risk of whatever is ailing him?"

"Vic, please, don't do such stupid things!" Jewel cried. "Lotty worries about you day and night. Don't do something that will break her heart, I'm begging you."

"But . . . could these men have contracted flu from farm dirt?"

"I don't know, but can't you for once leave something alone? At least until Lotty talks to the Cleveland Clinic?"

"Jewel, you suspect something, don't you?" I demanded.

"Anthrax," she finally blurted. "It could get into the lungs, make a doctor who wasn't expecting it not look for it. Don't go digging in contaminated soil!" She cut the connection.

Anthrax. Biohazard of choice for terrorists. Abortion clinics get threats of it pretty much every week, and of course the whole government mail apparatus was changed because of anthrax attacks following 9/11. I looked it up on the Mayo Clinic site, but it was hard to tell from the description of the symptoms if it could be mistaken for pneumonia. I fingered my lymph glands, checking for swelling.

"You are healthy as a hog, V.I. Warshawski," I said sternly.

More important was any risk I might bring Bernie, as well as the danger Cady could face if she went digging in McKinnon's land.

I texted Aanya Malik, Dr. Roque's technician, to ask if there was any chance he'd died of anthrax. She phoned me back almost instantly.

"Vic, about the anthrax. It is possible that spores are in the soil that Dr. Roque and Dr. Hitchcock handled, but then why did not the woman who sent the samples to Dr. Roque also have anthrax?"

"I don't know that she didn't," I said.

"You found her body. She was shot—that killed her. If she had been as sick as Dr. Roque, she could not have been driving that truck to begin with, believe me." She paused, fumbling for words. "I know that looking at the dead cannot be easy, but did she have black discolorations on her face or hands, something like a hard smear of tar perhaps?"

I pulled out my phone and looked at the pictures I had snapped. It had been dusk, the light was bad, and McKinnon's face was barely visible. It was mottled: she was old, and death had accentuated the liverish patches in her cheeks, but I didn't think I could see any tar-like smears. I forwarded the photos to Aanya.

"I will ask the pathologist who will do the autopsy to be sure to check for traces," Aanya promised. "Dr. Roque's children have agreed to let us have an independent autopsy of the doctor, and Dr. Madej, who will do that, can also arrange to work on Doris McKinnon. Although the anthrax bacillus itself dies quickly after the host dies, there would be traces. And I will show him the photographs you took of Ms. McKinnon."

I asked when the autopsy would be performed; she thought Dr. Madej would start work on it later this afternoon. "We trust Dr. Madej, Ruby—Dr. Roque's secretary—and I do. Dr. Roque himself trained Dr. Madej. He won't cut corners or make a cover-up."

"A cover-up?"

Aanya laughed in embarrassment. "Everything that is going on with Dr. Roque's death and Dr. Hitchcock's illness is so unreal—I feel as though I'm in one of those spy movies. Anything could happen, and I want to make sure that it does not. But that is not why I called. It's because of another strange event.

"Ruby and I, we were starting to go through things in Dr. Roque's lab, to see what open cases he had that needed to be sent to another pathologist. And I found the hand of an infant."

I pictured a baby's hand in a jar and asked a startled question.

"No, no, nothing that macabre—you have such a wrong idea of Dr. Roque! It is a tiny set of bones in a specimen case, dated and labeled. It came with the soil from Doris McKinnon."

The bits of bone Doris had dug up that night in the field. Not a badger or a raccoon but a human baby.

"What . . . Did he . . . Was there a report?" I managed to stammer.

"He estimated the bones to be about twenty-five to forty years old. He was able to get a DNA sample, but there was no match in any databases."

Another baby at the missile silo, with the age range framing the summer Cady was born. Another baby, one who'd been killed and left to lie there? Had Jennifer Perec produced a stillborn twin to Cady? Or Sonia, with her wild dreams about Matt and that journal entry describing hearing a baby crying—was it possible that Sonia had given birth but that she'd blotted out all memory of a pregnancy and delivery?

"Vic, you are still listening to me?"

"I'm here," I said, "but so bewildered I don't have anything to say. Could he tell the child's sex?"

"A girl, perhaps two or three months old."

"If I wanted you to try to match DNA from a living person, what would I need to send you? Would hair be enough?"

"Only if it's a living hair with the root attached. Saliva or blood would be better. What are you thinking?"

"Right now my ideas are like a white sauce that won't thicken, a mess of lumpy flour and milk. Get that bone case someplace safe, would you?"

I hung up and squatted down next to Peppy. "I wonder if that's the small object the marauders were looking for when they turned August's apartment and the Six-Points Gym upside down. Colonel Baggetto said they were missing a canister, but what if it was a baby's bones?"

Peppy thumped her tail once. Agreement. That meant I should follow my impulse and try to get a DNA sample from both Sonia and Cady, to see if the dead infant was related to either of them, to Cady's mother, or to Sonia as mother.

I texted Cady, asking if I could interrupt her workday for five minutes. "Something odd came up connected to Doris McKinnon's land. Would you undergo a DNA test?"

Cady was so excited that her text jumped off the screen, filled with absurd autocorrections. She broke for lunch at eleven forty-five; she could meet me at the Prairie Shores Café on Eleventh and New Hampshire.

That gave me time to drive to one of the big chain drugstores on Highway 10 and buy a few sterile sample kits and gloves. When I got back to midtown, Cady was hopping on the sidewalk in front of the café.

"What did you find? I can't go inside—everyone in there knows me. If they hear me talking to you about evidence at the silo, someone for sure will tell Gram. Did you find bones? My father's? The pearl ring my mother wore? It wasn't on her when they found her body, unless one of the deputies stole it."

I felt stricken. "Cady, I haven't found anything that definite. Some bones turned up that are old enough to have belonged to someone at the missile protest, but the person wasn't old enough to have been your mother or father. I can't justify asking for your DNA, but it could help to see if you are related to the dead child."

As I spoke, my words sounded lame to me, and Cady's excitement died down. Even so, she let me swab the inside of her cheek and watched me seal it up and label it. We went inside for lunch, but she was nervous and picked at her food. As she'd said, everyone in the café knew her—teachers, people from the courthouse across the park, friends of her grandmother. She couldn't focus on what anyone said to her. After stirring a bowl of chili for some minutes, so vigorously it slopped over onto her lap, she announced she had to get back to class.

I followed her outside, but she cut off my awkward apology.

"There's something else," I said. "Two men who handled Doris McKinnon's soil samples became gravely ill—one died, the other is fighting for his life. Sea-2-Sea is farming that land. There haven't been reports of other illnesses in the area, but the company could be suppressing that information. We need to know if Dr. Roque and Dr. Hitchcock caught the same bug and if they got it from McKinnon's soil."

"It's not very likely, is it? None of the farmhands from Sea-2-Sea are turning up sick."

"Nonetheless—"

"Nonetheless, you are trying to control what decisions I make, and, frankly, Vic, however well-meaning you are, that's not your call."

Bernie joined us at that moment. "There you are. Again you are not answering your phone. I went to the Hippo, but they could tell me nothing. I have been trying to do your work. I am sure the Protestants are hiding something."

It turned out she'd gone over to Riverside Church. Pastor Weld and Pastor Carmody had both read her the riot act when they found her hunting through the basement; according to her, if I'd been there, I could have entertained them while she, Bernie, searched for August—"Since only I care what has become of him. Are you doing any investigating today or only reading diaries created by *femmes folles*?"

"I'm going to visit one of these women right now. She's near death, so your hypervibrant presence might do her good."

"Maybe I can go over to Cady's school," Bernie said. "It is possible I myself will become a teacher."

"God help the children," I said, but I was relieved when Cady reinforced the idea: she could use a teacher's aide; budget cuts up and down the line in the state meant classrooms were bulging and support staff shrinking.

"As long as Bernie doesn't think she can start questioning my judgment," Cady added, with a pointed look at me.

I drove over to the hospital, my own spirits sagging. Sandy Heinz was on duty, fortunately, and told the security guard on the floor that it was all right for me to visit Sonia.

There were two large bouquets in the room, one from each brother. *"We're pulling for you, little bear, get well soon,"* Stuart had written. *"Go get those demon seals, little bear,"* Larry's card said.

I sat with her for a time. She was breathing on her own but still not conscious, and she seemed to have shrunk since my Saturday visit. I told her I'd read her journals and seen her sketches of Matt Chastain. "I put them out on Instagram and Facebook. I'll let you know if I hear anything. Your brothers love you, little polar bear."

Finally, with a nervous glance around to make sure the security guard's attention was elsewhere, I took out a sample bottle and swabbed her cheek.

I texted Aanya, saying I was going to drive the samples over to Kansas City to hand to her personally. She gave me directions to the lab, on the outskirts of the city.

On my way out of town, I dropped Peppy off at Free State Dogs and drove east, passing the Kanwaka Missile Silo. On an impulse I turned south to look at Sea-2-Sea's local offices. Since there were two rings of security fences, an outer one of eight-foot-high cyclone fencing with an inner ring of more attractive ironwork, it was hard to make out the details, but the complex seemed to comprise a series of Quonset huts, with a central drab brick office building in front of them. Whatever they did there must be mighty secret.

I hadn't seen either the sheriff or the colonel since we'd parted at the court on Saturday morning, but a Douglas County sheriff's squad car was parked across from barricaded front gate. When I stopped to look at the compound, a deputy got out and started toward me. He seemed to be photographing my license plates, which is always annoying.

"Can I help you, miss?" His tone wasn't inviting.

"I don't think so." I flashed a smile. "I'm wondering if I can help you, since you wanted my license-plate number."

"Routine precaution," he said, but he shifted uneasily, embarrassed at having been caught in the act. "I want to see—"

"Yes," I said sympathetically, stopping him before he could demand my license and insurance card. "I understand that Mr. Roswell is worried about hippies. I'm wondering if these mythical hippies should worry about anthrax."

"Anthrax?" He forgot about my license.

"I've been told Sea-2-Sea may be producing it here. Since it's a Category A bioweapon, I would expect a bigger protection detail than just one squad car. But I expect they're giving you antibiotics and a vaccine just in case."

I made a U-turn, spitting up gravel on his car, and left him in the road, staring after me.

45

HERE FOR THE DURATION

I DROVE ON TOWARD Kansas City, across the Wakarusa, past the place where I'd found Doris McKinnon in her truck on Friday, then followed Aanya's directions to the medical center. She met me at the entrance, so that I didn't need to go through security, and said if my swabs were good, she should have some results within the next day or two. I had wanted to see the bones she and Roque's secretary had uncovered, but she told me that the place where she'd secured them would take a good half hour or forty-five minutes to reach.

"Just as well that they're off-site," I said. "I don't know if that's what the vermin who invaded Dr. Roque's house were looking for, but better not to leave them where those creeps can get at them."

As I drove back to Lawrence, my thoughts churned uselessly. What did the army or Sea-2-Sea or Dr. Kiel, whoever was behind Douglas County's mayhem, need to find so desperately? I couldn't believe it had anything to do with drug manufacture. The U.S. Army wouldn't send a high-ranking colonel to a meth plant, and much as Nathan Kiel rubbed me the wrong way, I didn't see him as a drug lord.

I kept coming back to bioweapons. Roswell, the senior Sea-2-Sea executive, belonged to some group that supported rearmament. When I'd read about it, I'd thought of nukes, but the group could be interested in bioweapons as well. Dr. Kiel would know a lot about anthrax. Whether he knew anything about how to turn it into a weapon, he would still be someone the army or a private contractor would consult if they wanted to culture bioweapons in Lawrence.

If Roswell was producing weapons at the Sea-2-Sea compound, why would they also be growing crops nearby? As a cover for their weapons program? On the other hand, agricultural waste is spewed everywhere without a second thought; Sea-2-Sea might think nothing of selling sorghum grown in contaminated soil.

What about the spent fuel rods that Baggetto said he was looking for? Was that a cover, too? Baggetto had bugged my room. It could be to see whether I talked to anyone about fuel rods, but the story of the rods might be another cover story. Cover for bioweapons?

Bernie was still with Cady at the school. I drove to the B and B, where I returned to the databases with Dr. Kiel's research history. I couldn't find any articles that showed him involved with anthrax research. He'd started life working on something called *C. burnetii* in 1958 and had switched to *Y. enterocolitica* in the late 1970s. These germs had nothing to do with anthrax: the first was called a rickettsia; it gave you Rocky Mountain spotted fever. The second caused a nonfatal intestinal ailment.

By now it was three in the afternoon. How drunk would Shirley Kiel be? How choleric her husband?

The VW wasn't in the drive when I got to the Kiel house, and no one answered the front door. It was hard to imagine that both parents were at the hospital worrying over their daughter, but of course they might be at the grocery store or taking in an afternoon movie. My mouth twisted as I tried to picture the Kiels in some banal and harmonious activity.

I pushed my way through the heavy bushes along the side of the house to the back, where the sunporch overlooked an untended garden. A light was on; when I stood on a rusting garden chair, I saw Shirley, crossword book in hand, head back, eyes closed. Movement in her chest: she wasn't dead. Snoozing or passed out.

The chair began wobbling underneath me. I jumped clear as it fell over.

"Who are you?" A neighbor had appeared at the fence next to the Kiel house, a woman around seventy, holding a basket of plant bulbs.

"I'm someone who badly needs to speak to Shirley and Nathan about their daughter. Shirley's home, but she's not answering the door."

"Oh. Poor Sonia. Are you a social worker?"

"Private investigator."

She suppressed a smile. "Ah, the famous woman from Chicago who is uncovering all the sins and crimes of Douglas County. Shirley was complaining about you when I saw her at the farmers' market on Saturday. Gertrude Perec also chimed in, but Barbara Rutledge had an opposing view. You've provided us with a lot of entertainment. Nathan is probably in his lab, but if you want to wake Shirley, the back door is unlocked."

The town jester, that was me, racing back and forth between silo and river while the locals lined up to evaluate my performance. "You know all these people, and I don't. Do you know why Ms. Perec is so angry when Cady tries to ask about her father? I wondered if he was an old graduate student of Dr. Kiel's, but that made Ms. Perec really blow up at me."

The woman shook her head. "That's puzzled me all these years, too. It's somehow tied up in her great loyalty to Dr. Kiel. However, I don't know Gertrude well—we used to volunteer together at the League of Women Voters—but Cady's birth has always been a sore spot. Maybe while you're here, you can sort that out, too."

I made a face but thanked her for her advice on the back door, which opened with only a slight groan from the warped wood. The door led through a small mudroom to the kitchen. The Mixmaster was still on the floor, where it had been joined by a large pot.

"Ms. Kiel!" I shouted, careful not to touch the counters. "Shirley!"

I waited a count of ten, then skirted the appliances and went to the sunporch door. Shirley was straightening her skirt and patting her hair into place.

"Who— Oh, it's you." She wasn't happy, but her rancor was only at half strength.

"Yep. I'm here for the duration."

"Of what?" she snapped.

"Of Sonia and the attempt on her life. Of the story about Nathan and Matt Chastain. Matt, about his experiment gone bad—" I broke off. "Anthrax. Is that what Matt did that was so terrible?"

"Anthrax?" Shirley was bewildered for an instant, then gave a bark of contemptuous laughter. "If you think Nathan had anything to do with anthrax, you're going to be here an even longer duration. He's never worked with it. And neither did Matt Chastain."

The wicker chair I'd moved on Thursday was still where I'd placed it, but a set of books and crossword puzzles stood on it. I added those to a teetering stack on the side table and sat down.

"Then what sin did Matt commit that turned him into a 'subhuman specimen' in your husband's eyes?"

"My darling daughter's language. You've been talking to her? I thought she was in a coma."

"She is. That's something she said earlier." I started to ask if Shirley had been to the hospital yet but bit the words off: I wanted information, not a fight. "Regardless of the language, what did Matt do?"

"I don't know. He cultured the wrong specimen, or switched specimens in mid-experiment. Nate was beside himself. The army got involved because they'd funded the research. Nate had to go to Washington and explain himself. He must have done a good job—they renewed the grant, and Nate kept his job."

"Sonia saw something at the missile site back in 1983, whether—"

"She *thinks* she saw something. If you're believing the things she babbles—"

"Someone tried to murder your daughter yesterday. She'd begun recovering from her drug overdose and was coherent. Someone is afraid of what she'll reveal about events at the McKinnon farm, either three weeks or three decades ago. It would be incredibly helpful if you stopped hiding behind Cheese— behind Chesnitz's diagnosis and started listening to your daughter."

"Mind your own goddamn business," Shirley snapped. "We managed perfectly well in our own bucolic, hick-town way before you came muscling in from the big city to tell us what to do."

I glared at her. "You call this managing well? Your husband and you fighting day and night? Your sons so out of touch you didn't even let them know their sister was in the hospital? You're an intelligent woman. Don't you think you'd feel better—manage better—if you let the truth seep in around the edges?"

She struggled to her feet. "Don't preach at me. You know nothing about my truth, or my family's. You're not the one whose daughter tried to immolate herself on a barge on the river, imagining she could commit suttee because her fictional lover had supposedly died in a fire."

"You're right, I don't know those things," I said more quietly, "but I don't believe that Sonia made up Matt Chastain's death. Maybe she jumbled a lot of details together—she was fourteen, she was lonely and, like you, sensitive and imaginative—but she saw something that terrified her."

Shirley was appeased enough by the implied compliment to sit down again, but I couldn't get her to budge on what Sonia had seen thirty years ago. I finally gave up on it.

"Just one last question and I'll get out of your way. Who is Magda? Your sons told me—"

"Magda?" Red spots appeared on her face, fury sending blood to her head. "Has that bitch reappeared? I thought we were rid of her for good, little goddamn bitch of a sycophantic pseudoscientist."

I backed away involuntarily, as though her vitriol could eat through my own skin. The stack of books wobbled and fell over.

"Get out of my house," Shirley hissed, her face still blotched. "Get out of my house, and don't ever *dare* come back into it."

I stood on shaking legs. "Rid of her for good when? Last week or last century?"

She hurled her pen at me. Her aim was good. I got my hands up fast enough to protect my face, but my wrist took a stinging hit.

I retreated toward the kitchen but stopped long enough to say, "I called the hospital this morning. Sonia's still in a protective coma. I talked to her brothers yesterday. They were both distressed and wished they'd known sooner that she was hospitalized."

"If you dare bother my children again, I'll get the police involved," Shirley spat.

"Does that include Sonia?" I asked. "Have you been to the hospital yet?"

This time she threw a book, but I was out of range. I walked down the dusty hall and let myself out through the front door.

I wished I hadn't deposited Peppy at Free State. I could have used a little puppy therapy about now. As a poor second, I drove to the end of the street and lowered my car seat so I could lie back, eyes closed.

Shirley's anger was so extreme it singed. Who was the more damaging person in that marriage, Shirley or Nate? He was volatile and abusive, she was drunk and vitriolic. What a sea for a poor little polar bear to swim in. I found myself blinking back tears for Sonia.

I massaged my temples. Breathe into Shirley's anger, let it wash away from you. I thought of my own parents, my father's deep, protective love for my mother and the nights she and I had stayed up, sick with worry, while he worked the free-fire zones on Chicago's West Side.

My mother died when I was sixteen, on a cold March day. My father and I had spent the night in her hospital room, my father inserting himself between the tubes and wires in her bed so that he could cradle her in his lap. I was at her side, holding her hand. For sixteen years we had been a little triangle of love, with me as the apex they both supported. I'd spent too much time on self-pity, the loss of my mother heavy in my heart, weighted further by my father's death a decade later. I had never stopped to think how exceedingly lucky I'd been.

46

THE FIGHTING GERMS

I SAT UP AGAIN and looked up Kiel's university address: eighth floor of the Forschung Center for Life Sciences. The Forschung Center was on what they called West Campus, a sprawling extension of the university where giant research buildings sat. I drove up and down hills and found a public-policy institute, engineering, chemistry and physics, and finally the Forschung, tucked into a side of the farthest hill. Unlike the part of the campus I'd visited last week, there weren't any guard stations. Bonus for the weary detective: the Forschung had its own parking lot.

However, there was also a guard in the lobby, who asked my business with Dr. Kiel. I couldn't think of a clever cover story: I said I was there to discuss bioweapons, particularly anthrax.

Unlike the sheriff's deputy, the guard wasn't alarmed. I guess anthrax was all in a day's work at the Forschung Center. He called up to the eighth floor. Time passed. People came and went through the locked doors, which needed a key card for access; I couldn't get in unless I mugged someone in the parking lot to steal a card.

I checked my messages. Seventeen from Chicago clients, including one from Troy Hempel. Nothing from Lotty—her surgical day must be running long. Nothing from Jake. The only cheering message came from Mr. Contreras, happy he was leaving for home in two days: *"It's beautiful here, doll, but I want to be home. I miss you and the dogs and the little volcano on ice skates."*

I shifted uneasily, wondering what the volcano was doing. When I texted her, she assured me she was fine; Cady had invited her home to supper again. Cady's granny was super nice. Bernie didn't understand why I had a problem with her.

I wandered around the lobby, looking at portraits of bygone KU cell biologists. Noble P. Sherwood had a magnificent mustache and looked like Teddy Roosevelt. Cora Downs had done impressive work on tularemia when STEM women were as rare as unicorns. David Paretsky had done something unusual with peptides in a beast called rickettsia.

In a corner of the lobby, in the shadow of a display case, I came on a framed copy of the photo of "Dr. K's Fighting Germs," the picture of the lab team that had won a charity softball game I'd seen online in the *Douglas County Herald*. I was pretty sure one of the young men grinning in the background was the original of the face Sonia kept sketching.

I was heading over to the guard to ask him to check on Dr. Kiel when a young woman in a lab coat came out and looked at me doubtfully.

"Are you from Dr. Kiel's lab?" I asked. "It's V.I. Warshawski."

She ignored my outstretched hand. "He said to tell you he doesn't know anything about anthrax."

She was nervous; I wondered if Kiel had been yelling at her.

"He's bound to know more than I do." I smiled. "All I know is what the Mayo Clinic website had to say, but he can tell me things like whether someone digging up dirt on a farm east of town could have contracted it from the ground."

She hesitated. I said she could ask Dr. Kiel if it would be easier for me to discuss the situation with Colonel Baggetto. At that point she decided to take me inside—however nervous Kiel might make her, she didn't want to be a Ping-Pong ball bouncing between him and me.

We rode an elevator to the eighth floor. She revealed her name as Sue-Anne Tommason, from near Garden City. Yes, they were sick and tired of only being known for *In Cold Blood;* there was plenty more to Garden City than somebody getting murdered sixty years ago. "It was horrible when the *Capote* movie came out. It reopened all these old wounds and made us look like a national freak show all over again. You're from Chicago, right? And that's got way more murders than Garden City."

"Right you are, Ms. Tommason." I followed her out of the elevator and down the hall. "And that seems to be what we're mostly known for these days, that and Al Capone."

Tommason stopped outside a door that had Kiel's name on it, took a breath, and led me inside. She left me at the entrance, with a whispered command to wait a minute, and went through a door at the far end of the room.

The lab was a large, well-lighted place, but rows of high black counters made it seem smaller. Unlike the Kiel home, the room was clean and sternly tidy, with the kind of equipment that makes you think of Walter Mitty going *pocketa-pocketa*—big drums with hinged arm holders that moved up and down in a steady rhythm, racks of test tubes, shelves of beakers of all shapes and sizes. It smelled of chemicals, a biting scent with a musty underlayer. The smell was vaguely familiar, but I couldn't place it.

I wandered around and came to a tightly sealed glass case, a bit like a miniature greenhouse, with ventilation tubes leading away from a pair of canisters. I leaned over for a closer look. They looked like the canister in the photo that Colonel Baggetto had shown me, which supposedly held fuel rods.

"So you've switched from being an expert on my daughter's mental illness to an interest in wool-sorter's disease. Or maybe you think that's the underlying cause of her problems. It's an interesting hypothesis."

Dr. Kiel had come up behind me, the noise of the ventilators masking his crepe-soled shoes. Sue-Anne was hovering behind him with two young men about her age, also in white lab coats.

Kiel was bouncing slightly on his toes, a boxer already throwing the first punches. I supposed wool-sorter's disease was a nickname for anthrax; it would be a mistake to start the conversation by asking him.

"Those canisters—Colonel Baggetto told me the other night he was looking for one. Did it go missing from here?"

"What are you now? An investigator for the NIH? I don't need to account for my equipment to you or anyone else."

His voice was harsh, but he'd stopped bouncing. That made me think he knew about the canisters.

"You knew Dr. Roque," I said.

"Oh, yes. PH Roque."

"PH?" I asked.

"Publicity Hound," he snarled. "Oh, I know, *nil nisi bonum* and all that. Don't mouth pieties at me."

"I wouldn't dare," I said. "You know he died of a virulent strain of flu. And I presume you know that Dr. Edward Hitchcock, from the geology department, is in the Cleveland Clinic with a similar infection?"

I paused, but he didn't speak. The vein over his right eye started pulsing: danger sign. Sue-Anne and the two young men looked at one another. One of the guys shook his head slightly, a warning not to speak.

"Both of them were handling soil samples from Doris McKinnon's farm. That made me think of anthrax."

"Did it, now? Let's see: First you thought you were a mental-health expert, next you were with the NIH, inspecting my equipment. Now you think you're with the CDC, an expert on infectious diseases?"

CDC. The Centers for Disease Control. I didn't know what NIH stood for, and it didn't matter. Kiel thought broad insults would goad me into losing my temper, which meant I needed to be relaxed and smiling.

"I spoke with a doctor this morning who suggested anthrax."

Okay, Jewel Kim was a nurse, but Kiel seemed to be the kind of person who would sneer at nurses.

"Your Chicago doctors are surprisingly ignorant," Kiel jeered. "Or was it one of the cretins at the local hospital? Anthrax does not mimic flu. If that's all you wanted to know, you could have phoned me."

"I wondered who would want your daughter dead," I said. "You surely know that someone tried to smother her yesterday morning."

"You think her life has great value to society?"

I pulled a stool out from underneath the counter and sat. "I won't mouth pieties to you, such as everyone's death diminishes me. I do wonder whether you've spent so many years in fury that no other emotions can arise in you, but I'm only an investigator of human frauds and felonies, not of their hearts' deepest secrets.

"However, someone did try to murder Ms. Kiel yesterday morning. Even if you don't think her life has value, aren't you a tiny bit curious about who wants your daughter dead?"

His lips twitched. "I thought my wife and I had made it clear that Sonia's upheavals stopped entertaining us years ago. I assumed she owed money to a drug dealer who was tired of waiting for payment."

"You've watched too many episodes of *Breaking Bad*. Drug dealers may shoot each other on the streets, but they don't have the patience or the subtlety to break into an ICU in the manner that your daughter's assailant used."

Kiel was displaying a lot of nervous symptoms, from the twitching lips to the rocking on his feet, but he was so chronically angry and nervy that I couldn't interpret the symptoms: fear, guilt, knowledge, or just an insecure, volatile man who couldn't bear confrontation?

"I have a couple of visuals." I opened my tablet. I'd uploaded the Fighting Germs picture while I'd been in the lobby, and next to it I'd put a copy of one of Sonia's sketches.

"That's Matt Chastain, right, drawn by your daughter. But which one of those women is Magda?"

Dr. Kiel became very still. Even the vein in his forehead stopped pulsing.

"Magda. Who mentioned that name? Have you been talking to my wife?" The words were as forceful as ever, but his voice lacked power.

"Your sons," I said. "They were distressed at the news about their sister. They mentioned Magda when I asked about the experiment that went so badly thirty years back. What was that experiment?"

"Nothing you would understand."

"You're right that I can't tell a peptide from a pep talk, but I bet if you told me the basics, like why you had to go to Washington to defend your grant to the Department of Defense, I could follow along."

"You *were* talking to Shirley." His voice was recovering. "She loves to create drama out of the ordinary. Sonia was grabbing all the attention, with her delusions about Chastain, so Shirley began telling people that I was doing secret work for the Pentagon and that I'd been called on the carpet.

"Wrong, wrong, wrong. It was an ordinary grant review, but Lawrence had been the focus of enormous media attention because that ludicrous film, *The Day After,* was made here. That brouhaha was compounded by the fracas at the missile silo. The president wanted to be briefed. I went to the White House, I spoke to the president and his secretary of defense. Shirley all but accused me of being a fascist for meeting with Reagan—that's how unhinged she was. Sue-Anne!" he barked over his shoulder, "Go get that photo."

Sue-Anne Tommason trotted obediently toward his office.

"What is Magda's last name?" I asked.

"Why do you want to know?"

I smiled limpidly. "So I can find her dental records. So an independent pathologist can compare them with the X-rays of the teeth of the woman whose body disappeared from Dr. Roque's lab last week."

47

PLAYING WITH GERMS

I WAS GETTING BACK on the elevator, exhausted and frustrated, when Sue-Anne Tommason tapped my shoulder. She shoved some tightly folded papers into my jacket pocket and flitted back to Kiel's lab.

I waited until I was in my car to examine the pages. I'd been expecting a major secret—a hastily scribbled report of Dr. Kiel's involvement in anthrax research or an overheard confession to Matt Chastain's murder.

Instead I was looking at an offprint of a 1982 article in the *Journal of Cell Morphology*. "Phospholipase suppression in nuclear proteins during infection (*Y. enterocolitica*)." I sighed: this was one of the articles whose titles had stumped me when I first looked into Dr. Kiel's history last week. The only words I understood were "suppression in" and "during infection."

The work had been completed thanks to grants from the National Institutes of Health and the Army Research Council. It listed seven co-authors, starting with Kiel N. and including Spirova M. The only M in the list of authors.

I started to search for Spirovas on my tablet, but the sun had set while I was talking to Dr. Kiel. Floodlights were on in the parking lot and around the buildings, but away from the Forschung Center night was shrouding the West Campus. A mist was rising across the grass. I felt tiny and exposed on the hilltop, with dark prairie stretching out beyond me. A giant hound or, worse, a malevolent human could bound out of the mist while I was deep in databases.

I drove into town, to a strip mall near Free State Dogs. Students were laughing, holding hands, texting, as they went into the carry-out places. Their chatter felt reassuring. I parked under one of the streetlights and went back to my search engines.

LifeStory gave me a handful of Spirovs or Spirovas, no Magdas, and none who had been at the University of Kansas. I turned to newspaper databases, where I found her at once in the *Douglas County Herald,* lecturing in November 1981 to a meeting of the Lawrence Rotary Club.

Spirova had spoken about the grimness of life under Communism and how thankful she was to Dr. and Mrs. Kiel for opening their home to her. She was especially grateful for the chance to do research in Dr. Kiel's lab. When she heard him address a 1979 symposium on infectious diseases and bioweapons in Bratislava, she'd been overwhelmed by the depth of his knowledge.

> Dr. Spirova, although only thirty-two, is something of an expert on infectious diseases herself: she worked in the Soviet bioweapons installation in Těchonin, in eastern Czechoslovakia, before making her escape during a conference in Belgrade in 1981. It was a journey worthy of John le Carré: she fled with the clothes on her back to Vienna, flew to Montreal and made her way across the border into the United States on foot.
>
> "Is true, I am coming to this country not quite legally," Dr. Spirova said in her charmingly accented English. "I am needing political asylum. If returning to home country, to Czechoslovakia, I am in prison as traitor. Dr. Kiel obtained for me temporary residency permit; I can be part of his research family as well as his wonderful American home."

Spirova must have seen the same thing Larry and Stuart Kiel had—Shirley's drunken rages, incessant fights between Shirley and

Nathan. She was a refugee, though, and Kiel was her lifeline; she had turned Shirley and Nate into the all-American family.

The *Herald* had included her picture, a small, slender woman with fair hair pulled into a loose knot at the back of her head, curls falling out to frame an elfin face. In the photograph of Dr. K's Fighting Germs, Spirova was in the first row, her arm around Kiel. Camaraderie in the moment of victory, no doubt.

I couldn't find any other references to Spirova. I came on a September 1984 interview with Dr. Kiel, part of a series called "Hill and Valley," which presented alternating university and town personalities. Dr. Kiel was passionate about his work, about play, and about human rights. He and his wife, Shirley, had been involved in open-housing initiatives in Lawrence, but he had also opened his lab to a refugee from Communism—neither the refugee nor the country mentioned by name. His children got similarly short shrift: two sons away in college, nothing at all about Sonia, the bi-polar bear.

I hunted for Spirova's name in scientific databases. She'd co-authored four other articles with Kiel, the latest in April 1983. And that was the last mention I could find: no news stories, no work on phosphorylation, no membership in professional societies.

Shirley said she thought she'd been rid of Magda for good. Maybe Shirley had reported her to the FBI or INS and made sure she'd been sent back home, where she would have been incarcerated. The wheel turned; in 1989 Czechoslovakia became independent and political prisoners were being freed. If Magda had popped back up in Lawrence, though, why was it a quarter century after Czechoslovakia's Velvet Revolution?

My databases only skim the surface of international queries. They didn't turn up an M. Spirova at any Czech or Slovak research facilities. Magda could have gone underground, or changed her name, or married and taken her husband's name—this was fruitless. I closed the apps.

I walked over to Free State Dogs to collect Peppy. She was happy to see me, but she kept turning back to twine herself around the staff member who'd groomed her yesterday.

I walked her to the car with a firm hand on the leash. "You're all that stands between me and a meltdown, girl, so don't go leaving me for some young woman with a bouncy ponytail. It's bad enough having Jake swooning over foreign cellists without losing you, too."

Back at the B and B, with pasta, cheese, and salad from the market, I talked it over with Peppy. Dr. Kiel hadn't worked with anthrax, but whatever he'd studied, he'd been funded by the army as well as the National Institutes of Health—the NIH whose initials he'd flung at me.

Shirley said he'd been called on the carpet after the Matt Chastain experiment disaster. Kiel denied it. He'd shown me a photo of himself with Reagan and Caspar Weinberger, Reagan's defense secretary. It was meant to prove that he hadn't done anything wrong, and I supposed it did—no president poses with someone who's going to be a liability.

But why would a secretary of defense meet with a cell biologist, unless that biologist was doing something for the national defense? I brought my computer into bed and sat cross-legged in my underwear, trying to find out what work Kiel had done thirty years ago for the national defense. Not even my expensive databases could get Pentagon information.

I was frowning at the screen when Lotty called, her voice sharp. "Victoria! Thank goodness I've reached you. I've just been speaking with the clinical team looking after Dr. Hitchcock. He's suffering from pneumonic plague."

"Is that like bubonic plague?" I asked uncertainly.

"It's the most lethal form of it," Lotty said grimly. "Do you know him? Do you have any idea how he could have contracted it?"

I explained the chain of connections that had led me to his name but added that I'd never met him. "Is that what killed Dr. Roque? They were both handling some soil samples from a nearby farm."

"I don't know about Dr. Roque, but you don't contract plague from handling dirt. With bubonic plague you are bitten by a flea that has been dining on an infected rat or prairie dog. For pneumonic an infected person can cough or sneeze on you. If it had been anthrax, yes, the spores can lie dormant in the soil, but not *Y. pestis*."

"Why what?" I asked.

"Not 'why,' 'what,'" Lotty said dryly. "*Y* for *Yersinia*. The organism's formal name."

I pulled out the offprint that Kiel's student had given me. "Is it the same as *Y. enterocolitica*?" I had no idea how to pronounce it, so I spelled it for her.

"That's a related bacterium," Lotty said. "It's relatively harmless—can give you stomach cramps and fever for a few weeks but usually doesn't need antibiotics. How did you hear about that? You're not playing with germs now, are you?"

"I'm playing with people who play with germs," I said. "I just don't know what game they're playing."

"No one at the Cleveland Clinic knows how Dr. Hitchcock contracted pneumonic plague," Lotty said, "but if he was close to people you're dealing with, I want you to start a course of antibiotics right now. Get me the number of a twenty-four-hour pharmacy near you and go pick up the prescription as soon as you hang up. I'm going to start you tonight with a double dose. I'm also notifying the CDC in Atlanta, although I'm sure the Cleveland Clinic has already done so.

"If you're going to be near people or places that may be contaminated, wear a high-grade face mask. Don't drink alcohol while you're taking the drug: it lowers its efficacy. If you start spiking a fever or have shortness of breath or pain in breathing, get to the nearest ER at once. This is not a joke: left untreated, pneumonic plague has essentially a one-hundred-percent mortality rate. Do you understand?"

48

LATE NIGHT AT THE LIBRARY

I PICKED UP THE doxycycline prescription and took two tablets as Lotty had commanded. On my way back to the B and B, I drove downtown to look at the library: I was curious about the story in yesterday's *Herald* criticizing the library management for leaving its lights on in the middle of the night.

I parked across the street, my own lights off. There was one car in the lot, a late-model Acura, parked in one of the staff spaces. A light was on in the main reading room, but as I watched, it went out. A moment later Phyllis Barrier, the head librarian, emerged. She didn't look around but walked quickly to the Acura and drove off.

There seemed to be a reflection of a light in the basement. Many buildings leave lights on at night, for security or for the cleaning crew. Perhaps Ms. Barrier was monitoring the library, to make sure they kept on the right number. Perhaps the suspicions she seemed to harbor toward me made her want to check on whether the foreign detective was sneaking into her library after hours to use the computers.

I walked over and crouched to look in the basement window. A door was closing. I tried to visualize the library layout. There was a music lab down there, without windows, which held an industry-standard sound board. Ms. Barrier doubtless was letting music enthusiasts hold an overnight recording session.

Back at the B and B, Bernie had returned. I'd asked Lotty whether she should also be taking the antibiotic. Lotty, who usually opposed handing out antibiotics like Halloween candy, said in this case it was essential to err on the side of caution. I handed Bernie her own prescription, explaining the danger.

Her eyes widened. "Dr. Lotty seriously believes that one can become ill from the dirt on that farm?"

"Dr. Lotty is worried about our being around such a lethal organism. You're going home tomorrow, of course, but on the off chance that I've been in touch with whatever the source of the *Y. pestis* is, she thinks you should take a course of the drug."

Bernie nodded thoughtfully and took two of the tablets. I poured out the rest of the wine so we wouldn't be tempted to drink it. Bernie curled up in bed with me to watch *To Catch a Thief,* a movie designed to make you go to sleep happy. Instead, long after I'd turned off the lights, I kept feeling rats scurrying across the bedclothes. My arms and head itched from phantom fleabites.

In between the antibiotics and Cary Grant, I'd looked up pneumonic plague; the Web confirmed what Lotty had said, that it was transmitted via droplets in the air from an infected person or animal, but my semiconscious mind didn't believe that. At five-thirty, when I woke gasping for air, sure that pneumonia was clogging my lungs, I gave up on the pretext of rest.

I watched Peppy and Bernie enviously. Peppy opened one eye when I turned on the bedside lamp but fell instantly asleep again when she saw I was only sitting up with my phone, not going anywhere; Bernie didn't even stir.

I'd texted Aanya Malik as soon as Lotty and I finished speaking, to warn her of the possible cause of Roque's death: YOU AND RUBY AND ANYONE ELSE WHO'S BEEN IN CONTACT WITH HIS BODY SHOULD BE TAKING ANTIBIOTICS PROPHYLACTICALLY. She hadn't responded yet. I hoped that didn't mean she was already ill, too ill to look at her messages. The gestation period was one to three days, according to the Centers for Disease Control's website, and Aanya had last seen Roque on Thursday. I looked again at the clock—5:37, too early to call her.

If Dr. Roque had contracted plague and sneezed on the containers he sent Dr. Hitchcock, it's possible Hitchcock had picked up the disease simply from handling the jars.

But where had Roque contracted it? Not from the baby's bones: I'd asked Lotty that. Apparently *Y. pestis* wasn't as hardy as the anthrax bacillus. It wouldn't live in the ground or in a corpse for decades, so it couldn't have been in the soil samples.

I started a more serious search into scholarly articles about germ warfare. Much of the language was beyond me, but I gathered that the plague bacillus could be dried and sprayed over a targeted population, which made it possible to use *Y. pestis* as a weapon. Even though it was less stable than anthrax, it was so efficiently lethal that it remained a perennial favorite among germ warriors.

My eyes were dry and gritty. I turned off the light and lay back down, but I couldn't turn off the feverish churning in my head.

How had Shirley Kiel described Chastain's "colossal blunder"? He'd cultured the wrong specimen or switched specimens. Had he exchanged Dr. Kiel's pet organism, *Yersinia enterocolitica,* for *Y. pestis*?

If that was what had happened, it was criminal sabotage, not a blunder. I didn't know anything about Chastain, except that Sonia had been in love with him. I was guessing he was Cady Perec's father because in Sonia's youthful journal she'd recorded seeing him with Jennifer Perec, but I had to admit that was a leap. Gertrude and Kiel both thought he was a loser, but it was hard to believe Chastain would be so embittered by Kiel's endless insults that he would have started working with the plague instead of the stomach bug.

"Maybe he was a clumsy SOB," I said to Peppy, "but surely he wouldn't knowingly have endangered Jenny Perec or baby Cady."

I wondered about Sonia: she'd been a dishwasher in her father's lab. She was lovesick, she was jealous of Jenny. But even if she'd been unstable enough to try to hurt Jenny, I couldn't believe she would have known how to make a switch. You wouldn't leave *Y. pestis* sitting around in an air-freshener can where random people could spray themselves with it.

Magda Spirova, though . . . Kiel's sons thought she'd slept with their father when they met in Czechoslovakia. Say she came to Kansas expecting the affair to continue and instead found herself in a cauldron of Shirley's fury and Kiel's fears of exposure. She could have switched the bugs and then blamed Kiel's whipping-boy student. After all, she'd worked at a bioweapons installation in eastern Czechoslovakia.

I sat up again and went back to the *Douglas County Herald* story on Magda Spirova. Těchonin. The Web revealed that this was a dot on the map, not even a thousand inhabitants. The Russians made it famous, or infamous: after they consolidated control of Eastern Europe, they'd set up a bioweapons research site there. Among other things, they built giant fermenters to produce cool things like anthrax and typhus in huge quantities. Then they dried the bugs and figured out how to spray them over civilian populations. Magda brought that knowledge with her to Kansas.

Sonia had written in her journals that Chastain had been lying on the ground shaking and gasping for air. Maybe he'd been dying of pneumonic plague. Sonia had flung herself on him as fire was sweeping the field, and Kiel, in a rare moment of parental attention, had pulled her away. Her description of what happened next—I couldn't remember it exactly.

I got up and went to the drawer where I'd put her journals. They weren't there. I ransacked the room. The suitcase I'd brought from St. Raphael's was gone, Sonia's journals were gone, the sketches of Chastain—everything was missing. The only remaining proof that I'd ever seen those papers was the drawing of Sonia as polar bear, floating in a cup of lithium; it had ended up facedown under the bed.

I shook Bernie awake, to ask if she'd removed any papers and drawings from the room.

"No, Vic, I know you think I am a vandal, but really—that is too much! Turn off your death-ray eyes, please!"

"Sorry, Bernie. But that means that someone broke in here while we were both out yesterday."

Bernie watched while I examined the locks on the outer door, but the invader had been knowledgeable: no scratches or inept traces. I should have laid a trap. Should have, could have—didn't.

I was tired of pretending I wasn't under surveillance. I went out to the little common area and found the owner laying out boxes of dry cereal for breakfast. I asked her if anyone had come around yesterday looking for me, but she'd worked in Topeka the whole day; all she could tell me was that no one had left a note or phone message.

"Your reservation ends the day after tomorrow," she reminded me. "I have a family coming in Friday, and they'll be using my other room and the one you're staying in. And is that a relative with you? That will be an extra twenty-five a night for every night she's here."

I agreed absently. Basically I had two days to find out whatever I could and then—I guess look for another room or go home. I asked the woman if she had any peanut butter, and she showed me a drawer I hadn't noticed that held foil containers of jelly and peanut butter. I took several back into my room and smeared peanut butter over the mike under the desk. This got Peppy's attention: she climbed out of bed and gave the mike a thorough scouring. I'd love to know what my eavesdroppers made of that.

Bernie watched, giggling, and went back to sleep.

I sat back down, feeling Peppy's ears. I didn't usually examine her lymph nodes; how could I tell if they were swollen?

"We'll get through this together, girl, and none of that 'or die trying.' We are not going to die, and our enemies will be sorry they ever thought they could make us run or blink first, or whatever they thought we might do. We are tougher, smarter, stronger." I was only shivering because of the early-morning cold, not because I was scared.

I couldn't figure out any reason my predators had taken Sonia's papers. They didn't contain secrets. Or maybe they did, hints of something that people—Kiel?—had spent thirty years keeping under wraps. I rubbed my forehead. Think, Warshawski. People do it all the time. You can, too.

Matt hadn't been camping at the silo. Shirley said Kiel expected total loyalty from his students, no dividing your time with your family. Assuming Matt was Cady's father, surely he would have spent—most? much?—some of his time with Jenny and Cady. The plague bacillus could have been at the silo, not just in Kiel's lab. Matt carried it inadvertently perhaps?

Or—Sonia had cut out the innards of a book that dealt with secret tests on civilian populations.

I couldn't remember the exact title. Clouds and tests on human populations, I told Google. Yes, here it was: Titheridge, Edelwart, and Zehner, *Clouds Without Witnesses: Secret Weapons Tests on Human Populations*.

A review in the journal *Science* said:

> If you wanted to test the spread of disease agents in a lab the size of the Central Plains, the Department of Defense was eager to oblige. From 1940 until Richard Nixon outlawed bioweapons development in 1969, the United States Army and Navy conducted tests of how to spread anthrax. They diffused clouds of allegedly harmless anthrax analogs from airplanes over South Dakota, from generators on the tops of cars in St. Louis, Minneapolis, and Winnipeg. They sprayed the California coast from ships in San Francisco Bay, and dropped lightbulbs filled with organisms into the New York subway system. "It spread pretty good," according to one DOD observer.

The reviewer added:

> Since President Bush reinterpreted the Nixon directive in 1989 to allow for defensive bioweapons research, the United States has been involved in tinkering with genomes of a number of disease agents. Some of this work has been outsourced to private labs.

The old Buffy Sainte-Marie song went through my head: *My country 'tis of thy people we're dying.* I hadn't known that the United States conducted those tests: when I'd seen the book in Sonia's room, I'd assumed it referred to Russian tests.

I went back to the articles I'd found that explained how you turned a microbe into a weapon. You needed fermenters to brew large numbers of germs, then you dried them out, then you put them in lightbulbs or crop-dusting planes.

One of the articles had an illustration of a fermenter. It was a giant vat, the kind you see in beer breweries. If Kiel had been using something that big back in the eighties, where would he have put it? Out by the Kanwaka silo?

Too many things to put together. Short sleep and high anxiety didn't make my brain work faster.

"Time to be up and about," I told Peppy. "Run the riverfront, get some sheets of newsprint so we can write down our known knowns and our known unknowns."

I checked my messages. A reminder from Lotty to take my pills. With food. I woke Bernie again.

"I'm going out. Your dad is arriving at Kansas City on the five-fifteen from San Jose. He'll be here around seven. If you need me in the meantime, text, but you can call Lyft or Uber to get around."

I wasn't sure she'd heard me, but I stuck the doxycycline in my jeans pocket, pulled my computer, iPad, chargers together in my Faraday cage, and gathered various changes of clothes so I wouldn't have to come back here if I got wet and muddy.

Peppy and I ran a five-mile loop down near the river. By the end, some of my anxiety had eased and I felt better able to think.

The FedEx store across from the Hippo sold me paper. Inside the coffee bar, I sponged off and changed to my jeans in their washroom, then sat down at the counter to work.

I divided my sheet of paper in two: 1983 and today.

1983: The air force is annoyed that the protesters are outside the Kanwaka missile. They want to drive them away. The army is funding Kiel's research into *Y. enterocolitica;* why not spray some over the protesters, send them all vomiting into the local emergency room, and then burn the camp after they've left?

1983: When Doris went over to the field that August morning with food for Jenny and the baby, she'd seen the signs warning of hazardous waste. The signs had implied *radioactive* waste, but maybe that was a convenient cover.

1983: Unless Sonia's memory had become more melodramatic over time, Matt Chastain had died in the fire that swept through the protesters' camp. Cady Perec had looked for traces of Chastain in the cell-biology department files and come up empty. If a mother or sister had ever written Kiel wanting information about Chastain, those letters had been discarded.

Today: Doris McKinnon had found bones that she'd delivered to Dr. Roque. Baby bones, but maybe my invaders thought they were Matt Chastain's remains. Is that what they'd been looking for—in my place, at August's home and workplace? They were covering up his death?

Today: Dr. Roque died of pneumonic plague. Had he contracted it from the woman whose body I'd found in Doris McKinnon's kitchen when he started the autopsy? That didn't make sense. He'd sickened and died within hours of starting the autopsy, which even for *Y. pestis* must be a speed record.

Assuming it was Magda Spirova whose body I'd stumbled on, where had she gone after the calamity of 1983? Why had she come back now?

I put my pen down and went to the bar to order another coffee.

1983: Someone, likely Magda Spirova, switched plague bacteria with its less toxic sister. Kiel tested it at the Kanwaka commune. The army called Dr. Kiel to Washington to explain what went wrong, and he explained himself so satisfactorily that the president and his defense secretary had themselves photographed with Kiel.

If pneumonic plague had killed people back in '83 and was still killing people today, how had the organism survived all these years? Lotty had said it didn't last long outside, not like anthrax, so there'd have to have been a way to save a sample in a lab. I pictured Spirova carrying a cage full of infected rats with her wherever she went, a medieval witch with her rodent familiars. It was a discomfiting image, woman scientist as witch. Not my favorite stereotype. Anyway, if Magda had been involved, she'd done something modern, technically savvy. Maybe she'd stuck a test tube full of *Y. pestis* in a freezer and thawed it out when she reappeared in Lawrence.

However it happened, that was the secret that no one wanted me to uncover. They'd used plague on human targets, they'd successfully covered it up for over a generation, they didn't want it coming to light now. And who were "they"? Had to be the quartet I'd encountered in the hotel bar Thursday evening.

49

BABY BLUES

I STARTED TO TEXT Aanya again, to see if she knew anything about plague storage and preservation. Before I finished typing, a message came in from her, asking me to call:

I HAVE MUCH NEWS FOR YOU, SO IN CASE IT ISN'T SAFE TO TALK ON THIS PHONE, I'M GOING TO SKYPE YOU FROM THE SAME PLACE YOU SKYPED ME LAST WEEK. CAN YOU GET THERE NOW?

I took that to mean she would be at a library in Kansas City and wanted me to go back to the Lawrence library. I finished my coffee, put Peppy in the car, and walked the four blocks to the library.

When the video screens came up, I could tell that Aanya hadn't been sleeping. Her dark eyes had sunk into their sockets, and her narrow face looked even smaller, more pinched.

"Are you eating?" I asked.

A ghost of a smile flickered. "You and Ruby both. Ruby brought me her family's chicken-barley soup. She was so hurt when I turned it down, but I'm a vegetarian."

"Lentils," I said. "Come to Chicago when all this is behind us. I'll make you my mother's lentil soup. What do you have for me?"

The autopsy on Dr. Roque had been completed last night. "He had contracted plague, and perhaps that would have killed him, but he collapsed in the lab because somebody had stabbed him. The killer knew how to stay away from the cameras monitoring the autopsy room, so there is no recording of the attack. It is not possible to know who went into the lab and attacked him."

"You said you were listening to him as he was dictating," I reminded her.

"This person moved quietly. Dr. Roque did not cry out or say anything. Maybe it was even someone he was used to seeing."

If that was the case, it should make it easier for the police to find a suspect. "They wanted to remove the dead woman before Dr. Roque worked on her so that she couldn't be identified," I added, thinking out loud.

"Is that a reason enough?" Aanya flashed back. "The only consolation Dr. Madej could give me was to say that Dr. Roque was spared a painful death from the plague. And Dr. Madej thinks he and Dr. Hitchcock may both have contracted the illness from the soil samples."

"So someone deliberately contaminated the soil that Doris McKinnon collected?" I asked.

"Not necessarily deliberately. Since it came from a farm, if infected rats or chickens or even prairie dogs were nearby, they could have left plague in the ground. The organism occurs naturally in the wild. It isn't only the product of some diabolical plan to spread disease. It can sometimes survive in soil up to three months after an infected animal dies."

I told Aanya what I'd been thinking this morning, about Kiel's old experiment and the possibility of someone—Spirova—switching the bacteria.

"It is possible, yes, that such a thing happened thirty-five years ago, but believe me, Vic, those old microbes would not be still alive in that woman's farm. Three months or less would be a maximum lifetime for them outside a live host, and that is under the conditions that are most ideal for the bacillus."

She stopped for a minute to look at her notes. "Still, it is strange that so many people are contracting plague in Douglas County right now. Strange and worrying. I showed Dr. Madej the photos that Dr. Roque took of the woman whose body was stolen. Her body—her skin—was so damaged he didn't want to be on record with his opinion, but he didn't believe there were any signs of plague. However, he must inform the Centers for Disease Control and also local health authorities on account of Dr. Roque and Dr. Hitchcock."

"Yes, of course. Dr. Herschel in Chicago is also doing so, and she thinks the Cleveland Clinic has already notified them," I agreed. "If Spirova showed up ill at McKinnon's farmhouse, could she have infected August Veriden and Emerald Ferring? Have they died in hiding?"

"If she coughed on them, maybe," Aanya tried to reassure me. "If they ran away without being in direct contact with her or with fleas that had bitten her, they should be safe. After all, the woman who died in the truck, it was her house, am I right in saying this? And she did not die of plague."

"No, a bullet to the back of the head," I agreed grimly. "Guaranteed results, nothing as chancy as hoping a flea would bite the target."

We were both silent, depressed by the story we were uncovering. I started to end the conversation, but Aanya said, "I almost forgot: I have your DNA results."

"And?"

"Neither woman is related to the baby. But they are closely related to each other."

"Mother and daughter?"

"No. Siblings."

I sucked in a breath. "Sisters? But then—who is the dead baby?"

"I do not know. Until you send me more DNA from different people, I cannot make any guesses at all."

"Does this mean they have the same father or the same mother?"

Aanya shook her head, her smile glimmering briefly again. "That I cannot tell you. I am only a lab tech, not the archangel Gabriel, who oversees conception."

"What an unpleasant thought! Angels in the room at such a moment—as if surveillance by the NSA weren't enough of a burden."

At that Aanya actually laughed. She stopped, looking stricken. "I did not think I would ever smile again, but here I am, laughing."

"It's human, or life," I suggested. "We can't reside in grief forever any more than in joy."

"I know." The Skype video showed tears in the corners of her black eyes. "I know we cannot stop life from flowing on, we cannot reside always in grief, but I do not want to abandon Dr. Roque, not just yet."

When she'd hung up, I sat back in my chair, exhausted. I'd been so sure the baby would prove to have been Sonia's, or a twin to Cady. But this news—Cady was Shirley or Nathan's child? Or could Sonia and Cady actually be Gertrude Perec's daughters? Did that have anything to do with the plague years, or was it just collateral damage?

I opened my eyes: Phyllis Barrier, the head librarian, was looking down at me.

"We're glad that the library can be helpful even to strangers, Ms. Warshawski, but I do keep wondering what service we provide that you can't find elsewhere."

I smiled and stood up. "Libraries are refuges, Ms. Barrier. And yours is particularly welcoming, even in the middle of the night."

She bit her lip, wondering how to react. I delved into my backpack and produced a thin packet wrapped in tissue paper.

"One of your patrons left these at Doris McKinnon's farm. Please let her know that at night the lights in the basement are reflected onto the parking lot. Your board probably worries about the electric bill."

"I . . . You . . ." Barrier turned the packet over and over in her hands.

"Ms. Albritten moved your photo after the first time I visited her. She didn't want me to connect you to her. Maybe you were right not to trust me—I couldn't have kept them safe. In answer to your question, I come here to Skype to minimize the risk of outside ears hearing what I have to say."

I walked away without waiting for a response and returned to the Hippo, my mind on Cady and Sonia, not Emerald and August.

Could Cady be Gertrude's child instead of her granddaughter? I did sums in my head. Gertrude had been born in 1939 or '40; she'd have been forty-four when Cady was born. By no means out of the question. Maybe she'd had an affair with Kiel, didn't use protection because she thought she was postmenopausal, then pretended the child was her daughter's. Jennifer had died, so no one could question Cady's parentage. In that case, where was Jennifer's child? With Matt Chastain, either in death or in hiding?

It was a story, which meant it was only that. I drove to Gertrude Perec's house, where I found her working in her front yard. She looked up at me, but her expression was not full of love.

"Now what?"

I squatted on the ground next to her. "A complicated story. A difficult question."

She studied me without speaking, then sighed and put down her trowel. "Come into the house. Dog stays in the car."

Peppy was leaning out the car window, grunting her wish to be with me. I made the "stay" signal and followed Gertrude into the house, or actually the screened-in porch where I'd first met her last Wednesday.

"Are you ever going back to Chicago?"

"I hope so. I want to leave as much as you want me to be gone. The sheriff has ordered me not to leave until Doris McKinnon's murder is resolved. And of course until the people I'm looking for are accounted for. Maybe they contracted plague and died. It's been happening a lot lately."

She nodded, half to herself. "Word gets around."

"The county health department is supposed to issue an advisory. I don't know if they have yet, but the pathologist who was starting the autopsy on Magda Spirova had contracted pneumonic plague, which also killed Spirova."

"Magda! I thought—" She gasped.

"Thought what, Ms. Perec?" I said sharply when she broke off in midsentence. "Thought Dr. Kiel's friends got rid of her body before Dr. Roque could examine it? Or thought, like Shirley Kiel, that you were rid of her for good when she disappeared in 1983?"

"I don't have to answer your questions, about Magda or anything else."

"True." I sat back in the wicker chair and steepled my fingers. "You might want to answer Cady's."

"How dare you! I've never seen such arrogance, coming into a town of strangers and thinking you can tell us how to live. Last time you were here, you insulted the memory of my daughter with stories about Matt Chastain. Now you have a new theory? Do you make them up at night when you're lonely, just to poison the lives of people who have families?"

I flinched. Her rage had some kernels of truth in it.

"There's some evidence Matt Chastain died in a fire at the silo protest back in 1983."

"You've been listening to Sonia," Perec said scornfully. "Although I thought she was in a coma and couldn't speak."

"Everyone talks to everyone in this town," I complained, "but they don't talk to me, and they get peeved when I find things out on my own."

"What things have you found out?" Perec's throat contracted, strangling the words.

"Sonia Kiel and Cady are sisters."

"No! No, no, no!"

Her rising scream reached Peppy in the car, which made her start barking. I stood and signed at her to be calm, but it was several minutes before both she and Gertrude quieted enough for me to speak again.

"Doris McKinnon was digging up dirt samples on the land that the air force took from her and sold to Sea-2-Sea. She'd been told the land was too contaminated to farm, and then she saw that Sea-2-Sea was farming it anyway. She sent it to Dr. Roque to be tested—he was the black-mold specialist, so she figured he could sort out radioactive poisoning."

Perec was clutching the arms of her chair so tightly I could see the pulses in her wrists, but she didn't speak.

"While she was digging up samples, Ms. McKinnon came on part of a skeleton of a baby, probably born around the same time as Cady. She sent that to Dr. Roque along with the soil. I wondered if Cady had a twin who died or if Sonia's emotional problems might have been triggered by a pregnancy. She was fourteen that summer. I got DNA samples from both women. Neither is related to the dead baby, but the two are sisters."

"How did you trick Cady into giving you a sample?"

"I asked her for it."

"No," she said again, but it was a whisper. An instant later she started to cry, terrible jagged sobs that shook her whole body.

She would not welcome comfort from me. I went into the house and found the kitchen, found glassware, found water in the refrigerator. I filled two glasses and brought them with a box of tissues to the porch.

Perec took a glass from me. She gestured at a small round table. I moved it next to her chair and sat back down. Her sobs had already diminished; she sipped at her water and dabbed her face with a tissue, leaving muddy streaks across her cheeks.

I drank my own water: my throat was dry and raw from the stress. Or from incipient pneumonia. I surreptitiously felt my lymph glands.

"I wondered if you might be Cady's mother," I ventured.

"What?" The suggestion outraged her enough to bring some strength back to her voice. "My husband died when Jenny was a toddler. I thought you knew that—you know so much, busybody that you are."

I felt a perverse relief in her insulting me again—it meant she was recovering. "Sonia and Cady had a parent in common, perhaps two. I don't suppose the Kiels had a baby that you adopted."

She looked fierce, briefly, and then her face crumpled. She didn't start to cry again, but she collapsed back in her chair.

"I love Cady as my own," she whispered. "I do, I truly do, but—"

I waited, sitting still, making myself part of the porch furniture.

"I was so angry when Jenny got pregnant, and with Dr. Kiel's least promising student to boot. She was bright, outgoing, people followed her lead: she could have done anything with her life.

"Science—she was gifted, even Nathan—Dr. Kiel—who judges everyone harshly, saw how gifted she was. He got the university to offer her a full scholarship, and she started, in physics and international politics, and then she got sucked into the anti-nuke movement. Of course she met Matt Chastain through me—through my working for Dr. Kiel, I mean—and what she saw in him I'll never know!"

Her face worked, but she drank more water and managed to keep talking. "Jenny helped organize the protest at the silo. She had this ambition to make it like the one in England, and we fought over that, like we fought over everything the last year of her life. Oh, the nights I still lie awake tormenting myself with regrets. My darling, darling girl, all I did was fight with you. Why couldn't I show a little support? I knew you were right about the weapons, even if you were wrong about Matt."

She hugged herself; the wind was picking up, and she was feeling frail. I took a blanket from a settee and placed it around her shoulders. The only other thing I could offer was platitudes; those I kept to myself.

"She gave birth out there in that field, and those two women, Lucinda Ferring and Doris McKinnon, you'd have thought they birthed her themselves, they were so proud, so solicitous. I could have murdered the two of them, bringing Jenny here to show off little Cady, as if *they* were the grandmothers and I was some ignorant old-maid aunt. She had a strawberry birthmark on her left shoulder, just like Jenny's."

"Cady doesn't have one?" I asked when she'd again fallen silent.

She smiled, the kind you make when you don't want to cry. "Dr. Clayhorn, she was the pediatrician, she said birthmarks sometimes disappear spontaneously, but not usually inside a week. Nathan, Dr. Kiel, was always so solicitous of Cady's well-being. I didn't want to think about it. I wanted Cady to be Jenny's baby. The first year I worried that Matt might show up and claim her, even though Nathan promised that he'd left KU for good."

50

WHERE OH WHERE CAN MY BABY BE?

IF JENNY WASN'T Cady's mother, then who— Oh!" I felt a jolt, as if one of the Fates had stuck out a casual arm and whacked me between the shoulders. "Spirova had a baby at the same time as Jenny."

"She and Dr. Kiel argued about it; he wanted her to have an abortion, she wanted him to leave Shirley and marry her. She thought a baby would force him to choose her." Perec's head was bowed, her voice so soft I had to lean forward to make out the words.

"I presume if you knew, the whole lab did," I said. "Matt Chastain, too."

"I don't think so. I was Dr. Kiel's secretary. I saw and heard things no one else did, and I wasn't the kind to be sharing what I heard with every stray dog that barked outside Dr. Kiel's office." She gave me a sour look—I was one of those stray dogs, but I'd had the effrontery to barge in uninvited.

"Everyone guessed they'd had an affair when Nathan was in Bratislava. If Magda had asked me before making that dramatic escape out of Belgrade and so on, if she really did escape and wasn't just planted on us by the Russians, I would have told her he wasn't the kind of man who liked scandal. What he did on his trips never came home with him, at least not until she arrived." She stood and said brusquely, "I'm cold. We'll go into the house."

I was cold, too. I was glad to follow her inside to the kitchen, where she put on a kettle for tea and then disappeared up the stairs. The water came to a boil. I turned it off. I don't like tea—she could fix her own when she returned.

The kitchen overlooked the back garden, where birds were fighting over space at the two feeders Perec had set up. Birds covered the kitchen, too, painted on the stripes in the wallpaper around the breakfast nook, cut out of wood on the clock above the sink, even in the shape of the napkin and spoon holders.

Perec was gone long enough that I wondered if she was on the phone with Kiel. However, she finally returned, her hair damp from the shower, fresh makeup covering any remaining ravages of her weeping.

I seated myself in the breakfast alcove. "Did Magda come here for Kiel or because she was fleeing Communism—or both?"

Perec made herself a mug of tea and sat across from me. "With her you could never be sure about anything. She claimed she came here for freedom, but I think she wanted to live in the West, she wanted the kind of life you can live here if you have money and status. The army was glad she was here, I can tell you that much."

"Because she brought her special knowledge of biological weapons with her?"

Perec scowled. It annoyed her when I knew something she thought belonged to her as an insider. I wanted her annoyed—it would make her likely to tell me more.

"The army was funding Dr. Kiel's research," I prodded. "When the big mistake happened—when the plague bacillus was switched with *Y. enterocolitica*—he had to go to Washington to explain what had gone wrong. That was because people at the missile silo died. Including Lucinda Ferring."

I'd practiced saying "enterocolitica" in the car driving over and was pleased I could bring it out so fluently.

"She had the flu," Perec said thickly. "They called Dr. Kiel—those people at the hospital couldn't tell their right fingers from their right hand. They were always demanding his help. Anyway, he was the chief public-health officer for the county, even the state for a time. They called him in, and he cultured her blood, and he told them it was flu. It can kill someone, especially an older person, fast."

"Flu. No matter what he saw under the microscope."

She started to blaze up at me, but I interrupted. "Lucinda Ferring was his tech. She was in that lab. She was a black woman doing menial work, so she was invisible. I bet she knew everything you did and more besides, because you weren't out on the shop floor with the students and Sonia, who worked as a lab dishwasher. If someone—was it Magda?—was bringing *Y. pestis* into the lab, even if Ms. Ferring didn't know about it, she would have been exposed to it."

"You're trying to smear his name—"

"Did he give you a course of tetracycline about that time?" I cut across her again.

Her mouth opened in protest. Then came a horrified look, and she fell silent: memory had come back.

"He didn't bother with poor Matt or Ms. Ferring. Not even his own daughter, not until she fell onto Matt's dying body in that field." Sonia had written about it in her journal—she was burning, thinking she was in a fire. Burning, freezing, attached to a respirator. The 1 percent who survived pneumonic plague, but neither parent welcoming the miracle.

"Kiel went to Washington to explain himself to the army. If he put the blame on his dead graduate student, it would reflect badly on him—why wasn't he supervising his lab more closely? But the Czech bioweapons expert—what a lot of problems it would solve if she were responsible. What did he tell them? That he discovered she was a KGB agent, sent to steal U.S. germ secrets, that she actually conducted a trial diffusion for the KGB that killed a number of innocent people?"

"It *was* her fault," Perec said fiercely. "He had proof, he showed it to the army, and they came and took her away to Washington. They offered her some kind of deal if she would work for them secretly at

Fort Detrick. They gave her a new identity, Nathan told me, to hide her from the KGB. He said she wouldn't be bothering us again."

"And then she showed up here—when? a few weeks ago?—ready to blackmail Dr. Kiel, so she had to be disposed of, and how more artistically than with some of the pesky *pestis* that he'd kept locked away in a lab freezer all these years?"

"That's a lie!" Perec jumped to her feet, spilling her tea across the table.

I grabbed a handful of napkins from the bird-shaped holder and blotted the tea before it could slop onto me. "Okay, what's the truth?"

"Neither of us knew she was back here, not until you found her body. It was a complete shock."

"But everyone said that was Doris McKinnon," I objected.

"The army sent Colonel Baggetto here—Magda had disappeared, and they thought she might have returned to Lawrence. When he heard about you finding the body, he had his suspicions."

"Did they lead him to stab Dr. Roque?" My mouth felt as though it were filled with ashes.

"No one stabbed Dr. Roque. He died of the flu."

"Just like Lucinda Ferring." I was holding my temper by a thread.

Tea was pooling on her side of the table. She stared at it, as if it might turn into a magic well she could jump into.

"Cady," I said. "Lucinda Ferring found her in the field. She and McKinnon brought her to the hospital; she was dehydrated. And then someone called you."

"Nathan," Perec said in a dull voice. "He told me Jenny's baby had been rescued. They'd found Jenny earlier that day, drowned in the Wakarusa. The sheriff found her. Deputy Gisborne he was then. When Nathan told me Jenny's baby had made it, I didn't want to ask questions. I wanted something of my girl."

I didn't want to feel sorry for her, but I couldn't help it. She'd been squeezed in an intolerable vise—loyalty to Kiel, jealous fury toward Spirova, neither meaning anything under the crushing loss of her only child. Of course she wanted to believe that Cady was Jenny's baby. I couldn't say I wouldn't have done the same thing.

"Magda gave birth sometime that summer," I said. "Where?"

Perec hunched a shoulder, still staring at the tea. "She went to Aspen, or said she went to Aspen. There's a big conference there every summer, and she went off to present a paper. She left before she started really showing.

"I thought she'd had the baby in secret and placed it with a friend. She was still hoping Nathan would change his mind and leave Shirley. But I guess she was keeping her baby somewhere in Lawrence. Maybe when she realized Nathan wasn't going to marry her, she brought the baby out to the protest camp, hoping it would die from the plague test. She was crazy enough to do something that cruel.

"What am I going to tell Cady? What can I tell her her name is, even? What will it do to her when she finds out Sonia is her sister?"

Tears started falling again, not the sobs that had racked her earlier but those quiet, unconscious tears we don't even know we're shedding.

"Her name is Cady," I said quietly. "She's the person you raised, not the person Magda gave birth to. She's lucky that she came to you. You think highly of Nathan Kiel, but you must know how he and Shirley treated the three children who grew up with them."

She didn't speak, but some of the rigid lines went out of her cheeks.

I watched the second hand make a couple of circuits around the birds in the clock before I spoke again. "What made Colonel Baggetto think Spirova had come back here? Had she been in touch with Dr. Kiel?"

At that she looked up at me, the fierceness back in her face. "He talks to me. Who else can he trust? He saw her. He went out to that research place near Eudora, and he recognized her at once, even thirty-five years later."

"What was she doing there?" I demanded.

"I don't know. But Bram Roswell is as crazy as Magda, so whatever she was doing, it wasn't designed to bring peace and light to the world, you can count on that."

The meeting I'd stumbled on in the hotel bar last week, where Kiel was sitting uncomfortably with the colonel, Roswell, and the young man from the army staff college, that must have been to discuss Magda. How had she died? How had she landed in Doris McKinnon's kitchen?

And what part of it had August Veriden and Emerald Ferring witnessed? I didn't want to risk their safety by trying to find them in the library. If they were hiding in the stacks, under *F* for Fugitive or *W* for Witness, it would be child's play for Baggetto and Gisborne to follow me to them.

I stood, my knees stiff. Every joint stiff, actually. "You owe it to Cady to tell her the truth."

"You don't get to tell me what I owe to whom."

"You're right. I'm just the outside agitator turning Lawrence upside down. In some part of your mind, though, you've always known the truth—it's why you've resisted Cady's efforts to find out about her father. Do you know that she went through all the files in the departmental office, looking for Matt Chastain's records? What happened when his family wrote, wanting to know where he was?"

"Dr. Kiel told them he was doing important work for the government but that we couldn't disclose the location. Then he wrote that we hadn't had word from him for over a year and that the CIA feared he had died."

"A comfort to his mother, no doubt. Just as knowing how Jenny died was a comfort to you."

Her face was splotched with red. "Don't you sit in judgment on me. You have no right. You may think you're clever and that you know a lot, but you know nothing. You never had a child, you never lost a lover, you're like a cool breeze floating over the ground, not touching it."

51

KNOWN UNKNOWNS

I HAD JUST ENOUGH energy to find a park and sit on the cold ground with my dog. "Cool Breeze" Warshawski. Maybe I'd add it to my business cards. It would give me a certain swagger, like Cool Hand Luke.

"What a mess," I said to Peppy. "Poor Cady. This is going to hit her like a piano falling from the sky. The whole thing is a mess, from the death of Matt and Lucinda and Baby Cady Number One to now, with Doris McKinnon's and Dr. Roque's murders, and the attack on Sonia. Why do you think Magda Spirova came back to Lawrence?"

Maybe if I had something to eat and wrote it all down, it would make enough sense that I could figure out what to do next. I walked with Peppy to the bakery for soup and bread. They wouldn't let an emotional-support animal join me inside, so we trudged back to the Hippo. Anyway, the coffee was better there, and I could get a small whisky alongside it in case Peppy's support flagged.

As I sat at our usual spot, the high counter in the corner, my phone rang. Unknown local number, which turned out to belong to Bayard Clements, the pastor at St. Silas.

"Ms. Albritten!" I said. "Is she all right?"

"Sister Albritten is the Pillsbury Doughboy with the Energizer Bunny inside," Clements assured me. "I want to keep her that way."

My stomach muscles tensed as I waited for the next sentence: *Keep away from her.* Instead he wanted my help.

"Jordan, her son, you know, and his boy, they had to go home. School's in session, Jordan's wife is sick herself. No one from St. Silas can be with Sister Albritten around the clock, and I worry about her right now, especially tonight when she'll be on her own for the first time. I have to go to Atlanta this evening for a funeral, or I'd stay with her myself, but I won't be back until Friday."

"I'll do what I can," I said slowly, trying to imagine how my day might play out. "If I could get one of the women from Riverside?"

"As a last resort," he said sharply. "They live to gossip, and that's the fastest way for word to get out that Sister Albritten is home alone and vulnerable."

"Copy that, Pastor. I'll work out something."

What, I didn't know, but I didn't know the answer to *any* of the problems I was facing. Finding a way to look after Ms. Albritten would be a cinch compared to sorting out Cady's and Sonia's histories, finding August Veriden and Emerald Ferring, and unraveling what Dr. Kiel was up to with the colonel. Maybe I'd tuck Albritten into the Mustang with Peppy and let her ride shotgun as I drove madly around Douglas County, looking for dead women.

One problem at a time. I unrolled the newsprint where I'd divided events between "current day" and 1983. Under "Current Day," I wrote *"Colonel Baggetto came to Lawrence at the request of the army, not because of some bogus spent fuel rods but because Spirova's presence in Lawrence worried them."*

In 1983 Spirova had been furious with Kiel. In her mind he'd lured her to Kansas and then abandoned her. Had she switched those organisms in 1983 at the behest of the KGB or out of rage with Kiel? In either event he'd survived and thrived, while she'd been bound over to the U.S. Army. The army probably kept her on a tight leash when they first had her, but as the Cold War ended, I was guessing they cut her loose and didn't bother to keep track of her.

Even if revenge had been boiling in her mind for thirty years, why had Spirova waited this long to come back? She couldn't have counted on Kiel to stay alive until she got around to punishing him.

No, Spirova must have come back to Kansas for reasons that had nothing to do with Kiel but everything to do with bioweapons.

Gertrude Perec had said Magda was working with Bram Roswell out at Sea-2-Sea. Doing what? Perhaps she was taking her bioweapons expertise into how to destroy plants. Maybe that was what they were doing on their off-limits experimental farm—growing plants in order to give them lethal diseases.

I drew a picture of a corn plant with an ugly worm boring into to it. If Sea-2-Sea really was engaged in that kind of work, then the army probably knew all about them. In which case, instead of tracking Spirova to Kansas, Baggetto had brought her here as a consultant for Bram Roswell.

I started looking at Sea-2-Sea, not the rhetoric on their website ("Safeguarding America's Food Supply from Sea to Shining Sea") but deeper background. I skimmed reports to congressional committees, looked at work by investigative journalists who covered America's vast food chain, dipped into scholarly databases.

Sea-2-Sea didn't seem different from any other food giant: hideous work conditions in the fields to place on our tables those bright sparkling wines. Laboratories where plant and animal genetics were studied. Vast landholdings that drove small farmers out of business. Sea-2-Sea wasn't any better than their competition, but they didn't look worse.

When I'd first checked into Roswell, I'd noted that he was involved in some chest-thumping group. I went through my case notes. Patriots CARE-NOW: Concerned Americans for Re-Armament Now. Their website had the kind of rhetoric that made the hair on my neck itch: Obama was a terrorist Muslim who was selling out America to her enemies. America needed to become strong again, we needed to be feared, we needed to be vigilant against our enemies, we needed to be ready with first-strike capability.

Sergeant Everard came in and poured himself a coffee from the thermos at the counter. When he saw me, he called, "You found any more dead people, Warshawski?"

"I can't remember my body count the last time I saw you," I said.

He came over and knelt to scratch Peppy. "Sonia's still alive."

"That's good to know. I took some of her journals from her room at St. Rafe's on Sunday. Someone broke into my room at the B and B and stole them while I was out yesterday."

"That a fact? You file a report?"

"You think there's any point?"

"There's always a point, Warshawski. It lets the perps know that someone is paying attention. Even if they get away with it this time, at least the police have something on file if it happens again."

"The next time a Chicago detective comes here and starts poking into old business?"

He grinned. "Could happen, you never know. What was in the journals?"

"Old business," I said. "What happened at the Kanwaka silo, Matt Chastain dying of the plague—stuff like that."

That startled him. "He did?"

"All the signs point in that direction. I was just talking to Gertrude Perec, and she sort of confirmed it. At least she was aware that someone in Dr. Kiel's lab was playing around with plague germs out around the missile silo back in '83."

"Plague? Here, in Douglas County?"

"Yes. Here, in Douglas County."

He got slowly to his feet and perched on the stool next to mine. "And they covered it up, and now you're poking the wasp's nest and making someone really unhappy."

"Yes. In fact, I just heard this morning that the pathologist who performed the autopsy on Dr. Roque found that Roque was infected with pneumonic plague. That's what Roque's good friend Dr. Hitchcock is battling up at the Cleveland Clinic. Actually, the pathologist said he was notifying the CDC, as is Dr. Herschel in Chicago. They should be issuing an alert to the local public-health authorities. Two confirmed cases and a suspected third is alarming."

"Haven't seen anything about that." Everard touched an app on his phone. "Nothing's come through yet. You sure about this?"

"About which?" I said impatiently. "I'm sure there've been two confirmed plague cases here in the last week, but I don't know about the alert."

Everard touched a speed-dial button on his phone. "Sharene? Deke here. You know anything about a public-health warning coming into Douglas from the CDC in Atlanta?"

I heard the tinny clatter of her voice, music while he sat on hold, more tinny clatter, filled with exclamation points.

He looked at me bleakly. "Apparently the sheriff and our public-health director said it was premature to panic the people of Douglas County. You say 'bubonic plague' and everyone starts screaming and heading for the exits."

I felt a chill, a stiletto-shaped icicle, down the middle of my back. "Gisborne was the person who pulled Jenny Perec from the Wakarusa. He's popped up like a magician's rabbit every time I've been at the McKinnon farm or near the missile silo. What is his role in all this?"

Everard shook his head. "You and Ken don't hit it off, that's obvious, but that doesn't mean you get to accuse him—"

"Yes, when someone puts me in jail, it usually stops me from having warm and fuzzy feelings. He has the power in this situation, as do you, and your lieutenant, and so on. And it's your territory. All I have is a trail of events that show him trying to stop my investigation, along with his connection to many of the events I'm uncovering. He doesn't want a public alert on the plague? Who's he protecting?"

"Maybe he has more information than you do, Warshawski. You've done some smart fieldwork and made some lucky guesses, but that doesn't mean you know everything."

"No, you're right," I said quietly. "I understand this much: that I'm an outsider. Some days you feel you can trust me and some days you need to be loyal to your homies."

"To my homies? You think the Lawrence Police Department is like some big-city street gang?" His eyes were bright and hard.

"I grew up in a big-city neighborhood, which is essentially a small town where everyone is inside one another's business. We had plenty of feuds across our alleys and playgrounds, but you'd better believe we all banded together when someone from South Shore crossed our borders. I'm not accusing the LPD of corruption or lawlessness, just trying to understand why you stand up for Gisborne when you yourself have questioned his actions around the McKinnon murder."

Everard pounded his fist into his palm with such force that Peppy jumped up and anxiously started licking me.

The sergeant gave a bark of harsh laughter. "I cling to my homeboys, and I frighten puppies. Sorry, dog." He petted her head but turned and strode from the bar without saying good-bye to Simone and her friends, let alone me. Simone stared at me, questioning.

"Policy differences," I said, more lightly than I felt.

My phone dinged with a message from Cady: WHAT DID THE DNA ANALYSIS TELL YOU? ARE YOU GOING TO THE SILO?

I stared at the screen. I didn't want to lie to protect Gertrude Perec's feelings. I didn't want to break personal news to Cady myself. I finally wrote, YOU'RE NOT RELATED TO THE CHILD WHOSE BONES DORIS MCKINNON DUG UP. THE RISK OF PLAGUE OUT THERE IS HIGH: STAY AWAY FROM IT.

I started rolling up my newsprint notes when my phone rang. A second unknown caller with a Kansas area code. When I answered, it was a woman with a soft voice and a Kansas twang.

"Are you the lady who advertised about Matthew Chastain?"

I dropped the papers. "Yes. I'm V.I. Warshawski. Who is this?"

"Charmaine Long. I'm Matt's sister."

52

GOOD COUNTRY PEOPLE

CHARMAINE HAD DRIVEN in from Belleville, Kansas, the town where she and Matt had grown up. It was a neighbor who had pointed out the Facebook post. "We haven't heard anything in so long, I'd almost forgotten him. Where is he? How do you know him?"

"I don't," I said as gently as possible. "I was trying to find him because I think he was an important witness to something that happened in Lawrence thirty-five years ago."

Charmaine and her friend were staying at a motel west of town. I offered to meet her there, but she wanted to come into "the city," as she referred to downtown Lawrence.

I gave her directions to the Hippo. While I waited, I answered e-mails from Chicago, which was beginning to feel like a place I had known only vaguely, like a city where you spent a summer as a child but now can't quite remember.

I recognized Charmaine as soon as she came into the Decadent Hippo, not because she resembled Sonia's sketches of her brother, but because she looked around eagerly, as if Matt himself might appear at one of the tables.

She was an angular woman in her fifties, her salt-and-pepper hair cut in a straight line that didn't quite reach her shoulders. Her face was freckled from long hours in the sun.

When I stood to greet her, the light died from her eyes: she had hoped against all hope that her brother would be with me. I offered her something to drink; her eyes widened at the array of bottles behind the bar.

"I'm not much for alcohol in the morning. Not often ever, really, just Christmas and birthdays." Her tanned skin turned darker with embarrassment. "Does that make my small-town life obvious?"

I smiled. "I'm not much for alcohol in the morning, either, but they make good coffee here. I'm having coffee. There's tea, and soft drinks."

When Charmaine ordered coffee, Simone, sensing either drama or Charmaine's need for care, brought it to her at a small table in the corner.

We sat for an hour, her story coming out hesitantly at first, and then, as she became caught up in her memories, more fluidly.

The family hadn't wanted Matt to go to school at KU, but he won a scholarship and he was passionate about science. As a little boy he'd saved the money he made raking hay and running errands to buy a microscope kit over at the hobby shop they used to have in town. Their parents had been upset, but he was determined.

And then, after he'd been in Lawrence awhile, he began questioning the Bible story of creation. When he started his graduate degree, their parents learned he'd begun accepting evolutionary theory.

Charmaine gave a strained smile. "Maybe that doesn't seem shocking to you, but we were raised as Bible Christians. My parents couldn't talk him out of it. Dad brought Pastor Mulveney to the house to pray over Matt the last time he was home. Matt was respectful, but he said that though he'd never turn his back on Jesus, God gave us brains to use and learn, and what he learned had made him believe the evidence that geology and the stars gave us about the age of the world.

"Matt tried to get Mother and Dad to come to Lawrence, to see the people he was working with, but they said he'd turned his back on Jesus, he was damned forever; if they visited him, it would seem like they agreed with him."

She reached down to pet Peppy, to give herself a little breathing room.

"I can't tell you how hard a time that was," she finally went on. "I was four years younger and I followed him around like a duckling when we were growing up. I missed him terribly. My parents tried to forbid me to write to him, but I was nineteen, I was working in the local hardware store and the owner let me get my mail there. I kept his letters."

She'd brought one of the letters he'd written after that painful Christmas.

> Dear Sis
>
> I'm not trying to run away from you or from Jesus. The deeper I can see in nature, the more wonderful God's work looks. But He gave us brains and minds for a reason and I can't ignore what reason teaches me. If I could, I would. I'm so lonely, Sis. My professor who got me my graduate fellowship left to teach at a university in Washington and I'm working in the lab of the department chair, who thinks I'm lower than the dirt on the floor . . .

Poor Matt: condemned by his parents, called an incompetent loser by his thesis adviser. No wonder when he'd found love in Jenny Perec's arms he'd clung tightly to her.

"Even though I was writing him to tell him I still loved him, I didn't hear from him after that last summer. It hurt me deeply—I thought he didn't realize how much he meant to me. I started reading science books so I'd know how he was thinking, and I came to change my own mind about the creation story. I joined the Methodist church, which made our parents furious, and I wrote about it to Matt, but I never heard back from him."

She swallowed some cold coffee; Simone, looking over, brought a fresh cup without saying anything. "When I got married the next year, my husband, Gardiner, he drove me over so I could talk to the people Matt had been studying with. They told me he'd gone off doing secret work for the government and they didn't know how to reach him."

Her mouth was set in that smile you make when you're trying hard not to cry. "I'm five years older now than my mother was in 1983. Aging changes you, makes you realize how many things are more important than religion or ideology. Or made me realize—I don't think my mother and father ever realized that. My husband and I lost the farm in 2007, and then I lost my husband to cancer in 2011. I can't imagine turning away my own children because they believed something different than me, but my mother even burned all the pictures we had of him. I managed to save a few. That picture you put on Facebook, whoever painted that knew him pretty well—it looks just like him, like he did that last Christmas he was home."

"Did you know he was in love? I think he and his girlfriend had a baby girl, although I'm not a hundred percent sure just yet."

Charmaine's eyes widened in her sorrowful face. "A baby? What happened to her? Where are they?"

"I don't know, but the girlfriend died in a car crash about two months after the baby was born. And I think your brother and the baby died at the same time."

Tears formed in the corners of her eyes. First Gertrude Perec, then Charmaine Chastain Long. I was having a wonderful effect today on the women around me.

She wept silently, but finally said, "If he's dead, where was he buried? And the baby?"

I made a face. "I don't know for sure that he did die, but Jenny—Matt's girlfriend—was camping out as part of an anti-nuke protest east of Lawrence. A fire swept through their campsite and no remains were found. I've heard a rumor that I can't prove that Matt was there and died at the campsite. It's possible he survived, although the fact that neither you nor anyone else ever heard from him makes me doubt it. However, about a month ago, someone found part of a baby's skeleton out where Jenny was camping with the baby. Would you be willing to let me have a DNA sample? It might show whether that baby was Matt and Jenny's child."

Charmaine was eager to be tested if it meant learning one concrete thing about her brother, even it was the difficult news that all that remained of him was part of his dead child's skeleton. I paid Simone, and drove with Charmaine to a drugstore for another sterile kit.

When we'd paid for the kit, she let me swab her mouth and spelled out her name and address for the label. "If it turns out that baby's hand belongs to Matt's child, I want it," she said. "I'm the little girl's aunt, she should come home to Belleville with me and be buried with her people."

That seemed like a fitting request, although I wondered how Gertrude Perec would feel about it. Still, I promised I'd do my best to get the little hand to her.

When I dropped her at her car, she asked for directions to the missile silo. "If that's where his life ended, I want to see the spot. I want to walk that land."

"A couple of people out there have died from a rather serious illness recently," I said. "I can tell you how to find the farm, but it would be best if you didn't get out of your car. It's not clear what's going on, but there's an old Minuteman Missile silo there, and there might be some contamination."

When Charmaine had driven off, I texted Aanya to let her know I had another DNA sample to check against the baby. She offered to drive in to Lawrence to collect it—"You have been doing all the errand running so far; now it is my turn. Until I learn whether Dr. Madej has a place for me on his team, I am not having enough to do with my time except to sit and be unhappy."

I didn't want to tie myself down to a time and place to meet. I went back into the Hippo and asked Simone if I could leave a package behind the bar for a friend to collect. She agreed, on condition

I tell her what had made Deke Everard leave the bar without saying goodbye.

"You going to spread this through the county grapevine?" I asked sourly. "Dr. Hitchcock and Dr. Roque both contracted pneumonic plague, possibly from soil samples out near the old missile silo. The pathologist who did the autopsy thinks there should be a public health warning, but the sheriff thinks it's premature until they're sure they know the source of the infection. The sergeant agrees with the sheriff, I agree with the pathologist."

Simone took a step back. "This package, does it contain plague germs?"

"This package has zero to do with the plague. It has to do with trying to find the parents of a baby who died thirty-five years ago or so."

"Connected to Cady," Simone said.

"Not related to Cady at all, that much I know. Different baby, different daddy."

I wrote Aanya's name in black Magic Marker on a paper bag, stuck the box with the DNA sample in it, and borrowed some electrical tape from behind the bar to seal it shut.

Simone tucked the bag in a drawer filled with miscellany—lost glasses and phones, her own shoulder bag, a box of candles. "You ever going to tell me what this is all about?"

"If I ever know for sure what it's all about, I will definitely tell you."

53

DATE NIGHT AT THE MOVIES

EVER SINCE THE Cheviot lab removed the malware from my computer, I'd started seeing the Buick Enclave again. It wasn't definitely on my tail, but it seemed to be where I was too much of the time. I wanted an anonymous car, and I thought I knew where to find one.

I also was worried about Peppy: if someone wanted to push me away from the investigation, all they'd have to do is take Peppy out of Free State dogs and hold her hostage. But if I went into North Lawrence with her, the invisible poverty-stricken part of town, I could leave her with Nell Albritten and find a beater at one of the scrapyards.

I parked once again in the library lot. I packed my boots and change of clothes into my backpack, pulled my Faraday cage out of the trunk and tucked my devices inside, then walked with Peppy across the bridge, stopping frequently to see if anyone was following on foot. On the north side, I let her run along the river's edge. No SUVs lingered in the parking area, and no one followed us when we continued on to Nell Albritten's home.

Albritten greeted us with evident pleasure, stooping to pet Peppy.

I turned down an offer of iced tea. "Ma'am, I wonder if I could leave Peppy with you?" I explained my mission. One of the auto wreckers in the area would have a beater I could buy for a few hundred dollars; if my own errands turned dangerous I didn't want my dog's life at risk.

"She'd be company for you, too, now that your son and grandson have left."

Albritten made a wry face. "Bayard called you, asking you to keep an eye on me, didn't he? Your dog is welcome to stay here for a bit. She's a sweet girl. She'll be good company."

"If anything happens to me, will you call this number in Chicago?" I handed her a note. "Dr. Lotty Herschel will organize someone to come down to collect Peppy, and she'll also take care of . . . well, anything that needs taking care of."

"You really are expecting trouble?" she asked.

"It's all around me. I don't know why it hasn't hit me square in the face yet. My guess is the troublemakers haven't found whatever they were looking for when they went through August's home and place of work. They keep hoping I'll find August and lead them to him."

"Then it's just as well you haven't found him. If these villains catch up with you, I or young Bayard Clements will call this doctor of yours, and we'll look after your dog."

I gave her a quick embrace, feeling her shoulder bones through her cardigan. "I'd best be on my way if I'm going to get to the yards before they close."

Albritten grunted again. "I'll catch heck for this if word gets out, but I don't share the local view about you. I have a car you can use."

I didn't bother asking what the local view was, since I had a pretty good idea.

Albritten reached for a walking stick that was leaning against the TV. "You can fetch me a coat from the closet over there. The navy one."

She nodded toward her small entryway. I found a navy trench coat in the closet, with a blue silk scarf hanging around the collar, and helped her work her arms into it.

She led me slowly through to the kitchen, where a door opened into a garage. Everything in her home gleamed from polish and cleansers, and that included the garage, where plastic-covered bins stood on brightly painted shelves. In the middle sat a car, a dull-gray Prius. It didn't have any plates.

Albritten gave a grim smile at my sharp intake of breath.

"Jordan had ten fits when he saw it here. I guess you know where it came from."

"August Veriden's Prius was green," I said.

"Ed's daddy was a good friend of my husband's. They didn't mind doing me a favor. Painted it, changed some number plate, took out the spy eye behind the dashboard."

Whoever Ed was, he'd changed the VIN and disabled the car's built-in GPS signal.

I knelt down to look Peppy in the eye. "You're going to stay here, girl. You stay, you look after Ms. Albritten."

Peppy stared from Albritten to me with grave eyes and moved next to the older woman. I buried my face in her ruff. When I got to my feet, I felt as though I had lost my last friend on earth.

"We'll be fine, and you'll be fine," Albritten said. "Trust Jesus that far, young woman. The car keys are under the floor mat. Don't know why I did that—old habit and the first place anyone would look. You think you can get this business cleared up? Soon?"

"I'd better. I'm spending a fortune down here that I don't have, and I need to get back home."

"Husband waiting for you?"

"Friends," I said lightly, putting Jake to one side of my mind. "Friends and clients."

When I'd pulled out of her driveway and made sure the garage was firmly locked behind me, I drove over to Lou and Ed, the pair whose scrapyard advertised itself as "Breathing New Life into Old Metal." Albritten had phoned them after I left, and they had a set of Kansas plates ready for me. Two big men, taciturn, so alike that when they changed positions, I couldn't tell which was which. They looked me over to see if they agreed with Albritten's assessment that it was okay to trust me.

"You expecting cops to stop you?" Lou, or maybe Ed, asked, slapping the plates against his open palm.

"Sheriff might if I'm not clever enough to stay out of his way."

"What are you going to say about the plates being expired?" Ed asked.

Good question. "I'm borrowing the car from my cousin's husband's sister, over in Fort Riley. I didn't know the plates were expired, honest."

"Good woman." Ed swatted my shoulder. "Bat those baby blues, and they'll let you off with a warning."

"Not when they see my Illinois driver's license, they won't. And not if Sheriff Gisborne sees my name, so I'd best not do anything that makes them want to pull me over."

When Ed bent to screw the plate onto the back holder, a plastic-covered container dropped out. I knelt to inspect it: a small box, about five inches square, wrapped in thick plastic, taped tightly shut. Under a film of dirt, the plastic looked new, the tape fresh.

"I need a sharp blade." My voice came out hoarsely.

Lou felt in his coverall pockets and came out with a box cutter. I slit the tape, careful not to knick the box. Lou and Ed leaned over to watch, breathing heavily. The box was old, the surface rough from damp and age. I pulled it gently apart and found a second plastic bag inside, new plastic again, covering a small reel of film.

My hands were sweaty. I wiped my fingers on my jeans legs, but I was afraid to lift the reel. This is what August had found, what my troublemakers had been hunting for. Not the thumb drive, nor yet the baby's hand. A movie.

Lou, or Ed, went over to a supply cabinet and came back with a pair of latex gloves. "Good lamp over on that worktable." He jerked his head toward a high wooden counter where tools and engine pieces were laid out in careful stacks. He moved a fan and turned on a high-wattage work light.

With the gloves on, I carefully unspooled the reel, holding it so we could all see the tiny images, ghostly figures in the reverse coloring of a black-and-white negative. Before digital media, before VHS and Beta tapes, someone had shot film. This could be the sole copy of whatever it was.

I thought there were frames of a plane, of a woman with a baby in her arms—Jenny with Baby Cady Number One?—and maybe an aerial view of a campsite, but it wasn't possible to piece together a story by looking at the frames. I needed a projector, I needed a duplicator, I needed to dump this onto video and get a million copies made.

"Found that old projector once, didn't we?" Lou asked Ed. "We keep that or what?"

"Got it over to the house," Ed said. "Thought it would come in handy one of these days. You expecting anyone this afternoon? It's getting dark, maybe time to close up the yard for the day."

He turned to me. "Ms. Albritten didn't give us your name, just that you were a detective from Chicago helping out, but we've got to call you something."

"Vic. Your turn—how do I tell who's Ed and who's Lou?"

The men gave a rumbling laugh. "Ed has a mole on his left temple," Lou said. "I have the gold front tooth. Vic, you seal that box up and let me put it in my tool kit. You follow us out to the house, take it nice and slow so the sheriff don't pay you no mind."

It was just on five o'clock, twilight in November, as I followed their old Chevy truck north. Traffic was heavy, homebound commuters, until we passed the exit to I-70. The truck turned left and started up a hill. We were immediately in the country, on a side road that decanted us at a small farm. Ed waved me around the truck and pointed to a barn, where there was space for the Prius.

As I walked back, motion sensors turned on lights in the yard and behind the windows of a log-framed house that stood in the yard. The cabin was modern, not a historic relic, properly mortised and mortared, with skylights and solar panels on the roof.

A collie trotted around the corner of the house. He stood at stiff-legged attention until Lou said, "Friend," after which he sniffed me politely but unenthusiastically.

Ed whisked me inside while Lou went out to the barn to look for the projector. Ed said he wasn't going to close the shutters; it would only draw attention if a neighbor drove by. We'd go to the basement to watch the film.

Ed took a sheet from a neatly stacked pile in the linen closet under the stairs. I followed him to the basement and helped him tack the sheet to the paneled wall of what he told me was their storm shelter. It was minimally furnished—an old armchair, a daybed against one wall, a cabinet stocked with emergency food and water, a small bathroom in one corner.

"We don't sit down here much—we like being upstairs where we can watch the sky. After being in the yard all day or out poking through people's junk, we want stars and fresh air."

We paced nervously, not talking much, until Lou appeared with the projector. "Just needed a new cord. Got that laid on. Now, Vic, you got those slim fingers, not covered with cuts and burs like ours, you thread the film."

My slim fingers were thick with nerves, but I followed Lou's instructions on the threading order, and we had the projector rolling in a few minutes. The film started with the clacking noise of cellophane against spindles and the sparks of black and white that I remembered from childhood movies, and then we were facing a warning:

> Property of the United States Air Force. Classified. Top Secret. If you are watching this movie without proper clearance or authorization, you could face fines of $25,000 and up to five years in prison.

"You got clearance, Vic? Ed and I sure don't."

The three of us burst into nervous guffaws.

The film ran for just under thirty minutes. It started with a close-up of the missile with its warhead in the Kanwaka site, then panned the faces of the brave men who sat there in shifts, ready to answer their country's call if they needed to press a button to obliterate human life. This seemed to have been spliced in from a PR film; it looked more professionally shot than what came next, and it was the only segment that didn't have a date stamp.

MONDAY, AUGUST 15, 1983, 0800 HOURS

The ragtag protesters' camp. The numbers, never large, had dwindled; the tents were shabby, and you could tell that the ground was baked hard by the prairie sun. Jenny Perec was there with her baby, along with a dozen other people, most of them young, many wearing tie-dyed shirts or dresses with the peace symbol painted on the front.

The camera had contained a mike, but the focus had been on sight, not sound, so we got only murmured snatches of conversation. Ed, Lou, and I all jumped when a loudspeaker suddenly blared at the campers.

"Now hear this, now hear this: at six hundred hours tomorrow morning, a test of highly toxic materials will commence in this region. Vacate the premises by twenty hundred hours tonight. After tonight the air force cannot guarantee your safety."

The film showed chaos among the protesters. Some seemed to be confronting guards at the silo gates, others were huddled in a group by one of their tents. The film showed most of them packing their belongings into their cars or VW campers and driving away. I didn't see Jenny among them.

TUESDAY, AUGUST 16, 1983, 0600 HOURS

The filming began with the plane I'd noticed under the shop light. It wasn't possible to tell whether the plane was near the silo, but four men in protective gear were loading tanks under the wings, emptying stainless tubes that looked like Colonel Baggetto's missing fuel-rod container. Several men in uniform, wearing gas masks, were overseeing the operation. With them stood a trio of civilians.

I told Lou to stop the film so we could look at the civilians. Matt Chastain, Magda Spirova, Nathan Kiel. In 1983 Kiel had been a vigorous forty-eight or -nine with thick black hair like Sonia's, and sinewy arms and legs. Spirova and Chastain seemed impossibly young.

"Lady looks sly," Ed said. "Up to no good."

I looked more closely at Spirova's face. Ed was right; she was swallowing a smirk. Kiel was fussing with the equipment, but in the frozen frame he was facing the camera, saying something to one of the military men. I identified the three figures I knew to Lou and Ed, and Lou started the projector again.

We were above the protesters' encampment now, flying low, the plane trailing clouds of something—*Y. pestis*?—over the tents.

THURSDAY, AUGUST 18, 1600 HOURS

A jeep carrying men wearing protective gear drove into the camp. From the jerky quality of the picture, I guessed someone was filming in a following jeep or truck. I felt motion sick as the camera tilted and swung around. The crew in their protective gear were looking into the tents, giving thumbs-up to the trailing camera team, until they came to the tent closest to the silo. For a count of almost two minutes, the camera showed only the open flap to the tent.

Finally a man emerged, carrying a woman in his arms. She was either unconscious or dead, and I was guessing dead.

A man spoke into his walkie-talkie, but we couldn't hear what he said. For another minute or so, the camera swung between the walkie-talkie and the body on the ground, and then the cameraman stopped filming.

The next segment was so macabre I asked Lou to run it three times before I could finally believe it. A trio of cars arrived, traveling fast judging by the dust clouds. First came Kiel, fishtailing as he pulled up. Behind him a second car decanted Spirova. A beat-up Toyota squealed to a halt in front of Kiel. Matt Chastain jumped out and ran over to Jenny. Her body had been laid on the ground. Chastain flung himself onto it.

It took three air force men to pull him away and to hold him while he struggled. Kiel knelt and looked at Jenny and then looked up. His younger self displayed a wider canvas of emotions than angry spite. He was alarmed, but puzzled as well. Spirova's smirk appeared again, but only Lou, Ed, and I were watching her.

The air force men put Jenny into the Toyota and drove it away. Matt broke free and tried to run after the car but stumbled and fell. We saw blood spread across his left shoulder: he'd been shot in the back. Two soldiers picked Matt up and laid him in a cart attached to one of the jeeps, shoving aside camera paraphernalia and other equipment to make room for his body. The movie ended there, but on the third viewing I saw fourteen-year-old Sonia's face peering from behind one of the tents. They laid him on the cartafalque, Sonia had said in the hospital last week. The cart, Matt's cartafalque.

54

NOW THE WENCH IS DEAD

WHAT WAS THAT all about?" Ed demanded when the tail of the film had *clack-clacked* across the spindles.

"That was all about why Doris McKinnon and Magda Spirova are dead and why August Veriden and Emerald Ferring are in hiding." My voice was a thin croak; Lou went to the emergency supply cabinet and poured water from a gallon jug into a mug.

I drank it down and leaned against the back of the armchair, eyes closed. Magda Spirova came back to Kansas. In her journals Sonia wrote that she'd taunted "the Magpie," telling her she'd seen her in the movies. Sonia meant the air force's private film of the destruction of the protest camp—somehow Sonia had ended up with that film. Back in 1983 or now? She'd watched it, that was clear—it explained why Team Baggetto was so eager to silence her. Maybe it was why someone had stolen her journals from my room.

"How'd that movie end up behind the boy's plate holder?" Ed asked.

"Doris had it." I kept my eyes shut, trying to picture what might have happened. "Doris McKinnon. It's possible Sonia found it, or stole it, back in '83, during the chaos around the end of the camp. She took it up to McKinnon's house. Maybe it sat unseen there all these years. I don't know.

"Lucinda Ferring died right around the time of the fire at the camp. If Sonia or Magda Spirova or even Lucinda herself hid the film in McKinnon's house, it would have stayed hidden for a long time—it's an old farmhouse with a lot of cupboards and bureaus."

I could picture Doris coming upon it, the way you do—you're looking for that old bank statement from 1983 that proves the air force forced you to sell your land for nothing. You're scrabbling through every drawer and folder, and you stumble on this movie in an old box.

"She managed to watch it and was outraged and called Emerald for help. Or she found it and thought, 'Emerald's in the movies, she'll know how I can watch it.' I think that's more likely, because Emerald left Chicago so hastily. She had met young August, she knew he had film skills, and she paid him to come to Kansas with her—filming her origins story was a side project, not the main event. August could have borrowed a projector, maybe from his old film school."

I stopped to make a note—I should ask the Streeter brothers to find out if August had recently rented a projector.

"Doris and August and Emerald watch the movie, they know they're dealing with dynamite. Doris is furious with the air force for seizing her land and then turning it over to Sea-2-Sea. She wants samples to find out what they'd sprayed over her land all those years ago. Because whatever they sprayed killed Emerald's mother, Lucinda, who was Doris's close friend."

"They were in love. Don't beat about that particular bush, Chicago," Lou said. "That bit where they moved the girl's body into the car, what was that about?"

"That was about panic.They couldn't afford an autopsy to show cause of death. They decided to drive her to the river and make it look like she'd lost her mind and committed suicide. By the time she'd been in the water three or four days, you wouldn't stop to ask if that was where and how she'd really died."

"And what did those boys spray on the kids at the silo?" Ed asked. "It was a crop-duster plane. They pour pesticides on them?"

"Plague," I said. "Pneumonic plague, spread through the air, lethal ninety-nine times out of a hundred."

"That's criminal!" Lou cried. "Worse than criminal. Spraying innocent people? And that Dr. Kiel? He stood by and let it happen?"

"I think he thought the air force was conducting a test using his bug: it would give you diarrhea but not make you hideously ill. I think he was taken horribly by surprise. It's why he blew up at his poor young graduate student, the one who got shot in the back."

Ed and Lou digested that in silence for a moment. "What about now? If Ms. Emerald and young August were digging out in that field, will they come down with this pneumonic horror?"

"I don't think so." I told them what Lotty had said about the *Y. pestis* life span. It couldn't have survived in the ground all those years.

I stopped speaking mid-sentence. Roque and Hitchcock had contracted plague, and they had been handling McKinnon's soil. Doris didn't seem to have symptoms, though, so what was the story?

A jumble of images ran through my head. Colonel Baggetto and his missing cylinder. The snakes warming themselves on the glass top to a piece of the missile grounds. Patriots CARE-NOW.

I sat up straight again, and the doxycycline bottle dug into my thigh, warning me, reminding me to take another tablet. I swallowed one with the last of the water in my mug and got to my feet.

"This film is the hottest object in Douglas County right now. I need to get it someplace safe, but I also want copies so that this isn't the only testimony to what happened at that silo. If people think it's worth killing to get their hands on the film, then the sooner they know it's going out on the Web, the better. I don't suppose you know anyone who could copy this and keep it to themselves."

Ed and Lou looked at each other, silent communication between two men who'd spent most of their lives together.

Lou said, "We'll take the movie. Know a fellow over to Tonganoxie who can turn it into a video. In the meantime we have a safe. What about you? What's your next move?"

"I feel like the man in the story who flung himself on his horse and rode madly off in all directions at once. I need to talk to the colonel about his spent fuel rods and try to find out what Sea-2-Sea is doing on that land. But I'm going to start with Dr. Kiel—he has the least incentive to stay quiet these days."

"Okay, Chicago. You watch your back."

"Speaking of that—I left my dog over at Ms. Albritten's—Pastor Clements wanted me to keep an eye on her and that was the best I could manage."

I wondered why Bayard Clements hadn't approached the two men for guard duty, but as if reading my mind, Lou gave a snort of laughter. "That church parted company with us a long, *long* time ago. It was in the old pastor's day, but we found over the years we got on fine without all that fire and judgment. Seemed like the Bible text most churches like best is 'Judge fast before someone else judges you.' But we'll swing by Ms. Nell's place, make sure she's looking after your dog, or vice versa."

The two men led me up the stairs, checked the yard all around for visitors, escorted me to the barn for the Prius. "Be best if you didn't turn your lights on until you're back at the main road."

Ed said, "In the dark she's going to go straight into a ditch. We'll drive the truck down the hill. You can follow our taillights."

They led me as far as the train station, where they turned off to drive by the Albritten house. Having these unexpected allies, street-savvy guys with strong arms, made me feel easier than I had in days. I drove across the bridge and up past the university to Quivira Road, not exactly with a song in my heart and a smile on my lips but ready to face the wrath of the house of Kiel.

It was seven by the time I got there. I'd had to stop at a grocery store for something to eat—they urge you to take doxycycline with food, and I could see why: swallowing a capsule with a gulp of water had left me with fiery pains along my esophagus and stomach.

Kiel came to the door himself, a napkin in one hand and a fork in the other. "It's the dinner hour, or do they eat at midnight where you come from?"

"I can wait in the hall while you finish," I offered politely. "I wanted to tell you that I now know why someone has been trying to kill your daughter, first with roofies in her Moscow Mule and then by trying to smother her in the ICU."

"She almost died of a drug and alcohol overdose," he said. "She's been an addict for decades. Like her mother."

"Yes," I said. "Ever since she saw a soldier shoot your graduate student in the back. Matt was trying to get to Jenny Perec before her dead body was stuffed into her car. It's not the kind of thing you forget very quickly, especially not when you're fourteen and everyone around you says you're crazy, so they can ensure no one listens to you when you tell the truth in public."

Kiel stood glassy-eyed, not speaking. Shirley shouted from the back of the house, wanting to know who was at the door. When Kiel didn't answer, I called, "It's V.I. Warshawski, Ms. Kiel, with news about your daughter."

I turned back to Kiel. "What story did you tell Gertrude Perec? How did you keep her so loyal to you all these years? Her daughter was killed by the *Y. pestis* you helped spray around the protest camp. Her granddaughter was dead. You foisted off your own daughter on her—"

"What are you talking about?" he interrupted, the telltale vein above his right eye acting up. "I never 'foisted' Sonia on anyone, more's the pity."

"Oh, for God's sake. Cady. You encouraged Gertrude to believe that Cady was Jenny's baby, but Jenny's baby died of the plague. Cady was Magda's baby, but you helped create her. I can step you through the mechanics if you've forgotten how."

"So she wasn't lying," he whispered. "Doris McKinnon called Gertrude from the hospital, saying Lucinda had found Jenny's baby abandoned in the tent. I thought . . . I— What difference does it make? Lucinda died. I could see she'd been exposed to *pestis,* not *enterocolitica.* I couldn't think about a baby at a time like that, despite what Magda had said."

"Is that goddamn home-wrecking cunt still coming around?"

Shirley Kiel had appeared in the hall behind her husband, her head bobbing forward, her eyes glittering with alcohol and fury.

"Don't talk like that!" Kiel roared. "It's ugly, it's cheap, and it makes you—"

"Magda is dead," I said.

Shirley gave a crack of dreadful laughter. "Magda was in another country, and now the wench is dead."

"I guess it could seem like a joke, if you were truly perverse enough to laugh at murder. I don't know if you're a born sociopath or if you've spent so many years battling your husband that you no longer know what you're saying or feeling. Maybe that's the same as being a sociopath."

Shirley put a hand to her face, as if I'd slapped her. "That's not true! That's not fair."

"I'm way beyond what's fair. Fair would have meant you paying serious attention to your daughter when she was fourteen and making herself sick with longing over Matt Chastain. You couldn't have stopped his murder, nor that of Jenny Perec, but you could have protected your child from seeing those sights."

I felt a vein throbbing in my own forehead, my neck, too, and tried to steady myself. "What brought Magda back to Kansas this time, Dr. Kiel? Something to do with *pestis,* I assume, since Dr. Roque was infected with it and Dr. Hitchcock is fighting for his life."

He kept staring at me.

"Magda must have called you," I said. "Was she still bitter so many years later? After all, you sacrificed her to protect your research reputation."

"Yes, she called." He spoke in a hoarse whisper. "So many years had passed I'd begun to think I could live out my days in peace, without hearing from her again."

"What did she want from you?" I demanded.

"To taunt me, of course. She wanted me to know she could undo my career at any second with a phone call."

"What? To reveal your role in spreading *pestis* around the missile base?"

He nodded fractionally.

"Out of curiosity, not that it matters now, what actually happened? Why did you spray the camp?"

"It was a way of testing diffusion," Kiel said.

As soon as he started explaining himself, his voice became stronger.

He'd been working on *Y. enterocolitica* with army research grants. "Only for help in developing vaccines and other antidotes," Kiel added sharply. "I was hopeful that we could use *enterocolitica* in a fashion similar to Jenner using cowpox for the original smallpox vaccines."

The Department of Defense had carried out tests of airborne organisms in other locations; they thought rural Douglas County would make a good test site. And yes, Kiel admitted, it was a way of getting the last of the protesters off the missile base.

"I worked with the air force team to check the prevailing winds on the day we seeded the land. We mapped it all out, we knew which communities might be affected. After that, I started monitoring hospital admissions through the state's public health department. I expected to see a spike in GI symptoms. Then two people died of pneumonia; their families described the onset and the symptoms and I knew what I was looking at. I asked Magda. She blamed Matt and I was willing to believe her; he was constantly making mistakes in the lab. I alerted the air force. We got to the camp and they found Jenny, they shot Matt. They told me my career was over if I ever spoke about what had happened."

"Those pesky careers, they take a lot of care and feeding." My throat was tight; I could barely squeeze out the words. "When did you realize that Sonia was there?"

"How did *you* know she was there?" Kiel demanded.

"The film the air force was making of your test; I've watched it. Sonia's in it."

He didn't react to news of the film; his mind was absorbed by the events themselves. "Sonia . . . she'd been embarrassing me for months with her infatuation for Matt. Gertrude told me Sonia had been lurking around Jenny's tent off and on all summer, spying on Jenny and Matt. When we went out to prepare to burn the field, I found her—it was grotesque."

He made a gesture of disgust and turned his face away.

"She was lying next to Matt?" I asked. "He was dead, and she had his T-shirt on?"

"It was revolting. The soldiers who'd come out to do the burn saved her. A day hasn't gone by when I wished—" He cut himself off, realizing what he was about to say.

"Comfort yourself. Sonia also wishes she'd died that day. Why do you think she drugs herself? She wishes she could unsee everything you caused her to see."

"It wasn't my doing," he said angrily. "It was Matt, in his stupidity, letting Magda change the specimens on him."

"Nate is never responsible for anything that goes wrong." Shirley had been standing silent in the shadows behind her husband; her gibe startled me, but I stopped Kiel from snapping his own insult back at her.

"Why was Magda's baby in the tent? Why didn't she get the plague? Or get incinerated?"

He rubbed his forehead. "Magda knew I didn't want another child. She knew I wasn't going to leave my wife and marry her. Trade one harridan for another? I don't think so. Maybe she put the infant in Jennifer's tent to die, or maybe she thought it would be rescued. When Doris called from the hospital that day, I assumed it was Jenny's baby, miraculously saved."

The monstrous nature of his acts, and of Magda's, turned my legs weak. I had to clutch the doorjamb to keep from collapsing at his feet. Count ten, exhale, center yourself, there's more to ask.

"What brought Magda back to Kansas after all this time?"

"My evil daemon. You can't escape your fate. The Greeks knew that, but I never took it seriously until that army colonel showed up asking about her."

"Baggetto," I said. "Matt Chastain's sister came to me today. Do you know that his family cut him off because he was doing a biology degree and he'd come to accept evolutionary theory over biblical literalism? Do you know he'd been accepted into one of your colleagues' labs but he had to work for you because his mentor left for Seattle? You thought he was clumsy, but he was a boy who'd been in love with science since childhood.

"You take up so much space in the room that no one can breathe around you. You beat Matt down, you stood by while your older daughter collapsed, you let Magda Spirova sacrifice your infant daughter. You got yourself a pet psychiatrist who was willing to say Sonia was delusional and keep her endlessly medicated so you wouldn't have to think about that horror story in the camp.

"There's only one useful thing you can do right now: Call your pals, Baggetto, Roswell, the guy calling himself Pinsen. Tell them that by this time tomorrow the whole world is going to have a chance to view that air-force film. They can stop hunting for August Veriden and Emerald Ferring. They can leave Sonia alone."

55

MEN IN BLACK

MY LEGS BARELY held me as I walked to August's car. I wanted to see Baggetto, I wanted to tell him I knew his fuel-rod story was bogus, I wanted to find out what Spirova had been doing in Sea-2-Sea's fields, but I had no strength left in me.

I drove slowly to the B and B. Pierre should be there by now. I would pack Bernie into his car and then collapse into sleep.

When I pulled into the parking space at the back, my suite was dark. I felt a pricking at the base of my neck. Ambush? I edged into the room, flipped on a light. No one was there, but Bernie's backpack was on the foldout bed.

I removed my smartphone from the Faraday pack, fingers thick with fear.

PAPA'S PLANE MADE AN EMERGENCY LANDING IN DENVER. HE WON'T GET HERE UNTIL TEN, Bernie had texted. CADY WANTS TO GO OUT TO A FARM NEAR A MISSILE SILO, AND I THINK THAT IS WHERE AUGUST AND EMERALD ARE, SO I AM GOING WITH HER.

I called Bernie. "Are you with Cady? Are you already at the silo? Don't go in there—it's dangerous."

"You are only saying that because you have been too busy finding dead women to explore the only logical place where August could be."

"Bernie—it's not the only logical place. There are places in Lawrence that are much more likely—"

"Vic, I know you. I know you argue only to get your own way. I am with Cady. We can look after each other without a big sister on top of us."

She cut the connection. I called back but got voice mail. I tried Cady, but she didn't answer either.

Fury and fear washed through me. My body was so tired I could barely move, let alone think, but I needed to do both.

I got up and staggered into the bathroom, stuck my head under the shower to bring on a semblance of consciousness, put on a dry, clean sweater and pulled on my boots. My night-vision binoculars were in my Mustang at the library lot. So was my gun. They'd have to stay there.

I looked around for Peppy. It took me a minute to remember I'd left her at Nell Albritten's. My trip to North Lawrence, the film screening with Ed and Lou—those seemed to have taken place back in the Jurassic. Jake, my angry lover; Lotty, Mr. Contreras, Sal—all my Chicago friends felt even more remote than that.

I tried Cady and Bernie again before getting into the car but still just got their voice mail. My only hope of reaching them before Bram Roswell or the sheriff showed up lay in surprise. I tucked my phone back into its cage and took off. I circled the side streets until I was sure I was clean and then headed east, slowing at traffic lights but going through on the red.

Once I was clear of town, I pushed the accelerator up to seventy, bouncing in the ruts, pebbles dinging the sides of the car. East Fifteenth Street to the open country, south to Doris McKinnon's farmhouse, where I tucked the Prius inside her barn.

The direct route to the silo was across fields, but I wasn't about to attempt that at night, even with a full moon.

My boots crunched on the gravel. Around me, creatures slithered, twittered, rustled through dead leaves. Rats, badgers, owls—I wished I could be sure that was all I was hearing. Every swaying bush or dead cornstalk turned into a soldier training a nightscope on me, or Spirova's friends with aerosol cans of plague.

When I'm this frightened, I usually sing, but I didn't want to advertise myself. Breathe, Victoria. My mother's voice sounded in my head. *Relax,* carissima, *and breathe.* Naturalmente sembri un topo strozzato. *Of course you sound like a strangled mouse—you are not letting your body have any oxygen!*

Right, Gabriella. Deep breaths, down to my belly. Those breaths were one of your many gifts to me.

I'd reached the road to the silo. I stood still, squinting at the fields. A solitary spotlight on top of the silo's front gates showed a small car parked nearby. I went over to it and risked switching on my flashlight. No one was inside, but *Reporters Cover American History: Teacher's Guide* was on the passenger seat.

I squatted on McKinnon's side of the fence, trying to see any signs of motion in the field beyond or any darker shapes against the dark earth.

"Cady!" I called softly. "Bernie! It's V.I."

I called again but got no response. I walked back to the silo and shone my flash again through the padlocked front gates. Nothing was parked outside the heavy silo entrance. I slid through the same gap in the fence I'd used last week. Crossed the silo grounds at a cautious trot. Came to the place where the compound abutted Sea-2-Sea's land.

"Cady! Bernie!" I called again. "It's V.I. Warshawski. I can't see you. If you're in the field, tell me the way past the alarms."

No answer. I turned around, uneasy, listening for . . . I didn't know what. Had the two women gone to Sea-2-Sea's headquarters on foot, without Cady's car? If they'd been seized . . . I needed to go to Sea-2-Sea myself.

I skirted the back of the silo buildings, heading toward the county road on the west at the west side of the complex, but stopped abruptly: lights were seeping through the black paint on the windows of the old launch-control support building. It came from the section where the launch crews had worked and slept.

I hadn't tried to get past the padlocked doors to the support building when I was here before. I'd noticed that the locks were new and put it down to either meth makers keeping out the sheriff, or the sheriff and the air force trying to keep out meth makers. I swore silently: I should have been more diligent in my exploring.

I moved as silently as my boots would allow, up to the windows and through a crack in the paint. I could see a chair arm, the corner of a table, a man's hand chopping up and down as he made a serious point, but not the whole picture. I walked over to the entrance. The padlock had been removed; the door opened easily, silently, hinges and doorframe well oiled and planed.

As soon as I was inside, I heard their voices coming from the end of the hall. They were arguing. Baggetto was speaking, but I couldn't make out the words.

I walked down the hall, through the open door to the team meeting.

"I don't care what Kiel wants—"

Bram Roswell stopped in midsentence. Baggetto and AKA Pinsen were with him; all three stared at me as if I were an octopus who'd landed on a Ferris wheel.

"We wondered where you were, Ms. Warshawski," the colonel said. "You come and go, and sometimes you're very public about it and sometimes not so much so."

"It's always flattering to be missed," I said. "I wondered how sophisticated your surveillance might be. How did the peanut butter affect your remote mike?"

"Peanut butter!" the colonel said. "Was that the sound like sawing wood?"

I grinned, a savage rictus. "That was my dog licking it off. I hope she shorted the circuits. This seems like an uncomfortable place to meet, when you have the Oregon Trail Hotel close by. Or are you trying to restart the Minuteman program? The best place to do that would certainly be where a missile silo already exists."

"What we're trying to do is none of your business," Roswell said.

"That depends, of course, on what it is," I replied. "If this is a weekly poker game and you're hiding your winnings from your spouses or Uncle Sam, you're right—nothing to do with me. On the other hand, if you're releasing *Y. pestis* into the air and soil, it's the business of everyone in this county. In the whole country, really."

"How do you know about *Y. pestis*?" Pinsen demanded.

"Oh, please. It's not a secret. Dr. Hitchcock is at the Cleveland Clinic, fighting for his life. It's not what killed Dr. Roque, but he was infected—one of you heroes stabbed him before the pneumonia became full-blown."

The trio were momentarily quiet, and then Roswell said to Pinsen, "You were right about her—she's much too nosy. Better leave her here."

"I wanted to do that all along," Pinsen said, "but you thought she'd lead you to the actress and her sidekick."

"Have you found them?" Colonel Baggetto asked me.

I laughed. "Is that the best question army intelligence can come up with? Maybe you need to go back to that fancy army college and take Interrogation 102. If I found Ferring and Veriden, why would I tell you? But here's something I'll let you know for nothing: I found the object that you or your minions have been tearing the country apart looking for."

"What's that?" Baggetto asked.

"I kept stumbling on things that people might want to keep secret." I leaned against the wall, staying near the doorway. "A baby's hand, for instance, or the fact that Doris McKinnon had sent soil samples to Dr. Roque for analysis. When I saw the destruction in August Veriden's home and in the locker rooms at the gym where he worked, I knew you were seeking something small. I found a thumb drive with photos of the night McKinnon was digging on the Sea-2-Sea land, and I wondered if that was what you were looking for. It included footage of Sonia Kiel, and I knew the night she almost died outside the bar last week came from a deliberate attempt on her life."

"How could you possibly know that?" Pinsen said. "She's been an alcoholic and a drug user for thirty years. No jury would ever believe she hadn't OD'd on her own."

"I'm not a jury, but I have proof beyond a reasonable doubt. *You* were outside the Lion's Pride the night she collapsed. By the way, is your name really Pinsen? Are you really at that college in Fort Leavenworth?"

"What business is it of yours?" he said sulkily.

"I'm your boss," I said. "You work for me."

The men stared at me, bug-eyed, until Pinsen sputtered, "You are not here undercover. I have your complete life story laid out—every protest march, every parking ticket, every two-bit case you've worked. You have never been on the federal payroll."

"I wish you'd looked into my four-bit cases as well," I complained. "I'm a taxpayer. You and the colonel are both servants of the republic, not its masters. We citizens pay your bills. You work for me. Do you have Cady Perec here? She could explain it to you—she's used to trying to get twelve-year-olds to understand how the government works."

Pinsen made a gesture of contempt and walked to the window and back.

Baggetto said heavily, "His name really is Marlon Pinsen. He works for Homeland. Homeland Security. Monitoring WMD activity in the heartland."

"Oh, yes," I said sarcastically. "Those spent fuel rods. Get people afraid of nuclear explosions and they'll give you a wide berth."

Baggetto flushed but said, "What makes you think Pinsen poisoned Sonia Kiel? If he was at the Lion's Pride the night she almost died, so was half of Lawrence from what I can make out."

"When you guys were confabbing at the Oregon Trail bar the next night, I thought Pinsen looked familiar—and then I saw him in the background of one of the pictures I'd snapped while I was waiting for the cops. But you and he both pretended he was a cadet listening to you lecture. I still don't understand the point of that charade." I looked at Pinsen. "What did you do—pay those college boys to doctor Sonia's drink? The clincher, of course, was the attempt to suffocate her on Sunday. Who did you hire to do that?"

Pinsen scowled, but Roswell said, "You can't prove that."

"The hospital staff found fabric threads in her nose. They thought it warranted providing Sonia with a security detail."

"What did you find that you think I wanted?" Baggetto said.

"Right. That would be the movie the air force shot of the criminal use of *Y. pestis* on the missile protesters in 1983."

"You have it?" Baggetto jumped from his chair. "Hand it over, Warshawski. It's military, top secret, not for civilian use. And no crap about you being my boss."

"I've watched it," I said, "and I can see why the military wants to keep it secret, but it's too late. It's in production, and by this time tomorrow it will be all over the World Wide Web."

Baggetto leaned over me, hands against the wall next to my head. "You could spend the rest of your life at Fort Leavenworth, Warshawski. You have committed a very serious crime."

My heart started beating unpleasantly fast. He had six inches and forty pounds on me, not to mention all kinds of military combat training.

"Who has it?" Pinsen was behind him. "That lab in Deerfield you use?"

I ducked under Baggetto's left arm to glare at Pinsen. "You bug my car, my phone, and even my mail? I'll put it in my ad copy. 'Warshawski Investigations: So Successful Even Homeland Security Tracks Her.' I obviously solve problems that are too big for you."

"You don't run ads," Pinsen said.

"Marlon, she's baiting you," Baggetto said gently. He backed away from the wall and turned to look at his teammates.

"Can you trace where she's been today?" Roswell asked. "That'll tell you where she put the film. Unless she shipped it."

"If I could have traced her today, I'd have been on her already," Pinsen said. "But I know she didn't leave the county. Her car is still at the library, so she had to have picked up some other transport in this area."

"Hitchhiked," I said. "I can walk every place I need to be in Lawrence, but I hitched a ride out K-10 to get here."

"We'll do a sweep," Pinsen said. "In the meantime she stays here."

"You know I'm opposed to that," Baggetto said. "I'm opposed to your leaving the Perec woman here as well. Torture never produces reliable results. There's ample proof of that. All we want is the film, and once we have that—"

"I'm not risking any more damned leaks!" Roswell said. "That Kiel creature recognizing Fleming almost did us in."

"Fleming?" I asked. "Magda Spirova's witness name was 'Fleming'? What, she saw herself as a spy, like Ian Fleming?"

"Alexander Fleming," the colonel said stiffly. "She wanted to create something as memorable as discovering penicillin."

"Weapons-grade plague is a universe away from penicillin," I said.

"She started work on bioweapons hoping to find cures for them," Baggetto said.

"That was her propaganda," Pinsen snapped. "You fell for it, and it made you a questionable colleague."

"If you don't have a vaccine for your bug that you can give your own team, you've created a weapon that's a nightmare," Baggetto said. "I've been telling you that from the get-go, but you're so intent on your patriot games that—"

"They're not games. We are serious about getting this country back on the right track."

"I am the only person in this room with field combat experience," Baggetto said. "If you can't pay attention to what I have to say—"

"I am not going to have my work jeopardized any further," Roswell said, "and that's final."

"Roswell. Enough," Baggetto said, but Roswell blew a short tweet on a whistle, and the room suddenly filled with men in black.

I spun around, sprinted down the hall. I was almost at the exit when my body seemed to catch fire. I tried to keep to my feet, but my legs convulsed and I fell to the floor, writhing. Black-clad arms scooped me up, as easily as if I were a bouquet of prairie grasses.

I thought I heard Baggetto protest, but my ears were ringing, the men were all shouting, I couldn't sort one sound from another.

The man in black carried me down a ladder. Fifteen rungs, I counted, and then I was flung to the ground.

56

SNAKE EYES

I WAS LYING ON concrete. It was cold but soothing to my burning skin. My legs and arms kept twitching, as if I were a frog someone was running an electric current through. Tased, my groggy mind thought. The men in black had tased me. I could feel the pulsing where the darts had struck. My arm muscles were still hard to control, but my fingers found the wires trailing from the barbs. Five of them. Three people must have fired at me.

I smelled something familiar, acrid, musty—couldn't remember what I knew it from. Light glowed dimly behind me, showing that the ladder I'd been carted down ended in a concrete anteroom. I was facing a closed door. With an effort I turned my head. The lights were coming from behind a partly open door about ten feet away.

I shut my eyes and felt a wave of nausea sweep through me. I needed to sit up. I tried for deep breaths that would feed my quivering arms and legs, but deep breaths pushed the points of the darts against my skin.

When I exhaled, the darts released. I was wearing a windbreaker over my sweater; my clothes had protected me from the fullest force of the tase. I worked an arm out of the sweater. Bare arm and breast on freezing concrete: an ice bath. It roused me into a frenzy of action—namely, I forced myself to sit up. Shrugged myself free of the jacket. Pulled off the sweater.

Good job, Vic. You're ready for the Olympics. I still had my flashlight and my phone. I shone the flash on the jacket. Five darts. I pulled them out, dropped them on the floor, and worked my arms back into the sweater. I tried my phone, but the concrete bunker blocked any hope of a signal.

I grabbed the bottom rung of the ladder and pulled myself to standing. Walked on unsteady feet toward the lighted doorway, supporting myself by leaning on the rough concrete wall.

The musty, tangy smell grew stronger. When I pushed the door open all the way, I saw why: I'd found a lab, which looked and smelled like Dr. Kiel's. I'd smelled it the first time I came to the silo but hadn't connected the scent to Kiel. Another demerit on the detective's performance review.

A countertop held a dozen canisters—fermenters, like Kiel's—with hoses that snaked into a hood where an exhaust fan ran. A cylindrical machine against the facing wall was rotating slowly, making a clacking sound as an external set of rods moved up and down.

Three computers stood on the countertop near the door. Two seemed to be logging what the fermenters and the clacking machine were doing. The third monitor showed what was happening in the world aboveground. The room where I'd been talking to Baggetto and Roswell appeared in one quadrant, empty now except for one of the men in black, who was playing with his phone. The other quadrants showed the entrance to the silo grounds, the exterior of the launch-control support building, and a view of the Sea-2-Sea fields. I'd never had a chance of getting out of the building unscathed.

Since I could see the control room upstairs, the man in black could probably see me, if he looked up from his device. I craned my neck and saw two cameras in the corners, tracing an arc across the room.

A twittering and squeaking came from the far end of the room. When I shone my flash, red eyes reflected back at me. Cages full of rats. This time I couldn't fight the wave of nausea; I threw up the yogurt I'd eaten earlier.

It was then, bent over and panting, that I saw Cady Perec curled on the floor near the canisters. I shuffled to her, quickly, like a snail. Knelt down. She was alive, her breath coming in shallow puffs.

I shone my flash over her and saw the trailing wires to the darts in her body, one in the back, one in the shoulder, two in the hips. I pulled them out, and she whimpered, her eyes fluttering open. She looked at me in terror and tried to move away.

"Cady, it's V.I. Warshawski. We're inside the missile silo. We need to find a way out."

"V.I.? Vic?" She seized my arms in a fierce, convulsive grasp and burst into tears. "You found me. Thank God!"

"I was tased. Just like you. Where's Bernie?"

"I don't know." Her teeth were chattering. "We tried to sneak into the field, but I was wrong. The place I used to use—everything was like you said, covered in alarms. Soldiers showed up, it was like they were waiting for us. Bernie, when I screamed, she lay flat in a furrow. I don't know where she is now."

I had to hope Bernie had run to safety. She was small enough that she could have slipped away while men in black were torturing Cady. I hoped. I begged.

Even if Bernie summoned help, we couldn't count on its arriving—Baggetto would block any military response. Sheriff Gisborne would keep the local cops at bay. Cady and I had to save ourselves.

Bram Roswell and his band of patriots thought we would die in here, in the lab where they were growing pneumonic plague. They thought we would contract the disease. They imagined us choking to death. Then they could bury us in the experimental field.

"We have to find a way out of here." I pulled Cady upright and propped her against a cabinet door. "We cannot sit around feeling sorry for ourselves while we wait to die."

"I should have listened to you," Cady whispered. "When they brought me down here, they kept asking me insane questions about a movie the colonel wants to watch. It didn't make any sense. All the chemicals down here have made them crazy.

"They wanted to know where you were and where was your dog—they shot me again when I said I didn't know. Where was August Veriden, where was Emerald Ferring? If I'd known, I would have said. I told them you would be here if you weren't at the B and B—don't hate me, but they hurt me too much."

She started to weep, wrenching sobs like those that had racked her grandmother earlier in the day. I slapped her roughly.

"Listen, Cady, it's not like the action-hero movies. In real life, no one stands up to torture. You've done nothing that could possibly make me hate you. You've done nothing for which you need to feel ashamed. You're resourceful, you're a problem solver. And we have a major problem to solve. We need every skill set we possess to get out of this hellhole."

She stopped crying but looked at me apathetically. She needed more than a pep talk from me to summon the energy to save herself. I felt panic rising in me and swallowed it down, bile leaving a raw, bitter place in my throat.

Think for two, think for two, how do you do, I'm feeling blue, because now I must think for two. I needed someone to slap me.

"I'm going to go up the ladder," I said loudly. "You have to hold my flashlight so I can see what I'm doing."

She didn't respond. My own arms and legs were still quivering, but they were going to have to go to work. I hoisted Cady to her feet. Draped her right arm around my neck, put my own hand on her waist, and pushed her across the room. There was a sink by the door; I took a chance on the water and washed my face and rinsed my mouth, wet a paper towel and wiped Cady's face.

When I put my arm around her again, she was steadier. She gave a last gulping sob but stayed with me to the ladder, which was actually just steel rungs bolted into the wall. I thrust my flashlight into Cady's hands and ordered her to keep shining it on the ladder. I wrapped my clammy, twitching hands in my jacket sleeves and grabbed the rung above my head, pulled myself up, feet on the bottom rung.

Cady's arms were wobbly, and the light jiggled around, but she didn't drop the flash, and I could make out the rungs as I slowly climbed up. A hatch was almost directly overhead.

"Get me light right on the top here. I need to see this thing."

Cady tried, but she couldn't manage it. When she started to cry in frustration, I leaned against the wall, took my phone out, used the flashlight to inspect the hatch cover.

Reinforced steel from the days when a nuclear warhead sat nearby. A thick rubber seal fitted the hatch tightly into place. I turned the latch and pushed upward. It was clamped from the outside.

I climbed back down. Not a hard climb if I hadn't just been electrocuted and wasn't terrified in the bargain. Instead I was as winded as if I'd finished an Iron Woman. I squatted, panting, the pill bottle digging into my thigh.

"We're trapped, aren't we? We're going to die here."

Cady's dull, helpless tone so echoed my own mood that I became angry.

"These men are not going to manage our fate in the way that they did Doris McKinnon's or Dr. Roque's. We will survive and thrive," I said fiercely.

I pulled out the pill bottle and stared at it. I'd taken two tablets last night and three today. That left twenty-five, fifteen for Cady, ten for me. Three days' protection, maybe more if the pills took hold before the infection began, but I was damned if I'd sit down here checking my breathing and temperature every half hour.

I explained the situation to Cady. "I need you to take two of these right now to counteract what you've been breathing in here. They'll make you feel sick on an empty stomach, but that's better than what could happen to you without them."

"We could get a soda out of there." She pointed to the far wall, at a vending machine I hadn't noticed. "If you have any money. I left my purse in the trunk of my car."

I found a hammer in a drawer in the lab, which I gave to Cady, telling her to hit the lock as hard as she could. She gave it a few tentative blows and then swung her arm back and start whacking the machine. The lock broke, glass splintered from the front of the case, and cans rolled out around us, but she kept pounding until I grabbed her arm.

"That felt good!" She picked up a can of Sprite, handed me a Coke, and started a little victory dance in front of the vending machine. I high-fived her and handed her two of the antibiotic tablets to swallow.

I gave a hysterical laugh, thinking we were like Peter Sellers in *Dr. Strangelove,* shooting out the Coke machine to get coins for a phone call: now we had to answer to the Coca-Cola Company.

Faded black paint on a closed door by the machine announced it as the launch-control center. I switched on the lights and saw that Roswell had fixed it up as a kind of common room for his research team. There were couches, a couple of small tables where people could eat or talk or inject themselves with germs. A door in the corner opened onto a bathroom with a decontamination shower.

A kitchenette in the back included a fridge, bare except for a chunk of cheese and a pot of mustard; we found crackers in a cupboard and nervously helped ourselves to cheese and crackers, wondering if we were swallowing plague germs. An industrial clock hung near the refrigerator. One-thirty in the morning. How much time did we have?

Roswell had left the old launch-control console against one wall, its keys turned to begin the launch beneath buttons labeled TARGET 1, TARGET 2, TARGET 3. A framed poster captioned "America Held Hostage" hung above it, showing a beleaguered America attacked by hordes of Muslims, Chinese, Koreans, and Mexicans. Text in red letters over a mushroom cloud screamed, "IT'S 1 MINUTE TO MIDNIGHT, AMERICA. ALMOST TOO LATE TO FIGHT BACK. JOIN PATRIOTS CARE-NOW TO REPEL THE ENEMIES AT OUR GATES."

Another hatch was in the floor behind one of the couches, its cover locked into place with two arms. After some trial and error, we figured out that they had to be turned in opposite directions at the same time to undo the locks. When we lifted the cover, I lay flat and looked down, shining my flash around into a vast empty pit. I shuddered: this was where the missile had stood, a fat, sleek snake, never sleeping, ready for launch every second of the day.

I got back to my feet. "We'll climb down there as a last resort," I said to Cady. "Let's see what we can find in the lab."

Back in the lab, what we looked for first was protective gear. Cady and I both put on face masks, bonnets such as surgeons wear, latex gloves.

I went over to the ventilation hood above the fermenters. If they were culturing live *pestis,* the residue couldn't be going straight into the atmosphere, or people in the county would be dropping like medieval plague victims. Presumably they were sterilizing the steam or smoke that the fermenters were pouring into the air. At least I hoped they were.

We were roughly forty-five feet below ground, about the depth of a three- or four-story building. I tried to picture the grounds, but what came to mind were the snakes curling up on a hexagonal roof. The giant snake underground calling its young to its side. No, Warshawski: snakes seek out warmth. They had found a warm spot. Above the ventilation hood.

"Our way out," I said to Cady. "We're going to dismantle this little science experiment."

57

TANG SOO

CADY HAD MOVED past her panic into a numbed place where she could keep one foot moving in front of the other as long as I stayed upbeat, pumping oxygen into her heart. Our first step had to be to cover the camera eyes. The drawer where I'd found the hammer held a full tool kit, including a roll of duct tape.

Covering the far camera meant standing next to the rats. When I approached, the animals all rushed to the sides of their cages nearest me, squealing and clawing at the edges. They were hungry, and I looked like food. Were they covered with fleas that would jump onto us as soon as the rats died, or would the rats— Enough! My hands, my very skin, trembled with fear.

I found empty cages under the table where the rats were housed. With clumsy fingers I stacked the empties onto each other. My hair was wet under the bonnet as I climbed my makeshift ladder.

Cady stood as far from me as she could while she cut off a piece of duct tape to pass to me. My hands inside their latex gloves were numb with nerves. I dropped two pieces of tape before I held on to one long enough to cover the camera lens. After that, dealing with the camera near the door was child's play.

We watched the monitor. The man in black was dozing now. The clock on the computer screen read 2:20. It had taken forty minutes to cover the cameras. How much time did we have before the man in black noticed he'd lost his feed to the lab?

We couldn't find an OFF switch for the fermenters, so we unplugged a cord that connected them to a massive backup battery. We unplugged another cord that fed the machine with the clanking arms. In the silence that followed, the sounds from the cages filled the room, rustling, squealing.

I put my hands over my ears, pushing hysteria back inside, down to the bottom of my mind. Keep working, keep moving, think only of the next step to solve this problem.

I surveyed the fermenters. We needed to detach them from the ventilator. I didn't know what would happen if we took the nozzles off the tops, whether they would spew *pestis* all over the room. I wasn't convinced that the amount of doxycycline we were taking would protect us from a plague bath. Cady and I hunted in the drawers but finally went to the kitchenette in the equipment center for a box of foil.

I climbed onto the counter and carefully unhooked a hose from one of the fermenters. Vapor rose from the opening. I quickly wrapped it in foil and taped it tight.

I was breathing hard, my eyes fogging inside the protective mask. One down, eleven to go. One step at a time: Unhook the hose, cap the top with foil, tape it shut. Unhook, cap, tape. My hair was soaking, clinging to my scalp underneath the bonnet. When I glanced at Cady, her face was white, freckles standing out like orange stars.

After we'd wrapped the last fermenter, we carried them from the countertop to the other side of the room, where we stashed them next to the machine with the exterior arms.

I took wrenches and screwdrivers from the tool kit. Glanced at the monitor. Four A.M. The man in black was still sleeping, but someone would come to relieve him. Shifts change at seven usually. Three hours.

"You'll have to get up here with me," I told Cady. "That hood is heavy. When I get the screws undone, it's going to fall on me unless you can help hold it up."

We moved empty animal cages to the counter so that if the hood came down too fast, they would help break its descent.

The screws seemed almost welded in place. We sprayed with WD-40, we hammered on them, used the wrenches. It took a precious hour, but we finally lowered the heavy hood onto the bed of cages.

"Tang Soo," Cady said softly.

I looked at her, worried, wondering if she was hallucinating, but she gave a tired smile.

"The karate school I went to as a child, that was what we cried when we finished a kata. I need to rest."

We went back to the common room. Drank more soda, took another round of antibiotics, washed off in the shower, gave each other permission to sleep for fifteen minutes. I laid the map of America Held Hostage on the floor behind the console—the message of hate-filled fear only added to my own wire-taut nerves.

I fell deeply asleep as soon as I lay down. When my phone alarm jerked me back to life, my legs and arms felt too heavy to move. I looked over at Cady, sleeping soundly on the other couch. Let her rest, I told myself. One of us should have enough stamina for whatever heavy lifting lay ahead.

I pushed myself to my feet, ate another chunk of cheese, returned to the lab. Five-thirty. I removed the tape from the camera facing the rat cages. Its sweep didn't reach the ventilation hood, and it might buy us some extra time: if the watchers could see the room, they wouldn't worry that the other camera wasn't recording.

I climbed back onto the empty cages while the rats mewed nearby. I was starting to feel sympathy with them, all of us locked up down here, underfed and definitely unloved. There was a bag of rat pellets on a table behind the cages. If the way up was clear, I'd feed them before waking Cady.

"It's okay, boys and girls, we'll figure this out. One step at a time, one step at a time."

Maybe it's a sign of delusions setting in when you're crooning to rats. I hoisted my tired body onto the counter. Stacked cages directly under the ventilation shaft. Looked up and saw starlight through the scratched glass covering. Tried to stand. And found I was in an opening wide enough to take my head but not my shoulders.

I turned on my phone's flashlight and held my arm up the shaft, hoping against hope that I'd butted into a minor obstruction. Wrong. The shaft had been designed to keep people and animals out of the silo. A rat could get up and down, maybe a badger, but not anything as big as me.

I wanted to lie on the counter, cry myself to sleep. Cry myself to death. Is this the way you wish to go into that night? Mewling like a lost kitten while Roswell gloats over your plague-infested body? My cousin Boom-Boom used to chant Julius Caesar before he took to the ice: *Cowards die many times before their deaths; / The valiant never taste of death but once.*

I slid off the counter. Third period, coz, a minute on the clock, down by two goals, that's when you really start to fight. My pep talks weren't helping. I was demoralized, unable to think.

I stopped at the monitor to check the time. Six-fifteen. The shift would change—the shift had changed. The man in black was sitting upright, another man in black shouting at him. It was a silent movie, but the second man pointed at the computer screen on the tabletop: they could see the lab, they knew that something was amiss. Roswell came into view, wearing a T-shirt and sweatpants. He started gesticulating as well. The room began filling, men in body armor, men carrying massive weapons.

My heart thudded so violently it shook my chest and arms. I looked around wildly. The rats.

"We're buddies now, right? You're hungry, maybe you're sick, let's get you food."

I grabbed the bag of feed pellets and spilled it on the floor, made a trail that ended at the bottom of the ladder I'd been carried down. I could hear the men above me start to unscrew the hatch cover. I made my legs carry me, made myself run in a wobbly waddle back into the lab, opened the cage doors and waddled back across the anteroom to the launch-control center.

I shut the door, slid a heavy lock into place, shook Cady awake. "They're coming, a whole platoon of them! Get up, we need to go down this other ladder!"

I was screaming with fear. Cady shrank from me. It was gunfire outside our door that finally roused her into motion.

The door was heavy, but we could hear the men bellowing, could hear the shrieking of the rats, who were as terrified as Cady and I were. I hoped they were frightening the men in black.

We started down the ladder underneath the hatch in the far wall as the army outside began shooting out the lock on the launch-control room's door. Fifteen rungs down, just like the first ladder. My phone battery was dying, but I still had my pocket flash. I shone it around: we were in a tunnel that ended in a doorway about a hundred yards ahead.

We could hear the sounds behind us—the army had made it through the door to the launch-control room and started down the ladder. Fear, adrenaline—something boosted me. I sprinted the last few yards.

The door was locked with an arm that had to be lowered in a quarter turn. Old, rusted. Cady and I had to pull in tandem to yank it down. We wrenched it open and slid through as a volley of bullets struck it. We pulled up the arm lock on the inside, turned around: we were inside the missile holding pen. LEVEL 3 was painted on the door in heavy black letters. Old warning signs, the precautions to take before launch, but nothing about the precautions to take against an invasion by insane U.S. patriots.

There was an elevator to one side, but it wasn't working. We looked at each other, looked at the stairs.

"Tang Soo!" Cady fist-bumped me.

"Tang Soo," I agreed.

Neither of us asked what we'd do at the top if we couldn't get out. Die trying. My bravado of Monday night came back to mock me. Lotty would have some stern words for me if I died in this missile silo.

Level 2. We could hear guns blasting on the door into the missile chamber, but it would take them time to get through that mass of reinforced steel. We stopped briefly on the platform to catch our breath. Cady pulled a can of Sprite from a pocket and shared it with me.

"Tell me who my father is. If . . . if this is my last night on earth, I want to know."

I squeezed my eyes shut. "First, promise you'll save your reactions until we're safe. There's no time or energy for histrionics. Agreed?"

She nodded, eyes wide.

"Start climbing." I waited until she was two rungs up, followed.

"Jennifer Perec and her baby died in August 1983 in a disaster at the protest site. Magda Spirova—you know her name?—a Czech bioweapons expert who fled the Soviet bloc and came to work with Dr. Kiel? She had a baby with Dr. Kiel. Kiel and Spirova were reacting to the bioweapons test disaster. Spirova tucked the baby inside Jenny's tent. When Lucinda Ferring found you, she thought you were Jenny's baby. Doris gave you to your grandmother after Lucinda died."

"I—" She swayed on the ladder above me.

"No histrionics!" I grabbed her ankles. "Climb!"

She shuddered, lurched sideways, but I'd moved up behind her, was leaning against her. "Climb," I said in my fiercest voice.

She steadied herself and started up again. I followed, patting her legs after each rung: you're not alone, keep going.

Level 1. As we crawled onto the platform, the door at Level 3 burst open. The men in black started up the ladder. We pulled on the lock to the Level 1 hatch but couldn't budge it.

"We sit on the edge of the platform and kick them in the head as they come up," I said. "Unless you have a better idea."

The men in black fired up at us. The bullets sprayed the concrete platform, and we had to stand up, jump out of the way.

"We stand and kick." Cady's face was set in granite lines.

The fusillade echoed and reechoed in the vast chamber. The noise drowned any sound behind us, and Cady and I both screamed as the Level 1 door opened.

Peppy burst through, flung herself at me, and started licking my face.

58

CI SONO

I CLUTCHED PEPPY'S FUR, but she couldn't possibly be there: she was looking after Nell Albritten. I was dying. In the middle of the gun smoke and noise, I was being granted a vision of my dog. I held out my arms, sure that if Peppy were here, my mother would soon arrive.

"Gabriella! Gabriella, *ci sono, ci sono*."

"Not Gabriella," a man grunted. "Lou and me. You gals need to be out of here—now."

Thick arms lifted me. A black man, mole on his temple, I knew him. "Ed?" I said. "Peppy?"

"Ed it is. Dog's right here. Get the little gal, Lou, let's hump."

We were passing clumps of uniforms. Peppy whined and barked, staying so close to Ed that he stumbled over her. Someone snapped orders at Lou and Ed to stop—Cady and I had to answer questions—but the two men kept pushing ahead. My feet banged into the faces and backs of people in uniforms who were hustling past us.

We moved into fresh air. Helpless tears ran down my face. Air. I'd thought I would never see daylight, breathe fresh air again. Lou and Ed quick-marched to the road, to a convoy of squad cars. I saw their truck, pinned in the middle, with its slogan "BREATHING NEW LIFE INTO OLD METAL."

"Maybe you can breathe new life into old detectives." I could hear the manic edge in my voice as I started to laugh.

"Steady now, Warshawski," Ed said. "You got this dog worried enough without you falling to pieces on her, you hear me?"

"Bernie?" I said. "Bernadine Fouchard?"

"Little spitfire? She's safe. Deke Everard picked her up on K-10. She tried to break his nose before he persuaded her he was with the angels."

I laughed, weakly, a laugh that hurt my ribs. Ed laid me on the backseat of the cab, Cady in the front seat, where she'd passed out as soon as Lou strapped her in.

Peppy jumped in next to me and kept licking my face and hands. Ed climbed into the truck bed while Lou started the engine. Someone ordered Ed and Lou to stop—a cop or FBI, or maybe someone from the army, because suddenly soldiers seemed to surround us.

Lou said, "You'll have to shoot all of us, because these women aren't going anywhere but straight to a doctor. You want to talk to them, that will be when the doc says you can. No, don't go flashing that badge at me, because I'm not impressed."

And then we were bumping across corn stubble, driving away from the convoy. I was asleep before we reached the main road.

59

ENTERTAINING VISITORS

SLEEPING, WAKING, SLEEPING, a beeping near my left ear. I opened my eyes and saw a monitor, green lines on a charcoal screen. Seven A.M.

"No, it's too late, the shift is changing."

I choked out the words and tried to sit up. My legs were so heavy that shoving them over the edge of the bed exhausted me. By then I was surrounded by women wearing masks who were pushing me back into bed.

I was flailing in panic, lashing out.

"Victoria! Victoria, be calm. You're safe. Lie back, I'm here."

"Lotty? Lotty! How did they trap you? We have to leave now!"

"*Liebchen,* I'm your doctor, I'm keeping you safe. You're in the Lawrence hospital. You're in an isolation ward until we're sure you're free of plague. These nurses are taking good care of you. Lie down, you've pulled out your IV lines."

My breathing slowed; I was looking at nurses in masks, not Roswell's criminal army.

"Cady, is she okay, is she ill? I gave her hard news. Birth mother. Not Jenny Perec."

Lotty sucked in a breath. "I see. She keeps crying, wanting to know if her grandmother is still her grandmother. What is the name? Gertrude Perec? I will seek her out."

I was back in the cocoon of sleep before the IVs were back in my arms, but Lotty's presence was a tonic. I started waking, sitting, drinking fluids, and by Saturday, when my blood work came back clean of any *Y. pestis,* I was allowed out to the visitors' waiting area. Lotty was keeping the law at bay for another day, but she thought I should talk to Nell Albritten.

The old woman was in an armchair, the Reverend Bayard Clements next to her, Lou and Ed standing nearby.

"Turnabout is fair play, young woman," Albritten said when I thanked her for making the trip. "You saw to me, my turn to see to you."

"You owe your life to Ms. Nell," Lou said.

Albritten gave a rusty chuckle. "She owes it to that dog of hers. That sweet Peppy started walking in circles, whining. She knew you were in trouble, but of course I didn't understand that. I thought she was sensing someone outside my house. So I called the boys, and they set a speed record from that farmhouse of theirs, you'd better believe that."

She nodded for emphasis. "I still don't understand how a dog could realize a person was in trouble, but she knew, she knew."

"We've got her up to the farmhouse right now," Lou said. "She's happy there with our boy—seems to know you're okay. We'll keep her safe until you're back on your feet."

It was Nell Albritten who'd phoned Lotty—I'd forgotten leaving Lotty's name and number in case anything happened to me. By the time Lou and Ed had driven me to the hospital, Lotty was in Lawrence: she'd called in a favor from a wealthy man whose wife's life she'd saved, and he'd put his private jet at her disposal.

"How did you know I was in the silo?" I asked.

"We suspected the silo," Ed said, "but we didn't want to drive out there until we had some definite proof, in case you were in another part of the county altogether. We didn't know if that colonel had maybe dragged you off to Fort Leavenworth."

"Went against the grain with us," Ed said, "but we rode into town, went to Five-Oh, talked to the one man there we knew was reasonably straight."

"Sergeant Everard," I said.

"Yep," Ed agreed.

Everard had defended Sheriff Gisborne to me, but privately the sheriff's behavior was disturbing him. He knew that the sheriff was monitoring my position through the GPS signal on my phone. Everyone in the judicial center liked Everard; it wasn't hard for him to get the county dispatcher to share what they were seeing on their tracking software.

When I was using my phone's flashlight inside the silo, I was forty-five feet underground. For a brief moment, though, early Wednesday morning, a signal came across. When I was holding my arm up the airshaft and weeping with despair because it was too narrow for me, my phone had come online.

"The sarge got his lieutenant to let him mobilize all the Lawrence units, and the looey pushed on a deputy sheriff to override Gisborne and send county deputies out there. I don't know who called the FBI, but they got there, too."

"I thought I saw U.S. soldiers?" I said.

"Don't know who brought them along to the party," Lou growled. "Maybe they were trying to protect that colonel, or shoot him, who knows? Word around town is that the air force is concerned about a video that showed up online, something they say the colonel was sent here to seek and destroy."

"Oh, yeah?" I said. "Wonder what that might be."

Ed pulled out a phone and showed me a screen from YouTube. "Assassins in the Heartland" had received 1,217,836 views since going up two days ago. The freeze-frame showed Matt in the instant he'd been shot, before the blood flowered across his shirt back, just as he was starting to fall.

"People tell me the feds have been around, trying to find out who has the film and who posted it," Ed said.

"They getting any ideas?" I asked.

"What I *hear* is, someone put it up in an Internet café over in Kansas City, no way of tracing who did it. They got themselves a fake Facebook page and told the whole world to come see, and by now just about everyone in the world has been looking. Might be an international incident coming out of it. Russians are peeved, on account of that lady scientist, Magda, being part of their own old weapons program. A whole lot of other people are, too, according to the papers. Of course, you can't believe everything you read."

Sandy Heinz, the ICU nurse, appeared and said the guests had overstayed their visiting time. "We told you fifteen minutes, we stretched it to twenty, but it's been thirty now, so off you go."

It was Heinz who wheeled me back to my room.

"Sonia Kiel?" I asked her.

"She's coming around, more conscious hours than unconscious. Her parents still haven't been to see her, but one of her brothers—one of her actual brothers, because you'd better believe we checked his ID six ways from Sunday—anyway, he flew in from Boston. He's going to take her back with him when she's strong enough to travel. You think she's out of danger now?"

"I hope so," I said soberly. "Unless the people who were after her attack her out of spite. That video the guys were just showing me has all the information they didn't want Sonia to reveal."

Heinz gave a crooked smile as she helped me out of the chair and back into bed. "The hospital wants to send her to a nursing home. Cost saving, you understand—she's a Medicaid patient, and she's beyond her limit of days here. But your Dr. Herschel has been pushing our administrators to keep her here with a guard on her room until she's out of danger."

"The hospital should talk to Sergeant Everard," I said, alarmed. "I gave you an informal, unprofessional opinion. I don't want Sonia's life in my hands when I don't know what the bad guys are up to."

I was awakened an hour later by Bernie, who'd come in with Pierre before flying back to Chicago.

I'd never seen Bernie in such a subdued mood. She apologized to me, over and over, for coming down to Kansas against my wishes, for not listening to my warnings about going out to the silo.

"She will also be apologizing to her coach and her teammates. She knows that one more incident like this will be the end of her college life, right, Bernadine?"

"Yes, Papa."

I didn't believe this meekness would last, but it made a welcome change.

The next day Albritten came back, this time with Phyllis Barrier, the head librarian.

"Phyllis carried a heavy load for the last month," Albritten said. "She was visiting me that evening that August and Emerald showed up, wild with fear over what had happened at the farm. I wanted to call Pastor Clements, but Phyllis offered to hide them. After that she was the only person who knew where they were. She didn't tell me, and I didn't want to guess, but when you showed up like that, asking questions, noticing the missing photograph—we had a few bad days, not knowing how trustable you truly were."

Barrier gave a wry smile. "Librarians can't consult anyone, not even their lawyers, if we get a National Security Letter. I figured I was the best person to stand up to an interrogation. When you started snooping around the church basements, I was doubly glad we hadn't involved the churches. I'm sorry I didn't say anything to you that day you gave me Ms. Ferring's bra, but she's been wanting to thank you in person."

She turned her head, nodding. Emerald Ferring made a grand entrance from behind one of the potted trees in the atrium. She was wearing a caftan in a soft green wool that floated around her. August Veriden, in the signature black of the auteur, was almost invisible behind her.

Ferring thanked me extravagantly for my "life-threatening efforts in the service of truth." After a few moments of stilted conversation, she was willing to fill in the holes in what I'd guessed about the story.

When Doris McKinnon rented rooms to my mother and me, back in 1951, she opened doors to new worlds for us. For my mother it was a journey to true love, a love that took me a long time to accept. For me, Doris McKinnon enabled my journey to an education and to my vocation in the theater.

When my mother died, I had a hard time letting Doris be her chief mourner. My mother's church needed to do some changing as well. They managed, though, as did I: we've learned to change our hearts and our minds and become open to love in its many wondrous forms.

When Doris called and said she was disturbed by activity around her farm, I wanted to come back, to help her, and to make my own peace with the past. I'd been there in 1983 to support the protesters at the silo, I'd come back a month later for Lucinda's funeral, but I hadn't been in the town since.

Young August agreed to come with me, to video some of the scenes of my childhood for me.

When we got here, we found Doris in distress over her land, as you know, but her distress increased after our arrival: she pulled out a box of Lucinda's belongings that she hadn't been able to bear to go through in the weeks after my mother's death. She'd put these keepsakes away in a back cupboard and only remembered them as my arrival drew near.

We went through them, she and I, cozy in front of the fire, and then came on the basket that Lucinda had used for carrying supplies down to Jenny Perec in her tent. And in the bottom, under a hand-knit baby bonnet that Lucinda had originally made for me, we found the movie.

My old high school in Eudora had a projector that they let me borrow. We watched the movie in Doris's living room. We didn't know that poor, tormented soul, Sonia Kiel, was watching it with us through Doris's front-room window.

My mother had told me about the people in Dr. Kiel's lab. His unfortunate graduate student, Matt Chastain, and Magda from

Czechoslovakia, with her crazy jealousy of Dr. Kiel's wife. Sonia, with her sad, silly crush on young Chastain, and the way Dr. Kiel was forever taunting his own daughter. It was an unhappy story, but my world was filled with unhappy stories. I didn't pay much attention to Sonia's.

Sonia apparently kept telling people in Lawrence that she'd seen all these people—Magda and Matt, Jenny Perec and the babies—in a movie. Most people didn't pay attention, thought they were just more drug-addled ramblings—but the wrong ears did listen, as you well know.

August and Doris and I had been out for a drive. We came back to find Magda dead on the kitchen floor. We were badly frightened, as you can well believe. Doris kept her head the best. She sent us on to Aunt Nell—Ms. Albritten—while she stayed behind to collect her soil samples. She was obsessed with those. It was the last I ever saw of her.

We all sat quietly for a time when Emerald finished. I finally asked if she'd been in touch with Troy Hempel in Chicago—I hadn't heard from him.

"Oh, yes. I assured them that your work was essential for allowing August and me to come out of hiding. I don't know how long we could have stayed in the library basement before someone found us—thankfully it was you who alerted Phyllis to the danger of the lights we were showing. I've instructed Troy to pay you for your work. You've earned your fee."

Emerald was Doris McKinnon's heir. She had decided to remain in Lawrence, at least while she wrapped up the sale of the McKinnon farm. August was going to stay with her, to finish making his video about her life.

60

FAIRY TALES

MY CONVALESCENCE WAS slowed by an e-mail from Jake, a long-distance breakup letter.

> I love you, V.I., but you don't love yourself enough to stay away from danger. I can't continue like this, not knowing if you will live or die. I tried to persuade you to come with me to Switzerland, to start a new kind of life, but you seem to want to keep falling off cliffs without a safety net. I don't have the stamina any more for watching you do it.

While I was crying to myself in my hospital bed, Colonel Baggetto swept into the room. He was in uniform, all his medals in place, a junior officer at his rear.

Sandy Heinz followed him, took a look at me, and drew the curtains around the bed so that she could wash the tearstains from my face. She combed my dirty hair and brought me a sweater to put on over my hospital gown before she let Baggetto talk to me.

Jake's e-mail had left me at my most belligerent. "What's that West Point motto they show in all the corny war movies—'Duty, Honor, Country'? What duty were you fulfilling in betraying your country? And do you think you did it with honor?"

Baggetto pulled a chair over.

"You do not have my permission to sit," I snapped. "You nearly murdered me, you very nearly murdered Sonia Kiel and Cady Perec, and the deaths of Doris McKinnon, Magda Spirova, and Dr. Francis Roque can surely be traced to you. You should be facing a court-martial and a criminal inquiry instead of jangling your medals in my face."

"I know what this looks like, Ms. Warshawski," Baggetto said. "Let me have five minutes to explain."

"'Once upon a time.'" I scowled. "That's how all fairy tales begin."

"Once upon a time," he agreed. "Magda Spirova came to Kansas from the Soviet bioweapons lab in Těchonin, Czechoslovakia. Was she a defector, as she claimed? A spy, as the U.S. feared? Or a woman who'd fallen in love with an American scientist? I doubt we'll ever know the answers definitively, but after a year or two in Kansas she felt like a woman scorned: Nathan Kiel had slept with her during a big conference in Bratislava. When she got here, the affair continued in a desultory, hole-in-the-corner kind of way, but the harder she pushed on Kiel, the clearer it became he was never going to leave his wife.

"There were three people in Kiel's lab who had an idea of the affair—his technician, Lucinda Ferring; his most despised graduate student, Matt Chastain; and his devoted secretary, Gertrude Perec.

"Kiel was doing research on bioweapons for the army. Of course, by the 1980s, we—the U.S.—had signed onto protocols repudiating all bioweapons. But—and there's always a big 'but' with weapons—we were still doing research into cures or vaccines against other countries' bioweapons. That meant we had to grow our own organisms, because how can you test an anthrax or plague or whatever vaccine if you don't have any anthrax?" He gave a sour smile. "Kiel was doing some low-grade weapons work for the DoD on a *Y. pestis* relative."

"Yes, I know, *Y. enterocolitica*."

"How did you learn that?" Baggetto was instantly suspicious.

"I can read the professor's publication list, Colonel, even if I don't understand the big words. The air force asked Kiel to try out an aerosol version of his pet bug—it would make anyone who didn't vacate the camp sick to their stomachs, clear any remaining protesters out of the camp, and show the Defense Department how wide a radius the aerosol would reach. Someone switched *Y. pestis* for *Y. enterocolitica*. My money's on Spirova."

I could now say "enterocolitica" three times in a row without stumbling. I guess I'd brought something away from this wretched case.

"At the time Kiel blamed his graduate student," Baggetto said, "but you're probably right. No, I'm trying to be honest: you are right. I've read the classified reports."

"How lucky you are to have access to work done at taxpayer expense. The rest of us aren't so fortunate."

He flushed. "I'm not going to debate that with you, not now anyway. The DoD had a pretty good idea that Spirova was behind the switch. They wanted the whole ugly episode laid to rest. They gave Spirova the choice between working for them or being deported, and she figured the odds of landing in a gulag were better than those of getting a hero's parade if she went home. She changed her name to Fleming, as I told you, worked at Fort Detrick for about a decade. In the nineties we were being all lovey-dovey with the Russians, and we shut down a lot of weapons programs. The DoD let Spirova go and didn't think about her again. At least not until about six months ago, when we got whiff of a secret plague lab in eastern Kansas.

"No one believed it at first—conspiracy rumors float around the army, more maybe than in civilian circles. We all know that we can be sent off to fight at a second's notice, so we're on hyper-alert. Sometimes we don't know if we're fighting shadows or real enemies."

I rubbed my forehead. I was still unbearably weak, and having to listen to Baggetto spin his tale at such length was exhausting. I made a job of swinging my table next to me, pouring water, bathing my eyes.

Baggetto started to sit, but I shook my head: he hadn't earned it yet.

"Then a farmer in Douglas County died. The symptoms were consistent with pneumonia, which was listed as the cause of death, but Nate Kiel—he's still active in the public-health service—was worried. He sent a message to an old buddy at Fort Detrick. About that same time, the man who filmed the air-force video that you know about, he was dying. He made a deathbed statement that he'd shot the whole thing and lost the only existing reel. When the air force heard what was actually on the reel, they went to DEFCON Two without passing go. I was deployed to Fort Riley to keep a watch on the situation."

His voice was getting hoarse. He helped himself to a cup of my water, but I didn't try to stop him.

"When Emerald Ferring showed up with a filmmaker, I met with them, because filmmaker and missing film went together in my mind. After a morning with the pair, I knew, or thought I knew, they had nothing to do with the air force's missing reel. But then you showed up. Private detective, coming to Kansas, looking for a filmmaker. The army agreed you were worth keeping an eye on."

"And an ear," I said spitefully.

"Yes, an ear. I'm not going to apologize for bugging your room. I needed to know what you knew."

I gave a tight smile. "I would have told you if you'd seemed at all trustworthy."

The junior officer in the doorway was surprised into a coughing fit. Baggetto turned to frown at him: there went Junior's next promotion.

"Be that as it may, when you stumbled on Spirova's dead body, I knew that whatever you knew, whoever you were really looking for, you were close to the same quest I was on. I badly needed to keep tabs on you but, even more, on Bram Roswell at Sea-2-Sea. The morning Sheriff Gisborne and I found you at the silo, I let Gisborne know I sympathized with the CARE-NOW baboons. He introduced me to Roswell. We roped Kiel in. I could see what Roswell was doing, but it was damned hard to keep track of you."

I looked at my fingernails. They'd broken off in jagged pieces while I'd worked on the ventilator screws. They were black underneath, dried blood. A manicure wouldn't do much to prettify them.

"So your story is that you were infiltrating CARE-NOW? And AKA Pinsen—what was he doing?"

"He actually was working with them," Baggetto said through tight lips. "He *is* facing a court-martial, if that's any consolation."

The chronology of this was bothering me. "Be quiet for a minute," I said. "I need to think, and I can't do it against your voice."

He stood silent, arms behind him, a parade-ground posture. I shut my eyes so I wouldn't have to look at him.

"You say you only signed on after I came to Lawrence," I said, finally looking at him again. "But I came to Lawrence because someone had tossed August Veriden's workplace along with his apartment in Chicago. I assume they were looking for your precious movie. That happened about a week after August and Ms. Ferring arrived here."

Baggetto rubbed his own cheeks, dark with five o'clock shadow. "That was Roswell's private army. They were way out of control: one of them killed Dr. Roque and another pretended to be Sonia Kiel's brother so he could get into her hospital room and try to smother her. It was infuriating to see them acting like a vigilante force, but I couldn't get them to stop without tipping my own hand and I needed to stay undercover until I located the film."

"You don't sound very infuriated," I said bitterly.

"You want me to start pulling my hair out by the roots? Hear me out before you start preaching and condemning." He scowled resentfully.

"As you know, Sonia recognized all the players. She started telling anyone who would listen that she'd seen Spirova out by the silo—she kept referring to it as her lover's graveyard—but the thing that got everybody's tail in a knot was her screaming that she'd watched the film—'I saw her in the movies!' she kept saying about Spirova. That didn't mean anything to the staff at St. Raphael's, but it meant a lot to me. And when Pinsen got wind of it, he wanted her silenced. From what she was saying, we knew she'd seen the film out at the farm, but we couldn't find it when we searched there."

I nodded. "The messy searches were done by Roswell's army, the clean ones by you. Why did they pilfer the medical supply closet at the gym where August Veriden worked? They deal on the side?"

Baggetto made an impatient gesture. "Does it matter? I think they wanted to make it look like ordinary vandalism, not that they were after something specific."

My upper lip curled in distaste. "You searched Chicago and you searched Lawrence. You couldn't find the film, so you had to kill Sonia?"

"That was Pilsen: he got the college kids to put roofies in her vodka. They thought it was a big joke."

"I'll bet. We keep reading about the cool sense of humor guys at bars have."

It was convenient, putting all the bad deeds onto Marlon Pinsen. Just as Kiel and the army had done with Spirova in 1983. Pinsen would be court-martialed, Baggetto would go on to higher ranks, and we'd never know who really did what to whom.

"Of course, Spirova knew about the film. There was a night out in the Sea-2-Sea field—"

"Yes, I know about that. McKinnon was furious that the air force had sold her land to Roswell without giving her a chance to buy it. They'd told her it was contaminated with radiation, and she wanted proof one way or another."

"Yes. Well, Spirova decided she would infect McKinnon with *Y. pestis* and then search the house for the film. She brought an aerosol sample up to the house and contaminated the soil inside the jars, but Roswell didn't want contaminated soil going around the county—that would launch a full-scale investigation that might uncover his private patriot lab. He sent one of his private army after

Spirova. She was shot in the kitchen, where you found her. The underling took the aerosol samples away with him but didn't realize Spirova had already added it to the soil jars. I'm guessing that Veriden, McKinnon, and Ferring found Spirova's body and fled, but that's just a guess."

"I'm guessing Doris McKinnon came back to the house with August and Ferring. They saw Spirova's body and panicked. Doris managed to pack up the soil containers and get them in the mail to Dr. Roque before your pals knew about it. And then someone followed McKinnon and shot her," I said, leaning back against the pillows. "They reprised the murder of Jenny Perec: shot her, put her car into the Wakarusa at the same spot. Whose idea was that? Gisborne? He was the deputy who pulled Perec from the water."

"It wasn't quite that bad."

Baggetto and I both turned in surprise: Sergeant Everard had slipped into the entrance, next to Baggetto's adjutant, without our noticing.

"Hey, Warshawski." Everard came over to the bed and peered at me. "Want me to put those bruises out on Facebook? Proof to the world that you're an investigator who runs the extra marathon for her clients?"

"I don't want to frighten off cowboys and soldiers," I said. "What wasn't quite that bad about Gisborne?"

Everard sat on the edge of the bed. "He pulled Jenny Perec out of the Wakarusa. He didn't put her in there. That was the air force." He nodded at Baggetto.

"I'm with the army," Baggetto protested stiffly.

"Doing the air force's groundwork for them in eastern Kansas," Everard said. "Did you know how Jenny Perec was killed by the plague and her body put into the Wakarusa to make it look as though she'd gone off the road in a frenzy?"

Baggetto took a seat on the visitor's chair with a challenging look at me, but I let it go.

"I didn't learn about it until the day at the courthouse when

Gisborne got rattled by Warshawski here looking for the Perec file," the colonel said. "The file had disappeared, but I don't think it was Gisborne who pulled it. He started unraveling because he thought there was a traitor on the county staff."

"Yeah," Everard said. "One of his deputies was moonlighting in Roswell's CARE-NOW army. That was a blow. I kept telling Warshawski here that Gisborne wasn't a bad guy. He wasn't, but he got penned in pretty tight. He was giving Roswell and Sea-2-Sea extra security. Nothing wrong with that, but Roswell has a way of making it hard to leave once you're part of his operation."

"It was Pinsen who dug out the original story," Baggetto said. "He's with Homeland, so he has access to every secret act ever committed by possums in the dead of night. He knew that young Jenny Perec had died of the plague. He told Roswell, and Roswell got his citizen army to shoot McKinnon and put her in the river. That really unnerved Gisborne."

"He's stepping down," Everard said. "No shame in that either. Guy is sixty-eight; he's given a lot of service to this county."

"That's all very noble," I objected, "but I want to get back to the colonel. He says he was infiltrating CARE-NOW, but aside from letting Dr. Roque get killed and Dr. Hitchcock fight for his life with those contaminated soil samples, he stood by while Roswell's terrorists put Cady and me in the silo to die. I know you're not supposed to break cover, but how many bodies were you actually going to let stack up before you decided to break rank?"

"I did my best," Baggetto said through stiff lips. "I sent a signal to the First Infantry, and they marshaled a battalion. That was the unit that came to batter down the Level One missile-bay door."

"And now you'll go to Washington and get a promotion and a nice new assignment. I'll write my senator and beg him to make sure you don't come back to the Midwest," I said.

"Pinsen and Roswell are in federal custody," Everard said. "That should count for something. Dr. Kiel helped dismantle that horrifying lab in the missile silo. Sea-2-Sea is donating the fifteen acres around the silo to a nature preserve. But I'm with you. Not that my senators pay any attention to me, but maybe I'll go on Change.org and get a petition going to send Baggetto to some outpost overseas where he can do the least harm. Nepal, maybe, or one of those places near Russia that end in 'Stan.'"

The colonel didn't seem to think this was as funny as Everard and I did. He collected his adjutant and left, not even offering me a token salute.

61

THE SISTERS GROW UP

I GOT BETTER. LOTTY flew back to Chicago. I showered, collected my street clothes from the cleaners, picked up my luggage from the B and B, where the owner had packed it in her garage. I went to one of the many spas on Massachusetts Street, where they trimmed my hair and cut and shaped my nails. I looked more like an ordinary person, less like a battlefield casualty.

Lou and Ed let me spend my last few days in Lawrence on their farm, where the wind across the hills helped clean the misery of the last month out of my brain.

One evening I went to see Cady Perec, who was back with Gertrude.

"Vic, my whole world is upside down right now, but Gram is the woman who raised me and read me my bedtime stories. I feel like I'm living on a fake birth certificate, but I don't want to be Magda and Dr. Kiel's child. I feel like I belong to Jenny."

I smiled at her. "You have a right to the name she gave her daughter, Cady. A name to conjure with, to undertake bold deeds. I'm glad you don't want to give it up."

"I owe you a lot," Cady said. "My life in the silo—I can't ever repay that. Giving me the truth about my birth after all this time. It adds up to a huge debt."

I nodded at her. "It's the cliché of our era, to pay it forward, but that's what you do when you feel overwhelmed by gratitude. I don't want anything from you except to know you're doing your best in a world that's hard on poets and small creatures."

Gertrude couldn't quite forgive me for upsetting the narrative she'd imposed on Cady's life, but at least she offered me a glass of wine and a bowl of nuts; at least she let me talk to her granddaughter in the living room instead of on the cold porch. And she let me bring Peppy in with me.

The next day I went to see Sonia. She was in a nursing home, recovering her energy so she could join her brother Stuart in Maine. Three weeks without alcohol or those badly named recreational drugs had taken some of the coarseness out of her skin. She didn't have any memory of the events at the Lion's Pride, but she did remember watching the air force reel through Doris McKinnon's front-room window.

"I was there, you know, back in 1983. I saw it all. I saw them shoot Matt, I saw Magda steal the film from the air-force truck while everyone was arguing. She put it in the basket that Doris and Lucinda had left in Jenny's tent. I guess she thought she'd come back for it, but Lucinda took it up to the house.

"Later, after I recovered from the plague, Nate couldn't bear that I knew what had happened, so he was happy for me to be crazy. I became what everyone wanted, the crazy woman. I've promised Stuart I won't drink or do drugs while I'm living with him and Pietr up in Bangor, but that's the best I can do right now. Stay sober, keep away from Shirley and Nate. One day, one minute at a time, like all those slogans at St. Rafe's kept telling me."

"I borrowed your journals," I said, "and they were stolen out of my room. I'm sorry. The army has them—Bram Roswell's private goons had broken in and taken them, and Colonel Baggetto recovered them. They seem to be evidence now in a federal case against Marlon Pinsen and Bram Roswell. You may never able to get them back. Those beautiful pictures you painted of Lima and Autumn are gone, too. The only thing they didn't take was this."

I handed her the drawing of the bi-polar bear.

Sonia studied it for a long minute, then handed it back. "If you like it, go ahead and keep it. Who knows, maybe it will be valuable someday."

"Thank you. I'm sorry I violated your privacy, though."

She gave a lopsided smile. "You're only one in a long line. I'm getting a length of blue ribbon and making a cordon sanitaire to wear whenever I have to see a doctor or . . . or any violator. I get to have privacy, I get to get rid of CheeseNuts. You can keep the journals if they ever come back."

62

THERE'S NO PLACE LIKE HOME

I LEFT LAWRENCE THE day before Thanksgiving. Nell Albritten and Emerald Ferring tried to persuade me to stay for the big fete at St. Silas, but I needed to be home. Sergeant Everard took me out for a farewell supper the night before I left. One thing led to another, as they sometimes do.

"You could open an agency down here, you know," Everard said as I got dressed early Wednesday morning. "There's obviously an abundance of crime in Lawrence that none of us know about."

"You'd start imagining I was killing people to create work for myself," I said. "You'd start arresting me every time a dead body showed up in the county."

He laughed and helped me put Peppy into the car, along with my luggage and an enormous picnic basket prepared by the St. Silas women.

"You could be right about that, Warshawski. You could be right. Still, you go buy yourself a pair of red high heels, just in case."

I fished in my suitcase for my Magli pumps. "Got them, but they're taking me back to Chicago."

Much as I longed to be home, I backtracked to the middle of the state, west and north of Fort Riley to the little town of Belleville. I'd persuaded Aanya Malik to let me have the tiny hand Doris McKinnon had sent to Dr. Roque, along with her soil samples. Charmaine Long cradled the miniature case it was in against her cheek.

"Matt's little baby," she murmured. "My little niece. Thank you, thank you for bringing her home to me."

We talked through the afternoon, while I recounted once more the long hard story I'd pieced together. Charmaine, too, wanted me to stay for Thanksgiving, stay until Friday when she would have a private funeral for Matt and Jenny and baby Cady.

"I don't belong there," I said, finally extricating myself. "I need to go back to the place I do belong."

Peppy and I drove through the night, stopping in a motel outside Des Moines so I could sleep for a few hours. We crossed the Little Calumet as dawn was breaking on Thursday morning. The crowded streets of my childhood lay below me on the Skyway; the tower formerly known as Sears was silhouetted along Lake Michigan to the north. When we reached the South Side beaches, I pulled off the road to let Peppy swim. The water was cold, colder than the Kaw, but I stripped and jumped in with her. I needed the clear, cold waters of Lake Michigan to cleanse myself.

I toweled off under the shelter of a big rock and put on my good trousers, my rose cashmere sweater, my Magli heels.

When we reached our building on Racine, Mr. Contreras was waiting out front, tanned from his weeks in the Caribbean, smiling so widely his ears might have fallen off.

"You made it home safe, doll. You made it home safe. The doc kept me posted, or I would've been down there myself to patch you up. You come on in. People have been cooking, people are *desperate* to see you."

Lotty emerged from the hallway, Max Loewenthal beside her. Sal Barthele towered over them, August's cousin Angela next to her, with Troy Hempel and his mother nearby. Bernie came out from behind Mr. Contreras. She was starting toward me when Mitch gave a tremendous bark and broke through the throng. He jumped on me, knocking me to the ground. I lay there, laughing, and kicked my heels together.

THANKS

IN SOME WAYS this novel, which takes V.I. out of her comfort zone in Chicago and sends her to Kansas, is my own origin story. The story line was suggested by an event in my father's scientific life. He was a cell biologist at the University of Kansas from 1951 until his death in 2000; an experience he had at a rickettsia conference in Bratislava in 1964 underlies this novel.

The book is set in and around the town of Lawrence, Kansas, where I grew up. I have taken a number of liberties with the town, both its topography and its institutions. I've restructured the Lawrence Memorial Hospital to meet V.I.'s needs. I've filled in part of the ravine along the south side of the Kaw River to make room for Riverside Church. I've tampered with the layout of the Judicial and Law Enforcement Center and the workings of the county sheriff and the city police. I've inserted a missile silo into the Douglas County landscape, somewhere between the Pendleton farm and my own childhood home. I apologize for any land I may have misappropriated.

In Chicago, I have added an Area Six to the police department structure so that my fictional cops can operate without reference to any real police operations.

For the history of race in Lawrence, I've relied partly on my own memories and partly on *This Is America?, The Sixties in Lawrence, Kansas* by Rusty L. Monhollon and William Tuttle's *Separate But*

Not Equal. Langston Hughes grew up in Lawrence on the old east side, but for the purposes of this novel I've concentrated African-American life on the north side of the river.

As always, many people helped make this work possible. Professors Bill and Wendy Picking head the list, for taking time from significant professional obligations to advise me on biological matters. Dr. Raymond Zilinskas, who is an authority on biological weapons, was most helpful in the earliest days of my work on this novel.

Angela Wilson, formerly a district attorney in Douglas County, explained court procedures in Kansas for the moments when V.I. Warshawski inevitably ran afoul of the law. Jonathan Paretsky not only made that connection but drove me around the town and county to check locations.

Retired Lawrence police officer John Lewis has been most kind with his advice. As usual, I have taken liberties, some conscious, some inadvertent, with the advice I've received. Marzena Madej kept us all going in Chicago wihle I worked on this book: many thanks are due to her.

Finally, I'm grateful for the active support and insight of my editor, Dan Mallory, who has helped renew my confidence in my writing voice and in V.I. herself.

The chapter titles are dedicated to my husband and to the memory of Don Sandstrom, who cherished them.

I hope everyone will forgive my mistakes—this is a work of fiction and shouldn't be relied on for any political, personal, social, or economic data. Any mistakes are my misconstructions of what I read or heard; please don't blame the messengers.

All the characters in it are completely imaginary, except for the three professors whose photographs are in the lobby of the cell-biology research center that V.I. visits.

Note: I finished writing *Fallout* in August 2016, so no mention is made of cataclysmic events later in the year.

The sixteenth V.I. Warshawski thriller from the Queen of American Crime

CRITICAL MASS

Sara Paretsky

Private Eye V.I. Warshawski is roused one morning by an SOS from a woman on a farm south of Chicago. When V.I. gets there, she finds no woman – but a dead man in a cornfield, his body savagely mutilated.

V.I. is happy to leave the case to the local sheriff: it looks like a falling out among meth dealers. But back in Chicago, she learns that the missing woman is a protégée of her oldest friend and confidante, Dr Lotty Herschel, and is compelled to investigate.

What V.I. uncovers pulls her into a world of nuclear secrets and high-stakes computing, with roots reaching back to the Second World War. The detective soon finds herself in a hall of mirrors where she can't tell reality from video games, and her life is on the line. For V.I., this is her most profound, and terrifying, adventure yet . . .

Now available in paperback and ebook

The bestselling fifteenth V.I. Warshawski thriller

BREAKDOWN

Sara Paretsky

Carmilla, Queen of the Night, is a shape-shifting raven whose fictional exploits thrill girls all over the world. When tweens in Chicago's Carmilla Club hold an initiation ritual in an abandoned cemetery, they stumble on an actual corpse, a man stabbed through the heart in a vampire-style slaying.

The girls include daughters of some of Chicago's most powerful families: the grandfather of one, Chaim Salanter, is one of the world's wealthiest men; the mother of another, Sophy Durango, is the Illinois Democratic candidate for Senate.

For V.I. Warshawski, the questions multiply faster than the answers. Is the killing linked to a hostile media campaign against Sophy Durango? Or to Chaim Salanter's childhood in Nazi-occupied Lithuania? As V.I. struggles for answers, she finds herself fighting enemies who are all too human.

Now available in paperback and ebook

The unbeatably pacey fourteenth V.I. Warshawski novel

BODY WORK

Sara Paretsky

Club Gouge: Chicago's edgiest night spot, where a woman calling herself the Body Artist invites the audience to use her naked body as a canvas.

The show attracts all kinds of people, from a menacing cop to Ukrainian mobsters and Iraq war veterans. A tormented young painter comes too, and the designs she creates on the Body Artist drive one of the soldiers into a violent rage.

When the painter is shot, the police assume the shell-shocked veteran went off the rails. But his family hires V.I. to clear his name – and the detective discovers a chain of ugly truths stretching from Iraq to Chicago's South Side . . .

Now available in paperback and ebook

Do you wish this wasn't the end?

Join us at www.hodder.co.uk, or follow us on Twitter @hodderbooks to be a part of our community of people who love the very best in books and reading.

Whether you want to discover more about a book or an author, watch trailers and interviews, have the chance to win early limited editions, or simply browse our expert readers' selection of the very best books, we think you'll find what you're looking for.

And if you don't,
that's the place to tell us what's missing.

We love what we do, and we'd love you to be part of it.

www.hodder.co.uk

@hodderbooks

HodderBooks

HodderBooks